Count Julian;
or, The Last Days of the Goth

Available from the Simms Initiatives and the University of South Carolina Press

The Army Correspondence of Colonel John Laurens, ed.

As Good as a Comedy and Paddy McGann

Beauchampe

Border Beagles

Carl Werner, 2 vols.

The Cassique of Kiawah

Castle Dismal

Charlemont

The Charleston Book, ed.

Confession

Count Julian

The Damsel of Darien, 2 vols.

Dramas: Norman Maurice, Michael Bonham, and Benedict Arnold

Egeria

Eutaw

The Forayers

The Geography of South Carolina

The Golden Christmas

Guy Rivers

Helen Halsey

Historical and Political Poems (*which includes* Monody, The Vision of Cortes, The Tri-Color, Donna Florida, and Charleston and Her Satirists)

The History of South Carolina

Joscelyn

Katherine Walton

The Letters of William Gilmore Simms, Vol. 1

The Letters of William Gilmore Simms, Vol. 2

The Letters of William Gilmore Simms, Vol. 3

The Letters of William Gilmore Simms, Vol. 4

The Letters of William Gilmore Simms, Vol. 5

The Letters of William Gilmore Simms, Vol. 6 (exp. ed.)

The Life of Captain John Smith

The Life of the Chevalier Bayard

The Life of Francis Marion

The Lily and the Totem

Marie de Berniere

Martin Faber and Other Tales, 2 vols.

Mellichampe

The Partisan

Pelayo, 2 vols.

Poems, Descriptive, Dramatic, Legendary, and Contemplative, 2 vols.

The Remains of Maynard Davis Richardson

Richard Hurdis

Sack and Destruction of the City of Columbia

The Scout

Selections from the Letters and Speeches of the Hon. James H. Hammond, ed.

Simms's Poems Areytos

Social and Political Prose: Slavery in America/Father Abbot

South Carolina in the Revolutionary War

Southward Ho!

Stories and Tales

A Supplement to the Plays of William Shakespeare

Vasconselos

Views and Reviews in American Literature, History and Fiction, 2 vols.

Voltmeier

War Poetry of the South

The Wigwam and the Cabin

Woodcraft

The Yemassee

Count Julian; or, The Last Days of the Goth

William Gilmore Simms

Critical Introduction by W. Matthew J. Simmons
With a Biographical Overview by David Moltke-Hansen

The University of South Carolina Press

Pamphlet original published by the William Taylor & Co., 1845
Paperback published by the University of South Carolina Press
Columbia, South Carolina 29208

www.sc.edu/uscpress

Manufactured in the United States of America

25 24 23 22 21 20 19 18 17 16
10 9 8 7 6 5 4 3 2 1

ISBN 978-1-61117-575-2 (pbk)

Published in cooperation with the Simms Initiatives, a project of the University of South Carolina Libraries with the generous support of the Watson-Brown Foundation.

William Gilmore Simms: A Biographical Overview

David Moltke-Hansen

Introduction

Harper's Weekly put it succinctly in its July 2, 1870, issue: "In the death of Mr. Simms, on the 11th of June, at Charleston, the country has lost one more of its time-honored band of authors, and the South the most consistent and devoted of her literary sons" (qtd. In Butterworth and Kibler 125–26). Indeed no mid-nineteenth-century writer and editor did more than William Gilmore Simms to frame white southern self-identity and nationalism, shape southern historical consciousness, or foster the South's participation and recognition in the broader American literary culture. No southern writer enjoyed more contemporary esteem and attention, at least after Edgar Allan Poe moved north. Among American romancers (or writers of prose epics), only New Yorker James Fenimore Cooper was as successful by the 1840s. In those same years, Simms was the South's most influential editor of cultural journals. He also was the region's most prolific cultural journalist and poet, publishing an average of one book review and one poem per week for forty-five years.

Before his death Simms saw his national reputation fall along with the Confederacy he had vigorously supported and with the slave regime that many in the North had come to despise. Nevertheless reprints of most of the twenty titles in the selected edition of his works, first published between 1853 and 1860, appeared up until World War I. Thereafter only *The Yemassee*, an early romance about an Indian war in South Carolina, continued in print. The tide began to turn in the 1950s, when five volumes of Simms's letters appeared and a growing number of his works were issued in new editions. Publication in 1992 of the first literary biography, by John C. Guilds, and establishment of the William Gilmore Simms Society and the *Simms Review* the next year at once reflected and fostered this revived interest. Yet not until the 2011 launch of the digital Simms edition of the South Caroliniana Library of the University of South Carolina did scholars of southern, American, and nineteenth-century culture have the prospect of ready access to all of Simms's separately published works. With the University of South Carolina Press's cooperation, readers also will have access to sixty works in paperback editions by the end of 2014. Simms himself never saw nearly so many of his works in print at one time.

Clearly the decline in the critical standing of, and historical attention to, Simms and his oeuvre in the century after his death has reversed in the years since. The last three decades of the twentieth century saw more published on Simms than the previous hundred years (Butterworth and Kibler 126–200; MLA International). The last decade of the twentieth and first decade of the twenty-first centuries saw more dissertations and theses on him (forty-one) than had appeared in all the years before. This is not to say that Simms is yet given the attention directed to some of his contemporaries. For the first decade of the twenty-first century, the Modern Language Association International Bibliography lists roughly four times as many scholarly publications on James Fenimore Cooper, more than ten times as many on Nathaniel Hawthorne, and sixteen times as many on Edgar Allan Poe. Not surprisingly, therefore, Simms is not yet included in most anthologies of American literature, although he is a subject or a source in an expanding and ever more diverse body of scholarship.

To prepare to read Simms, it is important to see his writings in multiple contexts. He rarely wrote about himself outside of his more personal poems and his letters (some fifteen hundred of the many thousands of which survive). Yet he systematically drew on his background, personal experience, and relationships in his work. He also shaped that work through a progressively developed poetics and philosophy of life, history, and art. He did so in the context of his very broad reading of both contemporary and earlier Western literature and in the midst of multiple professional engagements and responsibilities. The richness and variety of these writings and involvements make Simms a key figure for future understanding of the literary culture, issues, and networks in mid-nineteenth-century America.

Background

Simms's family history reflected the dynamics that fueled the spread southward and westward of the populations, plantation economy, and society of the South Atlantic states. Simms's ancestry also reflected the Scots-Irish and English roots of what became identified as southern culture by the 1830s, a generation after the end of most immigration to the region. Two of Simms's grandparents, William and Elisabeth Sims, were Scots-Irish and migrated to South Carolina from Ulster. One, John Singleton, was an American-born son of putatively English immigrants, who had come to South Carolina from Virginia. The fourth, Jane Miller, was daughter of two Scots-Irish and Irish descended people—John Miller, of North and then South Carolina, and Jane Ross. Ross's family also migrated to South Carolina from western Virginia, where members lived cheek by jowl with other Scots-Irish families, who migrated to the Carolinas (White, *Ross*). Simms's father and Uncle James migrated in 1808 from Charleston to Tennessee, then to Mississippi. This was after the bankruptcy of the elder William's business and the deaths of his wife and their other two sons. Following the last of these losses, the elder Simms's hair turned white in a week. To his anguished eyes, Charleston appeared "a place of tombs" (qtd. in Guilds 6, 12).

For the son, however, Charleston was home—so much so that he refused to leave his maternal grandmother and move to Mississippi when his uncle came to get him in 1816. Then the fifth largest and by far the wealthiest city, as well as one of the greatest ports, in America, Charleston was at the peak of its influence (Moltke-Hansen, "Expansion" 25–31; Rogers). Cotton culture on the sea islands to the south, begun in 1790, and rice culture in impounded lowcountry tidal marshes meant that the port was filled not only with sailors of many lands and languages, but also with enslaved people of many African and Creole cultures and speech ways (slaves continued to be imported legally in large numbers until 1808). This street life made vivid the transnational nature of plantation agriculture and the fact that the developing region's dramatically expanding borders "were not just geographic; they also were human, historical, and intellectual" (Moltke-Hansen, "Southern" 19).

Even more important for the future author, the expanding region's borders and nature were taking imaginative shape. The West of the senior William Gilmore Simms and the first Creek War in which he fought, the Revolutionary War of the young Simms's maternal grandfather, the backcountry of many related Scots-Irish settlers, all these became grist for a lonely, energetic boy, who spent as much time with books as he could (Simms, *Letters* 1:161). The possibilities of such settings, incidents, and characters were not confined to history alone. Simms reported that he "used to glow and shiver in turn over 'The Pilgrim's Progress,'" while "Moses' adventures in 'The Vicar of Wakefield' threw [him] into paroxysms of laughter" (Hayne 261–62). Sir Walter Scott's Border and medieval romances and James Fenimore Cooper's Leatherstocking tales also deeply colored his imagination (Simms, *Views* 1:248, and Moltke-Hansen, "Southern" 6–15). As affecting were the ghost stories and Revolutionary War tales of his grandmother and the verses sent, and tales told, by his father.

These diverse tales became reasons to explore—in books, but also on the ground. As a boy, Simms ranged through the city and along the banks of the Ashley River, which fed into Charleston Harbor. He did so in search of scenes of colonial and Revolutionary battles and incidents (*Letters* 1:lxii). He first heard his uncle's and father's many Irish and frontier stories when they visited in Charleston in 1816 and 1818, respectively. He heard more on his trips to Mississippi during the winter of 1824 through the spring of 1825 and again in 1826. The first trip took him through Georgia and Alabama, where he saw elements of the Creek and Cherokee nations. At the time, Simms later reported, he was a boy "cumbered with fragmentary materials of thought, . . . choked by the tangled vines of erroneous speculation, and haunted by passions, which, like so many wolves, lurked, in ready waiting, for their unsuspecting prey" (*Social* 6). When he first got to Mississippi, traveling partly by stage, partly by riverboat, and partly by horse, Simms learned that his father had just come back from "a trip of three hundred miles into the heart of the Indian country" (Trent 15). Later father and son "rode together on horseback to various settlements on the frontier of Alabama and Mississippi" (Guilds 10–11, 17–18). Simms recalled as well "having traveled 150 miles beyond the Mississippi" (Shillingsburg, "Literary Grist" 120). The next year he returned to the Southwest by ship. "During this [second] trip he carried a 'note book.'" There he jotted episodes, encounters, stories heard, characters seen, and descriptions of the landscapes unfolding around him. He also wrote "at least sixteen poems" (Kibler, "First"; Shillingsburg, "Literary Grist" 123).

Simms took a third western trip five years later, writing letters back to the newspaper that by then he was editing (*Letters* 1:10–38). Together these three trips provided materials for his writings over more than forty years. "The first . . . produced mainly short fiction; the second inspired much poetry; . . . the first and third . . . yielded three novels written in the 1830s" (Shillingsburg, "Literary Grist" 119). This was, in part, because of the trips' timing. Sixteen years after the first trip, Simms told students at the University of Alabama that in the interval their world had changed from a howling wilderness into a place of growing civilization (Simms, *Social* 5–6). Had he not gone when he did, he would have been too late to see the frontier. Later travels took him many other places and also provided much grist for his writing. Never again, however, did he experience the frontier firsthand. Furthermore, on these later trips Simms was a practiced professional writer, no longer that boy haunted by passions.

Personal Life

After the ten-year-old boy's momentous refusal to leave Charleston, his grandmother sent Simms for two years to the grammar school taught on the campus and by the faculty of the nearly moribund College of Charleston. By then he already was "versifying the events of the war [of 1812]," just concluded, publishing "doggerel" in the local papers, and learning to read in several languages (*Letters* 1:285). His trip west a decade later helped him decide to pursue both literature and a career in law, but back in Charleston—this despite his father's urging that he stay in Mississippi. Upon his return home, he began to read law and also launched a literary weekly, the *Album*, which ran for a year. He became engaged as well to Anna Malcolm Giles, daughter of a grocer and former state coroner.

A year later the young couple married. This was six months before Simms was admitted to the South Carolina bar, on his twenty-first birthday, not long before he was appointed as a city magistrate. Although living up the Ashley River in the more healthful, less expensive village of Summerville, Simms kept a law office in the city. Shortly after using his maternal inheritance to buy the *City Gazette* at the end of 1829 and moving down to Charleston Neck, just north of the city limits where he had lived as a boy, Simms lost both his father and his maternal grandmother. He also found himself attacked because of his Unionist stance in the Nullification crisis resulting from South Carolina's rejection of a federal tariff. Then, in early 1832, Simms's wife died. Soon after, he took his four-year-old daughter back to Summerville to live and determined to sell his newspaper and leave the state for a literary life in the North.

Fueling his ambition was the correspondence Simms had begun several years earlier with an accountant whom he had published in his *City Gazette* but not yet met—Scots immigrant James Lawson. At the time Lawson, seven years Simms's senior, edited a New York City newspaper and, in addition to writing plays and poetry, was a friend (and, later, informal literary agent) to a wide circle (McHaney, "An Early"). Simms's trip north in the summer of 1832 saw the two begin a lifelong friendship, cemented as they squired ladies about and interacted with Lawson's literary circle. In subsequent years Simms multiplied the number of his friendships, in both the North and the South, making them in some measure a replacement for the family that he had lost. Lawson remained the closest of his northern friends, while James Henry Hammond, a future governor and U.S. senator, became his closest friend in South Carolina.

Late in 1833, after his Summerville house burned, Simms wrote Lawson to say that he was enamored of "a certain fair one" (*Letters* 1:73). Seventeen-year-old Chevillette Eliza Roach was the daughter of "a literary-minded aristocrat of English descent" with two plantations on the banks of the Edisto River in Barnwell District (later County) (Guilds 70). The courtship was protracted, as Simms felt it necessary first to clear debts that friends had bought up on his behalf. He also was determined "to marry no woman" before he was "perfectly independent of her resources, and her friends" (*Letters* 1:78). Therefore he did not propose until the spring of 1836. The nuptials took place seven months later, and as a result, Simms came to call the four thousand acres of Woodlands Plantation, with its seventy slaves, home. It was twenty years, however, before he took over management of the plantation and, then, only in the wake of his father-in-law's final sickness and death. Five years after that, he lost his wife, the mother of fourteen of his fifteen children. Nine of the children Chevillette bore him had already died, devastating Simms repeatedly. Five were still living (three sons and two daughters), as was Simms's daughter by his first marriage, who helped raise the youngest of her siblings. Those remaining children—even Gilly, who fought in the Confederate army—all outlived their father. Gilly and a brother-in-law ran Woodlands after the war, when Simms, though dying of cancer, was earning what he could by writing again for publications in the North and editing one or another South Carolina newspaper.

Career

The trip north in 1832 did not result in Simms moving there. Except during the Civil War, however, he returned almost every year. This was because the contacts he made, and the exposure to literary culture that he enjoyed, helped him define his future as an author. Earlier he had written fiction and criticism as well as journalism, filling the pages of several short-lived cultural journals and his newspaper, but between the ages of nine and twenty-six Simms had focused his literary efforts primarily on poetry. Beginning with his first book of verse in 1825, he had published five small volumes in Charleston. A couple had received positive notice in New York, and in the fall of 1832, J. & J. Harper issued the sixth anonymously from there, *Atalantis: A Story of the Sea.* Coming back the following summer, Simms had in hand for the Harpers a gothic novella, *Martin Faber,* and after his return south, he also would send the manuscript of his first two-volume border romance, *Guy Rivers: A Tale of Georgia.*

The reception of these and the romances and short stories that followed quickly made Simms one of the nation's most successful fictionists. He continued to issue poetry as well—roughly a collection every three years over the thirty-seven years that he worked as a professional author. But this output was dwarfed by the fiction—on average a title every year (counting several serialized works but not counting the many revised editions). Then there were the two dozen separately published orations, histories, and biographies as well as edited collections of documents and dramas and a geography of South Carolina. Add to these the revised editions and the further printings and issues of his own works and it appears that Simms saw a title coming off the presses at the rate of one every three months or so. Making that figure all the more astounding is the fact that, during more than a dozen of those years (the early-to-mid 1840s, the late 1840s-to-early 1850s, and the mid-to-late 1860s), he also was editing a cultural journal or newspaper. Furthermore he contributed reams of reviews and poems, hundreds of op-ed pieces and columns, and dozens of short stories and public addresses, which were never collected and published in volume form.

His career mapped an arc. It ascended meteorically in the 1830s and peaked in the early-to-mid 1840s, before beginning to descend. One reason was the popularity of the historical fiction that Simms began to write. When he left behind the law, his first newspaper, and the Nullification controversy, as well as his sadness, historical fiction was all the rage. Sir Walter Scott had fueled the craze, beginning with the publication of his first Border romance in 1814. He died in September 1832. Seventeen years Simms's senior, James Fenimore Cooper, the closest America had to a Scott at the time, was at the peak of his reputation and success, having started publishing his romances in 1820. Thus the way had been prepared for a writer of Simms's historical imagination and preoccupations. Within five years of his first trip north, moreover, Lawson's (and now his) circle became loosely affiliated with a nationalistic and Democratic group, self-styled Young America, this after Young Italy and similar ethnic, nationalist, European, cultural and political movements (Moltke-Hansen, "Southern"). Edgar Allan Poe and other members gave Simms's first fictions positive, if not uncritical, attention.

By the end of the 1830s, paradoxically, Simms, like Cooper, found his success attracting unauthorized editions of his works because Britain and America did not have an international copyright agreement. Further, in the wake of the panic of 1837, Americans bought fewer books. Simms's response was to diversify his portfolio. He turned to biography and history, including his hugely successful *Life of Francis Marion* (1844). He also returned to the editor's chair, overseeing one and then another cultural journal. These were unlike the ones he had edited in the 1820s: they included contributions by numerous authors, not just those from Charleston, but from the region and also the North. The ambition motivating the journals was to connect and promote Charleston intellectually. Consequently the journals more closely resembled metropolitan quarterly reviews in their offerings.

The mid-1840s saw Simms involved in politics, even serving a term in the South Carolina legislature. By the middle of the Mexican-American War in 1847, he had concluded that the South needed to become an independent nation. Thereafter, although he maintained ties with many in the Young America circle, he no longer promoted his writings as fostering Americanism in literature (*Views*). Instead he increasingly emphasized the ways in which his three romance series—the colonial, the Revolutionary, and the border—were making tangible and meaningful the origins and development of the future southern nation and the sad but inevitable consequences for Native Americans (Watson, *From Nationalism*; compare Nakamura).

Sectional politics colored more and more of Simms's perceptions, speeches, and private communications. The rising tide of abolitionism had him aghast. It also fed his growing sense that his position in American letters was slipping. He returned to editing, and his poetry, which was more often explicitly about the South, became increasingly patriotic in tone. Although his first biographer, William Peterfield Trent, insisted that Simms's declining standing reflected the change in literary fashion from historical romances to realistic novels, Simms in fact wrote more and more as a social realist in the 1850s (Wimsatt, "Realism").

The Civil War consumed Simms. As he wrote Lawson, "Literature, especially poetry, is effectually overwhelmed by the drums, & the cavalry, and the shouting" (*Letters* 4:369–70). He did manage to editorialize often and to rework and finish things long on his desk, including poems, a novel, and a dramatic treatment of Benedict Arnold, the northern traitor in the Revolutionary War. Then, in the wake of the Confederacy's loss and the failure of his vision for the South, he found himself recording the loss in a new newspaper, dealing with the trauma in his poetry, and becoming more existential and psychological in his fictional treatments. Simms's old New York friends tried to help. He did edit and see through publication a volume of Confederate war poetry. Yet it is a measure of his reduced stature that the several new romances he published appeared only in serial form. In part this may have been because he was in a sense competing with himself. Publishers were beginning to reprint volumes out of the selected edition of his writings. Many of Simms's works were available in book form, just not new works.

Associations

As the *Letters* testify, Simms had complex, overlapping networks of friends and colleagues. As a boy and young man, he received the friendship, patronage, and commendation of a variety of well-placed people in Charleston, including Charles Rivers Carroll. It was Carroll with whom he read law, to whom he dedicated his first romance, and after whom he named a son. Both men were Unionists during the Nullification controversy. So were Hugh Swinton Legare (later U.S. attorney general) and the considerably older William Drayton, as well as lawyer and editor Richard Yeadon and Greenville, South Carolina, newspaper editor Benjamin Franklin Perry. Also considerably older was James Wright Simmons, who had joined with Simms to launch the *Southern Literary Gazette* in 1828, when Simms was twenty-two. Through him Simms had direct contact with such British literary figures as Leigh Hunt and Byron (Kibler, *Poetry* 15).

The next group of influential friends and collaborators that Simms acquired were members of the Lawson circle and included such figures as Edwin

Forrest, the Shakespearean actor, and Evert Duyckinck, who published several of Simms's volumes in Wiley and Putnam's series Library of American Books, which he edited. Among the many others were poets and editors William Cullen Bryant and Fitz-Greene Halleck. Simms also made nonliterary friends in New York and Philadelphia, such as John Jacob Bockee and William Hawkins Ferris, the cashier at the U.S. Treasury office in New York who, after the war, helped Simms, Henry Timrod (poet laureate of the Confederacy), and others.

As a Barnwell planter, Simms met a widening circle of South Carolina's leaders and literati. For instance his acquaintance with James Henry Hammond began in the late 1830s and deepened into a friendship in the early 1840s. It was in the early 1840s, too, when he again was editing cultural journals, that Simms became friends with many southern writers. He regarded several of them, including Virginians George Frederick Holmes, Edmund Ruffin, and Nathaniel Beverley Tucker as members, together with Hammond and himself, in a "sacred circle." Uniting the circle were members' devotion to the South and a shared sense of the marginal status and critical importance of the life of the mind in a largely rural and unintellectual region (Faust, *Sacred*). Others of Simms's wide connections in the region did not interact as much with each other, but Simms long corresponded with Maryland novelist and lawyer John Pendleton Kennedy, Irish-born Georgia poet Richard Henry Wilde, Alabama lawyer and writer Alexander Beaufort Meek, and Louisiana historian and assistant attorney general Charles Gayarré, among others. By the 1850s, when Simms once more returned to editing a cultural journal, many of the writers whom he recruited were members of a younger generation. Poets Paul Hamilton Hayne and Henry Timrod were two. Often they and a half dozen others of Simms's and their generations met in John Russell's Charleston Book Shop and adjourned to dinner at Simms's Smith Street home, "dubbed 'The Wigwam'" (*Letters* 1:cxxxvi). Shortly before his death fifteen or so years later, Simms wrote Hayne, "I am rapidly passing from the stage, where you young men are to succeed me" (*Letters* 5:287).

Thought

The welter of Simms's works disguises unities and dynamics of the thought underlying them. From early on Simms was convinced that art ennobles or transforms, as well as gives voice to individuals and societies; therefore it must be cultivated assiduously. Without the potential for high artistic attainment, he insisted, societies are not ready for the independence and regard of free peoples. This is where Simms the historian joined Simms the poet. Societies develop, he argued (using the stadialism of the Scottish historical school), from imitation through self-assertion to achievement and also from savagery through strife to settled agricultural communities and, ultimately, to a hierarchical civilization supporting a rich artistic life. It was the job of the artist to help envision the goal, inspire the pursuit, and inform the process. That process was at once progressive and dialectical. Order, without dynamism, stifled development, as did the obverse—the dominance by ungoverned impulses or uncontrolled license. This was true in the individual, but also in societies as a whole. War was necessary for civilization, but its success was measured in the securities of the home, the center of cultural production and reproduction.

Whether in the public or in the domestic arena, "the true governor, as [Thomas] Carlyle call[ed] him—the king man—" guided rather than impeded the forces of change and progress (Simms, "Guizot's" 122). There were few such men with the capacity to lead. The same was true of nations. Neither all people nor all peoples were equal in either capacity or attainment. That was why Native Americans were overrun and Africans had been enslaved by European peoples in the New World. Indeed, Simms argued, "slavery in all ages has been found the greatest and most admirable agent of Civilization," giving education and examples to less evolved peoples (*Letters* 3:174). The degree to which a people had evolved mattered. That was why, he held, Americans had won independence from the most powerful empire in the world. They had done so through their Revolution, led by an elite that felt correctly its time had come (Simms, "Ellet's" 328). By mid-1847 that also was Simms's judgment for the South: the region had evolved enough to become independent (*Letters* 2:332). The hope inspired and then failed him and the people he sought to lead.

While not all men could rise to the highest rank, they all had the same responsibility at home. There the father was patriarch, protector, and head, while the mother was nurturer, moral instructor, and heart. There, too, children's characters and minds were formed by age twelve ("Ellet's"). Children's upbringing was critical to citizenship, and it was through her sons and the support of her husband, father, and brothers that a woman shaped the public sphere. The culture and character instilled in the child expressed and informed not just the household, but the larger society—the people.

"The history of peoples and their embodiments in institutions, states, and artistic productions—these were the great subjects" in Simms's view (Moltke-Hansen, "Southern" 120). Yet "poets were the only class of philosophers who had recognized" this until his own day, when at last "we now read human histories. We now ask after the affections as well as the ceremonies of society" ("Ellet's" 319–20). Peoples or races—that is, ethnic groups—were not unchanging any more than were their politics and their cultures. They either advanced or were overrun by history. Further, new peoples emerged, and old identities were submerged. The Spanish conquistadors were the creation of centuries of conflict with the Moors: their motivation was the glory of conquest, not the routine of trade or the plow. On the other hand, the English settlements in North America reflected the impulse to transform the wilderness into verdant farms and build society (*Views* 64, 178–85; *Social* 8). The same impulse drove Americans westward in Simms's own day and gave Americans their Manifest Destiny.

To explore these facts of the South's settlement and its place in international conflicts, Simms wrote all together, between 1833 and 1863, two romances set in eighth-century Spain, two set during the Spanish exploration and conquest of the Americas and two during the later English colonization of South Carolina, seven set during the American Revolution, and—depending on how one counts—perhaps eight set on the borders of the nineteenth-century South. After the war he published one more Revolutionary romance and two more that, like it, were set beyond the boundaries of civilization. He also left two unfinished romances, also set beyond society's normal reach. These late works, however, no longer had as their framing justification the cultivation of the South's future and civilization.

White southerners had their independence foreclosed by the war. In his last works, therefore, Simms found himself exploring the psychological, philosophical, and historical impulses that led to the Confederacy's demise and what, in the aftermath, it meant to be a good man and to build for the future, however impoverished. On the first score, he argued that the impulse to idealism behind abolitionism ignored historical realities, becoming inhuman in its consequences. On the latter score, he affirmed responsibility for one's dependents and the virtues of stoicism, as well as a continued commitment to the beauty and truth of art and the impulses to the cultivated life and fields. Therefore, in the face of the burning of his Woodlands home and library in February 1865—during Sherman's march and in the midst of desperate circumstances—he insisted that home, or the ideals and past characterizing its potential, still was at the center of true civilization, but only if elevated by art (*Sense* 8, 17). It was wrong to measure civilization by the getting, spending, and mad dashing, or material progress and utilitarianism, characteristic of both a capitalistic North and also many southerners. These traits he often had attacked even before the war, insisting that "the work of the Imagination, which is the Genius of a race, is only begun when its material progress is supposed to be complete" (*Poetry* 12).

Writings

Simms expressed many of his ideas most personally in letters and most cogently in essays, speeches, and occasional introductions to his books. But he illustrated them most fully in his fiction and poetry. By the time he arrived in New

York in 1832, he had formed many of the core ideals and beliefs that would shape his work. His application of them, however, modified his understanding over time. Growing as a writer and growing in knowledge and experience, he also grew as a thinker.

In his hierarchy of values, poetry came first. It was a prophetic calling as well as evocative of the deeply felt (or, sometimes, the fleeting) and thus testimony to the perdurance and transcendence of the beautiful and the human spirit. Yet, as Simms often ruefully reflected, prose spoke to many more people. That was a principal reason why he turned to writing prose epics or romances. He gave his most concerted consideration of poetry's value and roles in three lectures in Charleston in 1854. Over the prior three years he had given portions of them in Augusta, Georgia, Washington, D.C., and Richmond and Petersburg, Virginia. Entitled *Poetry and the Practical,* they did not see print until 1996, as Simms never found the time to expand them as he wanted. On the other hand, his last address on the same themes, *The Sense of the Beautiful,* was issued soon after he delivered it, also in Charleston.

Many of his important reviews have not yet been gathered, but Simms collected some in 1845–46, and *Views and Reviews in American Literature, History and Fiction* came out in 1846 and 1847 in two "series." Beginning with a consideration of "Americanism" in literature, the first series explored the themes and periods of American history for treatment by the novelist. Simms argued there, and in forewords to several of his romances, that fiction rendered the past more truthfully, interestingly, and tellingly than histories and biographies could because fiction—like poetry—required imagination to look beyond what is not known or expressed. The second series examined additional American writers and what distinguished them, for instance, in their humor.

Despite their early success, Simms's romances, novellas, and stories provoked mixed reviews. Poe eventually concluded that Simms had become "the best novelist which this country has, on the whole, produced" but also insisted that "he should never have written 'The Partisan,' nor 'The Yemassee.'" This was in a review of *Confession.* That novel, like the gothic *Martin Faber,* demonstrated, Poe contended, that Simms's "genius [did] not lie in the outward so much as in the inner world." Yet he nevertheless wrote of Simms's short-story collection *The Wigwam and the Cabin* that "in invention, in vigor, in movement, in the power of exciting interest, and in the artistical management of his themes, he has surpassed, we think, any of his countrymen." Other critics, especially in the genteel and Whiggish Knickerbocker circle, joined Poe in condemning what they considered to be the excessively graphic and vulgar qualities of many characters and scenes, and Simms's prolixity and sententiousness, in his romances (Butterworth and Kibler 64, 50).

The violent realism and earthiness of the romances did not result in realistic novels. Although Simms received early praise for his characterizations (particularly of women), he used the romance formula, with its stereotypic heroes and heroines, predictable themes, and conventional polarities. People were on quests or had lost their way or were fighting long odds or were carrying forward the banner of (and modeling) civilization or were mired in the slough of despond or were resisting all the claims of civilized society and behavior or were pursuing love interests. Deceitfulness, selfishness, and greed opposed honor, high-mindedness, and honesty against the backdrop of the South's development from the earliest days of Spanish exploration to the westward movement in Simms's own youth.

It was only gradually that Simms married the psychological acuity of some of his portraits of the interior struggles of his gothic characters and fiction to the historical romance. Helping him think through how to do so were the biographies he wrote in the mid-1840s, but also the incidents on which he focused particular fictions, such as the murder in *Beauchampe; or, The Kentucky Tragedy* (1842). However incomplete the blending of realism and romanticism or of stereotypical and socially individuated renderings through the 1840s, by the 1850s Simms fundamentally had made the transition to social realism in such works as *Woodcraft* and *The Cassique of Kiawah.* Indeed some scholars have considered *Woodcraft* the first realistic novel in America (Bakker; Wimsatt, "Realism").

In some sense disguising the transition is the fact that Simms also increasingly wrote as a humorist and, in so doing, often rendered his late narratives fabulistically, when not writing social comedy or stories of manners. This dimension of Simms's work was largely hidden, however, until the 1974 publication of *Stories and Tales,* volume 5 in the Centennial Simms edition. There, for the first time, readers had access in print to "Bald-Head Bill Bauldy." There, too, for the first time one could read together that story, "Legend of the Hunter's Camp," and "How Sharp Snaffles Got His Capital and Wife," which was published posthumously in *Harper's Magazine* in October 1870. These and other stories and tales made it clear that Simms was a fecund contributor to southern and American humor.

Humor let Simms take up issues that he could not otherwise address in print and still expect to be well received. He did so both during and after the war. The war also pushed Simms past the emerging fashion of social realism. Having destroyed the familiar, the preoccupation of much realistic fiction, the war made the liminal central (Shillingsburg, "Cub"). While his romances and tales had often explored life on the edge or in extreme circumstances, whether in war or on the frontier or on the verge of madness or in fanciful realms, it had done so against a backdrop of, and with the goal of affirming, social norms and development. In the war's wake that goal seemed absurd. Mythologized memories of a healthy past might nurture a sense of the beautiful but could not help one deal with the present. Thus Simms's conclusion, in a March 1869 letter to Paul Hamilton Hayne: "Let us bury the Past lest it buries us!" (*Letters* 5:214). Fifteen months later he lay dead in the 13 Society Street, Charleston, home of his oldest daughter, with the shell holes in the walls of the bedroom he had shared with several children.

Posthumous Reputation

The twenty years after Simms's death saw him often respectfully treated, first in obituaries, later in memoirs and columns, and also in literary dictionaries and encyclopedias. Yet Charles Richardson's 1887 *American Literature: 1607–1885* proved a harbinger of a shift: Simms, Richardson observed, was "more respected than read," having "won considerable note because he was so sectional" and then having "lost it because he was not sectional enough," although he showed "silly contempt for his Northern betters" (qtd. in Butterworth and Kibler 130). Five years later Trent's biography of Simms appeared. It was the first full-length, scholarly treatment. Its central thesis was that Simms's environment frustrated his abilities: the South was inimical to art and the life of the mind, and Charleston high society's hauteur marginalized Simms despite his talent and character. Trent's second thesis was that Simms's commitment to the romance and his romanticism meant that his works had become largely unreadable in an age of literary realism. Although Vernon Parrington and later scholars recognized Simms's impulses to realism, the two theses long shaped Simms criticism and, indeed, also helped frame study of antebellum southern literature and intellectual life (Parrington 119–30).

A Virginian born in 1862, Trent was a progressive who wanted a New South radically different from the old. He saw his pioneering study of Simms as an opportunity to criticize what the Civil War had made untenable. From his perspective the Old South was not the expanding and rapidly developing environment, with a deep history, that Simms portrayed, but a place where slavery stultified and stunted the growth and progress displayed by the North. Southern—especially South Carolinian—writers occasionally challenged Trent's agenda and conclusions, but those critiques had little impact. Not until after publication of the Simms letters in the 1950s did scholars begin to consider the author in the historical and contemporary contexts that he had rendered in his poetry and fiction. And not until after the centennial of his death did a growing number of scholars, having concluded that southern intellectual history was not an oxymoron, begin to study in detail the culture in which Simms participated and to which he contributed so voluminously and variously.

Some of these scholars also have had agendas: they have wanted to see Simms included in the American literary canon, for instance, or they have wanted to defend the heritage that in their view Trent, and so many others, inappropriately belittled or ignorantly dismissed. More fruitfully, other scholars have begun to reframe the understanding of nineteenth-century American intellectual life by stripping away preconceptions that characterized earlier evaluations of Simms and his contemporaries. They are closely examining the historical record and transatlantic and other contemporary contexts and developments in the process. Although the pursuit of canonical status in a post-canonical age seems quixotic at this point, the explosion of the canon is leading to more varied fare being offered and may, therefore, mean that Simms, once his work is widely available, will be more often anthologized as well as studied. Defensiveness about Simms and the antebellum South may warm the hearts of like-minded people, just as critics of the Old South have been encouraged by shared presuppositions and disdain. Yet dueling cultural ideologies do not advance comity and may only reinforce mutual incomprehensions. Continued, deep research in original sources and the theoretical reframing that Atlantic history, the history of the book, and other perspectives offer—these approaches promise most for further study of Simms, his works, and his world.

Works Cited

For amplified readings by and on Simms and on his world, go to http://simms.library.sc.edu/bibliography.php.

Bakker, Jan. "Simms on the Literary Frontier; or, So Long Miss Ravenel and Hello Captain Porgy: *Woodcraft* Is the First 'Realistic' Novel in America." In *William Gilmore Simms and the American Frontier,* edited by John Caldwell Guilds and Caroline Collins, 64–78. Athens: University of Georgia Press, 1997.

Butterworth, Keen, and James E. Kibler Jr. *William Gilmore Simms: A Definitive Guide.* Boston: G. K. Hall, 1980.

Faust, Drew Gilpin. *A Sacred Circle: The Dilemma of the Intellectual in the Old South, 1840–1860.* Baltimore: Johns Hopkins University Press, 1977.

Guilds, John C. *Simms: A Literary Life.* Fayetteville: University of Arkansas Press, 1992.

Hayne, Paul Hamilton. "Ante-Bellum Charleston." *Southern Bivouac* 1 (October 1885): 257–68.

Kibler, James E. "The First Simms Letters: 'Letters from the West' (1826)." *Southern Literary Journal* 19 (Spring 1987): 81–91.

———. *The Poetry of William Gilmore Simms: An Introduction and Bibliography.* Columbia: Southern Studies Program, University of South Carolina, 1979.

McHaney, Thomas L. "An Early 19th-Century Literary Agent: James Lawson of New York." *Publications of the Bibliographical Society of America* 64 (Spring 1970): 177–92.

Moltke-Hansen, David. "The Expansion of Intellectual Life: A Prospectus." In *Intellectual Life in Antebellum Charleston,* edited by Michael O'Brien and David Moltke-Hansen, 3–44. Knoxville: University of Tennessee Press, 1986.

———. "Southern Literary Horizons in Young America: Imaginative Development of a Regional Geography." *Studies in the Literary Imagination* 42, no. 1 (2009): 1–31.

Nakamura, Masahiro. *Visions of Order in William Gilmore Simms: Southern Conservatism and the Other American Romance.* Columbia: University of South Carolina Press, 2009.

Parrington, Vernon L. *The Romantic Revolution in America, 1800–1860.* Vol. 2 of *Main Currents in American Thought.* New York: Harcourt, Brace and Company, 1927.

Rogers, George C., Jr. *Charleston in the Age of the Pinckneys.* Columbia: University South Carolina Press, 1980.

Shillingsburg, Miriam J. "The Cub of the Panther: A New Frontier." In *William Gilmore Simms and the American Frontier,* edited by John Caldwell Guilds and Caroline Collins, 221–36. Athens: University of Georgia Press, 1997.

———. "Literary Grist: Simms's Trips to Mississippi." *Southern Quarterly* 41, no. 2 (2003): 119–34.

Simms, William Gilmore. *Atalantis: A Story of the Sea: In Three Parts.* New York: J. & J. Harper, 1832.

———. *Beauchampe; or, The Kentucky Tragedy.* 2 vols. Philadelphia: Lea and Blanchard, 1842.

———. *The Cassique of Kiawah: A Colonial Romance.* New York: Redfield, 1859.

———. *Confession; or, The Blind Heart. A Domestic Story.* 2 vols. Philadelphia: Lea and Blanchard, 1841.

———. "Ellet's 'Women of the Revolution.'" *Southern Quarterly Review,* n.s. 1 (July 1850): 314–54.

———. "Guizot's Democracy in France." *Southern Quarterly Review* 15, no.29 (1849): 114–65.

———. *Guy Rivers: A Tale of Georgia.* 2 vols. New York: Harper & Brothers, 1834.

———. *The Letters of William Gilmore Simms.* Edited by Mary C. Simms Oliphant, Alfred Taylor Odell, and T. C. Duncan. 6 vols. Columbia: University of South Carolina Press, 1952–82.

———. *The Life of Francis Marion.* New York: Henry G. Langley, 1844.

———. *Martin Faber, the Story of a Criminal; and Other Tales.* 2 vols. New York: Harper & Brothers, 1837.

———. *Poetry and the Practical.* Edited by James E. Kibler. Fayetteville: University of Arkansas Press, 1996.

———. *The Sense of the Beautiful: An Address . . . before the Charleston County Agricultural and Horticultural Association, May 3, 1870.* Charleston: Charleston County Agricultural and Horticultural Association, 1870.

———. *The Social Principle: The Source of National Permanence. An Oration, Delivered before the Erosophic Society of the University of Alabama . . . December 13, 1842.* Tuscaloosa: Erosophic Society, University of Alabama, 1843.

———. *Stories and Tales.* Vol. 5 of *The Writings of William Gilmore Simms.* Centennial edition; introductions, explanatory notes, and texts established by John Caldwell Guilds. Columbia: University of South Carolina Press, 1974.

———. *Views and Reviews in American Literature, History and Fiction.* 2 vols. New York: Wiley and Putnam, 1845 (1846).

———. *The Wigwam and the Cabin.* 2 vols. New York: Wiley and Putnam, 1845–46.

———. *Woodcraft, or Hawks about the Dovecote: A Story of the South, at the Close of the Revolution.* New York: Redfield, 1854.

Trent, William Peterfield. *William Gilmore Simms.* Boston: Houghton, Mifflin, 1892.

Wakelyn, Jon L. *The Politics of a Literary Man: William Gilmore Simms.* Westport, Conn.: Greenwood Press, 1973.

Watson, Charles S. *From Nationalism to Secessionism: The Changing Fiction of William Gilmore Simms.* Westport, Conn.: Greenwood Press, 1993.

White, William B., Jr. *The Ross-Chesnut-Sutton Family of South Carolina.* Franklin, N.C.: Privately printed, 2002.

Wimsatt, Mary Ann. "Realism and Romance in Simms's Midcentury Fiction." *Southern Literary Journal* 12, no. 2 (1980): 29–48.

Critical Introduction

COUNT JULIAN

W. Matthew J. Simmons

Traditionally two of the more critically maligned works of Simms's oeuvre, *Pelayo: A Story of the Goth,* and its ostensible sequel, *Count Julian; or, the Last Days of the Goth,* are nevertheless valuable resources to scholars of Simms and nineteenth-century literature generally. While their value may not be immediately apparent based on aesthetic merit, these works show Simms struggling to articulate some of his key philosophical concerns, and they provide two of the most fascinating textual histories of all of the author's many works. Also, *Pelayo,* at least, is a much better novel than critics have traditionally acknowledged. So, while these romances of Gothic Spain may be two of the author's minor novels, they nevertheless are among Simms's most intriguing attempts at writing historical, and even philosophical, fiction. Because of this, they deserve renewed critical attention, in spite of their limited aesthetic successes.

Simms's interest in medieval Spain may seem uncharacteristic for an author most well-known for his novels about the Revolutionary War and the early days of the American Republic. Yet, as Stanly T. Williams's excellent "Spanish Influences on the Fiction of William Gilmore Simms" points out, Spanish culture and language were "a key to themes and backgrounds which were to be important in [Simms's] fiction and poetry. Everything suggests 'his preference for Spanish [language and culture], or at least a consciousness of its potential treasures for him as a novelist, either through a knowledge of Spain itself or of the history and legends of Spanish-America." (223) Certainly, the hazy history of late Gothic Spain, with its tense mix of Germanic, Hispano-Roman, Jewish, and Moorish populations, provides rich fodder for romances of the type Simms produced. Yet, it is nevertheless curious that the author would leave his robust explorations of the American scene for such a radically different fictional setting, especially considering the great commercial and critical successes of his Revolutionary and Border Romances. To make sense of Simms's ambitions for these twin novels of "the last days of the Goth," we need to consider the origin of the novels and the possible social and personal pressures he would have been feeling in the late 1830s. Both novels point to what is perhaps the central theme in Simms's work, an issue *Pelayo* and, in its own vexed ways, *Count Jul-*

ian, would allow him to explore from a new perspective: the relationships between history, art, and the literary vocation.

Both *Pelayo* and *Count Julian* had their genesis in a short piece of juvenile verse-drama, a project Simms abandoned as a young man, only to find himself returning to in the late 1830s. Writing to his literary agent and friend James Lawson in October 1841, Simms recounted this part of his literary biography, noting that "I have in my possession now a Tragedy partly written when I was 17-18 – founded on the apostacy [*sic*] of Count Julian. From the materials of this tragedy, my romance of Pelayo was evolved" (*Letters* 1: 285). As Williams's essay suggests, Simms did have a longstanding interest in Spanish culture and language, and thus his youthful foray is unsurprising. Yet, the question remains: why did he return to this project approximately a decade and a half after putting it aside?

Simms biographer John Caldwell Guilds posits an explanation for the author's choice by contextualizing it within the major social pressures Simms himself was likely feeling at this time: so recently married into the lowcountry gentry from "which he had felt rejected since boyhood," the author "was encouraged by his new peers ... not to forsake the great literary traditions of Europe, to which they still looked, with something akin to awe, for cultural verification." (81) Always conscientious of the fraught position of a professional man of letters in the antebellum South, Simms needed to legitimize his vocation, especially amongst his new social milieu. By leaving his work on America and her history for the time being and taking up a project derived from European history, Simms, in Guilds's reading, hoped to show the Charleston elite that his work was of real and significant merit.

In *Conjectures of Order,* Michael O'Brien notes the singular importance of history, and historical literature and knowledge, to the southern elite in the early decades of the nineteenth century: during this time "historical literature grew in force as a species of knowledge deemed to explain the human experience and, in its ubiquity, came then to engross a greater share of Southern culture than before or since." (591) Southerners read a wide variety of historical texts, especially standard Classical sources like Thucydides, Herodotus, and Livy. While most medieval historians were ignored, those of early modern Europe, like Edward Hyde, Earl of Clarendon, and Voltaire were regularly examined. Hume and Gibbon "were ubiquitous and even enjoyed" (594). These historians all evidenced a traditional view of the role of history, one that "told the stories that clarified the lineaments of this mixed human race;" they "told historical tales of transhistorical significance, whose value was to encourage the morally great and to warn against the immorally forceful" (597). Surely Simms was exposed to several of these historians, as his own approach to history reflects this traditional stance. Simms believed the role of an historical text was not merely to rehearse the significant actions and events of the age, but rather to reveal truths in expressing things of "transhistorical significance."

Thus, Simms's abandoning of eighteenth-century America for eighth-century Spain is perhaps unexpected, but not out of character for the writer who believed that the latter contained relevant truths about the former. Simms explored the ramifications of this fact in these two novels. The social pressures Guilds notes likely did weigh heavily on the author, yet these did not paralyze him. Rather, his understanding of the purposes of history as a humanistic pursuit and literary wellspring would suggest to the author that Medieval Spain could be just as valuable to the modern American writer as it would be to the Spanish or Islamic novelist of the nineteenth century. Further, orations like *The Social Principle* and *Self-Development* show Simms's view that the Spanish conquest of America was based in a culture heavily affected by centuries of warfare with the Moors, fighting that began at the time in which Count Julian and Pelayo lived. Thus, we can surmise that the author understood the two places and periods as, in some important ways, directly connected.

Backgrounds – *Pelayo: A Story of the Goth*

Pelayo was published by Harper & Brothers, in two volumes, in 1838. Though technically anonymous, it was attributed to the author of *Mellichampe*, *The Yemassee*, *Guy Rivers*, *The Partisan*, and *Martin Faber*. Because this is the only edition of the novel to emerge before the present volume, the publication history of the book is not extensive. The story of *Pelayo* is nevertheless complex, providing an example of the struggles Simms often endured in realizing his artistic vision.

Simms's earliest forays into writing *Pelayo* were during his late teens in the mid-1820s, when he engaged in writing a verse-drama about the legend of Count Julian, influenced by poems on that and related subjects by Sir Walter Scott and others. At some point in the late 1830s, the adult Simms reconsidered this work. While there is no definitive evidence of when he returned to writing *Pelayo*, Simms's first mention of the novel in his extant correspondence was a March 1837 letter to James Lawson: "the Harpers ... have the entire MS of Pelayo," he told his friend and informal literary agent. He also remarked that the book turned out to be a "much longer work than I had intended it to be, and has cost me more time & thought than I had anticipated" (*Letters* 1: 99). Simms's comment that he struggled mightily with *Pelayo*'s production provides evidence in favor of Guilds's argument that Simms was out of his element with this novel, perhaps indeed producing something out of social necessity, rather than out of artistic vision. Further evidence about the frustrations Simms faced are found in a letter to Lawson from September of the same year. He complained that he was "literally doing nothing, unless turning into prose, the verse passages of Pelayo be considered doing something. It is labor, but labor without profit" (*Letters* 1: 116). While it is unclear how much the publishers wanted changed from the time of their reception of "the entire MS" to this rewriting of the "verse passages" six months later, it is clear that the overall process was exceptionally taxing for Simms; while Harper & Brothers had the full manuscript in March 1837, *Pelayo* was not published until the spring of 1838, over a full year later.

Simms's reference to these "verse passages" of *Pelayo* alludes to the work's genesis as well as to possible reasons for the novel's uneven quality. In its published version, three poems, representing songs and ballads sung by characters at key moments, constitute all of the verse in the novel. Yet, the aforementioned letter shows that Simms reworked – with difficulty – more extensive verse passages into prose, suggesting a much larger initial presence of verse in the work. Simms seems not to have overhauled these extensive verse sections, but to have engaged in a sort of odd translation from poetry to prose. Mary Ann Wimsatt notes that the fidelity of *Pelayo* to its verse origins is seen most manifestly in the novel's dialogue, where "the speech of the characters is lofty and archaic, depending heavily on asides and soliloquies. That of Pelayo in particular is filled with metaphors, conceits, word-plays, and paradoxes, in attempted imitation of Renaissance drama, and is streaked with a grim humor redolent of the Jacobean stage." ("*Ivanhoe* and Simms" 259) The effect of this is often jarring, as characters often seem as if they fell from the pen of an Elizabethan playwright instead of a nineteenth-century novelist.

By choosing to use language in this way, Simms limited the novel's chances at real aesthetic success. He marred a sophisticated narrative and philosophically intriguing exploration of history, citizenship, virtue, and justice with prose that was too often prolix and leaden. If Guilds is correct, and Simms's proximate goal in writing *Pelayo* was to earn respect from the Charleston elite through invocation of European subjects and forms, then Simms certainly succeeded. However, this same success is also the chief source of the novel's failings; while *Pelayo* is a much more intelligent, challenging, and fulfilling novel than Guilds allows, Simms ultimately did not reach the levels such a sophisticated work would seemingly demand because of his myopic fidelity to the work's juvenile source and his resistance to deviating from the confines of the European traditions of the Romance and the stage.

Simms dedicated *Pelayo* to William Hayne Simmons, a Charleston-born physician descended from Henry Woodward, "the first English settler of South Carolina" (Simmons xi). While such a dedication seems to further validate

Guild's reading, Simmons's precarious position in Charleston society complicates this straightforward picture. Although a descendant of Charleston's literal first family, Simmons was not a wealthy man. While a physician by trade, Simmons thought of himself as a man of letters. In 1821, at the age of 37, he "decided to pull up his roots" in Charleston and leave for Florida (xiii). Though Simms was then only 15, the two men maintained a professional and personal relationship over the years, something that was surely aided by Simms's close friend and literary collaborator James Wright Simmons, the younger brother of William Hayne. As late as the 1840s and '50s, William Hayne Simmons contributed poems to the *Southern Quarterly Review* while Simms was editor of that journal. Simms also included several works by Simmons in *The Charleston Book* and promoted Simmons's work to Evert Augustus Duyckinck, another friend and an influential figure in the mid-century New York publishing world. Simmons wrote on the early history of Florida, and dedicating the book to him reinforced the connection between that history and the fall of Gothic Spain. Because Simmons, like Simms, also had greater ambitions than inheritance, Simms may as well have been including his Florida friend in the search for the cultural respectability that Guilds believes the novel represents.

Backgrounds – *Count Julian; or, The Last Days of the Goth*

Derived from the same juvenile source material as *Pelayo* and conceived of as its direct sequel, *Count Julian* soon took on a life of its own, and its publication history is perhaps the strangest in the entire Simms canon. Several striking delays resulted in *Count Julian* being published more than seven years after *Pelayo.* The extended breaks in composition were both frustrating and confusing to Simms, as the aesthetic failures of *Count Julian* bear witness.

Soon after the publication of *Pelayo,* Simms was already at work on its sequel, as evidenced by a January 1838 letter to Lawson. Work on *Count Julian,* though, proceeded "rather slowly" (*Letters* 1:139). By March of 1839, Simms had made significant progress, but an unforeseen circumstance would severely delay the work, and perhaps ruin all chances of it being either a fitting sequel to *Pelayo* or a strong novel in its own right. In a letter of 30 March 1839, Simms asked Lawson to "call on the Harpers & see if they have received any M.S. from me, of the sequel to Pelayo" (*Letters* 1:142). This manuscript contained the first five books of *Count Julian,* but was lost at some point before or during its delivery to the publishers. According to family legend, Simms was separated from the manuscript because he was instructed by a psychic to avoid the ship from New York to Charleston on which he had already booked passage (Guilds 393n). The author's luggage – including the *Count Julian* manuscript – was already on board. Though unable to retrieve his belongings, Simms followed the advice of the psychic and canceled his passage on that ship, which sank off of Cape Hatteras. Miraculously, the trunk containing the manuscript of *Count Julian* washed up on shore and eventually was found. Simms did not recover the manuscript until 1841, as evidenced by his noting in a letter from October of that year that the work "has now only recently been restored to me" (*Letters* 1: 281). Because the early 1840s was one of the most productive eras of Simms's career, he was busy with other projects when the manuscript finally made its way back to him. As a result, he did not restart composition on *Count Julian* for at least another year and a half. Thus, nearly four years had elapsed from the time Simms began work on *Count Julian* to when he resumed its composition in mid-1843.

These intervening years created a significant obstacle to the easy completion of *Count Julian*: quite simply, Simms seems to have forgotten his original plans for the novel. Despite this, he made arrangements, as he often did, to have the book published before it was completed. Park Benjamin was contracted to bring out the still-unfinished work by August 1843, thus giving Simms very little time to complete a work he now found unfamiliar. To make matters worse, Simms had to forward the incomplete manuscript to Benjamin as part of his arrangements with the publisher. Not in possession of the original manuscript for a second time, Simms wrote to Lawson that he hoped his agent would encourage Benjamin to make "immediate progress, with the novel, as it will be impossible for me to prepare the sequel until I get the printed sheets which precede. I have not read the thing for years" (*Letters* 1: 365). Perhaps predictably, Simms did not finish in time for August publication.

In October 1843, just as Simms seemed to be wrapping up the novel, new delays occurred. Benjamin seemingly had yet to print proofs. A vexed Simms wrote to Lawson to "see Benjamin on the subject of the novel. My understanding was that they were to put it to press instantly, or as soon as possible. Instead of this, here is 1 ½ months, and no proof yet ... Do see them about it, and unless they are willing to proceed at once, or if they show any reluctance, let the MS. be withdrawn" (*Letters* 1: 375-76). When he eventually did receive and review the proofs, Simms told Lawson "I very much fear that Count Julian will be a wretched failure. This is *entre nous*. It seems to me from reading some 40 pages of the proofs that it is monstrous flat. Heaven grant it may get better as it proceeds" (*Letters* 1: 416). By April 1844, Simms had still heard nothing about the novel's publication; ultimately, Benjamin never issued *Count Julian*.

While the business and legal details of the end of Simms and Benjamin's relationship are unclear, by early 1845 Simms had moved on to working with two other possible publishers for *Count Julian*: Burgess, Stringer and Co. and J. Winchester. The author continued to struggle with completion of the novel, and his relationship with these publishers was soon strained, just as it had been with Benjamin. He wrote to Lawson in February, "As soon as [Winchester] sends me the proof of what he has, I will finish the story .... This I cannot do, unless I rewrite and reinvent all that portion which he retains. You will also get from Stringer the printed volumes & retain them for me. I do not care to urge the work upon him, altho he was pledged for it" (*Letters* 2: 39). By June, both publishers were gone, and William Taylor had purchased the rights to *Count Julian*. Simms was soon able to finish the work, but there were still delays, as evidenced by his pointedly asking Lawson in November 1845, "Why has Taylor delayed the Count?" (*Letters* 2:115) The nature of these delays is unclear. While the copyright was secured in 1845, it remains unclear whether the work was actually brought out to the public in late 1845 or early 1846; compounding this confusion is discrepancy in the date printed on the title page and cover. Though otherwise identical, the cover is dated 1846, while the title page reads 1845. Whatever the actual publication date, Taylor did publish *Count Julian*. While Simms's long ordeal was finally over, the novel's strange and troubled composition and publication history is reflected in its overall poor quality. Until the present volume, the 1845/46 Taylor edition was the only publication of the novel.

One of the more curious features of *Count Julian* is Simms's dedicatory epistle to John Pendleton Kennedy, the Baltimore lawyer and congressman most famous as author of *Swallow Barn*. Simms invoked Kennedy as a sort of surrogate through whom he could offer an apologia for *Count Julian* to the public, in anticipation of the criticism it was sure to receive. In the dedication, Simms noted that Kennedy would "easily understand how much of the encouragement of the author depends upon the reader's sympathy, and how much the just decision upon his labors result from a correct knowledge of the circumstances under which he has toiled," (*Count Julian* v) circumstances Simms would soon relate. He described the work's beginnings as a drama and lamented the "absurdity" of 'theatrical management in modern times" which lead to the work being "consigned to the closet" (vi). Simms then explained how this drama was later brought out of "the closet," and reworked to produce *Pelayo* and *Count Julian*.

Mentioning the latter work, Simms declared to Kennedy that while it was not "worthy of you, my dear sir, it is yet frankly laid before you as one of the best testimonies of my own abilities and of my respect for yours" (vii). Though Simms called it a testimony to his own abilities, he also seemed to know that there were things about *Count Julian* that could have been changed. The novel could have been made better, but "such an attempt would involve an entire remodeling of the structure — a change of plan and purpose — of elements and attributes — of scenes, places and characters — and, in the somewhat mournful language of Scott, in similar self-review, I resolved to 'let the tree lie where it had fallen.' That tree, my dear sir, is at your feet" (viii). In many strange ways, this dedicatory epistle both admitted and tried to excuse the great flaws of *Count Julian.* It was Simms's hope that Kennedy "will find some fruits [within the novel] which, if not of the richest flavor, or the noblest size, will at least possess a not ungrateful relish for your lips" (viii). His friend could, thus, soften the harsh critical judgment he likely knew to be coming.

Critical Reception and Evaluation

In comparison to the great successes Simms had with other works in the 1830s and '40s, both novels were relatively unnoticed upon their release and have seen very little critical attention since. Mary Ann Wimsatt notes that of six journals that regularly reviewed Simms's works, only the *Knickerbocker* reviewed *Pelayo;* the causes of this dearth of criticism are unclear ("*Ivanhoe* and Simms" 251n). Nevertheless, the journals that did consider *Pelayo* provided generally positive reviews: though later often at odds with Simms, the *Knickerbocker* recommended the work, and described it as a novel that will satisfy readers that "kindle at passionate language, and stirring dramatic incident" (qtd. in Butterworth and Kibler 40). The same review also commented on the fact that Simms's narrative departed from pure, factual history — a prescient recognition, as the coming years would see Simms's intellectual energies deeply involved in trying to theorize the proper relationship between art and history. The *Ladies' Journal* also recommended *Pelayo,* noting that it "will not only be read, but will be remembered, for there are such scenes in it which cannot leave the mind" (41). In the case of *Count Julian,* the novel was critically damned from its first appearance, with the *Knickerbocker* caustically noting that "there is more life in the sleeping beauty of a wax museum" (67). Simms's Kennedy-invoking dedicatory gambit backfired, succeeding only in further compromising the work's reputation: reviewers saw Simms's apologetic stratagem as insulting to Kennedy, a novelist who was highly regarded at the time, and critics were vitriolic over this *faux pas.*

Both novels have been almost completely critically disregarded in the twentieth and twenty-first centuries. Guilds dismissively calls *Count Julian* "ill-advised" (195) and describes *Pelayo* as "a derivative piece below the standards of an author of Simms's caliber." He suggests that the positive reviews of the latter during Simms's life are "attributable to the taste of the time and the reputation of the author, not to the sagacity of the reviewers" (81). Mary Ann Wimsatt provides the fullest twentieth century treatment of each novel, devoting two essays to considering their place in Simms's canon, as well as their connections to works by other major writers.

In an essay exploring the parallels between the Spanish fictions of Simms and Washington Irving, Wimsatt finds *Count Julian* related to Irving's *Legends of the Conquest of Spain,* a work also about the "accession of Roderick to the Gothic throne of Spain, his various crimes which culminate in the rape of Count Julian's daughter, and Julian's subsequent betrayal of Spain to the Moors" ("Simms and Irving" 33). She notes that while "the influence of Irving on Simms is strong and evident," throughout the work, "Simms did not, apparently, make much specific use of Irving's story," in the first five books of *Count Julian,* and instead drew on the ninth-century account of the Moorish historian Rasis – the same account that Irving used as his source material. However, Book Six, the novel's final section, leans heavily on Irving's *Legends,* adapting phrases and descriptions from that work (33-34). Wimsatt agrees with earlier dismissive assessments of *Count Julian,* calling it "derivative, digressive, frequently melodramatic and tedious," and argues that it does "not challenge even the relative mediocrity of Irving's work" (34). But in an essay that examines the influence of Scott's *Ivanhoe* on *Pelayo,* Wimsatt examines that work closely. *Pelayo,* she argues, is a novel that helps us understand Simms's place in the nineteenth-century Anglo-American intellectual and literary climate, and suggests that "Simms's indebtedness to Scott extends far beyond the fragmentary borrowings previous writers on the subject proclaim" ("*Ivanhoe* and Simms" 253). Wimsatt contends that these, and other, features help to redeem the work, despite its "prolixity, melodrama, and slightly salacious sexuality" (260), concluding that the work thus deserves wider critical attention.

Reconsidering *Pelayo* and *Count Julian*

Wimsatt's assessment of *Pelayo* leads in the right direction. While an imperfect novel that suffers from unnecessary digressions and jarring stylistic choices, *Pelayo* is nevertheless a generally exciting, readable book, with real adventure and intrigue. But what makes the work truly interesting are the ways Simms attempts to take it beyond an historical adventure story and make it into a novel of ideas. The work opens with a brief examination of the historical circumstances of medieval Spain, including a recounting of the degenerate kingship of King Witiza and his overthrow by Don Roderick. Simms shows that the downfall of Witiza, and other like governments, is due to misrule, excess, and an overall abandonment of virtue. The Goth, Simms tells us, "had sunk from all the attributes of that forward valour and manly simplicity of character" (*Pelayo* 17). Looking to illustrate transhistorical truths, the author prescribed revolution as the cure for such vicious government; though they are marked by violence, suffering, and "horrors" that are "lamentable," revolutions "are injurious to places rather than to people. The great bulk of mankind grow wiser upon them, and the discovery of a new abiding-place, like the discovery of a new truth, must always afford an added empire to thought, and a wider realm to the wing of liberty" (13).

Simms's concerns in this novel were not different from those he advanced in his romances of Revolutionary America – he asked how a government loses its virtue, and what the proper response of a people should be to a government marked by vice, excess, and loss of "manly simplicity of character." How do we understand the forward march of liberty, and what role do people from different stations of life play in this movement? How is government legitimized, and can a ruler who lacks in virtue still be a legitimate ruler? Perhaps most importantly, what is the role of singular great men in the progress of liberty? These last two questions are the most pressing explorations in *Pelayo*, as the novel sees the deposed King's sons, Pelayo and Egiza, conspiring to restore the rule of their family and overthrow the vicious and lustful "usurper." Yet, after his defeat of Witiza, Roderick is declared King by the Gothic nobles – not by himself. He thus is able to claim to be technically a legitimate ruler, who has the support of at least some of the people. This complication figures in the brothers' attempts to build a conspiracy against Roderick with the nobles who did not support his ascendancy. They first attempt to persuade Julian, Count of Cueta and the most accomplished soldier in Spain, to support their cause. Yet the virtuous Julian refuses the princes' offer, as he sees Roderick's rule as legitimate, right, and proper because it has been proclaimed by a large number of his fellow nobles.

Despite his ostensible legitimacy, Roderick, because of his fundamentally lustful and tyrannical nature, is Simms's villain; Pelayo and Egiza's quest to overthrow him forms the novel's central action, as the brothers are Simms's representatives of liberty and nobility. In this way, Simms essentially wrote the history of Revolutionary America back onto that of medieval Spain. A key moment in the novel is when Pelayo is able to gain the political and military support of Spain's Jewish community, who answer to the leadership of the desert warrior Melchior. Under Roderick, the Jews continue to be a people in peripatetic exile; Melchior is certain that, under the rule of Pelayo, his people will finally have a place to belong, a country and a government that will provide them with the assurances of liberty, security, and justice. In talking to Melchior about the Jews' support of his bid for the crown, Pelayo makes promises to Melchior that a contemporary of Simms would have recognized as positively Jeffersonian. The young prince promises that, under his kingship, Jews would have "the same freedom with the rest, to hold their faith and their wealth — their several thoughts — to shape themselves in life — pursue their venture, whether in worship, or in toil, or in trade, each with his single mood, with no restraint, save of wholesome laws that all obey" (*Pelayo* 87). As Pelayo journeys throughout the Spanish countryside, he makes similar promises to other groups. Spain, then, is to be a multi-ethnic kingdom, ruled by a government based in notions of justice and liberty — ideals that would echo on the other side of the Atlantic a thousand years later.

As he reimagined eighth-century Spain as a prototype for the American Republic, Simms did a credible job of discussing virtue, liberty, and equality. This is especially apparent in his sympathetic and nuanced presentation of the Jewish characters and Pelayo's impassioned defenses of their patriotism to suspicious Christian Spaniards. The author's repudiation of the anti-Semitic stereotypes of avarice, licentiousness, and the hatred of the Christian are compelling and artfully done. Although one character, Amri, does indeed fit these stereotypes, his vices stand in stark contrast to the virtues of all the other Jewish characters. Furthermore, Simms linked Amri to the equally despicable Christian nobleman Edacer to show that moral degeneracy is the fault of the individual, not the race. Simms took a seemingly Aristotelian approach to virtue in the novel. While Amri, Edacer, and Roderick are clearly flawed because of their *lack* of virtue, the almost monomaniacal pursuit of justice and liberty on the parts of Pelayo and Melchior, at times, illustrates that an excess of virtue can itself become vice. Their pursuit becomes tedious, and the demands that Pelayo places on his brother Egiza, like those that Melchior places on his daughter Thyrza, do much to show a flaw of even heroic men — they can fail at simple human decency in favor of abstract ideals.

Simms's adherence to the conventions of the Romance leads to one of the most powerful *and* problematic aspects of the novel: needing a "dark lady" to parallel the virtuous and pure Thyrza, Simms develops a subplot around a Gothic prostitute named Urraca. This subplot presents her love for Amri, and her desire to leave her profession and commit herself fully to him. Amri, however, manipulates Urraca to satisfy both his lusts and further his political ambitions. Eventually finding her to be an impediment to his aspirations for power, Amri attempts to eliminate Urraca by convincing the enslaved Zitta to poison her mistress, a plot Urraca learns of and tries to turn back against Amri. Simms elegantly presents this series of events, using this subplot to provide readers with some of his most robust explorations of love, ambition, and, most interestingly, slavery itself. The relationship between mistress and slave is well-realized, moving, and morally nuanced; Simms here questioned the purposes and ethics of slavery, providing readers with a moving example of the complexity of his thought on the subject. As in other places in his *oeuvre*, Simms also shows himself unafraid to discuss sexual ethics forthrightly, a feature of his fiction that deserves greater critical attention. Finally, the closing scene of the subplot is incredibly beautiful, shockingly violent, and one of Simms's most emotionally realized scenes generally. Taken together, the story of Urraca, Amri, and Zitta is one of the real highlights of *Pelayo.*

Yet, this subplot is also vexing. It seems, at best, to be only tangentially related to the rest of the novel, and feels shoe-horned into the book. It does little to explicate or complement the main action of the story, and causes *Pelayo* to be seventy-plus pages too long. Finally, it seems a waste to use the incredibly compelling figure of Urraca in a context where her story is little more than a digression. Simms would have done much better to devote a short story or novella to telling this story; that he shoves it into Book IV of *Pelayo* is disappointing with regard to the narrative potential for Urraca's story, and frustrating as a jarring and emotionally demanding digression from the rest of the novel.

Taken as a whole, *Pelayo* offers a fascinating exploration of liberty, freedom, justice, notions of virtue, religious tolerance, and the inevitable flaws of great men participating in a great endeavor. It is, of course, full of aesthetic shortcomings, too: the tediousness of its dialogue, its overall prolixity, and the aforementioned subplot concerning Urraca, Amri, and Zitta. Yet, despite these flaws, *Pelayo* is a much stronger novel than has been previously argued. Reading its understanding of revolution and the pursuit of liberty and justice alongside Simms's more familiar romances would, I think, give us a deeper insight into the author's philosophy of history, government, and the artist's place in these pursuits.

Count Julian was billed as the sequel to *Pelayo,* and it in many ways wants to explore similar themes. Yet, the work is messy and often frustrating to the point of un-readability. The narrative jumps in unexpected and confusing ways. Pelayo himself is absent from *Count Julian* until its close, in what seems like a hackneyed attempt at continuity between the two works. Yet, perhaps the incredible composition and publication history of *Count Julian* suggests that we cannot, in any really reliable way, read this as a sequel to *Pelayo* except in terms of inspiration. Read as its own novel, *Count Julian* explores religious zealotry, romantic love, desire for power and money, and animal lust as obsessions that control an individual, leading to hubris and error. While there thus may be some similarities in theme and setting between the two books, Simms's work in *Count Julian,* especially with regard to religion, sets it significantly apart from *Pelayo.*

Count Julian's plot centers on Toledo, where Pelayo and Egiza's uncle, the Archbishop Oppas, is enacting his own schemes against Roderick from within the royal court. The morally degenerate Oppas is a holy man only in title, and shows no concern for neither piety nor the justice and liberty sought by his nephews. Rather, his goal is only the fulfillment of his lust for Roderick's queen, and he engages in complex machinations to achieve his goal. Chief among these are his manipulation of Romano, a mentally unstable religious zealot who harasses Roderick with Old Testament-style prophetic warnings. Oppas also seeks to manipulate Count Julian, who, at the novel's opening, is still loyal to Roderick. The twisted archbishop convinces Roderick to send Count Julian to fight the Moors, and persuades Julian to send his beautiful daughter, Cava, to Toledo for protection. Oppas knows that Cava's beauty will fire an insatiable lust in Roderick, and the twisted Archbishop predicts that the king's rapaciousness will lead to Cava's rape and Julian seeking vengeance against Roderick for the sovereign's vile action; in the ensuing chaos, Oppas hopes that he will be able to claim Roderick's queen as his own bride. Complicating matters is the presence of Prince Egiza, who met and fell hopelessly in love with Cava during the action of *Pelayo*. Having abandoned his brother in the mountains outside of Cordova, Egiza seeks to rescue his beloved Cava from the rapacious king. During his rescue attempt, Egiza makes an attempt on Roderick's life. This proves fruitful for Oppas's schemes, and the plot moves forward until Julian has, at the novel's climax, denounced his faith, declared loyalty to the Caliph, and joined forces with the Moors so as to effect his vengeance against Roderick for the rape and ruin of Cava.

The plot is convoluted, and *Count Julian* deserves its reputation for being an overwrought and tedious potboiler. Yet, in examining how positive impulses like religious devotion and romantic love can, in fact, lead to error and vice, *Count Julian* gives the reader pause, and asks us to reconsider what we know about Simms's overall project. Clearly Oppas and Roderick are evil. But several of the other characters, like the love-obsessed Egiza and the piety-obsessed Romano, are much more ambiguous in their morality and virtue. There are also unambiguously good and heroic characters. Chief among these are Egiza's jailer, Guisenard, and the muleteer Toro. These men are marked by a sober restraint that contrasts to the lustful excesses of Oppas and Roderick; by a sense of duty to others that nevertheless resists the destructively obsessive regard we see Julian and Egiza holding for Cava; and by a simple and humble Christian faith, in stark contrast to the irrational, bombastic, and dangerous zealousness of Romano. They are not the ridiculous, salacious caricatures that define the novel's other male characters, nor the helplessly pathetic shells we see in Cava and the Queen. Instead, Simms showed examples of real virtue in these men, and they seem to be the only fully human characters in the novel. Again, it is as if Simms was proposing true virtue in an Aristotelian sense, and only

Guisenard and Toro, among all the characters in *Count Julian*, are able to find the golden mean.

Yet, these two men are only minor characters, involved in plots merely complementary to the main action of the novel; that such liminal figures are *Count Julian*'s most heroic characters is deeply unsettling. What is even more disturbing is how quickly, and with what great and egregious violence, Simms killed these characters. Their deaths are the two most beautiful and completely realized scenes of the novel, on par with some of Simms's most powerful scenes generally, but Simms so jarringly ripped these characters from the narrative that readers cannot help but view them as literally hopeless. In this way, they seem to be a fitting metonym for the entirety of *Count Julian*.

Perhaps the difficulties in composing *Count Julian* made Simms unable to write a hopeful novel, and these scenes are the frustrations of the writer made manifest. Even if the hopelessness of the work can be attributed to the author's palpable frustrations, the Simms scholar must nevertheless contend with the darkness inherent in these scenes, especially with regard to religion. In *Count Julian*, prayers are not answered, except in death. Simms insinuated that the rape of Cava occurs underneath the gaze of an icon of the Blessed Virgin, and Toro's call to Mary to save him results only in death. Guisenard's simple, rational piety is destroyed by Romano's mad fundamentalism, and Oppas literally molests those who come to make their confession to him. A harrowing moment of mob violence results from attempts to convey the corpse of a "saint" to a church. All of these scenes of religious depravity lead to the novel's climax, Julian's apostasy, where he declares that all faiths are nothing more than "national superstitions." Faith, as Simms presented it, portends to be as much a sin as lust, greed, or wrath. The reader interested in understanding how Simms thought of religion must necessarily visit *Count Julian*. While Simms himself was broadly Christian, if not a churchman, the dark, proto-naturalistic world of *Count Julian* forces us to question just how orthodox his understanding of religion truly was, at least at this moment in his career. Exploring these questions makes *Count Julian* a worthy and rich source of study for the Simms scholar — even if it is, in many ways, a bad novel.

Both *Pelayo* and *Count Julian* have deep and profound aesthetic shortcomings, and the cynical reader could see their presentations of big ideas as attempts by the author to cover up their weaknesses as novels. Yet the truth of that is up to the scholar to decide. Both works, despite their flaws, deserve real attention, precisely because these two imperfect romances of medieval Spain try to explore some of the most profound questions that Simms took up in his oeuvre: the nature of virtue, the role of government, the purposes and ends of liberty, the place of faith in personal and public life, and the dangers that accompany all of these. Perhaps Simms could have explored these ideas sufficiently in a work of the Early American Republic, fictional territory on which he surely had much more aesthetic successes. But, convinced of transhistorical truths, he used his prerogative as an artist to explore other shores, and saw them as equally able to tell his society about itself and its moment, while at the same time telling about another people and their historical and cultural situation. If this is a flaw on the part of Simms, it is a flaw of ambition – the only flaw we would ever wish on our truly great artists.

Works Cited

Butterworth, Keen and James E. Kibler, Jr. *William Gilmore Simms: A Reference Guide*. Boston: G.K. Hall & Co., 1980.

Guilds, John Caldwell. *Simms: A Literary Life*. Fayetteville: The U of Arkansas P, 1992.

O'Brien, Michael. *Conjectures of Order: Intellectual Life and the American South, 1810-1860*. 2 vols. Chapel Hill: U of North Carolina P, 2004.

Simmons, William Hayne. *Notices of East Florida*. 1822. Ed. George E. Buker. Gainesville, U of Florida P, 1973.

Simms, William Gilmore. *Count Julian; or, The Last Days of the Goth*. Baltimore and New York: William Taylor & Co., 1845/1846(?).

——. *The Letters of William Gilmore Simms*. Ed. Mary C. Simms Oliphant *et al*. 6 vols. Columbia: U of South Carolina P, 1952-2012.

——. *Pelayo: A Story of the Goth*. New York: Harper & Brothers, 1838.

Williams, Stanley T. "Spanish Influences on the Fiction of William Gilmore Simms." *Hispanic Review* 21.3 (1953): 221-28.

Wimsatt, Mary Ann. "*Ivanhoe* and Simms's *Pelayo*." *Studies in Scottish Literature* 12.4 (1975): 250-69.

——. "Simms and Irving." *Mississippi Quarterly* 20.1 (1966-67): 25-37.

COUNT JULIAN;

OR,

THE LAST DAYS OF THE GOTH.

A HISTORICAL ROMANCE.

BY THE AUTHOR OF "GUY RIVERS," "THE YEMASSEE," "THE DAMSEL OF DARIEN," "RICHARD HURDIS," "BORDER BEAGLES," "THE KINSMAN," &c.

"Count Julian, call'd the Invader: not because
Inhuman priests with unoffending blood
Had stain'd their country; not because a yoke
Of iron servitude oppress'd and gall'd
The children of the soil: a private wrong
Rous'd the remorseless Baron."

SOUTHEY'S RODERICK.

Baltimore:
WILLIAM TAYLOR & CO.
CORNER OF NORTH AND BALTIMORE STREETS.
New-York:
WILLIAM TAYLOR, 2 ASTOR HOUSE.
1845.

TO THE

HON. JOHN P. KENNEDY,

OF BALTIMORE, MARYLAND.

My Dear Sir:

In taking leave to use your name in connection with the present publication, I presume still farther to address myself, through this medium, to other readers than yourself. You, I trust, will indulge me in this freedom, as, from your declared sympathy with the man of letters, and your own well-known and much admired achievements in the same field—achievements which you have but too prematurely forborne to follow up—you will easily understand how much of the encouragement of the author depends upon the reader's sympathy, and how much the just decision upon his labors result from a correct knowledge of the circumstances under which he has toiled, and what have been his aims in the scheme of his performance.

The work which follows has a history of its own apart from the very romantic history from which its materials have been drawn. This history concerns me rather than my book, and concerns the reader, who limits his curiosity to the simple detail of the story which he reads, still less than either. To all those, however, who would follow in the progress of an author's mind, through the successive steps and periods in his career—who are curious to note the stages by which he has advanced from one labor to another—there may be found, in this brief letter of explanation, something of equal interest and use.

The conquest of Spain, by the Moors, was an event which, at a very early period, seized upon and influenced my imagination; and, at the immature age of seventeen, I had planned the rude draught of a tragedy upon the subject. When reading law at nineteen, this performance was elaborated to completion, and its scenes and subjects shared my thoughts in a disproportionately large degree with Chitty and Blackstone. That, in an early, and, perhaps, an evil hour, I left the latter for more congenial authorities in art, need not be wondered at after this statement, as the simple fact need not now be more particularly insisted upon.

The drama, thus written, was submitted to the manager of a theatre—was accepted, announced and put in rehersal. But theatrical management in modern times is something of an absurdity. The secondary position which the author holds to the actor—reversing the order of things, as they were when the drama was successful—of which my first associations behind the scenes soon gave me sufficient evidence, was quite too offensive to my self-esteem to be endured patiently. My tragedy was withdrawn and quietly consigned to the closet. With a passionate fondness for the drama—with a pressing conviction, not yet surrendered, that, as a literary man, in this department of fiction lay my *forte*—I was yet thoroughly satisfied that the day had gone by, or had not yet come, when it would be becoming in the man of pride and character—of sensibility at least—to present himself at the door of a manager, soliciting to be heard through this medium. I felt that nothing but necessity—the defeat of theatricals on every hand—the utter desuetude of the drama—would ever open the eyes of the actors to the suicidal course which substitutes their art for that of the poet in whose labors only do they find exercise and employment. I took for granted then—and subsequent experience confirms all my conjectures—that the day must come, when, in the utter neglect of the stage by the great body of the public, the manager would discern the secret of its renovation to lie in the novelty of the fiction itself, and not in the variety of styles in which different actors would present to the multitude, the same old story with which they had become a thousand times familiar. For that day, however reluctantly, I was prepared to wait, sooner than forfeit any of my self-respect by unmanly concessions to a system falsely recognised as a legitimate medium of communication with the public.

But I was not to wait idly. There were other fields of exercise, and I availed myself of them to make my acquaintance with the public—in what manner, and with what degree of success, is known to no one better than yourself. My books were favorably entertained, and, after having repeatedly illustrated the histories and peculiarities of my own people, in works of fiction, I began to turn my eyes to those of other lands with the view to obtaining novelty in my materials. I am not sure that I was right in this. An author, to whom the *locale* of his action is so very important (as it is with me) to the spirit of his narrative, is perhaps always more happy in his achievements when he looks at home.

In this search I was reminded of my almost forgotten tragedy. I relieved it from its lock-up, reviewed it, and proceeded to convert the story into prose. The work grew beneath my hands. The material was copious. A certain duplexity in the action suggested its division into two parts, and the first of these parts took a definite form, before the public eye, in the shape of a "Story of the Goth," in two volumes, entitled "Pelayo." This work was written in the beginning of 1836. In the close of that year I wrote the greater part of the sequel—which is now for the first time presented to the reader, in the romance which I have honored with the inscription of your name—"Count Julian, or the Last Days of the Goth." Not worthy of you, my dear sir, it is yet frankly laid before you as one of the best testimonies of my own abilities and of my respect for yours.

There is a further history peculiar to this story. The five first books, constituting six in seven parts of the volume, were sent to the publishers early in 1837. They miscarried. My agent for their transmission, with culpable remissness, had neglected to take any memorandum by which he might recal the name of the person by whom they were sent; and months elapsed—and finally two years—before they were recovered. Meanwhile, a terrible revulsion had taken place in the monetary affairs of the country. Trade was stricken down—enterprise palsied—and literature, as one of the luxuries, less essential than bread, and beef, and beer and brandy, was among the first, in her various departments of art and education, to succumb to the paralyzing catastrophe. "Count Julian" lay upon the shelves. The sixth book was only in part written, and I had no motive to finish it. The loss of the manuscript for so long a time, of the first five books, and the doubts which I naturally felt that they might never be recovered, made me resolve to expend no more time on the composition. I turned to other labors, and, in the study of new histories, and in the preparation of other fictions, I ceased to bestow any thought upon that which had been already productive of so much annoyance.

At length, the work was inquired after by the publishers. The sequel of "Pelayo" had been promised. It was demanded. Offers from more than one publishing house prompted me once more to take up the abandoned papers, and prepare for their completion. In this attempt, I was led to discover that my mind had experienced a vast transition, in many respects, since the work was originally undertaken in 1836. My standards had undergone a change, as I fancy, for the better. I had acquired a better knowledge of my own strength—I had learned more justly to estimate my own defects and deficiencies. I had learned, in brief, to write with a greater degree of reference to the inimitable and unperishing principles of art, rather than with heed only to the capricious and frequently diseased appetites of the multitude. I need not say that, in the perusal of what had been already written, I saw how much there was that I could change for the better. But such an attempt would involve an entire remodelling of the structure—a change of plan and purpose—of elements and attributes—of scenes, places and characters—and, in the somewhat mournful language of Scott, in similar self-review, I resolved to "let the tree lie where it had fallen." That tree, my dear sir, is at your feet. I am not without my hope that you will find some fruits upon its branches, which, if not of the richest flavor, or the noblest size, will at least possess a not ungrateful relish for your lips, and for those of our very gracious public, to whom, as to a brother in the art, I commend your literary fortunes quite as frankly and sincerely as my own.

Very respectfully,

Your friend and servant,

W. GILMORE SIMMS.

WOODLAND, South Carolina, May 1, 1845.

COUNT JULIAN;

OR,

THE LAST DAYS OF THE GOTH.

BOOK FIRST.

CHAPTER I.

A PROFLIGATE king and a discontented people, bad counsellors and ambitious subjects, are each of them enough for the overthrow of any kingdom. They were all combined for the overthrow of the Gothic monarchy. Roderick—it was already the prophecy of the seers, who were numerous in Spain at this period—was destined to be the last king of the Visigoths. The signs of evil in the land were numerous. Commotions in the city, rebellions in the mountain—marvels in the heavens, and tremors in the earth—betokened the coming changes to the uninformed and superstitious. To the more thoughtful and the better taught, the actual condition of things spoke for themselves. The day was at hand—a day of blood, carnage, and singular moral not less than political revolution—in the dawn of which—a dawn preceding a long and disastrous night—a moon, according to the prophecy, should give light in place of the sun, and by its baleful and unnatural lustre, the land of the Christian was to suffer through long and successive ages of blight and eclipse. But, as if it were not enough that these changes should be effected by the ordinary tendency of events, the men high in place and unapproachable in power, those who were most to be injured by such revolutions, madly contributed to their promotion; and, wholly blind in the desperate wilfulness of his sin, Roderick himself, like another Nero, bore the torch which was to fire his kingdom and consume his power. He gave a loose rein to his own lusts, when his toil should have been to check the lusts of those around him; and thus precipitated, by his madness, the madness of those whom it was his true policy and becoming duty only to restrain and guide. But Providence had willed the destruction of the Goth. His closest counsellors were his secret enemies, and had commerce with his foes. From them he imbibed an unhappy and unwise distrust of those who were his truest friends. Oppas, one of the two archbishops of the kingdom, had insinuated himself into the blind king's confidence, not by the wisdom and virtue of his counsels, but by adroit appeals to his moods and desires. He was not too proud to serve his monarch as a creature, when he found that the vanity of Roderick did not permit him to esteem a counsellor; and, by a thousand successful but unbecoming acts, he found that favor in the bosom of his prince, which enabled him to mislead, and in the end to destroy him.

In his secret chamber the archbishop now meditated other plans, not merely for confirming his empire over the mind of Roderick, but for misleading him to his ruin.

It was his aim to make his master as unpopular with the priesthood and nobility as Roderick had made himself with his people. He had already done much toward these objects. He had secretly persuaded the king, not by any direct charge, but by dishonest and adroit insinuations, to distrust and consequently to offend many of his best nobles, whose absence from court, and retirement to their several castles, had been the necessary result of these operations. Their removal from his own path was not less an object with Oppas than the misunderstanding which it was his aim to occasion between them and their sovereign. But he had not been able utterly to banish from the court the good and the sensible. There were some few who still held their ground, solicitous to serve their monarch and their country, regardless of self, and who bore patiently the hourly injustice, the cold and scornful slight, and sharp rebuke, to which their perseverance continued to expose them. Failing to drive them away, Oppas changed his means of attack, and now labored industriously to misrepresent their purposes, and undermine their reputation.

To affect the priesthood was a leading object with the archbishop; and, unfortunately for Roderick, the indifference of the king, openly expressed, upon all matters of religion, contributed in no small degree to facilitate the labors of the conspirator. Roderick, at a very early period, had thrown aside the mask which he had worn upon coming to the throne. He had then deemed it advisable to conciliate the nobles and the priesthood, and he had greatly succeeded with both of these powerful castes. He had raised the standard of rebellion against his predecessor, Witiza, in defence of the privileges of the former, which had been assailed in his father's person; and the priesthood was readily persuaded to regard their cause as identical with that of the nobles, when they remembered that Witiza had yielded but little deference to their power, which he sought to circumscribe, and, on one occasion, had even bid defiance to the head of the Roman church, threatening, in reply to rebukes from the papal chair, to reward his soldiers for the conquest of Rome itself, out of its own treasury. Having the power of these two classes, Roderick had succeeded in his rebellion. His usurpation was made legal; and, for a brief season, all parties were apparently satisfied with his elevation. But, too soon for his own security, the reckless usurper threw aside the friendly disguises which had gained him so much. With the consciousness of power, came the confidence, too readily acquired by princes, in its stability; and Roderick now gave himself but little care to conciliate any class or character. He yielded himself up to the vices of his predecessors and of the times. He adopted all the effeminacies of the voluptuous Greek and the debased Roman; and the nobles who resisted his pretensions to absolute sway, and the priesthood which rebuked them, equally became the objects of his anger or his scorn.

It was the policy of Oppas, connected as he was with the growing conspiracy against Roderick, to foment the discontents of these classes, while stimulating the king with every counsel to continue and increase their provocations. In this labor of sin he was indefatigable; yet, though he employed numberless agents, who were always busy, the archbishop was adroit enough in his machinations, not only to escape detection, but even to avoid suspicion. It may be that there were some of the nobles who saw into his secret soul, and conjectured his base purposes; but so carefully did he conduct his game, and so great was his seeming influence with the king, that none was able to show cause of suspicion, and but few would have dared, having the proper evidence, to have declared against him.

Still, though at present thus secure, the time was approaching when he felt that it would be necessary to practice all his address to avoid the jealous scrutiny and apprehension of the king himself He was aware that an outbreak was at hand, when his nephews, the two princes Egiza and Pelayo, would lift the standard of revolt in the Asturias; and he well knew that nothing then but shows of the most devoted loyalty would suffice to protect him from suspicion. This difficulty was before him now; and alone, at midnight, in his chamber, the archbishop revolved the matter in his mind. While he mused, a private signal reached his ear. He rose instantly, and admitted one who seemed to have been expected. The stranger was one of those upon whom the arts of Oppas had been practiced in part already. Something, however, was yet to be done, to the completion of his purposes. The person who entered, and who now seated himself so confidently yet unobtrusively in the presence of the archbishop, was a priest, and one who had a great influence among his fellows, being endowed with the popular gift of eloquence in a wonderful degree, and being at the same time one of the four persons, chosen for their venerable appearance and known wisdom and sanctity, to be keepers of that famous and strange fabric in Toledo, which was known as the House of Hercules.

This 'house,' so called, was one of the greatest supposed wonders in all Spain, and was regarded by the people of the country—the natives being understood, and not the Goths—with a feeling of superstitious fear and veneration, which made it an object of national care and consideration. It was a mountain, in which there was a cavern and many secret and subterranean passages. Many were the strange stories told concerning it; and, in that time of marvels and general superstition, when religion was only dawning as it were upon mankind, and all was twilight and shadow in the spiritual world, the popular story was the source of a most prevalent faith among the people. It was said of this cavern that it had been the work of Hercules, who, when he first came into Spain, raised it there in the course of a single night, building it on the inside of the most costly materials, and leaving a written prediction, which was contained within its walls, concerning the future destinies of the nation. Wo and nameless miseries were denounced against that person who should endeavor to obtain possession of the secret which it concealed; and such had been the fear inspired by the denunciation, that the monarchs of that country, reckless and vicious as in every other respect they may have been, had never once dared to penetrate the sanctuary; but, in respect of the prediction, or perhaps with a due regard to the popular superstition, they had each of them, previous to the time of Roderick, affixed a heavy lock to its gate of entrance, that it might be the more readily recognized as a place sealed up against idle curiosity or an improper thirst to know that which the due progress of events would necessarily reveal. At this day, it matters little to inquire the source and secret of this superstition. The probability is that it was one of the thousand arts of that venerable power, known to all nations and ages, which seeks to maintain its sovereignty by practicing upon the credulity of the weak and unsuspecting. The House of Hercules was in the possession of the Gothic priesthood. It gave them at all times a certain, and perhaps supreme command over the fears and the feelings of the Spanish people. It was confided to their direction, and a selection of four persons from their body were appointed to keep it. It does not appear that these four persons were kept from the knowledge which was denied by the monarchs of Spain—arbitrary though they might be in all things else—to themselves and their subjects. They had each of them, up to the time of Roderick, placed an additional lock upon its gate, the better to secure its secrets. That duty was yet to be performed by the reigning sovereign. But Oppas resolved that Roderick should not perform this duty. He resolved that this should be one of the appointed modes which the king should employ by which to offend the priesthood. This, however, was a secret resolve of his own mind, to be pursued with cautiousness. While he spoke with the venerable Romano, who, by the way, was the chief of the four keepers of the House of Hercules, and who was himself both straight-forward and simple in all his purposes, Oppas suffered nothing of his internal schemes to be seen or conjectured; but he strove rather, though still with the view to the promotion of his own evil objects, to insist as strenuously as his brethren upon the performance of this duty by the king.

"It was bad enough, Romano," he proceeded, "bad enough that king Roderick should permit the accursed Hebrew, because of his gold, to fester in the kingdom, a stink as he is in the nostrils of Heaven and Holy Church; but what was to be looked for at the hands of one who has a countenance and a hand for the heretic Arian? Doth he not hold terms with the heathen, and those who are the known enemies of Holy Church? Doth he give heed to prescribed rites and the blessed ordinances? He makes no confession; though well I know he hath a bosom full of black and uncleanly thoughts which should bring down his proud knees day and night, at rise and set of sun, in humility before the altar, if he dreamed of, or dreaded, the wrath which is in store for him, and which hourly gathers increase. What cares he for my exhortings, or for thy eloquence, Romano, which might move any other heart than his? His neck is stiffened, and his heart hardened, like that of Pharaoh. God forbid that he provoke Heaven's wrath too far: God forbid that we be called upon to avenge his ordinances!"

"Yet, my lord bishop, I would say God's will be done!" said the other. "If it be so that Roderick shall still farther continue to defy Holy Church, and give so little heed to her messengers, I trow not what we shall do to avoid the duty which shall be assigned us. I would not that Roderick should continue blind; I would that he should come to a knowledge of his danger; and therefore, father bishop, I would have thee say——"

"I have said, Romano—I do say," replied Oppas, interrupting him. "It is the counsel for ever on my lips, and I have warned him as one that had been sent; but his thoughts are of the world and its pleasures only. He thinks but of wine and wassail; the voluptuous woman is his master; and the prayers and preachings of the church avail nothing. The servant of God must speak, having more fire on his tongue than I, ere Roderick shall be brought to hear."

"Could I but be brought to speak with him in private, father bishop——"

"Would he suffer it?" said Oppas, quickly. "Alas! Romano, I fear that Roderick is one upon whom a mark is set for destruction. For what saith the blessed St. Cyprian? 'What shall be hoped of the king that is wilful and heareth not—that hath sin in his eye, yet seeth not—that shuts his ears against the word that is spoken, and laughs at the teacher? He shall perish; and man can not save him!' Is it not so with Roderick, my brother? Thou shalt see for thyself, Romano. Thou wilt soon go to demand of him, that, as in all time aforepast, he do as the kings of Spain have ever done, and place a new lock upon the gate of the House of Hercules——"

"Thou dost not think him wilful to refuse?" demanded the priest, quickly.

"Heaven send him better wisdom, my brother," said Oppas, with much outward piety; "but I greatly fear me that he will. He hath too little reverence for the church to heed thy requisition; and the mystery of Hercules will be to him but a blinding superstition, which he doth affect to hate and to despise!"

"Now, out upon his profane thought, if such be a part of it!" exclaimed the pious Romano, with a holy horror. "What doth he know of the mystery of Hercules, that he should despise it? What is it to all the kings of the earth, who are but mean and mortal things, that they should presume to fathom the Incomprehensible, and declare what is worthless and what is good?"

"Alas! my brother; it is because the kings of the earth are mortal, that they so presume. It is their ignorance which breeds their presumption, Romano. Roderick is one of them, and he challenges danger as a thing that can touch him not; and he has learned to look upon the messenger of death as a summoner for subjects only, and not for those who sway. This is the woful blindness of which St. Cyprian has told us: it is the blindness of Roderick, Romano."

"But wherefore, my lord bishop, should Roderick withhold himself from this duty, which the kings of the Goth have ever been prompt before to perform?" demanded Romano.

"I say not, brother, of a certainty that he will, but I greatly fear it, as I know the nature that is within him. It is enough that none have ever done so before of the Gothic kings that Roderick will be bold to do it. It is a boast with him that he may dare when others would dread—that he can do what other kings may not even think."

"But the people, lord bishop, the people of Spain—who have been taught to hold the mystery of Hercules as their pledge of safety—will they forget the prophecy, which says that Spain shall be lost by the king who shall unfold the mystery; will they suffer Roderick, in his blind impiety, to do such rashness? Assuredly they will not, lord Oppas!"

"Alas, Romano, of what is it thou speakest? The people of Spain!—where are they—who are they? Roderick will have no let to his mood from any, and our good argument shall yield him none; and if the will so prompt him, he will search deep into the sacred mystery, in despite of the prophecy which denounces wo to the monarch who shall fathom it."

"It must not be!" cried the stern Romano; "the mystery must not be unlocked, my father. We were lost if it be so. The denunciation is terrible against the monarch, and against the people, and against the land, if it shall be opened. Better that we should perish first, my father!"

"Or he, the wrong-doer!" said the archbishop, in a low but inquiring tone, while he laid his hand upon the arm of his companion. "What says the prophecy, Romano? 'Spain shall be lost to the king that shall penetrate the House of Hercules, and seize the mystery thereof?' There is a meaning in this for each ear, Romano. Truly may Spain be lost to the monarch, yet Spain may not be lost to herself. She may be lost to the tyrant, Romano, but not to the people: she may be lost to the Arian, and to the Manichean, and to the profligate, my brother; but, if her sons be true, and the fathers of her church be true, she will never be lost to the banners of the blessed Jesus. Seest thou not, my brother?"

"I apprehend thee," replied Romano. "It is true, as thou sayest; but though the evil fall only on the wrong-doer, and the loss of Spain be only to her present ruler, yet would I not that the mystery should be laid open to the impious and profane eye, my lord bishop. The holy things of the church are not for the contemplation of the Arian. His finger must not touch, his eye must not see, his tongue must not defame, the relics which are given to our keeping. The trust is sacred, and we should keep it so, or consecrate the sacrifice which gives it up to the sacrilegious ruler with our blood, my father!"

"Thou hast spoken like one, my brother Romano, to whom the gates of Heaven have already been unlocked!" said the archbishop, with an air of the profoundest reverence. "Thou hast spoken boldly of our duties, and, as thou sayest, it shall be so. The martyrdom of the saints will be a kindred sacrifice with the profanation which thou speakest of; and God give us strength, my brother, to bear his cross meekly, but fearlessly, whenever the earthly ruler shall so decree in his tyrannical dictation. But let us hope for better things, Romano. Let us hope that Roderick may not be thus wicked—that he may do with thee and thy trust as the kings of Spain have ever done before, and place upon the mystery of Hercules the lock which thou shalt bear him. It is the only lock, my brother," continued the archbishop, and speaking with increased significance of tone and manner; "it is the only lock which should bind him to his church, my brother; and should he reject its ties, Romano"——

He paused with the inquiry, and looked in the face of Romano, as if seeking for an answer from him. The eye of the zealot glared with an unspeakable fury, which was a sufficient answer. His reply in words, though full of meaning, had not the same emphasis of expression which distinguished his look.

"If the lock binds him not to the church, my lord Oppas, then is the church not bound unto him. It is with the church to bind and to unloose, to bruise and to heal, to slay as well as to save!"

"My brother, the truth is living within thee!" exclaimed the archbishop, with well-affected enthusiasm; "truly is thy lip touched with the live coal from off the altar, and thou speakest with the voice of Isaiah. Thou hast said what I have thought, but what I could not so well or so boldly have said. The church has all the powers which thou hast named; and the positive command to use them in his holy cause has come from God himself. But though we shrink not from their use, my brother, we must use them wisely, not precipitately. Roderick must do this wrong ere we so punish. Let us not idly prejudge him, with the blind wilfulness of children. True, he hath already done much, and left much undone, for which he merits sore punishment from the church; and I fear me that, in his heart, he is an Arian—though his lip, when he first came to the throne, had freely enough spoken otherwise. But I will not judge him, nor shouldst thou, my brother. Better that we should be thought slow in our duty and lukewarm in our love for the church, than that we should minister to error by premature judgment."

Romano evidently listened with impatience to this long and hypocritical harangue of the archbishop. Not that he knew or suspected his hypocrisy. No! He gave his superior only too much credit for his indulgence to a heretic, as Romano had already learned to consider Roderick, through the artful tutoring of Oppas; and was only impatient to launch forth in anticipation the thunders of the church upon one whom he was now well-assured would soon render them necessary. His reply was marked by this spirit, and gave the archbishop only another opportunity the better to practice upon the fanatic.

"I dare not think with you, my lord Oppas, in this matter. To be slow in our duty is to refuse its performance—and to be lukewarm in our love for the church, is to pursue the blessed Jesus with a deadly hate; for he that is slow is overtaken by the enemy, and he that is lukewarm is won over by his arts."

"Thou art right in what thou sayest, my brother; but thou errest when thinking that I would counsel either sloth or lukewarmness. I said that it were better we should seem slow and lukewarm in the eyes of the rash and headstrong, than that we should go madly forward to do injustice in our judgment, though it be upon one like king Roderick, of whom there is but too much cause for believing that he looks kindly upon Arianism, even if he has not the accursed sin already in his bosom."

"And that is enough for judgment!" said Romano. "He that is not with me is against me, and he who lifteth not spear and sword in my behalf doth arm the enemy to my undoing. The blessed scriptures are full of precept; and we may not pause to denounce judgment upon the backslider!"

"No, surely, that we must not, good Romano, when the church is in danger. But——"

"And is not the church in danger? What greater danger than when the king which it hath chosen for its protection, heeds not its prayer for safety?" was the demand of the impatient zealot, who, in his sacred fury, did not hesitate to interrupt his superior.

"But we know not that he will refuse, Romano!" said the archbishop, willing now to soothe in some degree the devil he had raised, as he was satisfied of its readiness, when the proper time should arrive, for the execution of its intended purposes. "But we know not that he will refuse, Romano; we must await the season and the summons. It is enough for us, my brother, that we understand our solemn duties to God's holy church, and shall not be ignorant of the performances required at our hands in the hour of our Saviour's need. When we know the path and feel the duty, it is easy for the appointed to go therein; and I trust when the hour cometh, Romano, that I may be but as firm as thee!"

Romano grasped the extended hand of Oppas, while a scowl of the fiercest enthusiasm overspread his pale and thin features. The flatteries of the archbishop made him already thirst for that martyrdom which he now imagined was at hand, and a secret prayer revolved in his mind, having its origin in the selfish ambition which possessed him at that moment, that Roderick might refuse the application from the keepers of the House of Hercules, that he might be the first victim in a cause which must embalm his memory certainly in the odor if not in the actual enjoyment of sanctity.

"Let us await patiently the hour, my brother. Thou needest not fear to wait for thou canst not be tempted. Thou art strong to do and to obey; and the church will call its servant, perchance, when thou lookest not to hear such a call, but never when thou art unprepared. Thou hast but to remember, as I said to thee erewhile, that the prophecy of the ancient house thou keepest hath a meaning for either ear; and though Spain may be lost to the king, it does not follow thence that she will be lost to herself, or to the church. It is for such as thee, Romano, that the church will reserve its highest duties. She may call upon thee to save her, Romano; but whether she call upon thee, or upon me, or upon any more worthy and devoted of the brotherhood, it is my prayer that we may be always ready, with girded loins and unshrinking hearts, to do her bidding!"

"Amen!" said the other, crossing himself devoutly as he spoke, and preparing to retire. Enough had been said for his purpose, and, too good a politician to risk all by saying more, Oppas did not seek any longer to detain him. Contenting himself with repeating a few of the heads of the preceding dialogue—such as he conceived the best calculated to confirm the zealot in these views of the powers of the church, and the propriety of employing them, even upon refractory princes, in cases of extreme danger to its authority—he then suffered him to depart. Romano retired to the House of Hercules, prepared to work according to the feelings and principles laid down by his superior, and which that wily intriguer well knew he would soon enough diffuse among his brethren.

CHAPTER II.

With the departure of Romano, the archbishop, in soliloquy, gave a greater freedom to his secret and true thoughts. He laughed scornfully as he thought upon his late companion

"A man," said he, "to work upon the many—to rouse them into rage until no lion of the desert shall be less easy to tame or conquer—whose words shall fall like so much heavenly manna around them, and so readily persuade and prompt—yet what a child himself!—how easy to be won, to be beguiled, and carried from the truth, which he really loves, to the blinding falsehood, which if he do not hate, it is only because of his utter incapacity to see!"

He called a page, after this soliloquy, and proceeded to prepare certain papers which lay before him.

"These lords," said he again, in a half-syllabled manner, "these lords, whom Roderick hath banished, at an instance the source of which he suspects not, are in Andalusia. They are rash, and rage against him. They must have counsel. It were pity that so much good anger, which might produce noble performance, should suffer waste. These advices will better teach them; and their proud stomachs shall not fail to gorge the counsel, as they shall know nothing of the counsellor!"

The page stood before him.

"Ha! thou art there, Ewitza? 'T is well. Go down to the inner court and learn if the couriers be yet arrived from Cordova. The couriers of the church, boy; remember!"

The boy disappeared.

"The church is a good mantle," said Oppas, with a most innocent chuckle, "and like charity covereth many sins. But for its vestment my couriers would not so safely pass with their precious burdens."

This passing commentary did not, however, interfere with the various matters of business which still lay before the archbishop for his disposal. Various dispatches were prepared with the haste and readiness of one expert in his vocation. Over most of these, as he singly arranged them for the couriers, he spoke freely to himself of their several objects, their character, and of those to whom they were to be delivered. All of these dispatches more or less affected the conspiracy which he had in hand; and, though addressed to wholly different persons, no two of whom were to be moved in like manner, yet it may be said, in behalf of the good judgment which the lord Oppas had of men in general, that but few of his dispatches ever failed utterly of the effect they were intended to produce.

"This!" said he, as he lingered long upon one billet ere he passed the gold and silken cord around it, "this should be the torch, the blaze of which should kindle all the rest. This is for Roderick. He shall fire the pile: by his own hand, in his wild passion, shall he effect his own destruction. It cannot fail: his lust is now a madness—an incurable disease, and this cannot but mislead him."

He turned the billet in his hand—once more read over the contents, which were written in a style carefully disguised. When he had read, he folded it, penned the inscription in the same assumed writing, folded the silken cords about it, and placed it in his bosom, out of sight, saying as he did so:

"This will serve to-morrow; and if Roderick flame with its tidings, as I am sure he must, then will our desires have play not less than his! Julian will be sent far from sight, and the army be removed to the African coast—taking all hindrance from the path of Pelayo. What follows next, but that the wronged father should bring the same army to our aid, and rouse up the nobility to side with him—even those who are friendly to the usurper. This done, what matters it whether that great brag of the court and twisted feather, the dangling Edeco, leads the forces of the Goth? Were it the best army that ever Spain sent out against the Scipios, it were sent out to ruin under Edeco. God keep him in the grace of Roderick, so that he may still continue to be the espatorio—sword-bearer it should rather be, for truly, doth he bear it rather as a burden than as a weapon—rather as a thing that, as it carries honor, must be carried in its turn, than as a thing it were a grace to carry, and which should call for eminent grace in him who carries it."

The page by this time had returned, and, advancing, he laid sundry packets before the archbishop; on all of which the cross was drawn in deep red lines. Oppas made a sign to the bearer to wait, and breaking the silk of each he proceeded to its perusal. When he had done, he gave him the sundry dispatches which he had made up, and commissioned him to send off the couriers with them straight.

"This," said he, taking the one billet from his bosom, on which he had so much relied, and addressing the boy, "this thou wilt dispose of, Ewitza, so that the page of Edeco shall possess it, yet see thee not. Thou canst place it in his hands after night, to-morrow, having well chosen a disguise for thy concealment."

"I can, my lord!" said the swarthy boy, whose dark eyes shone with a quick, arch, and intense fire: "I can, my lord," he repeated, as the archbishop watched his countenance.

"And with the secrecy I require, Ewitza?"

"As thou requirest, my lord!"

"I trust to thee; I know that thou wilt do it. Leave me now; thou hast done thy service for the night."

The boy retired, and the archbishop was alone. He looked out upon the stars, and with that mingling of religion and superstition which was the prevailing feature of the time, and from which the wisest and the worst were not entirely exempt, he demanded of them that success in his purposes which he had nevertheless toiled diligently to secure by merely human means. One star, a dark red orb, shining over the distant and frowning rock known as the House of Hercules, particularly fixed his attention. Bright sparks seemed to shoot out from its sides, and while he gazed he fancied that an eye looked forth upon him from its centre.

"It is the eye of a god," said the priest, "perchance the eye of Hercules himself, watching over his temple. Would that the skill were mine to read its language! It might be, then, that I should not"——

He paused and looked around him upon the chamber, as if he heard some one stirring within; then turning his gaze again to where the star had shone, he was filled with new courage as he saw that it had sunk from his sight behind the mountain, and was no longer visible, no longer watching its temple.

"It is favorable, that sign," he exclaimed; "if the god withdraw his guardianship, what care we for the human keepers; what care we for the mummery and the mystery, if it makes for our cause that it be thrown open to the impious gaze of the intruder? Roderick shall break the seal, rather than close it. I will move his vanity to the measure; for well I know that it must work wo to the monarch who shall do so. It will work him wo with his people, if not with Hercules. The church shall rise against him—the Iberian slaves shall grow strong, having its sanction—and the kingdom shall be lost to him for ever. It will be our weakness and lack of spirit, if it shall then be lost to us."

Complying with a habit of body rather than a feeling or sentiment of mind, the conspirator retired to his devotions; and when these were finished, sought his couch for those slumbers which his protracted and earnest toils throughout the day had long before rendered necessary.

CHAPTER III.

Let us now penetrate the royal palace of Toledo, at present in the occupation of the usurper Roderick, and that incomparable woman, Egilona, his wife; a woman superior to her time, in sense and in virtue—but one whose charms, though great enough to win her the homage of a Moorish not less than a Gothic monarch, were yet not equal to the task of securing the affections of one so capricious and reckless as king Roderick.

The palace of Roderick—king of the Romans, as the late Gothic sovereigns were pleased to style themselves—had become the dwelling-place of Roman ostentation and Asiatic luxury. The throne blazed with gold and jewels of immense value; the commonest utensils of the household were formed of the most costly materials; the robes, dresses, and equipment were of a texture which the early Goths would have laughed to scorn for their silken effeminacy; and all objects of contemplation and enjoyment, announced that rapid progress from the extreme of savage privation and necessity to the refinements—so called—of civilization, to which the Goths may ascribe the downfall of their mighty empire. The luxuries which enervated them, at the same time invited the invader; and both the Moors who succeeded, and the Goths whom they overthrew, learned in due season to deplore the wooing and too well beloved possessions, which, however willing they might have been to die for, they had not the strength or courage to defend.

King Roderick sat upon his blazing throne, having on his head the horned crown of Gothic royalty, and covered with robes richly embroidered from the neck to the heels, the folds of which swept the floor in a long train behind him. He was a monarch of a noble and imposing presence, with a face full of authority, an eye haughty and commanding, and a lip that curled with an imperious and stern expression. Egilona, his queen, sat below him, upon an inferior seat, and her eyes were turned up and watchful of his features with a fond but earnest look, which at moments grew even into sadness. Her features were very beautiful, and not less amiable than beautiful. In the midst of a court where all was vicious, and where sensual indulgence had a full guaranty in the universal practices of all, not the slightest suspicion had ever assailed her purity; and though Roderick had ceased to love her with that regard which so much beauty might well have awakened in any but a blunted sense, he at least never ceased to respect her in consideration of her many virtues and her gentle bearing.

On either hand of the king stood an espatorio, or sword-bearer, of whom there were four, one of whom always kept guard in the ante-chamber of the Gothic monarch. The espatorios on the present occasion were Edeco and Favila—the former, a favorite of the monarch who contributed greatly to his debasing passions by ministering, as his creature, to those sensual indulgences to which, in his hour of prosperity, Roderick had unhappily given himself up. Edeco was a servile minister, a fop, a thing of feather and pretence, who spoke after a manner of his own, and whose ambition was to emulate the effeminacies not less than the extravagances of the other sex. Favila was a simple noble, having the royal blood of the old stock in his veins, but without much character of any sort, and one who would readily fall in with the prevailing influences of the time, good or bad. There were many ladies and nobles in attendance, all richly attired; for Roderick was a monarch to whom the glitter of jewels and the glow of silks and costly embroidery were grateful beyond all reasonable measure. But the archbishop Oppas was absent from the assembly, and it was for his presence that the king most earnestly looked.

But though late in attendance upon the court, Oppas had been already long since busy with his ministry; and ere the king had made his appearance that morning before his attendants, the wily conspirator had taken care, though keeping himself free from any apparent connection with the proceeding, to prepare the mind of Roderick against the anticipated application of Romano. It was to obtain further knowledge on this subject that the king looked round upon his courtiers, and at length ordered that the archbishop should be summoned. Before the command had well escaped his lips, the door opened and the desired personage made his appearance. The king addressed him instantly:

"My lord bishop, you are waited for. What men are those without?"

Romano and his associates had followed the archbishop, and now awaited in the ante-chamber for the summons to the royal presence.

"They are the men, oh king!" replied the archbishop, "who keep the House of Hercules."

"The House of Hercules—what house is this?" demanded the king, who affected ignorance of the whole matter.

"It is a mystery, oh king!" continued Oppas, "no doubt of highest though of secret value. It is called the 'Mystery of Hercules,' though it hath many other names."

"Make us wise in them, my lord bishop," said the king.

"I have little knowledge in this matter, oh king!" replied Oppas, "and not much, if any, beyond that of the noble gentlemen I behold around me; which is a knowledge, I believe, commonly possessed by all the people of this country who come of the native Iberian stock"——

"The native Iberian stock!" exclaimed the king, scornfully. "What idle mock is this, my lord bishop? What secret should the native Iberians keep from their sovereign, I pray? What are they that they should thus presume in secrets, in mysteries, and houses of Hercules? Of a truth, this is a matter for grave heed and close inquiry, and we'll have more of it, my lord bishop. Give forth thy other names for this mystery; we will hearken patiently, even though we hearken without gain of wisdom."

"These are old names, oh king! by which the charge of the keepers of the House of Hercules hath ever been known; and each of them hath a signification which ancient times hath affixed to it. One is the 'Perfect Guard,' by which it would seem that he who hath established the mystery would have shown that the secret should be made inviolable"——

"Ha! it were no wisdom of Hercules to think to bind the Goth! But go on, my lord bishop."

"'Pleasure and Pain,'" continued Oppas, "is another of the names set to this mystery, having its meaning also; for it is said"——

"We will read this signification ourself, my lord bishop. The 'Pleasure' is for the king of the Romans; the 'Pain'—thou shalt have it thyself, lord Oppas, to share between thy native Iberians and the keepers of the mystery. What think you, is the division not an equal one, my lords?"

And the wild, scornful laugh of the sovereign was but the signal for a kindred echo from all around him—all save the queen and her ladies, the archbishop himself, and one of the lords in attendance whose name was Bovis, and who was one of the best counsellors, though perhaps one of the least attended to, of the king whom he served.

"Another name, oh king!" said the archbishop, with a gravity of countenance which the mirth of the sovereign and of the court had not shaken, "another name is given to this mystery, having a higher meaning, which should not move your scorn, my lords—'God's Honor,' and the 'Secret yet to Come,' are no irreverent titles to our regard, oh king! These are the names of the House of Hercules, and of the mystery thereof. By all these names, from the time when Hercules slew Geryon and built this house, hath it been known even until now."

The archbishop crossed himself devoutly, as he concluded; but the king burst into a loud laugh, and as he was about to speak, seemingly with scorn of what he had heard, Egilona, the queen, turned to him, and her hand was laid gently upon his arm, and her eye looked up in supplication to his face, while she spoke in a gentle and sweet voice—

"'God's Honor,' oh Roderick! remember it is 'God's Honor;' and there can be no king's honor unless there be 'God's Honor.' Speak not in wrath, speak not in scornfulness of what thou hearest, oh Roderick! for it is holy. Let that name—'God's Honor'—be a spell to keep that secret which may seem to us but a childish folly."

"Go to, Egilona!" said the king, gently but quickly; "these are not things of thy discernment. Have done; we will hear others speak."

"Then hear *me*, Roderick!" cried the lord Bovis, advancing. "Hear me! I would counsel thee to leave this House of Hercules and its mystery, as a thing not calling for thy heed. It is enough that the native loves it, and deems it sacred—let it not be seen that thou scornest the thing of his affection, for then"——

"Enough, enough, good Bovis," exclaimed the king, impatiently; "thou hast the trick of the aged Santon, and makest thunder when thou pleasest."

"Alas, Roderick, would that I could make thee to heed the real thunder when thou but hearest it!" responded Bovis, turning away his face from the monarch in mortification, as he saw that his exhortations must be fruitless, and that Roderick was predetermined in his purpose.

"Doubtless this mystery hath gold and silver in it," said Edeco, in a mincing tone, seeing the humor of the king, "it may be robes of a curious fashion are there wrought. I would have a sash from its walls, my lord bishop, could it yield me one of a most cunning and light texture. These silks, by the burning lance! are unendurably heavy upon the shoulders."

The affected speech of the effeminate favorite was as great a provocation of mirth as any of the good things of the monarch, for which mirth was necessarily expected, and the courtiers generally laughed, and the king spoke with a kindred humor to the favorite; but Egilona looked upon him sternly, and the face of Oppas was turned upon the ground. The latter saw, and was satisfied to see, that matters were going on according to his desire, though he affected to look with gravity and sorrow upon the open scorn which the king expressed for the sacred things of which he had spoken.

"'God's Honor,' my lord bishop," said the king, "is truly a title to our devout regard; yet we know not but that 'God's Honor,' in the House of the pagan Hercules, is made a cover for man's sin. We will hear more of this matter from thee, ere we summon these men to our presence. Where is this house, I pray thee?"

"Here, in Toledo, oh king!" replied the archbishop. "Hard by the ruins of Erviga, the enchanted tower takes a large and holy space from the press of the city. It seems but a common rock, heaved suddenly up from the bosom of the broad valley; and yet, even as a tower, it is built up with a crafty skill and a most consummate art. So fame gives it out; of my own knowledge I can say nothing. It hath doors and windows within, all well secured, yet there is without but one single gate of solid brass, most cunning of design, having upon it a thousand clasps at the least;

whereto each monarch of Spain, before thyself, oh Roderick! hath set anew a lock, having due observance to the commands of Hercules securely to preserve his mystery which he hath therein concealed. To pray thee to do in like manner with the kings aforepast, do the men stand without. It is for this purpose only that they come."

"For this they come in vain!" was the sudden and resolute reply of Roderick. "I were no king in Spain, if stale conceit like this should bind me down submissive to an idle mock, that to my mind, lord bishop, would seem greatly to trench upon ground that is holy. This Hercules—this pagan Hercules—what is he better than the accursed Mohammed to us? He should, of a surety, lose dominion where the cross of Christ is held high in honor by truest worshippers. But, let the men appear."

CHAPTER IV.

The doors were thrown open, accordingly, and the four keepers of the House of Hercules, clad in long yellow robes, were ushered into the presence of the king. They were headed by the stern ascetic, Romano; his long, white beard streaming down upon his bosom, giving a ghostly and venerable appearance to his thin, pale, hollow cheeks. In his united hands he bore a huge, heavy lock of brass; and with a fearless and unblenching manner, resolute and unabashed, he at once approached the throne, and stopped not till he had passed through the double ranks of courtiers, who made way on each side, and stood immediately in the presence of Roderick. He was closely followed by his brethren; but the king did not suffer them to advance so far, ere he spoke, and arrested their approach.

"Well; wherefore come ye? Why bring ye that massive keeper? Speak! What would ye? Who are ye? What would ye have of the king?"

The words and manner of the king were stern and ungracious, but Romano was no ways daunted. He met the fierce glance of Roderick with a glance of defiance, and as full of resolution, if not so fierce, as that of the monarch. It was indeed this bold demeanor on the part of Romano which had chafed the usurper, whose nature was imperious; and the impunity with which he had swayed having made him reckless, he was not readily disposed to recognise in an inferior any feature that did not speak for his servility. But Romano had been previously aroused by what he heard from Oppas, and by his own subsequent reflections on the same subject, and he was unwilling to abate a jot of his pride or his purpose. Without seeming to regard, however, the particular language of the king and his stern deportment, Romano, with eminent and calm dignity, replied as follows:

"God, sire, hath given you power—the monarch chosen of the people of Spain. The troubles of the strife are all over, and thy duties begin. It were well, then, if now, like all our kings, you seek with us the House of Hercules, whereof we are the keepers, and with this sacred lock, after the manner of your predecessors, bind its great secret fast"——

The king now interrupted him, for it seemed as if Romano would have spoken further

"And wherefore this?" demanded Roderick. "What is the secret thou wouldst hold so fast? What is it to us, what is it to the monarch of Spain, that we should do as thou requirest? Why is it our duty? Speak! And yet beware!—beware, old man, that thou dost not trifle with us! I suspect ye! I know not that ye do not conspire in that same House of Hercules against our throne. There be traitors all around us, it is said; some we have banished, it is true; some, with their heads, have paid a heavier forfeit. Beware of this, sir keeper! Speak for thy trust."

The brow of Romano grew dark, as he heard this speech of the king; his lips quivered—his eye kindled, and, with hand uplifted, advancing as he spoke, he thus addressed the king:

"I serve the living God! king Roderick; and, serving Him, I cannot be a traitor to any of the mortal kings of earth."

The brow of king Roderick darkened, and he replied, briefly:

"Ay, if thou servest him rightly; mark you that."

The response of Romano was instantaneous:

"He is thy judge, and mine, king Roderick; let Him decide for us both; to Him I leave it for judgment, as must thou also."

"Thou errest, sir priest. The judgment shall be with me, if I find thee a traitor. So, look to it, and go no more wide of thy business. Speak of thy charge, and tell us of this House of Hercules. What of thy mystery? Unfold me that. And hearken me, old man; let thy discourse be smooth, if you are bent that it must be free. I am not meek of temper. See that thy story has fitting language, but give it no sting; or, whether thou willest me to be thy judge or not, I will not scruple to send thy head, white as it is and venerable, along with some others to our city gates. Beware!—but speak."

The fierce eye of Roderick looked into one not less fierce, when he sought to daunt by his gaze the enthusiastic Romano. But the difference of look was in favor of the priest, whom a constant contemplation of holy things had elevated and strengthened. There was a dignity mingled with the fire of his eye which Roderick could not quell, and the influence of which he did not entirely escape. Romano replied instantly, advancing still nigher to the king as he did so, with his hand extended until the huge lock which he carried waved directly in the face of the monarch:

"And if thou didst this wrong, king Roderick," were the solemn and stern words of the venerable man, "and if the righteous and all-judging Heaven, for its own high and hidden purposes, looked down and suffered it, God's will be done—not mine; not even thine, oh Roderick! though thy own hand performed it. We are but creatures of Providence, and nothing of ourselves. If God ordains that thou shouldst slay me, I may not murmur, either at his laws or at thy performance. I will but pray to be strengthened against the hour of trial, so that I may not tremble at the stroke of the headsman, or deny my Master when questioned of the faith that is within me."

"The holy man!" exclaimed Egilona, reverently, and with folded hands. "I pray thee, oh Roderick! that thou wilt speak him kindly."

Roderick frowned only, as he heard these words, but did not answer the speaker. His eye glared only upon Romano, whose dignified manner had the effect of rebuking the violence of the king, while his language was too little objectionable to yield the latter any occasion to speak the anger which he felt. While he hesitated, with this feeling, to speak at all, the conscious Oppas came to his relief.

"Wilt thou not hear the venerable Romano, king Roderick?" said he. "He will doubtlessly unfold to thee all that thou wouldst know, touching the holy house, much better than any here."

"Ay, let him speak his story," said Roderick, "but reserve his sermons. We'll have no more of them. To the secret of thy charge, sir priest. What of this house which ye call holy?"

"Which wise men, before our time, oh king! have pronounced holy; and which other wise men have confirmed as such. It is holy; and the secret which it contains is even holier than the house which holds it. By all prophecy, that secret is of mightiest power, and if revealed before the fitting season, will be of great evil to the kingdom."

"That is thy fear, not mine!" said Roderick, scornfully.

"'T is wisdom's fear, oh king! though, perchance, it be none of thine!" replied the fearless Romano.

The king half arose from his seat in anger, but the queen Egilona laid her hand upon his arm, and he maintained his temper, while Romano, without seeming to note his emotion, thus proceeded:

"This sacred trust comes down to us, oh king! from Hercules himself, who founded Spain and this Toledo, which thenceforth, he prophesied, should be the mightiest city of the realm. Then did he prophesy of the fate of Toledo, and of all Spain. This prophecy"——

The king interrupted him with something of eagerness in his tone and manner:

"What said he? What was the prophecy?"

"'T is that we keep, oh king! within the House of Hercules; and that we might maintain it truly, he prepared a spell, such as no magic but his own might foil, and there he sealed it fast."

"Thou know'st it not?" demanded the king

"I do not, Roderick."

"Well!"

"Around it, then, he heaved this dwelling, which is loftier far, oh Roderick! than thou with all thy strength can hurl the smallest stone!"

"Well, what of that? I trow the boast were but a small one; 't were no great brag in mighty Hercules to build so high a house."

The sneer of Roderick was followed by his own and the unreserved laughter of his courtiers; but Romano continued his description of his trust, without seeming to regard them:

"Four lions, oh king!" he proceeded, "form its foundation. These are of brass, and made with the nicest art; yet are they so large that not one of all thy warriors, though mounted on the tallest charger, can reach with his extended arm to their gigantic necks."

"'T is a silly tale," said Roderick; "hast thou no better matter for my ear, old man?"

Romano replied gravely, and with rebuking language:

"The tale, oh king! is little, of a truth, if the willing and obedient ear find not its import. 'T is enough for the church, oh king! that Heaven gives its commands; it is not for us to ask what is the scope of wisdom in our Ruler, or challenge His decree. Were it so with us, oh Roderick! then might'st thou find a traitor in each poor Iberian who might claim example from the license of Holy Church to doubt thy justice and defy thy rule."

"Ha!" exclaimed Roderick, with a fierce scowl and furious gesture; "wilt thou not be warned, sir priest, of thy folly ere it be too late? Beware! I tell thee; guard well thy speech; it chafes beyond thy thought. Beware!—beware! On with thy tale of Hercules."

A slight smile mantled the lips of the priest, as he listened to this language, and beheld the emotion which he had awakened in the king. It was then that he felt himself the minister of Holy Church in probing to the quick the feelings of one whom he held to be quite too regardless of her claims. He proceeded, nevertheless, without comment, in his narration:

"He then built up the tower; yet he built it not in human sight. None saw the building. No inquisitive ear heard the clear hammer ring; no eye beheld the stroke The night beheld the plain—a level plain, smooth as this floor, oh king! The morning saw this tower, like some huge rock, resting upon it."

"Quick labor that!" exclaimed Roderick. "See, Edeco, that you give this in counsel to our artisans; so shall our gardens flourish, Egilona, and our new palace spring at our approach, on the other side of the Tagus. Would he were here, to give them some strong words, that old Hercules!"

Edeco made some corresponding remark in reply to that of the king, at which the courtiers generally laughed; but Romano, as if he felt that their punishment would come sufficiently soon, did not pause to denounce it, but his bosom beat with indignation. Roderick bade him proceed, and he continued his description:

"And yet, oh king! that mighty tower, having such a sudden and unexpected birth, is wrought with such true art that it holds not a single stone which may match in size with thy hand. Yet are they still most large, as they are most precious. Jasper and marble are most common and least worthy of its materials, and they shine upon its walls like the loveliest chrystal. A greater wonder than all this, oh king! is that, though all these stones are so deftly joined together that they seem but of a single piece, yet no two among them are of the same color!"

"A nice builder he!" said Roderick, contemptuously, "that mighty Hercules!"

Romano continued, without seeming to heed the interruption:

"They further show, oh king! that they are of holy workmanship, as they do record—being linked together with such intelligence—all deeds aforepast, all great achievements, as if written in some endless chronicle. Having thus done, Hercules did then predict what should come hereafter, and the secret thereof is the charge assigned to us for keeping in that holy house."

"That shall we read!" exclaimed Roderick, as the aged Romano concluded; "that shall be read, if there be truth in what thou sayest, old man! The future and the present shall be ours, even as the past, if it be that courage to defy your superstition is all that be needed to the purpose. I have no dread of your spells—of your pagan spells; and we should nothing fear, my lord Oppas, having the cross of Christ above our heads, to grope for this secret in the House of Hercules. What say you?"

"Now Heaven forbid! king Roderick," replied the lord Oppas, in a well-affected horror. "Now Heaven forbid that you should seek to usurp the secret of the 'Perfect Guard.' We would not have it so."

To this speech, seemingly injudicious, but really designed as it was, Roderick at once replied, with the fiercest emphasis:

"Why, who are you, my lord bishop, that will not have it so—that would bind me with the will of my subject, and impose upon me a fetter which a king only knows how to break? Truly, good bishop, thou hast greatly forgotten thyself to hold me such discourse."

"Pardon my zeal, oh king! that moved my lips to so much freedom. But I would remind thee of the Iberian people, who regard"——

"Pshaw! lord Oppas; thou dost prate to me of dogs and vermin," exclaimed the king, with that common phraseology of scorn which the Gothic sovereigns and people usually employed, when speaking of the natives of the soil.

"Yet, oh Roderick! remember that, of all the kings who have gone before thee, none have dared"——

The fierce king silenced his speech at this word. The archbishop well knew, ere he spoke it, what must be its effect

"Enough, sir priest!—enough! I dare! I—Roderick, king of the Romans—I dare! Give way!" And the king rose as he uttered these words. But the lord bishop was disposed to clench the resolve of the king by an opposition which he well knew would be fruitless, and would only furnish additional provocation to the monarch's temper.

"And yet, king Roderick," he began, "it is my thought"——

The impatient and irritable despot at once interrupted him:

"Thy thought is insolent, my lord bishop!" he exclaimed, "if it will suffer me none. I will not heed thee, and need no further counsel in the matter. I am resolved!"

"Yet I pray thee hear him, Roderick," said Egilona, appealingly. "Thy error is always too great an impatience, Roderick; I pray thee to curb it. Hearken to the venerable father—hear the good bishop—hear him, I pray thee, Roderick, for my sake hear him."

"And wherefore hear him?" exclaimed Roderick. "I know what he would say, and am resolved against it. I am no fool—no suckling, to be led by babes and priests and sucklings! Hear me—hearken, sir priest!—you with the lock! I will that no further guard shall be kept over that pagan mystery which thou keep'st. I will possess this secret; and henceforward, if it be necessary, I will maintain this house. Lead the way, then; I will not fear to look in upon old Hercules, and hear what he may tell us. Bid our guards nigh, Edeco; and have some implements ready. Lead on, old man; guide us the proper way."

"I will not lead ye!" exclaimed Romano, throwing himself directly before the path of the tyrant. "I will not lead ye to sin! I will show neither slave nor sovereign the path to evil!"

The hand of the king was uplifted as if to strike, but the lord Bovis interposed, and strove to persuade the king; while others, the lord Oppas among them, undertook, though without success, to quiet the aroused enthusiast, Romano. Nothing daunted by the threatening action of the king, and unrestrained by the appeals of those around him, he continued to struggle and approach, speaking all the while in denunciation of Roderick's design:

"Strike, if thou wilt!" he cried to the king; "strike, if thou wilt! I do not shrink from thy blow, king Roderick, and do not fear even death at thy hands. I stand up for the cause of God, and am ready to die, if need be, in his service. Yet hear me, Roderick; I do denounce upon thee a dreadful doom, if with thy unlicensed hand, defying Heaven, thou dost usurp this holy secret!"

"Fool and madman, away!" cried Roderick, scornfully, and full of wrath, to the now furious Romano. "Thy doom is dreadful to the coward only—it shakes not me. Away! Take him away, my lords! I will not strike thee to the earth, old dotard; thy gray hairs plead for thee against thy folly. Perchance thou hast been more wise in thy youth: thou art sadly foolish now! Take him hence, slaves; let him not vex us further."

"Thou art doomed!" cried Romano, as he struggled with the guards.

"Thou liest!" replied the king, with scorn. "Go, mutter thy doom to thyself. I heed thee not. There is no bolt in the unmeaning cloud. I stand in its defiance."

"Thou art cursed!" cried the old man, gasping for breath, and still striving to approach the person to whom he spoke: "Thou art cursed! In Heaven's name I curse thee! I"——

"Take him hence!" cried Roderick, becoming hoarse with his own suppressed anger, at what he deemed the insolence of the priest.

Again the lord Bovis spoke to the king, in low tones, and sought to dissuade him from his purpose:

"Heed not the old man's anger, I pray thee, king Roderick," said the sagacious noble, "and yet give heed to it, as it shows thee what may be the anger of others if thou dost usurp this secret. What though thou scorn'st as idle—and well thou may'st—this story of Hercules and his house, yet a wholesome policy would have thee forego thy purpose. Close up the door, rather than open it. Take the huge lock, and fasten the old tower, though it hold nothing. What matters it to thee what are its mysteries, so that they are innocent?"

"Ay, but how know I that, Bovis?" cried the king, exultingly, and interrupting his counsellor.

"By its undisturbed age till now. It hath always been held so, king Roderick, even by the most jealous of our sovereigns. Leave it untroubled now. Its claims are modest enough; would that thy professed friends and favorites had as few! Let it have what it asks. To thee its secrets are nothing; but it behoves thee much not to offend those to whom its secrets are every thing. Remember, thou art scarcely seated in thy throne. It were not wise in thee to check these churchmen, who are too powerful to be trifled with, and scarce honest enough to be trusted."

Such was the sagacious counsel of Bovis, one of the king's best counsellors. It struck Roderick with considerable force, but he had not the courage to recede from his error. His reply was characteristic:

"There is much in what thou sayest, Bovis—much more than in any of these dooms of Hercules. But the truth is, I am roused now to look upon the ancient builder and hear his secrets. I must have my way. Besides, it is my humor thus to punish the insolence of these people, who would bandy speech with me, and seek to baffle me in my desires. I will make them know and fear me."

"Is it not rash?"—the counsellor began, but the king silenced him.

"No more! I've heard thee, Bovis. I am resolved to unlock the cavern, and thou plead'st in vain to move me from my purpose. I will search the house of our progenitor, and read his prophecies; see where he lies in state, or holds his court—and, with the aid of Holy Church, give defiance, if it shall so please me, to the old pagan and his dooms and thunders. Thou, my lord bishop, thou shalt lead the way, and lift the cross"——

Oppas started, with a look of profoundest horror, as he heard these words.

"Pardon me, king Roderick! but I may not do as thou wouldst have me."

The king laughed scornfully at what he deemed the superstitious timidity of the bishop.

"What, thou art coward like the rest, my lord bishop? Well, truly, we are surrounded with feeble men, who need a fitting example to be strong. Be it so, then; I will lead the way, though I lead it alone. The doom be mine, if any doom there be—and mine the profit, sirs."

"Yet, oh king! would I warn thee, ere thou mov'st in this, that thou invad'st the law and break'st the pledge which thou hast given."

To tell Roderick of laws, the archbishop well knew was only to stimulate him in his desire to abolish them; and the king, as Oppas expected, repeated his resolve with accumulated obstinacy.

"Now, by the Cross! my lord Oppas, which thou bearest this day, I swear to enter into this pagan house—I swear it! The law!—I tell thee, priest, my pleasure is the law. Away, there, with that madman!"

Romano, seeing the king's intention to proceed, had again thrown himself in the way before him. The last words of Roderick were a command to his guards to remove the aged zealot. But with their utmost endeavors they could not silence his speech:

"Over me thou walk'st!" exclaimed Romano, in defiance to the king. "Yea, Roderick, if thou art bent to move upon this bold sacrilege, thou shalt first trample this lowly body into dust."

"Why, so I will!" cried Roderick, leaping forward.

The queen seized him by his robes, and implored him to forbear; but he pushed her away, and hurried forward to the spot where the lord Bovis and others were endeavoring to silence the furious Romano. They interposed between him and the angry monarch; but even while they bore him back, the priest shouted his curses and defiance.

"I call on God to hear me!" he cried aloud, and shook his massive lock at the approaching Roderick. "He hears!—He sees!—I look for Him to blast thee, Roderick, ere thou canst rush upon me! Now!—now!—His thunder! Thou wilt hear it now! I hear it! Now!—now!"

Romano's hands were stretched to heaven as he uttered these words, and his whole air and manner were those of one who listened for the bellowing thunder which he invoked upon the sacrilegious king. There was a momentary pause, as if all waited the storm which was to blast, so earnest was the expression of Romano, and such was the tacit reverence which his manner inspired. But as Roderick drew nigh unharmed, the countenance of the venerable man lost its confidence, and looked the disappointment which he really felt. A moment after, he sank within the arms of his companions through sheer exhaustion.

"Thrust him forth, slaves!" cried Roderick, "but harm him not. His gray hairs and his madness plead for him even against his tongue."

CHAPTER V

Obedient to the commands of Roderick, the soldiers in attendance proceeded to thrust Romano forth from the presence; but, though greatly enfeebled by exhaustion, this was not to be done without difficulty. He struggled still to maintain his ground, and to resist the strong arms which grappled him. The efforts that he made for this purpose were much beyond his natural strength; but he had been an ascetic, and his looks belied the vigor which had grown exceeding great through severe abstinence. His morbid imagination was also active to strengthen him beyond his ordinary nature. While he strove, the white foam gathered around his mouth, and the clenched teeth shone fearfully through the pallid lips, like those of some famished wolf. He was borne back from the pathway of the king, who had now risen; but still, as they hurried him backward, he continued to shake his lock and hurl his curses at the tyrant; the lock being conspicuously, but perhaps unconsciously, raised in one hand, and the cross which he commonly wore extended in the other. Roderick scorned the priest's feeble efforts too much to be greatly enraged with him, and he contented himself with saying to Romano, as he was hurried from his sight:

"Does thy God hear thee? Thou wouldst have him blast me, wouldst thou? old dotard, as thou art! But thou invok'st Him in vain! I laugh at thy curses, and spare thee for thy insolence because of thy excess of years and folly!"

"Wait but a while—but a little while, proud Roderick! I see the bolt that is hidden from thee; I hear the voice and the thunder! God speed them to his own glory!—God speed them to thy confusion! Go—go to thy crime!—speed to the sacrilege thou aim'st at! But the vengeance is on its way, and thou but hurriest to meet it! Go, then, Roderick, to thy doom! I blast thee with Heaven's curses!—I mark thee as one that Heaven has marked for vengeance! The bolt is shot—I see it; and thou canst not fly! The shaft is aimed, and thou art without shield to breast it! Thou fliest—but thou fliest in vain!—the red sulphur chases thee!—the fire is upon thee!—thy crown is torn from thy brows! Spare me, oh God of mercies! spare me the sight!"

Raving thus, even to exhaustion, the venerable Romano fell upon his face, still struggling with those who held held him, and muttering still, though incoherently, the curses which he continued to invoke upon Roderick.

"Away with him!" cried Roderick, hoarsely; "away with him!—he speaks folly!"

Although the king affected to despise and to disregard the holy man, it could be seen by those around him that he trembled even while he spoke, with sudden emotion; while Egilona, with many tears, sought to prevail upon him to forego his purposes. But the heart of the king was hardened against her solicitations. Too much prosperity had blinded him to truth or prudence; and a false and unhappy pride—a deluding self-esteem—prompted him to continue firm in his first resolution to explore the cavern. The very interposition of those about him, who were most worthy of his consideration, as it made him jealous of their adhesion, strengthened him in his perverse judgment; and an adroit remark of the archbishop, who deplored, in the king's hearing, but not in the hearing of Romano, the excess of zeal that had been shown by his holy brother, confirmed Roderick in the contempt which he had expressed for Romano's ravings. He silenced their further pleading by a fierce repetition of his resolve:

"Lead on, with thy soldiers, Edeco! I swear by the horns of the crown, to find this secret, if there be any, and abolish this idle mummery, if there be none. The House of Hercules is the house of the Goth; shall he be ignorant of what it holds? Lead on, then, I say, and no more of this howling!"

The lord bishop Oppas with a secret heart exulted in this movement, though his hands and eyes were still uplifted in a sort of holy horror. He still continued to urge the king, but without avail, until he saw him depart on his way, with all his guards and many courtiers. When left to himself, the archbishop uttered his exultation aloud:

"It is done!—his madness is better than that of Romano. We shall succeed; between the zealot and the tyrant the game is certain. Now, let Hercules speak what he may, well I know the language of the church; and these Iberians—these despised Iberians—shall they not hear of this scorn of their giant and themselves? That is my care. They shall hear it all!"

He hurried away, with these words, to his own palace, from the towers of which he beheld the procession of the king—a motley procession of nobles and guards—some following through obedience, some through curiosity, but all with mingled emotions of doubt and confidence. The Mystery of the House of Hercules was a faith so popular, and held to be of such marvellous import in Spain, that there were but few even of the higher classes of the people that were not in some degree the subjects of its influence. The natives hung about the procession at a respectful distance; and had Roderick deigned to study or to examine the faces of those who came near him, he would have seen much to induce a pause in his progress, if not a repentance of his headstrong resolution.

Meanwhile, the king, doubly resolute in his purpose because of the strong opposition and entreaty he had met with, made his way toward the isolated pile which was distinguished as the possession of Hercules, and which, with other marvellous feats of that demigod in Spain, gave him a title to be recognized as the tutular divinity of the country. The tradition says of this fabric that—"When Hercules the Strong came to Spain, he made in it many marvellous things, in those places where he understood that they might best remain, and thus when he was in Toledo, he understood well that that city would be the best of Spain, and saw that the kings of Spain would have more pleasure to dwell therein than in any other part, and seeing that things would come after many ways, some contrariwise to others, it pleased him to leave many enchantments, made to the end that after his death his power and his wisdom might by them be known. And he made in Toledo a house," &c. Then follows a description of this house, part of which has been given by Romano to the king, and we forbear repetition. "And he commanded"—continues the tradition—"that neither lord nor king of Spain who might come after him should seek to know that which was within, but that every one instead should put a lock upon the door thereof, even as he himself did, for he first put on a lock and fastened it with his key."

But the violent spirit of Roderick, as we have seen, brooked no such dictation. In vain did sundry of his nobles, while he continued his march toward the enchanted tower, urge upon him to forbear, and give up the hidden quest; he heeded them not, but with a momently increasing train he at length reached the rocky dwelling which he had resolved to enter. But this was no easy matter. Many were the locks already affixed upon the brazen gate, for which there were no keys—and bolts, and other modes of securing the entrance, had also been adopted by those whose solicitude had ever been to keep fast the secret of Hercules. But these were obstacles only, and not preventives, in the way of the usurper. He commanded pincers and other appliances to be brought, with which lock after lock was broken. Vainly but earnestly did the faithful Bovis, and others whose sense of duty was paramount to all other considerations, plead to the last with the inflexible and wilful monarch In the old "Chronicles of the King Roderigo," there is a rude representation on wood of the opening of the enchanted tower. A slave with huge instruments is breaking the locks. Near him stands Roderick, in his royal robes. At his feet a priest kneels, endeavoring to dissuade him from his purpose. A Gothic noble, also, holds up his hand in warning to that mad temerity which seemed reckless of all consequences. But they counselled and implored in vain. The heart of Roderick was haughty and unyielding, like his countenance. The slaves proceeded with their labors, and at length, to the great delight of the usurper, the last lock was broken and the last rivet drawn which secured the massive gate against his progress. At that moment a dreadful shriek was heard to issue from the cavern, and a noise like thunder. The workmen threw down their instruments and fled in affright. All shrunk back from the entrance but Roderick, who, noways alarmed, advanced resolutely and laid his hand upon the gate. At this moment the lord Bovis once more rushed between, and with earnest address implored him to forbear.

"It is not too late, oh Roderick! to forego thy purpose. I speak not in fear of Hercules or of his enchantments; but look upon these sullen slaves, who crowd the walls of the city, and from the hills gather round to gaze at us. Already is rage mingled with the religious horror upon their faces; and they but wait as if to hear the command of their god, calling upon them to destroy thee. Pause, oh Roderick! while yet in time. It is not too late!"

But the heart of the king was hardened, and the fiat had gone forth for his destruction. Who can save him whom God would destroy? The supplication of Bovis was in vain.

"It is too late, Bovis! Shall I confess to these vile dastards that I fear them? Shall I say that I believe in their folly, and shrink from the direction of my own mind? No!—it is too late! It might have been wiser not to have moved upon this business; but it will not be wise for me to leave it now. The king who recedes from his resolves, encourages the resolution of the slave, and is no longer a proper monarch. Let me perish ere I do this! Thou art answered, Bovis."

"I am—but not satisfied, oh Roderick! with thy answer. If thou wilt give me none other, I will share thy danger—I will go with thee into the cavern."

The king warmly grasped the hand of his faithful counsellor, and his eye glistened, but he said nothing in reply. Boldly throwing aside the gate, which swung easily round at his touch, he darted into the cavern, and was instantly followed by the equally resolved but more rational Bovis. They had scarcely entered when the gate, of itself, swung back and closed upon them, shutting them in from that anxious but timid crowd who waited without, and who, in the general silence that followed the departure of the king from sight, now began to imagine a thousand terrible dangers for him and for themselves.

They had not waited long, however, before the massive gate was again thrown open, and the king rushed forth followed by Bovis. But he did not return with the same confident countenance with which he had departed. His eyes were wild, and seemed starting from his head, in the extremity of his terror—his sword was bared in his hand—the hair was erect upon his brows, and the thick sweat fell from him like rain. He grasped the arm of Bovis and stared wildly in his face; but the words that fell from his lips had no meaning for the crowd. It was well that they stood away from the cavern's mouth, and that the dimness of twilight was around the two, so that the consternation of the king was not so clearly seen by the people as by his companion, who did not seem so greatly the victim of his apprehension. He strove to soothe the king, who spoke in fitful and incoherent language.

"Be calm, oh Roderick! I pray thee; let not the people see thee thus. Remember thou hast the robes of a king about thee, and thine eye should have the fire of an eagle. For shame, Roderick!—it is not becoming in thee."

It was thus that he strove to chide into subjection the weakness which the king exhibited; but that was not so easy a labor.

"Thou saw'st it!" exclaimed Roderick; "the king—myself—him that was Roderick! Was not that Orelio he bestrode? It was!—and he fled! I saw it—with mine own eyes I saw it!"

"I saw a horse and a man upon him in flight, or something that had the look of man and horse," replied Bovis, with indifference.

"'Twas Orelio—my own sable steed, Orelio; but the flying caitiff who bestrode him—tell me, Bovis, that it was not Roderick. Thou dost not think that he would fly thus from the accursed Moslem! Thou darest not think it of thy sovereign!"

"Speak not thus, for the people approach us. Be calm—be firm—strive with thyself, oh king!—so that they may see nothing of thy fear, which will strengthen their superstitions."

The wisdom of Bovis was unheeded by the king:

"But the rider of that steed?" he said, wildly.

"Was unlike thee, oh king!—for he fled from his foe; and thou hast never done a thing so base. The rider was affrighted; and I pray thee, my dear master," said Bovis, dropping his voice as he spoke, "to forbear the look and the speech which will bring thee too closely to such a likeness. Thou wast not the flying slave, for thou wert beside me all the while, and didst pursue him with thy weapon"——

"Ay, and would have slain him, Bovis, but that he sunk from before me into the engulfing earth," exclaimed Roderick, fiercely. "Wherefore I ask thee, Bovis, did he sink? Why did he not await my stroke? Canst thou tell me that?"

"I can tell thee nothing, my dear master, for the matter is beyond me. But this I know, that thou lettest it trouble thee too greatly. It is a foul trick of the fiend; or, it may be, a trick of the accursed priesthood, whom thou hast been but too reckless to offend."

"Perchance, perchance; and I would, Bovis, that I had given heed to thee at the first. It were better.——But wherefore—canst thou tell me—wherefore, when I hurled my sword at the flying fugitive, wherefore did it come back to me with the point turned unto my hand, as if it had been caught, and so hurled to me again, by another arm? Canst thou tell me that, Bovis?" demanded the monarch.

"We will think more of this hereafter, oh king!—but now let us meet thy lords"——

"But the speech, Bovis—that dreadful voice!—I hear it now! What said it? Ha!—Dost thou remember? It rings fearfully through my brain. 'Thy kingdom'—'t was thus it said"——

"Heed it not, Roderick!" said his counsellor; but the king continued:

"'Shall be taken from thee!' Said it not that, Bovis?"

"Nay, Roderick, I know not—I gave it no heed," was the reply.

"It was; but I fear them not! Let them come—the accursed Moslem—let tnem come! Shall we fear? They little know my strength. I am strong, Bovis; I fear nothing. The dream is passing away. I am once more Roderick. Bid our nobles come nigh!"

And, truth to say, the delirium had passed away from the mind of the king when he came to think on those dangers which were only human. He resumed his composure; and when the courtiers once more gathered about him, he was the same fearless spirit, and imperious sovereign, who had led them forth that morning.

CHAPTER VI

But the consternation of the king, when he first emerged from the cavern, had been sufficiently visible to such of the people as were bold enough to advance beyond their fellows. The nobles sagaciously beheld nothing and spoke of nothing that they saw; for they well knew that there is no knowledge more dangerous to the inferior than that which shows him the weakness of the superior. The weakness of the tyrant is the scourge of the slave. But in the absence of the nobles there was no such check upon the sullen Iberians.

"Didst thou behold his eye?" said one. "Looked he not like one who had been blasted?"

"And his hair!" said another; "how it rose and stiffened upon his head; and the sweat poured from him like rain!"

"He hath it truly!" said another; "the good Romano warned him how it would be, but he heeded it not. He hath it now!"

"But that is not all!" exclaimed a fourth; "that is not all, my brethren, that ye shall see. It is but a warning he hath had of what is to come. Think you when Holy Church curses, that he who is cursed lives? No! We know not what Roderick the Goth hath seen, or what he hath heard; but of a surety he hath seen and heard matter of fear which is to come. Hush!—the lords move slowly, and may hear us; and for the native to speak in the ears of the Goth is accounted insolence."

"They do say," murmured the first speaker, in a subdued voice, "they do say that the king defied the Cross, and spit upon the holy man Romano. If he did"——

"Can he live?" demanded another. "Something dreadful will happen."

"I will not sleep to-night," said the fourth speaker, "for of a truth great Hercules will avenge his wrong upon Roderick. I look to see it before the morning dawns. And, lo! my brethren, behold! Look at that great bird which has just lighted upon the holy house, as if he had been sent from Heaven as a messenger. Look!"

"I see it! I see it!" was the cry of each; and every eye was turned to the rock, on the topmost pinnacle of which an eagle had alighted, as he had probably done for a hundred years and a thousand times before, without attracting the same degree of attention.

"Let us all watch, my brethren!" said the first speaker, solemnly, "for, of a truth, something dreadful is to happen. It cannot be that this will pass over. Hercules will have his dues, and the blessed Romano will be avenged. My blood boils to think how he hath been scorned by Roderick, and thrust away at his bidding by his soldiers. Of a truth, had any one of the nobles who stood beside Roderick when he came from the holy house, but said to me, 'Brito, cast a stone at his head,' I had done it."

The timorous crowd shrank away from the bold speaker, who was thus unconsciously embodying the popular mind; and, one by one, they left him to those musings which they esteemed too dangerous to participate, but which were sweet to him—doubly sweet—as they were now for the first time entertained. But he was not left entirely alone. When the crowd had gone, a stranger—wrapped in a close disguise—approached him from behind a ledge of the rocks which were at hand. Brito started from his place of rest and watch as he beheld him, and his hand clutched a sharp knife which he carried in his belt.

"Fear nothing," said the intruder, seeing his action.

"I do not fear much," was the reply of Brito; "but thou comest so suddenly upon me. Who art thou?"

The stranger, without answering his question, replied thus by another question:

"Thou art a serf of the count of Saldano, him that is banished, art thou not?"

"I was!" replied the slave, sullenly; "but he is no master now!"

"He was a noble master once," said the stranger; "but of this I would not speak I heard thy words but now, Brito, spoken among thy fellows."

"Well!" exclaimed the slave, while his hand once more clutched his knife.

"Thou wouldst have hurled a stone at the impious Roderick, had any one bade thee from among the nobles?" said the stranger.

"Ay, that would I! I said it to my fellows, and I fear not to say it to thee," replied the man.

"No, thou need'st not fear to say it to me. Thou speak'st aptly. I, too, would freely have hurled a stone at the tyrant, and should have asked for no one to bid me."

"Wherefore didst thou not?" was the natural reply of the Iberian.

"It was not time!" was the reply of the stranger, uttered in low but firm and emphatic tones. "When I would hurl the stone, Brito, there will be many more to do as I do, should my aim or strength fail me. Dost thou heed?"

"I do; but thou confusest me, stranger."

"Wherefore?"

"I know not; but it is so. I am confused, and many strange thoughts are in my brain."

"Let me arrange them for thee, Brito. Thou wouldst have struck the tyrant, had any one of the nobles commanded thee? Wherefore shouldst thou look to them for command? Regard thine own limbs. Have they strength in them? What are thy muscles? Can they not bend and heave, and are they not elastic for all strife and trial? Look'st thou ever in the water which ran at thy feet, and saw'st thou ever thine own face, and looked it less like that of a man than Edeco's? Wherefore look to him for a word of authority, when thou art not less—ay, when thou art far more—a man than he? What is the difference between you? Hast thou ever asked, Brito?"

"I have not—I know not, stranger; but some of these thoughts have already come to me, confusedly," said Brito.

"I knew they had, or thou hadst not spoken as thou didst. But hearken to me, and I will show the difference between Brito and Edeco," said the stranger. "A feather makes it."

"A feather!" exclaimed the serf.

"Ay! a feather—a feather, and a robe. Speak to me, and shout, Brito; I would hear thy voice."

The Iberian shouted aloud, until the deep valley rang again with the thrilling sounds.

"Didst thou ever hear the royal espatorio speak?" demanded the stranger.

"I have," was the reply.

"Had he a voice like thine?"

"Of a truth, he had not," said Brito.

"What then?" said the stranger. "Thou hast better limbs and sinews—better lungs for speech, and, since thou hast looked in the brook I need not tell thee that thou hast a far nobler aspect than Edeco. What is the difference between you? The feather, Brito, the feather—nothing more."

"Yes, more," said Brito.

"What?"

"The king's favor," said the other.

"A feather too! I marvel what were the value of the king's favor to Edeco, when the stone hurled from thy hand has taken his master in the forehead! But little, I tell thee, Brito; but even that little shall be made up to thee if thou wilt go with me. Thou shalt have the feather and the robes, Brito, and the favor of a king."

"I would not have the favor of king Roderick," responded Brito, quickly and sullenly, "since he hath banished my master."

"Thou shalt have the favor of a king, but not of Roderick, Brito. Come with me."

"I would wait awhile, stranger, and see if aught comes from the holy house. Hercules will of a surety avenge his wrong upon the tyrant."

"Thou seest now!" said the stranger. "It is from Hercules that I come to thee, Brito. He hath chosen thee, with a thousand others, to minister to his revenge upon Roderick. Come!"

With a mind crowded with conflicting and new thoughts, the serf followed his mysterious guide. The stranger had touched the key of thought in his mind, and had fired the train which ages had prepared and events were still preparing. That night Brito was dispatched with missives to prince Pelayo; and it was thus that the lord bishop Oppas gained a new instrument in the cause of revolution.

That same night, sleeping in the arms of the pure and beautiful Egilona, Roderick started from his dream of fears, in the consciousness of a wild and sudden terror.

"The palace flames!" he cried, in alarm, arousing his still slumbering queen. At the first moment of awakening, such, indeed, was the impression upon both. A bright red glare covered the walls and the chamber, and almost blinded them with the intensity of its reflection. But, looking forth, the king soon discovered the true occasion of the blaze. The flames rose vividly, but in the distance; and it required no second look to tell him that it was the towering House of Hercules that sent forth such an immense body of light. The pinnacle of the mountain was clearly in his sight, the flames rising and winding around it and shooting up in pyramidal glory even into heaven. The superstitious apprehensions of the king, which he had quieted greatly before his return to the palace, were once more aroused; and while the trembling Egilona hung upon his arm, he crossed himself, and muttered his regrets for entering the enchanted premises, against the will and wishes of all beside himself. It was sweet and singular then, to see Egilona chiding his self-reproach, and encouraging him against his superstitious apprehensions. She derided the serious fears he had begun to utter, though she had been the most urgent ere the attempt was made to discourage him against it. But Roderick was not so easily satisfied, though the words of the queen tended greatly to soothe his apprehensions. The scene in the cavern, of which the queen knew nothing, and the knowledge of which he had enjoined upon Bovis to withhold from all, was present in its fullest force to his mind; and the dreadful cries which now began to assail his ears, as if they were the cries of demons dancing around the blazing ruins, helped to strengthen his original fears. He could bear it no longer, for he heard his name occasionally amidst the uproar, which by this time had awakened the household. Favila, one of the royal espatorios, who slept in an adjoining chamber, clapped his hands for admission, and the king bade him prepare his guards, while he attired himself in his armor in order to go forth. He was soon equipped and in readiness to ascertain and meet the danger, whatever might be its shape; for, however great might have been his faults and deficiencies, the want of courage was not among them. It gave him pleasure to see the stern lord Bovis beside him, as he emerged from the palace; for, though it was not often his custom to heed the counsel of the wise and honest, he still found a singular degree of confidence in having beside him such a counsellor. When they arrived at the scene of the conflagration, it was singular to behold the spectacle. It was not merely the trees and shrubs which covered the rock that seemed to burn, but the rock itself. Red flames seemed to shoot out, like jets or tongues of fire, through a thousand crevices upon and all around it, which the eye had never seen before. The whole interior of the cavern appeared to be on fire, and the heat was insupportable except at a considerable distance. Yet, from its capacious jaws came a thousand confused and conflicting cries. Voices seemed loud in debate within, and ever and anon one voice, preëminent over all, cried aloud—"Wo! wo, to Roderick, who hath possessed himself of the secret! Wo to Spain, that hath suffered it! Wo!—wo!"

"Now, would that I knew the secret of that cavern!" muttered the lord Bovis to himself, but sufficiently loud to reach the ears of the king.

"What secret?" demanded Roderick.

"The secret of its passages to and fro, in and out, Roderick; for, of a surety, these priests are now howling within."

Even as he spoke the cries ceased, and all was silence. In a few moments more the flames overspread the pinnacled tower, and seemed to possess a perfect mastery within. Crash after crash of the falling stones announced this to be the case, and at length the entire front of the fabric went down, unfolding for a moment, only to close up for ever, the spacious jaws of the enchanted tower.

CHAPTER VII.

It were not just if we should say that these seeming marvels had no effect upon Roderick, when they affected the greater body of the people. It was his pride to conceal his sufferings and apprehensions. Whatever he believed or feared, was a secret between himself and the lord Bovis, who, whatever might have been his anxieties or his apprehensions, certainly entertained none of supernatural dangers. On the contrary, he regarded the wonders which so imposed upon the fancies and fears of others as coming entirely from human origin; and in his argument to the king, both before and after his visit to the enchanted tower, he referred to a human policy alone as that which should keep him from his purpose, and when consummated, which should strengthen him to meet its consequences fearlessly and wisely.

"I fear not Hercules," he would say, "but I misdoubt these priests, Roderick, whom thou art but too ready to offend. Beware, for of a truth I tell thee that the word of the church is of more power with the Iberian—ay, and with thy own people—far more, than any word of thine."

But Roderick was insensible to danger coming from men like himself. The moment he was relieved from his superstition, he was relieved from all other forms of fear. The argument of Bovis, which went to persuade Roderick that the marvels which he saw were of priestly contrivance, only aroused him to anger against the church. In due proportion to the feeling of scorn which he was ever disposed to entertain for his enemies, was his recklessness now of those earthly dangers which his faithful counsellor warned him against; and it was to the lord Bovis a subject of regret that he had indicated the source of those wonders to the king, which had so annoyed him; for he now saw that he had but let loose an angry enemy upon the priesthood, whose fury would be such as inevitably to blind him to those dangers upon which he was bent to run in aiming at their ruin.

"I will pursue them, Bovis, I will drive them from my kingdom! The pope himself shall feel me; and, like Witiza, I will tell the proud pontiff that from his treasury shall my soldiers be paid!"

"It was Witiza's folly that he so spake, oh king!" said Bovis, gravely; "he lost his crown by that and other like madnesses."

"I will not lose mine, Bovis; yet will I have my revenge for this insolence."

"Yet be not too quick to anger, oh king! Remember, I have but given thee my opinion of this priesthood, and that is not the thought of any other of thy nobles. It were neither wise nor just to do aught against them until thou art sure."

"I will be sure," replied Roderick, "and if what thou sayest be true, the saints shall not save them!"

That day Romano had an interview with the lord bishop Oppas. The fire which burned in the eye of the venerable zealot was like that of madness. His figure appeared to have grown, and to have expanded; and the belief to which he had been persuaded, and, indeed, to which he had persuaded himself, that he had been chosen as a divine instrument, had elevated his mind, and warmed his spirit into the most fearless fury of fanaticism. The subject before them was the recent destruction of the tower.

"The people cry aloud in horror," said Oppas, "and speak of it, Romano, as an immediate act of Heaven."

Romano smiled, but said nothing. Oppas watched his countenance narrowly, however, and saw that he had much to say.

"They speak," he continued, "of most wondrous things. They say—for many of them watched all night—they say that 'they beheld an eagle fall right down from the sky, as if it had descended from heaven, carrying a burning fire-brand, which it laid upon the top of the house, and fanned with its wings,' until it blazed, and thus came the fire, which, as we know, was dreadful and all-consuming. Didst thou hear this story, Romano?"

Another smile overspread the lips of Romano as he heard this legend, which was the tradition for ages after among the common people of Spain; and Oppas saw by his smile that the ancient man knew a far truer story of the conflagration. He replied:

"The story is an idle one, my brother Oppas; it was no bird, no messenger from heaven, which consumed the house. It was this hand, my brother, that bore the torch and set the fire to the house within. These hands piled the fuel; and, with my brothers, I sang praises to Heaven, even while the flames danced around us and licked the high walls overhead. We saw them cling like serpents to the roof, and we cried aloud in our rejoicing. A divine spirit seemed to move us all, for we shouted and clung to one another, even while the flames gathered strength and body, and there seemed no escape for us but by passing through them to the far secret passage which opens upon the Tagus. Yet when we would have gone, for the roof began to crumble and the wall rocked around us, the flame-wall suddenly parted from before us at the mouth of the narrow passage, even as the waters of the sea divided at the bidding of Moses before the flight of the Israelites; and we knew from this sign, and from others, that the blessing of God was upon our work, and that He would now have us leave it."

"And sayest thou, Romano, that this work was thine, and not that of Heaven? Methinks it doth not become thy humility to say so, and thou hast grown proud because the Lord hath so distinguished thee above all thy fellows. It was Heaven's deed, and not thine, my brother—though thy hands may have been employed by the Blessed Father to do his purposes. They were then no longer thy hands, but the hands of Heaven, Romano; and thou shouldst be heedful not to let thy heart forget its place of humility, in the high honor to which it is uplifted."

"Thy reproof is just, my brother, and the scourge to-night shall be the penance which shall subjugate my vain and rebellious flesh."

The venerable zealot folded his arms upon his breast and looked up to heaven as he spoke these words, with an aspect of most towering humility. His pride had been duly increased by the artful sophistry of Oppas. But the archbishop had not done with him.

"Thy speech was a vain one, my brother, for the deed which thou didst had a voice in thy own heart, which counselled it. Wilt thou say that that voice was thine own, my brother? Alas, no!—whence came thy authority?"

"Of a truth," said Romano, "it must have been a voice from God."

"It was, Romano; and because thou wert within the chambers of the house, and not without to see with thine own eyes, wilt thou pretend to deny the things of their sight to others? Wilt thou, in thy heart's vain confidence, presume to say that because thy hands were chosen to put the fire within which consumed the house, that God sent not another messenger, even from the heavens, to light the flame without? Know'st thou not that the flames raged even more furiously without the tower than they could have done within?"

"There is reason in what thou say'st, my brother. Thou art strong, and I am weak," replied Romano.

"Truly do I believe, Romano, what the people declare; and further, my brother, inasmuch as thou wert chosen by Heaven to do thy spiriting in secret, hidden by the thick walls of the cavern from the sight of all, so do I hold that it was meant that thou shouldst say nothing of thy service to Heaven. Wilt thou boast, my brother, of thy aid to God? Wilt thou clamor for thy recompense before the day of reward cometh? Wilt thou forget the command of the scripture, and suffer thy left hand to have knowledge of the doings of thy right? and—greater sin—wilt thou cry aloud to the people, with a mighty voice, of that performance which God has made thee to execute in secret? In truth, Romano, this were a heavy sin."

"It were, indeed, my brother; but I trust to have mercy. I have spoken but to thee of this matter."

"It is well; and it may be that Heaven has suffered thee to speak thus much in my ears that I may counsel thee, and declare to thee thy penance. I do counsel thee, my brother, to hear and to believe the testimony of the people, for assuredly do I hold it to be the truth. The eagle which brought the brand from heaven to destroy the tower was an outward sign to the crowd, significant of what thou didst within; and the marvel which they saw is yet further to be expounded, my brother, for thy benefit. The eagle was emblematic of thy spirit in this great service, and its coming from heaven indicated the source of thy ardor. The lighted brand which it bore was thy heavenly gift of eloquence which is required to enkindle in the cause of God the true worshippers of the Cross in Spain; and was not the tower which it destroyed a sign of the power of this usurper, Roderick, who had desecrated it, as he has desecrated all other holy things of this realm to his most unholy purposes."

"It is light which I see, father Oppas—a glorious light!" exclaimed Romano. "I have been blind before. And thou, too, art honored in God's employ, as thou hast been chosen to declare to me the truth."

"Remember then, my brother, that as God sent his eagle with the lighted brand, that his purpose might be seen of the people, and has dispatched thee with a secret counsel to a secret performance, it follows that thy doings should be hidden in thine own heart, and thou shouldst only speak of that which Heaven intended should be known. The eagle bore the fire and destroyed the tower, my brother; not thee—not thee!"

"Of a truth it was the eagle, lord bishop. Forgive me, Heaven, that I made a vain boast of my own feeble toils in this service!"

The point of the bishop was obtained, and the popular story was generally circulated, and as generally credited, with many additions. It was said further—for fear becomes fancy in such cases—that "after a while there came a great flight of birds, small and black, which hovered over the ashes of the tower; and they were so numerous that, with the fanning of their wings, all the ashes were stirred up and rose into the air and were scattered over the whole of Spain, and many of those persons upon whom the ashes fell appeared as if they had been besmeared with blood. All this happened in a day, and many said afterward that all those persons upon whom the ashes fell died in battle when Spain was conquered and lost; and this was the first sign of the destruction of Spain."

CHAPTER VIII.

In a few days Roderick had regained his usual elasticity; and, as in all similar cases, the matter which had caused so much surprise and fear soon ceased to be remembered, or was only remembered to be laughed at. But a deep and restless feeling had been awakened among the priests and among the people. The total disregard which Roderick had shown for the accustomed privileges of the one, and the venerated superstitions of the other, sunk deep into their minds, and with the feeling of general insecurity which his recklessness had produced, necessarily came the desire to be free from his power. It may be supposed that neither the intrigues of the archbishop Oppas nor the simple zeal of Romano were spared in promoting this desire. The effects of their industry may be seen anon.

Roderick, in the meantime, having recovered from his alarm, as the tempest appeared to have passed unharmingly over his head, relapsed into his wonted indulgence of lust and license. Unhappily for himself and for his kingdom, the pure charms and gentle virtues of his incomparable queen, Egilona, failed to restrain him from the most unbecoming vices. Edeco, his creature, and the pander to his unholy passions, seldom left him, and his influence over the mind of Roderick, acquired through the love of pleasure which was the predominant trait with the monarch, was unapproachable by better and wiser counsellors. With Edeco to minister, and his own lustful imagination to conceive, the king resumed his career of indulgence, to which the adventure of the holy house had offered some little check, if not rebuke; and the court became once again, as it was before, the theatre of wild excess and abandoned debauchery. But the usurper was destined to receive another warning, if not a confirmation of the old. It is in the written history of kings, that they seldom go utterly unadvised of their errors; and the narrow economy which in ordinary life preserves the ploughman from destruction, would avail with not less adequate certainty to the protection of the king. It is not less true, however, that high station is apt to blind one to humble dangers. The monarch is too apt to disdain, as unworthy of contemplation, the pedestal upon which he stands.

There was one true courtier, who clung firmly to the Goth, and with little but his self-approval for his guerdon, scorned to counsel in any other than the language of honesty. This was Bovis. Even as Roderick was about to speed to some pleasures, or rather excesses, to which he had engaged himself for the day, this nobleman arrested his progress. His manner was solemn but urgent, and the king seeing it, and fearing counsel which might interfere with and rebuke his proposed indulgencies, would have hurried away from his counsellor; but Bovis was too honest, too faithful, to suffer him to escape.

"Nay, good Bovis, nay; not now—another time," said the king.

"There is but one time, oh king! for our duties," replied the plain-speaking and stubborn counsellor.

"Again!" said the king, while a stern frown gathered on his brow at the pertinacity of Bovis.

"Again, and yet again, oh Roderick! when I strive against the king in the king's behalf."

"Thou art too pressing, Bovis."

"Not a whit, oh king! if thou wilt hear me. Be not angry with thy servant, I pray you, my master; my zeal is in your service, not in mine own. Not to serve you thus would be to wrong thy service, and do myself wrong."

"I do not reprove you, Bovis, that you neglect me. You shall not, with such a show of self-reproach, fasten yourself upon me." And Roderick waved his hand as if to dismiss the unwelcome counsellor; but the faithful follower was firm.

"The tidings come, oh king!"——

"'T is well! Another time! Seest thou not, good Bovis, that our mood would be free from toil to-day. We will hear you at some fitter hour, when you may discourse your will to us, and we will meditate upon it, and plot and plan, if it will please you, then—but not now. I 'm bound for pleasure now."

"But few words have I to say, oh king! and they are needful Wilt thou not hear me?" said Bovis.

"Can I else than hear thee?" replied the impatient monarch, turning full and fiercely upon the speaker. "Can I else than hear thee, when with thy fullest, freeest assail of voice, thou perchest on mine ears, and with a note of discord, like the jay's, though with far less variety of plumage to the sight, still and anon thou rendest me with thy clamor? Free me of that!"

Firmly but respectfully the counsellor replied:

"It is my love of thee, oh king! and of thy kingdom's good, that prompts my free duty into active zeal. I would have thee hear me, even though thou chidst me in return."

"'T is ever thus," said Roderick, "it is still the good of my kingdom, or my own good, and my good subject's zeal. This is the plea for each unhouseled owl, grown sagacious, and noteful of the tempest. Would I be thoughtful, they assail my thought, and thrust their own upon me. Would I pray, they come between me and the holy man, zealous to teach me of their priest's avail, beyond the reach of any prayer of mine. They make confession for me—decree my penance: would they could give me absolution!"——

"Not thus, oh king!"——

Bovis would have interrupted the current of his master's fretful declamation; but Roderick continued, without giving heed to the interruption.

"Still the same, whether in fight or festival, they chase away all my personal sense or thoughts, solely to requite me with the recompense of theirs. Nor even when I love are they less heedful to compel me into a passion according to their discretion. They are still nigh, and when I crave one woman, bring me ten, all the while chiding me with most saintly discourse of the wrong, and the folly, and the deadly sin, and preaching with seasoned words of fear, and fast, and fleshly abstinence. I'm not myself—I cannot be myself, nor rule myself, nor have thought, or wish, or will, for myself, in the presence of such zealous guardians of my own and my kingdom's weal as thou, Bovis."

"Thou art pleased to jibe, Roderick. I have not been the thing thou speak'st me," was the calm and dignified reply of the statesman, to the irritable rhapsody of the king.

"What wouldst thou, then? Speak out at once, and leave me. I thirst for unrestraint."

Roderick seated himself as he yielded this permission, and Bovis—who was a man of stern sense and direct purpose—at once replied, addressing himself to the business on which he came:

"From Cordova we learn, oh king! that Melchior, the famous outlaw, otherwise known as Melchior of the Desert—he who delivered up Auria to the Moor, and for whom the late king Witiza offered such heavy reward—has returned from Barbary, and is somewhere hidden in Spain, and it is thought even in the city of Cordova itself. Couriers have come from Edacer, who advises us that a Jew whom he hath in pay is now close upon the trail of the hoary rebel, and he hopes ere long to dispatch his head to you."

"For which he would have a goodly recompense. Is it not so, Bovis? The weight of the traitor's head in treasure was Witiza's offer for the precious possession. Would he had left the treasure that should pay for it! 'T will task us to provide it, and the brethren of the rebel must be assessed. There is no mode else. Is this all, Bovis?"

"No, Roderick; I have other matters of great regard for thy ears."

"I could have sworn it! But go on; dispatch them quick," said the impatient monarch

Bovis, without being moved by the sarcastic manner and words of Roderick, proceeded thus:

"Another comes, who reports that Pelayo, the late king's younger son, toils busily in rebellion; that his followers already begin to grow in the Asturian Passes, and that it is the thought of Edacer that he hath also dared to move within the circuit of Cordova, where his Jewish spy reports him to be found."

"Tell me of a boy! Why, Bovis, thou hast grown womanish and feeble. What are these boys of Witiza? Both young and sinewless, unbred in arms, having no wealth, no followers. Let them send out a force and bring their heads, and talk no more of them."

"'T is easy said, oh king!"——

"And easy done, my lord Bovis, if that my people be not worthless and my nobles unfaithful. But no more of this, thou art answered. Hast thou further speech with me?"

"I have, oh king! The Moor is on our shores!"

"Ha!" cried Roderick, starting quickly from the seat, in which he rather reclined than sat, his whole countenance filled with sudden astonishment and alarm.

"What is 't thou say'st, Bovis? Didst thou say the Moor—the Moor?"

"The Moor, oh king!"

"Then there is truth in it. The accursed house! Thou saidst the Moor, lord Bovis?"

"I said the Moor was on the shores of Spain."

"And why didst thou not speak this to me at first? Why tell me of Jew traitors and Gothic traitors, when thou hadst to tell me of my enemy—Roderick's enemy—the enemy of the Goth—the accursed Moslem? Go, bid them arm! Let the big trumpets sound. Array the force of the kingdom. These infidels must be met, and with all my power. Go, Bovis, let them arm. I will myself lead them to battle. I fear not—I will not fear!"

"There is no need, oh king! You speak but rashly. The Moor is few in number; and a small force, led by a trusty captain, will avail. You must not leave Toledo."

"Wherefore?" demanded Roderick.

"There are enemies to Roderick in Toledo, more fearful than any that he hath in Africa."

"Ha!—who?—what?" demanded the king.

"Another time, oh king! we'll speak of this. It is enough now that we attend to the business of which I tell thee. It does not need that thou shouldst lead the force that is to protect thy borders. Send a good captain"——

"Let Edeco go!"

"A fool!—a fop!" exclaimed Bovis, indignantly. "No, Roderick, keep him here as thy pander to pleasure, since thou must have such a needful officer. But send a man, and a tried captain upon this duty. Sent thy missives to the count Julian; is he not the governor of Ceuta? Let him go to his command. There is not a better captain in thy kingdom."

"Thou say'st well, Bovis; thou pleasest me. Let him go. Send dispatches to him with first speed, and let our commands be urgent upon him to drive back the infidels."

"It shall be done, Roderick," said Bovis, preparing to go; but it was now the disposition of the king to detain him.

"And thou think'st that the force of count Julian will avail, Bovis? The number of the Moor is small. Art thou sure that it is small, Bovis?"

"Quite sure, oh king! And the force of count Julian is a veteran force, to which the Moor can offer no equal."

"Let him speed straight, Bovis. Take thou all the direction of this proceeding, and command thou, in my name and behalf, whatever is needful to be done. Ha! Edeco!"

The fop entered at the moment, and the man of business, who heartily despised so shallow a creature, departed from the presence.

The parasite and puppy, who was the fair representative of a species not yet extinct, approached the king with the look and manner of one who was satisfied that he had in his possession the means of giving pleasure. The monarch saw this in an instant, and prepared himself accordingly to receive it. In that moment the intelligence of Bovis, and the apprehensions which it had inspired in his mind, were forgotten; and, bidding the fopling advance, he demanded his tidings.

"Eh, my master; has that camel-faced counsellor, who has a name so befitting—has he gone, and will he not disturb us?" was the reply of the mincing courtier

"He is, Edeco. What wouldst thou say?"

"I very much dislike his proportions, oh king!—and his speech is sometimes unsavory to me."

"Fight him then, Edeco," replied the king, with a laugh of mingled scorn and good nature.

"Why, so I would, Roderick, but that my nose objects. To slay him, I must be near him; and after such contact I fear me that all the waters of the Tagus would fail to purify my garments."

"Thou dost right, Edeco, at whatever reason, not to seek Bovis in fight. He would swallow thee at a bound."

"Then, oh king! would he swallow a greater delicacy than he has ever eaten before, and one far too choice for his coarse appetite to esteem. Should he be so unfortunate, he should then die of his own self-infliction, for greatly I fear me his taste would be spoiled for all other food. But I have that for thy royal taste, my master, which is more becoming for our speech. Behold this paper, Roderick; read—read for thyself. It were too great a feast for me to partake of twice in the same hour It is the music to thy dainty supper, which thou hearest. How it sounds! Tink-a, tink-a, tink-a, tink-a, tee! Would that I had grace of musical speech! Dost thou read the character, oh king? It is fairly written, with a fine reed, else would I not have looked upon it, for a bad character offends a nice sight; and then what a pleasure thou hadst lost, Roderick; what a pleasure of sounds and sights—tink-a, tink-a-tink-a, tee—how sweet is the discourse! 'Eye,' and 'lip,' 'cheek,' and 'heaving bosom'—thus it runs; I could not forget. And so pure, too!—a virgin mine!—ah! ah!—ah! I have had dreams of these in the spring-time, when, in my youth, I did strive with a maid of Andalusia, and was not overcome in the conflict. I shall never handle arms again; but it is pleasant to be reminded of them. Dost thou read, oh king! Is it a sweet discourse?"

"Truly, Edeco, thou wast born beneath the seven stars, that all fought for thee. Thou art lucky. Where got you this? I will love thee for ever, if the tale be true."

"Read it again, oh king! I have a musical ear, though the seven stars denied that I should have musical speech. Read it, Roderick, read it aloud: Tink-a-tinka, tinka, tee!"

The epistle, which was one written by the archbishop Oppas, was addressed to Edeco, but in a hand so disguised that it was impossible to suspect the writer, even if the sanctity of his profession had left him, like the rest of the courtiers, open to suspicion. It ran thus, and the king read it sufficiently loud to be heard by Edeco, but not loud enough to be heard by any casual listener. Roderick was more prudent in his amours than in his politics, though sufficiently reckless in both for his own not less than the ruin of his people.

"Doth Roderick delight in beauty?" said the epistle; "and does Edeco know not where to seek it for the master who so greatly favors him? Wherefore does he not look upon La Cava, otherwise called Florinda, the young daughter of count Julian, of Consuegra. Is she not the beauty who would please my lord, the king? Look on her eye; is there a bright star shining in the dark heavens alone, that is like to it in excellence? You shall place it in the centre of the court, and the princely ladies upon whom ye have looked so long, even until ye could see them not, will be dark spots and sullen clouds beside it, and they shall grow blind while it blazes. Is it her cheek that ye would look upon? If you look not too long, ye are hardened into stone, and feel not. That cheek is soft and rose-like, even as an evening cloud which hangs in the sun's pathway, and gathers his sweet smile as he goes. Does this move ye not? Then mark her lips, which have the curl of the leaf and the flush of the flower, and which only pant as they have not pressure. Is her lip nothing to a taste so dull as Roderick's? Then regard her bosom, which heaves up, pure, slow and white, even as a little foam-crested billow, that rises and swells and shrinks back without a murmur, when the sky is fair, and the evening smile rests on the rocks, at the foot of the rugged Calpe. Bright and black her tresses fall upon her shoulders in a sort of bountiful tribute to the rounded beauties which, though they sweetly shadow, they can never obscure; and for her form, ye have seen a long white figure of fleece in the sky of Andalusia, which the truant breeze has pressed here and there, until it grew into the shape of some godlike messenger speeding on a work of love. Even so lined and moulded as it were by the breathing rather than the finger of Heaven, is the shape of the lady Cava. Does Edeco hear, and shall the king not see? Would he see her, let him ask why she comes not to court; let him bring her there, where she shall shine in his bosom. Let him send the count, her father, upon some far and troublous service, and let La Cava be his sweet charge in the royal gardens at Toledo. Sweet gardens for so divine a bird—bird most fitting for such blessed gardens."

A bright glow overspread the face of the king, as he read this inflammatory epistle. His quick fancy, sudden to light up, and overwhelming in its fire, was instantly aroused by the description which he read. Nor were the words of Edeco, his profligate minister, calculated to subdue his passion. Everything that could be said by the habitual lips of the licentious courtier, was said, in order to add fuel to the flame already burning in the bosom of his master; and nothing now would satisfy Roderick but possesion of the unconscious but selected victim. This, however, was a resolve more easily taken than executed. The power of count Julian was immense: his popularity greater than that of any one nobleman in the nation, and in addition he had command over a certain portion of the military force of the kingdom, which he had often led, and the men of which were devoted to him. To dishonor him was to create an enemy too powerful wantonly to provoke; and, however reckless in most respects, Roderick paused ere he proceeded. It needed the artful suggestions of Edeco to spur him on. It needed that he should frame plots, for the consummation of his unholy purpose; and from him came the base suggestion that the mind of the maiden herself might be moved to consent to her own shame, and thus the sin might be concealed, for a season at least, from the knowledge of the devoted father. With the provocation of his lusts, the reflective faculties of Roderick grew obtuse, and in due proportion as his baser desires predominated in his mind, did his more generous resolves sink down. It was one of his first objections to any attempt upon the maiden, that he had just dispatched a courier to count Julian, commanding him upon his duties to the frontier, in order to encounter with the invading Moors. The honorable first feeling of the king revolted at the thought of doing a wrong to one who was even then about to toil and battle in his service; but this suggestion, instead of silencing the vicious Edeco, only furnished him wiih an additional argument.

"And wherefore send the courier, oh king? Let him be recalled. Speed yourself upon the mission; and while you give his command in person to count Julian, he cannot fail but tender you the guardianship of La Cava. Let your words be mixed up with whatever matter of grace and honor you please to suit his ear, so shall he the more readily confide to you a trust, which—if this letter be true—shall, indeed, be the sweetest bird that ever sang in your garden."

"It shall be so," said the too easily persuaded king. "Ho! there," he cried to the attendants; "one of you speed quickly to the lord Bovis; say to him that I resolve not to send to the count Julian, and bid him recall his messengers. Away!"

The lord Bovis sought in vain to know the particular reasons which had so suddenly prompted him to undo that which was most wisely done; and he was not the more satisfied as he saw that Edeco must have been the king's counsellor to this end.

"I pray that you may not repent, oh king! that you have been persuaded to withdraw your missives to count Julian. Well do I know there is none other in your realm better able to contend with the Moor than he."

"I know it, Bovis; and though I recall the messenger, I do not thereby recall the message. No, good Bovis; your counsel is in my mind, and Julian shall be our lieutenant in Africa; but I, myself, will give him his commission, and advise him of his duties. In an hour and I will be on the road to the castle of count Julian, nothing doubting of a hearty greeting from an honored servant."

"Of a surety, oh king! such will be your greeting from Julian. Would that all your friends were half so true and warm in your service. May I attend your majesty?"

The inquiry of Bovis was put hesitatingly. He was bewildered by the suddenness of Roderick's resolves, and fearful that some unseemly motive had induced it, as he ascribed its adoption to the counsels of Edeco. The king denied him, though in a kind manner and with a compliment, the boon which he desired.

"No, Bovis; Edeco shall command the guard which shall attend me—and such command, I trow, would be to you ungracious. You shall stay here and keep watch while I am absent. Egilona shall rule through thee."

The rugged but honest counsellor turned away—he had his doubts and his fears, but he could say no more.

In a little while and Roderick was on his way to that secluded dwelling of count Julian, where—ignorant as innocent—the young and beautiful Cava had dwelt till now, happy in her own innocence, and in the passionate fondness, the almost jealous love, which her proud but noble father bestowed upon her. But one dream had yet warmed her fancy to any attachment other than that which bound her to her sire. But one image came between her mind's eye and his commanding person. Her thoughts, though now warmed to love, were yet most pure and undesiring; and, although the will of her father stood in opposition to her heart's new-born devotion, it had not provoked her to murmur at his denial or to seek to break through his restraints. If she loved Egiza, she loved him with the thought that there would come a time when her love would be acceptable in her father's eyes: she did not think of its indulgence on other terms. Perhaps, indeed, she did not think of it at all. Life, with her, seemed only a feeling—duty, an instinct—and love, an emotion. To call her feelings by names, or to inquire into their consistency with one another, was no part of her mind's employment; and her heart, as yet, was quite too young, and too well satisfied with itself, to call in its assistance.

END OF BOOK FIRST

COUNT JULIAN;

OR,

THE LAST DAYS OF THE GOTH.

BOOK SECOND.

CHAPTER I.

The sun was fast sinking in the western heavens, and but a few bright rose tints remained, resting like so many smiles of a gentle spirit upon the gray hills over which he had lingered, when a man in the prime of youth, but weary and wayworn, descended one of the jutting ledges of rock which covered the scene in every direction. His dress was torn and soiled with dust and mire, and his tread was feeble and tottering. He went forward with an anxious step which might have been a hurried one but for his physical inability to make it so. It was evident that he had travelled far, and had suffered much from hunger and fatigue. His cheeks were sallow and sunken—his eye dim and spiritless, yet sometimes it lighted up with an expression of pride and energy, which spoke for concealed character that had once known lofty purposes, and had been prompted and taught in a high condition. From his neck depended the short thick sword which the Iberians preferred to use. It was without sheath of any description, and the dint of many strokes might have been seen upon both of its keen edges. Fresh stains were also plainly apparent upon its once polished surface, and distinguished its wearer as one to whom danger had been recently and fearfully familiar; though his desolate condition might well enough instruct the observer to believe that his share in the strife had been less than fortunate. Feeble though he seemed, he did not pause for rest when he descended the tedious rocks over which he came, though the green and smiling beauty of the little valley through which he wound, might well have tempted one less weary to repose. But the traveller went forward, and after a momentary hesitation began to ascend the hill which terminated the plain and lay directly in his path. It was painful to behold his toil in this endeavor—so feeble had he become that nothing but the most unrelaxing resolve of mind could possibly have sustained, while nothing but a conviction of the last importance could have carried him forward. He reached the peak of the eminence, and the last gleams of the sun fell cheeringly around him. He turned his sad eye upon the inspirer, and stretched out his arms in the same direction, as if he implored strength to pursue his way. While in this attitude the waning orb sank suddenly from sight, and a cold chill fell upon the heart of the wayfarer. His eye turned upon the space which he was yet to overcome, and it looked dismal and uninviting. Once more he gazed wistfully toward the western summits, and sweetly did they lie at rest with the purple haze and the various drapery of evening around them. Then, as if he had too long delayed, he again set forward, and plunged down the steep passages with a reckless determination that seemed desirous to forget fatigue while invoking danger. Night closed around him ere he reached the bottom of the valley, and when he did so his strength utterly failed him. He could go no further. He sank down by a little hillock, and, in the first moment of despondency, he refused to hope.

"Why should I struggle longer with my fate!" he exclaimed, mournfully, while his cheek rested upon his hand, and his eyes peered into the bosom of the earth before him, as if he would there look for shelter and repose; "wherefore resist; why not yield, and let the strife cease? I have striven long and hopelessly—I have lost all—I am myself lost. With my own hand I put away the crown of my ancestors—with my own lips have I rejected the service of my people. What remains? Wherefore should I live?"

His arm relaxed in the support which it gave to his head, and, as if he would yield the struggle for life in compliance with the suggestion of his lips, he sank forward upon his face without effort, and lay supine upon the earth. But he lay not long in this manner. The mourner was young, and not utterly hopeless, though he thus declared himself. He started from his dream of despair—he raised himself from the earth, and the new-born emotions of his soul found utterance from his lips, having no check in that evening solitude.

"Yes—there is one! She remains; and, having her, I have lost nothing. Let the throne go to my brother. It were a toil to govern which I should not seek, having my heart only filled with the one image of delight. She demands the sacrifice—she forbids the step; and that is enough! She will reward me for the loss, if loss there be; and, with her to cheer my solitude and fill my home, I know no solitude. I lose no kingdom. I am still a king; prince of possessions far more worthy than any I resign."

To an imagination so fond and fervent, the pictures which the young man had drawn before his mind's eye, had the effect of almost making him forget his weariness, and he lay musing upon them for some time in silence, unconscious that the night was thickening fast around him; making further travel difficult, if not dangerous, among the hills. He started from his dream at length, with a sudden knowledge of his difficulties. His momentary rest had brought with it a certain degree of refreshment; and his fancies had filled him with new courage to pursue his way. He started to his feet, and in the uncertain light which hung mist-like and vaguely around his path, he set forward without hesitation. An hour later, and he lay motionless at the opposite foot of the hill he was now about to ascend—stupor growing fast upon his senses, and the feeling of despair, which he had just baffled, coming over his heart with a darker gloom than ever. He resigned himself to his fate, and his eyes closed; but a falling torrent at a little distance, unseen though heard, vexed him with its trembling murmurs, and he vainly strove to sleep. While his eyes were closed, a voice mingled with the waterfall and provoked his attention. The voice was evidently calling at the foot of the hill, and from the very valley in which he lay. He opened his eyes, and a new hope came to his heart. He, too, cried aloud; and his desperate accents seemed to him like those of a feeble boy. Again did he cry aloud, and he was answered. While he looked, a light gleamed before his eyes, and he shut them the next moment in utter oblivion. When he again opened them, he found himself upon a rude couch of straw, in the humble cottage of a peasant.

"Where am I?" he demanded, hastily.

"With friends," was the kind answer; and a woman stood beside his couch.

"Rest—do not fatigue yourself," she said. "You are feeble—you need sleep"

"And food," said the traveller. "But tell me; how far is it to the castle of count Julian, of Consuegra?"

"It lies near at hand," was the reply; "but a short two leagues from the mountain; you may see its towers in the sunlight."

The traveller seemed satisfied, and the woman brought him food. While he ate, her husband came in, and described the situation in which he had been found. It was with difficulty they persuaded him to forbear continuing his journey that very night, so anxious was he to set forth when he learned that the castle of count Julian, for which he inquired, was so near at hand. But his frame refused to answer the desires of his mind, and even while he spoke of going forward, he sank into a deep slumber.

The next morning, after partaking with the cottagers of their humble breakfast, the traveller resumed his journey, and in a couple of hours the castle of count Julian stood before him. But he did not approach it as was usually the wont of visiters to do. He carefully avoided the public entrance, and the ordinary paths. Sinking into the rear of the building, he sought shelter from passing observation among the trees and hills. Here he waited patiently, watching the castle all the while, until at length, as if an auspicious moment had arrived, he went to a secret place in one of the rocks with which he seemed to have been previously familiar, and drawing from it a bow and quiver, he approached a spot visible only from the eastern wing of the edifice. Advancing from the cover of the trees into a clearer space, he shot three shafts into the air, in an upright line; then, gathering them up, he again sank back into the close cover, and awaited the result.

A keen and watchful eye in those towers had marked the flight of the arrows; and after a brief space of time, the lovely lady Cava, the daughter of count Julian, stole through the shade of the thicket to meet the stranger.

"My lord, my true lord!" she exclaimed, as he folded her to his bosom; "you are come to me at last; and oh, how happy does your coming make me! Why have you lingered from me so long? I feared, Egiza, I feared that some harm had befallen you."

"Dear Cava, your fears were idle!" exclaimed the youth, while he clasped her fondly to his breast. "You see me at last—safe—unhurt, and as true to you as ever."

Her eye caught the stain of blood upon his garments, and they bore other traces of the strife in which he had so lately been engaged. The color went from her cheek as she surveyed these tokens.

"This blood upon your clothes!—speak—tell me, Egiza, your hand has been mingling among the men who fight."

"It is true. I have been striving against my enemy—against the enemy of my people—against the tyrant who usurps my throne"

"You cannot mean it, Egiza!" exclaimed the maiden, withdrawing herself from his embrace.

"It is true, Cava; and I fought perforce. It was no merit in the eyes of my people that I took arms in their behalf. I could not help but fight since I was assailed."

"And you were defeated, Egiza!" demanded the maiden, anxiously.

"No! thank Heaven, we were not defeated. The good cause triumphed in the fight. I waited but for that. I saw my brother a conqueror over his foe, and free. I saw him with the crown of his people—my crown—upon his head. I heard him hailed with the plaudits of my countrymen; while I—alas! Cava, if thou shouldst love me not, if thou shouldst be untrue to me, I am lost!"

"Nay, doubt me not, my dear lord!" exclaimed the maiden, at a loss to account for the deep expression of anguish, and the acute, wild fire that gleamed forth from the face of her companion. He proceeded:

"Yes, Cava, I am still Egiza to you, though it may be to none other. I have been true to you, though they proclaim me false to all beside. Do you believe my truth—will you receive my vows—will you give ear to the protestations of one whom all men call traitor?"

"Alas! my lord, your words are strange to me, and full of terror. What is it that you mean?" was the reply of the apprehensive but fond maiden. "Who is it so foul of speech as to call you traitor? You are all truth, and I would believe it from no lip, not even that of my father."

"Bless you, bless you, dear Cava! for the word. It is sweet, it is every thing to my soul," was the fervent response of Egiza; but, after the pause of a moment, his manner and his language changed: "I am a traitor," he exclaimed, "it is true what they declare, my Cava; I am a traitor to my people—'tis you have made me so."

"I, my lord?" she replied in unaffected astonishment.

"Ay; but I blame you not, my beloved. Freely do I bear the scorn—calmly do I hear the reproach, so that it come not from thy lips—so that thou love me not less because of it. Oh Cava! I have come to you, indeed—but how poorly do I come! I am still true to you, but how false to my people. To be yours, my Cava, I have robbed others—to win you, you know not what I have lost, and forfeited."

"What lost—what forfeited, my lord?" she demanded.

"My country—my crown—my brother's love—my people's homage, their reverence, their service—all. They have taken from me all—pride, station, friends' love, people's service, and honorable name!"

"Alas! it is not so; you do not mean it, Egiza! And it is I that have done this, that have caused this evil? Oh, my lord, unsay your words. Tell me that you but toyed with my childish fears—that you meant not the cruel speech in sooth."

"'T is true!" he responded, gloomily; "'T is all true."

"Speak—tell me how!" she asked in terror.

"I have met my people—the nobles of Iberia—in solemn council. They proffered me the crown of Spain"——

"You took it not!" she hastily exclaimed.

"I thought of you, my Cava; I feared that it would rob me of your beauty, and I refused it."

The gladness of Cava's heart, as he spoke this, was visible in her eyes; but they met with little of a glad response from his. Sadly he proceeded, for the memory of his brother's scorn, and the unconcealed indignation of his nobles, was present to his mind.

"They would have doomed and slain me," he proceeded.

"But you escaped!" she exclaimed. "How?"

"My brother spoke for me, and though he spoke for me in scorn, he yet saved my life—saved me for you, dear Cava."

"Heaven save him for it with blessings, my dear lord. We owe him much."

"Much, much!" was the ironical and bitter response of Egiza. He proceeded:

"He saved me to my own shame, and for the scorn of others, dear Cava—nay, even, perhaps, for thine."

"Never, oh never! Speak not thus, Egiza. Why should I scorn you?"

"Have I not shrunk from the danger of this war, to head which they implored me? 'T was I, dear Cava, who first set on the nobles, after my father's death, against his murderer. I was the first to shrink from them. I leave them to the danger—I desert them at the season when every sword is needful in their ranks, and every head is numbered. This is my shame, dear Cava—my deep shame. For thee have I done this; for thee have I given up my father's throne, and suffered dishonorable words to blot my name. Wilt thou not scorn me for it, like the rest?"

"No, Egiza. Nor will they scorn you, who are wise. This war is hopeless. How can your people attack king Roderick? Where are the soldiers, the arms, the money? 'T is madness but to think it."

"The greater reason, then, my Cava, that I, who have wrought them to this madness, should be the last to leave them. If the cause be so hopeless, I should be the first to meet with its dangers, and not the first to desert them because of its hopelessness. Seest thou not that if thy argument be strong, the greater is my shame to leave them. Thou takest to thy heart, my Cava, one who is scorned of all but thee."

"I will not think it, my Egiza; but if what thou sayest be true, I will love thee more for the scorn of others. Do I not know that it is for me thou hast risked this danger and incurred this shame. 'T is I have wrought thee to it; and shall I heed the error, if it be error, which makes me thine the more certainly—which comes of thy stronger love for me. No, Egiza, I will but pray Heaven that the power be mine to requite thee with that love for which thou hast yielded up so much."

"Thou wilt requite me?" he asked, hastily.

"I will be thine, Egiza; or, I will yield myself to none other."

"But wherefore the doubt, my Cava? Is this all? Canst thou not say that thou wilt certainly be mine?"

"My father, Egiza."

"What! Thou waitest for him to give me to thy arms? Alas! Cava, he will never give thee to me. Has he not drawn weapons upon me? Dost thou forget when last we parted, when Pelayo came to my succor, and saved me from bonds or death? What hope is there that he will yield thee to my prayers, when such has been his temper."

"He will relent. He denied thee when thou wast a foe to king Roderick, but when he hears that you have left your people, and refused the crown, he will relent—he will yield me to thy prayers; for greatly, dear Egiza, does my father love me."

"Would it were so, Cava; but I fear me much that he will not so readily confide in my pledges—he will not believe my promises."

"Fear nothing, Egiza; he cannot doubt thy truth—I know he cannot!" said the relying maiden.

"But if he does, my Cava"—— The lover paused in his speech.

"Alas!" exclaimed the maiden, as her head hung down droopingly at this suggestion of denial.

"If he does withhold thee from my love, my Cava—if, heedless of my prayers and thy consentings, he should deny me to thy arms—say, what, what wilt thou say?—what, then, shall I do, that the happiness of both be not lost for ever?" exclaimed the lover.

"Indeed, indeed, I know not!" said the maiden.

"Let me teach thee," was the quick response. "Thou shalt fly to my arms, my Cava; a priest shall be in waiting to wed us; and, far away from danger, in the seclusion of the mountains of Asturia, we shall enjoy happiness and defy danger

Wilt thou fly with me, Cava; wilt thou share with me the life I offer thee, should thy father deny thee to my prayer?"

"Stay!" she cried—her hand uplifted, and her eyes turned upon a distant road, which wound around the brow of a neighboring mountain. The eyes of her lover were upon her, and he urged her reply to the demand which he had made. But her mind had received an interruption, and she did not heed his earnestness.

"Stay—a moment, dear Egiza; look to the road from Toledo. What is it that thou seest?"

He turned his eyes impatiently in the prescribed direction, as if all objects but that of his quest had been of no importance—none, at least, which should interrupt his pleadings.

"I see men," he replied; "a goodly troop, shining with armor: but what is this to us, my Cava?"

"They seek my father," said the maid.

"But do not seek us. Let them speed, dear Cava, as they may; but hearken, dearest, to the prayer I make thee. Thou hast heard what I have said—what I would have thee say. For thee, and at thy wish have I yielded all; wilt thou yield all for me? Should thy father refuse my prayer—should he deny thee thine—wilt thou then free thyself from his power, and rely on mine? Speak, dearest, and make me happy by a word"

"Alas! Egiza, what would you have me say—what would you have me do?"

"Be mine—be mine!"

"Why, so I would be. Doubt not, my lord, that my father, who truly loves me, will yield me to thy prayer, knowing how much I love thee. He is kind—loves me beyond all human things, and gives me all things I love. Wait but a while, my lord—give thyself time to seek him, and to make thy worth be known to him, and all will go well, even as we wish it."

"I pray it may be so, my Cava—but should it not--say that he should deny me—say that he holds me as an enemy, or that he would give thee to some other noble"——

"I would not wed another!" exclaimed the maiden.

"Thanks, many thanks, dear Cava!—but say that thou wilt wed with me, and I will bless thee from my soul."

"Alas! I know not—the thought is strange—I know not how to answer."

"Dost thou love me?"

"Canst thou ask?" replied the maiden reproachfully; and she half withdrew from his arms, which at this time were locked around her.

"Nay, Cava, chafe not with me. I speak like one most desperate. I am desperate. I have but one hope left. 'T is in your hands. Speak and save me, Cava—or, if thou dost not love me as I would have thee love, speak and destroy me."

"Oh, I am thine, all thine, Egiza; wherefore dost thou doubt me thus, and vex thyself? I will be thine—thine only."

With an almost frantic embrace he drew her to his bosom, and, for the moment, such were his feelings, he had no other mode of speech.

"I hold thee bound, my Cava," were his words at length, when he broke the silence which his intense pleasure had imposed. "Should thy father withhold thee from me, and deny my prayer, thou wilt still be mine. Thou wilt heed my summons; thou wilt come to my signal as thou comest now."

"I will, believe me, Egiza; but I must fly thee now. Look! the strange troop approaches, and my father must not know of my absence from the castle, should he demand my presence to receive them."

The stirring sounds of the trumpet rang with a lively note as the troop wound their way over the rocky defiles. Egiza surveyed the glitter of their armament with a melancholy feeling, and his mind busied itself in comparing the gorgeous trappings of the chiefs who led them, with his own miserable appearance. A jealous sentiment rose to his lips.

"Thou wilt look on these gallant warriors, my Cava, and in thy thoughts thou wilt compare them with the sorry looks of Egiza. Their gilded trappings will shine in thy eyes, till thou turnest from the thoughts of him who seeks thee in so poor a fashion."

"Thou dost me wrong, Egiza. I will remember nothing but the trappings thou hast given up for my love, and remembering these, I shall not regard the glitter which I behold on others. Be as sure of the love of Cava, as thou hast made her confident of thine. I leave thee now, Egiza; I will come to thee to-morrow, and we will speak more of this matter. I will, when thou hast permitted me to speak, declare to my father, all that thou hast now unfolded to me. Be not impatient, my lord, in this matter; my love is too strong for thee to make it needful that thou shouldst hasten the season when it may be thine."

The gorgeous cavalcade which they beheld descending the hills, had now reached the main entrance of the castle. They heard the martial summons of the trumpet clamoring for admission, and the maiden hurried away from her lover, in her solicitude to gain her chamber ere the arrival of strangers, while Egiza sank among the covering hills with which he was familiar, and which had often already afforded him a shelter.

CHAPTER II.

THE maiden had but little time to effect her object, and gain her apartment, so wilful and exacting is the devoted love—so impetuous and rapid had been the approach of the strange warriors. The cavalcade was that of the Gothic monarch, whom we have seen setting forth on a double mission for the castle of his lieutenant. With that reckless hardihood of vice which distinguished his reign, and led to his downfall, he came at the same moment to exact service from his subject, and to inflict dishonor on his name. In his corrupt mind he already revelled in the charms of La Cava, while her brave father was doing his battles and defending his country from the infidel invader, But while purposing this deadly wrong to a faithful subject, king Roderick was yet too well aware of the danger which he was about to incur to suffer his secret thoughts to be known by others. He too well knew the fierce and jealous nature of count Julian, who had come of the old Roman stock, and he was not ignorant of the great influence which he possessed over the veteran soldiers whom he had so often led to victory. To his creature Edeco, alone, from whom—and the anonymous epistle of Oppas—the base incentive had come, did he communicate his design. With more caution, therefore, than he was accustomed to employ, he resolved upon pursuing his present object; and when he met count Julian, who had come forth to the castle entrance to receive him, his manner and language, though free and kingly, were yet singularly circumspect, for one so habitually reckless.

"You do your poor noble honor, my lord king, when you so ride forth to see him," was the salutation of count Julian, while he held the stirrup for the monarch to alight.

"Ay, my lord; and had I known that your castle held so lovely a spot in com mand, I should not have been so slow to seek thee out. Truly the air is grateful, and the hills—they rise around thee like a natural rampart. Wert thou a rebel, count Julian, it would need a goodly force to undo thee in thy stronghold."

"It is thine, oh king! and little prospect is there that it will be held against thee or thine. The air, as thou sayest, is grateful; and in the sunset, the hills wear a look which will delight thine eye far more than now. But let us in, my lord; thou shouldst need refreshment. Thou wilt find a cup of choice wine grateful after thy toilsome travel among these hills."

"The thought is good;" and the king alighted while he spoke. The grooms came forward and took charge of the horses, while, following their master's example, the nobles in the train of Roderick alighted also, and, at the bidding of count Julian, followed them into the castle. When they had drunk and been refreshed, the lady Cava descended from her chamber, and the eyes of Roderick for the first time rested upon the features of his chosen victim. He whispered to Edeco, when he beheld her:

"The billet speaks truth only; there is nothing half so lovely in Toledo."

The favorite ventured no reply, but his finger was lifted to his lips as if in caution, for he saw the eyes of count Julian were upon the king, and the pride and jealousy of the warrior were well known to him. But Roderick, though he strove, could scarcely keep his eyes from the maiden. His glance riveted hers, for it was the first time that she had beheld the king, and she looked upon him with a wonder and admiration, no less fearless than innocent. And truly might she regard him with admiration, for the person of Roderick was extremely noble. He was taller than the general race of men, yet so proportioned and symmetrical as to command no regard in this respect, save when standing by the side of others. His face was full and his eye commanding. His forehead was rather broad than lofty, and his look, though it was not wanting in intellectual expression, spoke more for the love of sway, the pride of pomp, and strong passions, than for the good mind which he possessed naturally, but which the sudden gain of unlooked for power had either entirely perverted or kept in subjection. These gave an air of animation to his manner and countenance, which could not fail to attract the eye, and win the admiration of those he looked upon kindly.

After a brief space of time given to ordinary subjects, and when the beautiful Cava, at the command of her father, had retired from the presence to attend to such concerns of the household as were fitly entrusted to young maidens, in those days, the king addressed himself to count Julian upon the obvious subject of his visit.

"I have brought you a heavy charge, Julian," he said, "and I look for you to be as heedful in our cause, of the honor and security of the nation, as you have proved yourself in the time of our predecessor."

"There are none to challenge the faith of Julian of Consuegra, I trust, oh king!" was the reply of the count, who looked round while he spoke, with searching eye, among the nobles who attended the sovereign. "The faith which I have pledged to you, king Roderick," he continued, "I have ever kept, as I now again pledge myself resolute to keep it. Declare thy will, oh king! and receive my service."

"I believe thee, Julian; I meant not to question thy honor by my speech, but, declaring my firm confidence in thy ability, again to give it employment."

"I am ready in thy service, oh king! Command me as thou wilt, in honor, and my sword and life are thine."

"I had deemed them so, Julian, ere I came to thee. Advices have reached me that the insolent Moslem again threatens us with invasion. The post at Ceuta is again thy charge. We require thee to move for it by the morning, and do thy best to chastise the foe."

"Now, this instant, oh king! it thou wilt, I am ready to depart!" was the immediate answer of the count.

"I knew thy promptness, Julian, but it will not need that thou shouldst depart before the dawn, unless thou shalt deem it important to thy toils. Nor, indeed, canst thou well do it, since it is our purpose to be this night thy guest. We will depart together in the morning, and thou shalt ride with us to our royal city of Toledo, where it is the will of the queen Egilona, that thy fair daughter, of whom she hath heard, should abide until thy return. She shall be handmaid to the queen during thy absence, and her happiness and instruction shall be our care. Does this disposition please thee, count Julian?"

"It does, oh king! since this were but a wild and lonely region for my daughter to abide in when I am absent; and still less would it suit that she go with me to Algeziras, when the cloud of war hangs over the coast. In the presence of the noble Egilona my daughter will learn the lessons of truth, and be confirmed in the gentle virtues which I have toiled, and not in vain, to impart to her mind. Thou hast well determined, oh Roderick! and I will not spare my sword in strife with the Moor, remembering the sacred charge which I leave in thy protection."

The object of the lustful monarch so far had been pursued successfully; and his exultation could scarcely be concealed. The watchful Edeco beheld it, in his quick, hurried glances, in the sudden flow of blood into his cheeks, and in the passionate movements of his person. But these signs entirely escaped the observation of count Julian, who, though jealous in the last degree of the honor of his name and family, yet had not the slightest suspicion of the meditated bad faith of the sovereign who had just yielded to his hands so great a trust; and one which would so readily enable him to revenge himself for any such wrong. Nor did the reckless spirit ot Roderick, thoughtful only of personal indulgence, permit him to perceive the extent of the security which he had thus given to Julian, for the honor of his daughter. It he did, he was but too well disposed to defy consequences, to seek the correction of his error. With a blindness which was like fatality, he gave to the man whom he was about to wound in the most sensitive part, the command of a post, the most important in his kingdom, and the exclusive control of ten thousand veteran soldiers. But this thought troubled neither the mind of the monarch, nor that of his creature, Edeco. As his sword-bearer, this man slept that night in a chamber adjoining that of Roderick, and having access to it. When they were retired for the night, he gave a loose to those congratulations on the success of his project, which he knew would flatter the hopes of the king, whose foul appetites were all in activity. He exaggerated the charms of La Cava, dwelt on her gentleness, which he mistook for weakness, and with the peurile affectation of the fop discoursed of those topics which belong rather to the vicious profligate. It need not be said with what impatience Roderick longed for the departure of Julian, and the possession of his unconscious daughter

But what could exceed the agony of soul of La Cava, when she was apprised by her father of his intention to remove her to the court. She would have pleaded against his purpose, but that she had no pretence for doing so. To declare to him the near neighborhood of her lover, might be to compromise his safety. To declare to him how deeply she loved Egiza, would be no reason why she should not be removed to Toledo, unless it could be shown that the supposed rebel could, in a moment, reconcile himself to the usurper, and receive her immediately, in the eye of the nation, as his wife. The more the mind of Cava reflected upon these matters the more did their difficulties increase. Her own reflections yielded her no satisfactory counsel, and she could only hope, by seeing Egiza before her departure, to learn from him what remedy might yet be found to relieve her from the approaching difficulties of her situation. The anxiety increased to agony, when, after several attempts to steal forth, she found it impossible to succeed. The courtiers and guards of Roderick were numerous, and they filled all the grounds of the castle. Night came on at length, and she gave up the desire in despair. She slept not, or only slept to dream of sorrows, and she rose the next morning only to realize them. At an early hour, assisted by her father, she entered the covered carriage which had been prepared for her, and, escorted by Roderick, who closely attended upon the vehicle, she set forth, sick at heart, and paralyzed in hope, upon a journey, every step of which carried her further from her lover. Did she imagine it only, or was it the face of Egiza, that peered down upon their progress from the brow of the mountain, as they wound their tedious way through one of its gorges? Did he know of her departure—did he doubt her truth? How much would she have given that moment to have breathed but a single sentence in his ears.

CHAPTER III.

It was while they wound through a lovely valley, on their approach to Toledo, that they encountered a procession of holy men bearing the image of the Virgin. They were returning to the house of the fraternity, which picturesquely crowned an eminence that stood at a little distance and within sight. Though engaged in holy offices, the brothers did not think it unseemly to pause in their progress to gaze upon the royal cavalcade, which was so much more gorgeous, if not so much more imposing than their own. It was this purpose of curiosity which Roderick had ascribed to them, but it may be that there was yet another motive, for, as the king approached, one of the venerable men emerged from among the crowd which gathered upon the hill-side to let the royal train pass, and threw himself directly in the way of their progress. Once seen, the countenance of that singular man was never to be forgotten; and long ere the king drew nigh, he was troubled with the recollection of circumstances which had not a little annoyed him when they had taken place. The person was that of Romano, who had been the chief keeper of the house of Hercules. He filled the very spot over which they were compelled to pass, and he seemed resolute to maintain his position. His hands were uplifted as much in sign to his bretheren—who looked on with mixed feelings of veneration and dismay—as to the heaven to which they were raised; and with his white beard streaming to the wind, his uncovered and shaven crown, his wild, fierce, and even haughty expression—as, in his secret soul, he held himself the representative of God in his anger—he was altogether the embodiment of a majesty before which even that of Roderick was compelled to quail. While the monarch drew nigh, and when within hearing, the words of Romano were heard addressed to his company:

"Witness for me, witness for me, my brethren, that I do what God has appointed. That I stand without fear in the presence of the tyrant, and denounce upon his head the wrath which is to come. I call ye to heed me now, my brethren, as ye shall be asked for your testimony hereafter; look upon him, the enemy of God, walking in the vain confidence of his earthly power—behold the servant of Heaven, humbled of earth, and despised of man, yet strong of heart, as I feel that a power greater than that of earth, and a sovereign before whom this tyrant is a shadow and a worm, is my confidence and support. Witness for me, my brethren, witness for the father and the king, whose servants ye are!"

"Now, what does the old dotard mean?" demanded the king of those about him, as these words reached his ears. "Ride forward, Edeco, and command him from the path."

Edeco rode forward as he was bidden, but Romano heeded him not:

"Not for thee—not for such as thee, are the words of Heaven. Thou art the creature and the worm. I have no mission for thee. But I have that for the ears of thy master which shall make him tremble in his secret soul. Bid him ride forward and learn my message. Bid him haste that he may hear it. Let him not delay to receive what I do not delay to impart." And he turned from Edeco to the brethren, while he continued to speak:

"There is a Daniel for every Belshazzar, my brethren, since by God's abundant mercy it is that He wills not the death but the repentance of any sinner—no, not even the vilest and the worst, which is always he whom power and the vain conceits of earth have hardened into the enemy of Heaven. It may be that He means not the destruction of this mortal, and that I am but to warn and to terrify, that the repentance of Roderick may be free and flowing, and abundant like his sin. I know not—I but speak as I am bidden: and I speak not for myself. If my words this day, fall not upon unheeding ears, like good seed washed upon stony places, then am I thrice blessed, since I am the minister of God's indulgence rather than of his punishments. Let us pray, my brethren, that it be as I have said. Pray quickly, all, for the sinner approaches."

He crossed himself devoutly as he uttered these words, while his lips murmured the prayer that he had prescribed to his brethren. A universal murmur of supplication went through their ranks, in compliance with his suggestion, for the venerable Romano had long been regarded among his fellows as one chosen of Heaven

But the wrath of Roderick was scarcely restrainable when Edeco bore back the answer of Romano. Hastily leaving the side of the carriage in which Cava rode, he made his way to the front, and a few bounds of his steed brought him directly in the presence of the zealot.

"Madman! wretched and reckless fool! get ye from my path!" cried Roderick, fiercely, while his teeth were gnashed with such vexation that his words were scarcely articulated.

"I do my duty!" cried Romano. "I speak for thy Master, Roderick. It is for thee to hear!"

"Take him hence!" cried the king to the priests. "It is ye who encourage this madman in his insolence. Take him hence, ere I strike him to the earth."

But the timid priests manifested no disposition to interfere. The words of the king were far less imposing to their senses than those of Heaven's messenger, as they believed, or affected to believe, that Romano was. They only huddled more closely together as the king spoke, as the timorous sheep crowd with apprehension when the howl of the wolf reaches their ears, at evening. This movement only left Romano more distinctly opposed to the king, and the soul of the venerable enthusiast seemed to expand in its confidence, as the isolation of his person, which it left more exposed to danger, served to increase the commanding character of his appearance.

"I need no encouragement from man!" exclaimed Romano. "I am commissioned by Heaven, and the glory of my commission gives me the strength which I need."

"Get from the path!" exclaimed the monarch, hoarsely.

"Not till I have said Heaven's judgment, or, it may be, its warning only. That shall be as thy pride or thy humility wills it, oh Roderick! when thou hast heard me."

"Will no one drag this miserable madman away?" cried Roderick.

A dozen of the king's attendants sprang forward at these words, but ere they could lay hands upon Romano, the brotherhood had closed around him, with their uplifted and extended crosses; they seemed to defy the soldiers, who shrank in hesitation, as they feared to encounter that power which ruled monarchs, and had shaken them from their thrones. The zeal of Romano received new encouragement from these signs. Encircled as he was, by the priests, he showed no token of apprehension; he extended no cross for his own protection, but with hands stretched out to heaven,

"Be witness," he cried, "be witness of this violence, and of my faith in Thee, oh Father of the Universe! I fear not the shaft of the tyrant, while I speak Thy vengeance upon his head."

The fury of Roderick was indescribable, but Romano, utterly unaffected by it, proceeded to address him:

"I call upon thee, oh Roderick! to read the writing of heaven—it is upon the sky before thee—it is written in flames and blood, and it is spoken in words of thunder. Look there—as upon a wall," and he pointed to the eastern heaven, while his eyes watched the same quarter with a devotion that conclusively proved to his brethren, if not to the king, that he really saw what he called on them to witness. It is indeed more than probable that many among them saw it also, and even the eye of Roderick, like that of his followers, turned once involuntarily in the same direction.

"It is there!" cried Romano. "The letters—ye see them, ye see them! Ye cannot help but see them, for they are written in flame. They have a deadly meaning, oh Roderick! and the writing is for thee. It is fitting that, as thou hast been the Belshazzar of this land, that as thou hast been voluptuous, and profligate, and cruel, that as thou hast scorned the words of the wise, and trampled upon the things that are holy, that thou shouldst have the warning and the doom pronounced against thee which was written by the Eternal finger on the palace walls of the Assyrian."

"Madman—away—away all, or I urge my horse upon ye!" exclaimed the king, and he advanced as he spoke, though his limbs seemed to be feeble, and he trembled even while he proceeded, with an ague that seemed to have arisen from his fears, though it was most probably in consequence of his anger. The monks half receded as they witnessed his movement, but Romano yielded not an inch, nor showed any apprehension. With exulting eye as he witnessed the tacit homage which the king by his seeming apprehensions, paid to his ministry, he continued to speak in the same fearless and enthusiastic strain.

"Wo! wo! Behold the writing: 'MENE, MENE, TEKEL, UPHARSIN!'"

Roderick urged forward his steed, but the wild look, the free, enthusiastic action, and the supernatural elevation of Romano, seemed to have its effect upon the horse, not less than upon his rider. The noble animal reared and receded, sinking back upon the crowd that followed.

"Orelio! Orelio!" exclaimed the king, patting the steed upon his neck while striving to urge him forward.

"Take counsel from thy beast, oh king!" cried the zealot, whose exultation was now unbridled. "He has a better knowledge than his rider of what is due to Heaven's messenger. He will not move forward till my mission is completed!"

"We shall see that, madman!" cried the king, and he drove the rowels into the

the sides of the reluctant animal. Romano neither shrunk back as he beheld these efforts, nor paused in his speech.

"The writing, the writing is before thee, Roderick. Hear, and be wise in season, for, of a truth, even as He spake to Belshazzar through the prophet Daniel, doth the Lord of Hosts speak to thee through my lips. He hath numbered thy kingdom—He hath finished it."

"Dog!" cried the now desperate king; and he snatched a javelin from one of the soldiers.

"Thou art weighed in the balances and art found wanting!" continued the fearless enthusiast.

"Not in strength to punish thy insolence am I wanting." cried Roderick, hurling the shaft with a desperate arm. Heedless of the bolt the zealot continued:

"Thy kingdom is divided,"—— the arrow quivered in his thigh, and the sudden pang of the wound broke the sentence of his lips, which was concluded by a slight cry, the involuntary acknowledgment of the suffering flesh. In the next moment, the snorting and terrified steed was driven forward by his raging rider, and the feeble but erect and fearless form of Romano, was hurled aside and thrown against the rocks. A cry of horror rose among the monks, as they beheld the injury done to their comrade—an injury esteemed by them a sacrilege. They gathered around him where he lay, and raised him up in their arms; and, even while Roderick rode on with his train, his denunciations followed the monarch, and filled with gloom and apprehension such of his company as honored the existing forms of religion, and regarded with respect those superstitions of the time, which held a sway among the Iberians of far more potency than any in possession of the throne.

"Wo! wo!" was still the burden of that voice: and even the fears of Roderick were aroused when he coupled what he had witnessed in the cave of Hercules, with the report of the Moorish invasion, and these words of Romano, which he continued to hear, even when out of sight of the enthusiast, and which predicted to him the loss of his kingdom. It needed not then that Roderick should desire free access to the daughter of Julian, in order to prompt him to urge the instant departure of that warrior for the protection of the coast. Even in his voluptuous fancies, there came to his mind dark pictures of his land's distress, his own overthrow, and scenes of strife and bloodshed, which a prescient imagination might safely paint to a tyrant and usurper, and which the coming time was not slow to realize, in all their truth, and with increased and indescribable terrors.

"Now the garden which the king Roderick had made for the gentle queen Egilona," says a chronicler of the time, "was of a curious and a foreign elegance. It stood upon the banks of the golden-bedded Tagus, and the sweet murmur of the waters as they rolled on beside its walls, made a fitting refrain for the pleasant bird-music that was for ever heard from within. Aromatic shrubs, which had been gathered and brought from the far east, filled the air with fragrance; and, after the Moorish fashion, gushing fountains were made to jet from the complaining well, so that an ever-going murmur kept the solitude of the garden wakeful. The trees, many of which were of distant lands, brought by the Roman conquerors into Iberia, were carefully trained into curious shapes, and made to yield the goodliest fruits; and Roderick commanded that a hundred of his Moorish slaves should be busy at all hours, in the building of the garden, and of the palace which stood in the midst of it, so that, long ere the people had dreamed of the curious labor, which was carried on, within the massy walls which surrounded it, the nice perfection of king Roderick's wish had been attained, and the palace and the gardens sprang into existence as it were by magic, in the brief space of a single night. Thither in the oppressive days of summer, would the queen Egilona retire, and secure from intrusion relax from the toils of the court, and attended only by her favorite maidens, enjoy the perfect privacy and the soothing luxuries of so charming a retreat."

It was to this garden of delight that the enamored, but as yet cautious Roderick, conveyed the lovely Cava. It was here that the queen received her, and, pleased with her sweet and modest appearance, nor less so with the singular simplicity of her manners, she took her almost immediately into favor. While count Julian remained in Toledo, and for a brief season after his departure, the king, with an exercise of forbearance which was unusual with him, did not approach the maiden, and Cava might have enjoyed almost perfect happiness in that fairy abode, the beauties and sweetness of which had sunk into her soul, but that her heart was too full of the desolate Egiza. When her father departed for his command at Cueta, the tears of the maiden were unaccountable to him, as they spoke for the secret sorrows which he did not conjecture. He left her with reluctance as he beheld her grief, for she was as the apple of his eye, and something of a mournful presentiment weighed down his heart, as he uttered his hurried language of farewell. It was with an earnest solemnity of manner, that he yielded the sacred trust to king Roderick.

"Be her friend and protector, oh king! while I serve in your wars abroad. It is my wealth and my joy, my treasure and my blessing, which I yield to your protection; and should it please Heaven, Roderick, that I perish in the strife with the infidel, I pray you to remember that though you should lose a soldier and a faithful servant in me, it is not fitting that you should suffer my child to feel that she has lost a father."

Roderick scrupled not to promise the noble soldier, and Julian departed, half relieved of the gloom which had weighed him down. It had been well for Roderick, and well for all, had he been less free to promise, or more scrupulous in performance

---

CHAPTER IV.

Meanwhile the hapless Egiza, poised on a ledge of rock which overhung the great pass leading to count Julian's castle, watched with straining eyes the departure of the glittering cavalcade which bore away the dear object of his affections. He saw count Julian riding beside the usurper, and he readily conceived that the maiden of whose dress he caught partial glimpses through the covering of the carriage, was the lady of his love. His conjecture was confirmed as he listened to the dialogue of two peasants which took place in the valley just below his place of watch. He descended as the cavalcade passed on. Without a thought of what he should do—without any distinct purpose in his mind—he hurried in pursuit. From rock to rock he kept upon his way, without fatigue, without hunger, but with a singular feeling of thirst which prompted him to stop at every spring or brooklet, and drink like one who had famished long with the desire. In this pursuit, he was not at any time far behind the travellers. Their progress, in that hilly region, was necessarily slow. More than once he caught sight of them, as rising to the peak of one eminence, he beheld the last glimpses of their train stretching away over another; and when he came to the spot where the adventure of Roderick with Romano had taken place, he found the venerable old man surrounded by his brethren, and feebly striving, with their assistance, to ascend the little mountain on the brow of which stood the dwelling of their fraternity. But the movements of the feeble old man were necessarily slow, and the yearning eyes which they cast upon the new comer, evidently called for his more vigorous aid. He, too, began to fail from the fatigues of his journey, but the excitements of his soul sustained him; and when, all in a breath, the monks told him of the impious violence of Roderick, Egiza warmed into new strength with their narrative, and lent the aid of his vigorous arm in sustaining the enfeebled Romano up the mountain. It may be supposed that the version which Egiza heard of the transaction, was wanting in most of the circumstances which might have qualified the degree of criminality in the violence of Roderick, and, perhaps, to many minds might have even justified it. The tale they told was one of unmitigated tyranny on the part of the king; a tyranny for the punishment of which they did not cease, all the while, to invoke the thunders of Heaven upon his head. Romano did not speak until the tale was fairly ended. He did not seem to think the matter of sufficient importance to demand the attention of one having the business of Heaven. But when the monks had concluded their story, he fixed his eyes upon the gloomy features of Egiza, and suddenly demanded whither he went.

"I know not, father," was the sad reply. "I care not—to the city—to Toledo."

"We will journey together," responded the other, "let us first take refreshment, since it is not written that the mortal, though he be called to the performance of duties different from those commonly given to mortality to perform, should live on heavenly manna, only. Brother, wilt thou give cheer to the aged servant of God, and to this good youth who has come to our help. I ask thee in the name of the father."

The solicitation was in truth a command. The entire possessions of the brotherhood were at the bidding and disposition of Romano. But little time was given by the two to the business of the feast. The zealot was never yet a voluptuary, and, with such a burning passion at his heart as love—love denied, love doubtful, or love apprehensive—youth has not often cared for food, however the need of physical nature may have demanded it. They were soon satisfied, and once more on their way together.

Romano led the way with a confidence of step and manner which did not arise from the vigor of his frame. His was the strength of the mind, the strength of mind even in its weakness—a strength which is always terrible in its insanity, and which, though incoherent and without power in all things but one, is yet singularly powerful to perform in that one. The few words which he had already uttered, impressed Egiza with wonder and respect; but when, as they proceeded, he beheld the erect carriage of the aged man, and beheld the deference which all paid to him who met him, when he watched the eloquent fire that flashed out at moments from his eyes, and perceived the ready instinct by which the decision and the words came from his lips, and were sustained by his resolute bearing, the youth began tacitly to give credit to the claims which Romano urged, to be the special messenger of God. It is true that Egiza, had he given himself the trouble to reason on this matter, would not have suffered such a thought in his mind; but youth is the season for feeling, perception, impulse—not reflection; and, in those days, reason had never yet dared to lift its voice, in question, for an instant, of the venerable superstition. The awe which gradually came over his bosom as they thus pursued their way together, was the tribute of youth to age, of passion to reflection, and credulity to the ancient hypocrite of ages.

When the two reached Toledo it was night; and, for a moment, Egiza paused ere he entered the walls of the city. Romano paused also, as he beheld the indecision of the youth. He gazed upon his face intently, and seemed desirous to read the thoughts in the mind of his companion. These thoughts were various enough, and not so easily followed. He, the rightful heir to the throne, stood before the royal city of his birthright and feared to enter it. He was a stranger without a home—an outlaw without hope; one whom any one might slay, and find not only impunity, but reward for the deed. It would be too much to say that thoughts like these did not press heavily upon his mind in the few moments which he yielded to hesitation at the gates of Toledo; but his fears, if he felt any, passed away in an instant.

The monk laid his hand upon his arm:

"Where goest thou?" he demanded.

"I know not. I have no home in Toledo," was the desolate reply.

"But thou hast business?"

"No; I know not," said Egiza with similar tones of self-abandonment.

"God provides a home for the homeless!" exclaimed he. "God provides labor for the unemployed. Thou hast duties, young man, or thou wouldst not have life. Art thou heedless of this? art thou ignorant of them?"

Egiza was silent. It is not often that princes are taught that they have duties and labors like common men. Seeing him hesitate, Romano proceeded:

"Go with me, my son, and when thou wouldst have comfort, confess to me thy griefs. Thou hast them. Life must have sorrows, or Heaven would own no joys; nor, if it did, should we desire them. Go with me, and, be sure, the God who gave thee life will find thee employment."

Still the youth hesitated. He was unwilling to commit himself to a companionship which might stand in the way of his pursuit, and though he wished to go instantly to the palace of his uncle, the archbishop Oppas, he was apprehensive that in so doing he might compromise either his own or his uncle's safety, and possibly both.

"Hast thou heard, my son," said Romano with gentleness, "I have asked thee to keep with me."

"Where goest thou?" demanded Egiza.

"I go now to the dwelling of the most holy father, the lord bishop of Toledo."

"What! the lord Oppas?" exclaimed Egiza.

"Even he!" said the other. "Hast thou knowledge of him."

"No!" replied the other, after a brief pause, in which he deliberated upon the propriety of falsehood in such a case, and found a justification for it in his own mind, in his dangers and necessities; "but I have heard of the venerable father, and I would see him; perchance, it may be as thou hast said, that God will provide with fitting toils the wayfarer who hath none."

"Thou hast the proper spirit, for heavenly furtherance," said Romano, "and it may be that I am the chosen instrument for guiding thee on the way to thy labors. Let us go together."

And the two entered Toledo: Romano full of wild fancies of heavenly anger, the overthrow of tyranny, the upraising of the abused church, and the healing of its many wounds; and Egiza divided between hopes and fears of a humbler, a more selfish, earthly nature. He knew the danger of his present movement, but he did that for love—and he felt the shame—which he had not been bold enough to do for his throne and country. He had grown reckless from frequent risks, and desperate from privation, and almost indifferent to detection; and with a boldness which, in time of sudden peril, is perhaps, the best protection, he fearlessly went with his conductor into the very heart of the city, where stood, in the near neighborhood of his uncle's dwelling, the palace and the dangers of the usurper.

Romano at once proceeded to the dwelling of Oppas, and was instantly admitted.

At first, Egiza thought to remain behind, waiting an opportunity to see his uncle alone, but his companion bade him follow close, and, with something like indifference, careless whether Oppas should recognize him or not, in the presence of Romano, he obeyed his directions. He relied upon his inferior garments, soiled and torn—the length of his hair and beard, which he had left untrimmed, and his unexpected coming, effectually to disguise him from the scrutiny of his uncle until such time as he should think fitting to declare himself.

But the keen eye of the archbishop discovered him, as soon as Romano, having told his own story, brought him forward. Egiza, at a glance, saw that he was known, and pressed his finger upon his lips in sign of secresy. But such precaution, with one skilled like Oppas in all secret arts, was unnecessary. He did not seem to heed the prince, but bidding the servant conduct him to another chamber, he advised Romano that he should take his companion, for the time, into his own protection. For a long while did the archbishop and Romano converse together, the former urging new measures upon the latter, which he seemed rather to educe from the mind of the zealot than to prompt with his own. Such was the occult skill of the former; and great indeed, was the service, which, under his instigation—which he deemed to come from heaven and of his own head—the latter performed in promoting the insurrectionary purposes of the ambitious Oppas.

When Romano had taken his departure, the archbishop called Egiza, and they conversed long in secret together. The lord Oppas did not spare his reproaches of the prince for the desertion of his brethren and of his people, of which he had already heard through his emissaries; until at length the language of Egiza grew fierce and scornful.

"Thou speakest, my lord uncle," said he, "as if I might look but for little help at thy hands. I care not for this, but am I to believe that thou wilt give me up to the slaves of Roderick? If thou art resolved on this, or if thou but meditatest it, as from thy harsh speech it would seem not unreasonable to apprehend, I am ready. Go to your tyrant, and declare to him the truth. Why shouldst thou not have the money for my blood as well as another."

"Thou hast taken a tone from the mouth of Pelayo, my son, in this thy language," was the mild reply of the archbishop, whose policy it was rather to conciliate than offend. "But let us," he continued, "let us speak no more of this or any matter again to-night. Thou art weary, and this makes thee angry and impatient; I, too, am troubled with labors of greatest weight, and these make me stern, and perhaps unjust. Come, my son. Let me lead thee to a secure chamber, and in the morning I will procure thee a fitting disguise; for in Toledo we must move with caution. Remember, Egiza, the guards of the tyrant are around us; his spies are busy in his service ever; and however reckless thou mayst have become touching thy own safety, thou wilt be heedful not to expose thy person needlessly, when thy safety will affect that of another."

With the dawn, Romano was again a visiter in the dwelling of the archbishop Couriers had arrived during the night in Toledo, and the defeat and death of Edacer the govornor of Cordova, at the hands of an insurgent, under the lead of Pelayo, the brother of Egiza, was generally known in the city.

"The arm of God shows itself at last," exclaimed Romano. "His thunder, that only spoke before, is now winged with the red lightning, and the shafts have stricken to the hearts of the tyrant's followers. Thou hast heard, my lord Oppas."

Egiza had given his uncle the intelligence but a few hours before, but the archbishop was heedful not only not to say this, but to forbear admitting that he knew of the events at all, until he received them from the zealot.

"And Julian has departed for the coast," said Romano. "What warrior will lead the force against Pelayo, my father? Will it be the silken slave, Edeco—the piebald, pasteboard minion that the king so loves? If it be, then of a surety hath God decreed that he shall go mad like Nebuchadnezzar of old, that out of his own performances he may perish."

"Of a truth, thou speakest his doom, my brother," replied Oppas, with solemnity. "God worketh out his judgments in fear and wonder, in many secret ways; and it is a wholesome propriety, that which makes crime sooner or later the minister of its own punishment. We behold in trust and fear, my brother, yet we behold not calmly or idly. We contribute unconsciously to the good work, and the rightful judgment of heaven, and like the blind bolts of the storming clouds, we go upon errands of destruction, and know not what we do, till the victim lies before us. Sawst thou not much that was a mystery to thee in the youth whom thou brought with thee last night?" said Oppas, abruptly, seeming to change the subject, but, of a truth, coupling the inquiry in the mind of his hearer with all that he had previously said.

"Of a truth, I did," replied Romano, musing idly; for the drift of Oppas was beyond his search.

"He is young, yet sad; he is strong, but his limbs lack service. He seems like one quick to strike—to slay if need be, but God has not yet given the victim to his knife. Wherefore so much sadness in his youth; why is he separate, as it were, from all other men, and all other ties? Can it be, my brother, that such as he is chosen for great service?"

"Wherefore not!" exclaimed Romano. "God loveth those whom He chasteneth, and if this youth have sorrows early, he hath strength also, and he hath an appointed service which shall lead him to high favor."

"I think not that he came to your help upon the mountain without advisement—I think not that he came to Toledo without a business. My brother, is he not an instrument given into thy hands?"

"Truly, it would seem so, my father, though I thought not this. Verily, thou art of the seed of those whom the generations which are gone of time, held wisest of men."

"Yet were this instrument—which thou must see was put into thy hands—but an idle one, harmful to itself, and harmless where the just Providence would make it hurtful, unless it have its sheath. The minister of vengeance were but a failing minister, if he walked at midday, and concealed not his secret purpose. The youth must be habited, my brother, in a guise which shall not be unfitting for him who is appointed to a holy purpose, and which must be effectual to hide his purposes from the sinner for whom he is sent in punishment, even as the red bolt is hidden in the black cloud until the moment ere it smite with death."

The zealot was convinced.

"I will bring thee a garb of my own for the youth," he said as he hurried away with this object. The disguise of a monk enveloped the person of Egiza, and he walked the streets of Toledo with impunity. He urged his inquiries with comparative prudence, and the circumspect archbishop adroitly helped him to such intelligence, at intervals, as he thought might best promote his own various, if not sometimes conflicting objects. The stern soul of Oppas looked forward to the time when the crime, which was yet only in contemplation, but which Roderick meditated, and of which Cava was the victim, might find its sudden avenger in the arm of Egiza.

"Let him strike!" exclaimed his archbishop to himself, as he meditated these important matters in the secresy of his closet. "Let him strike, and strike successfully, and I care not though they hew him in pieces a moment after. He can serve us only as he strikes the tyrant, and yields a victim who is worthless to us in all things beside."

This cold-blooded policy he encouraged, and many opportunities were secured to Egiza for frequenting the various places in the city which it was known that Roderick sought. Bribes, judiciously administered, and never without success in a court where no other god than gold was worshipped, procured access even to the palace for the apparent monk; and, with these opportunities, the unhappy prince soon knew all that he most desired to know. From common rumor he learned that the lovely Cava was an inmate of the gorgeous palace that stood in the royal gardens, upon the golden-sanded Tagus, and around these walls he daily wandered, with a wistful eye, and a burning and sleepless hope. Devoted to the one purpose, and reckless in its pursuit, or thoughtless of the danger, he meditated nothing less than to scale the walls, and in spite of the guards who watched them, to penetrate the gardens, behold with his own eyes, and bear away, if possible, the only object for which he cared to live, and without which, he was not unwilling, at any moment, to perish.

CHAPTER V.

THE fierce passions of the tyrant, clamorous for their victim, could hardly be restrained until the departure of her father. He had scarcely gone when he bade the miserable creature, Edecó, who had grown skilled in long pandering to his master's views, prepare the way for the contemplated sacrifice. But the stunning intelligence of the revolt in the neighborhood of Cordova, the defeat and death of Edacer, and the successful flight of the insurgents under Pelayo, whom they had crowned their king, offered a brief interruption to the progress of his crime. Right gladly, however, even then, so much moved had he been by the charms of Cava, would Roderick have set aside the cares of empire, and given himself up to the lascivious objects in his view, had he not possessed a true friend and faithful counsellor in the severe lord Bovis. He would not suffer the king to be untrue to himself. It was to his palace in the pleasure gardens on the Tagus, that this stern counsellor came to rebuke him for his sloth, and urge upon some particular measures for the general safety. This trusty nobleman, when he saw the loveliness of count Julian's daughter, as she appeared in the train of the queen, readily conceived the reason why Roderick had himself borne to Julian the foreign commission with which he had invested him; though he did Julian the injustice to suspect that the brave count had connived with the king—as was but too much the practice of the court—at the expense of his daughter's virtue.

"Another, and yet another!" he said to himself as he surveyed with feelings of pity, the evident innocence and surpassing beauty of the maiden. "Poor butterfly!" he continued, "thou little knowest the price which thou payest for thy gilding. It is, indeed, all gilt, the mere dust which glitters, and which the pressure of the unlicensed hand, and the lustful lip, will tarnish and remove. To-morrow will another like thee take thy place, and all thy satisfaction will be to know that she who has succeeded thee, and for whom thou wilt be scorned, will in time be superseded by another, and share in thy disgrace."

Such were the unuttered thoughts of the stern Bovis, as he beheld the glittering pageant of the court in which the wondering Cava first appeared before his eyes. Nor did he spare the king himself, in uttering similar language.

"My lord king!" he said, "thou hast brought the daughter of count Julian to court. May I ask of thee hast thou paid him her price, if thou hast not"——

He paused.

"And if I have not," said Roderick, "what then?"

"Send for him instantly, take from him the commission which thou hast given him, and with all possible haste thereafter, let his head crown the great gate of Toledo"

"And wherefore thus?" demanded Roderick.

"The girl is too fair, oh king! too fair to be long innocent in a court like thine, and if thou wrongst her, and hast not secured the blindness of her father, thou hast made him too strong for thy safety by this commission."

"Pshaw, Bovis, thou hast the art of dreaming dangers, and thou findest enemies in thy faculty, where other men behold but rushes. Go to—give thyself no heed to this matter, but speak of the business which I gave thee in hand. What of Edacer; hath he not sent the head of the rebel?"

"He hath sent nothing; but I look for his couriers to-night, when we shall, I doubt not, be apprised of his success."

The couriers brought other tidings, as we have seen; and for a moment the consternation of the court was great. But only for a moment. The dream of sloth and luxury was too soul-subduing in that region to keep it for any length of time aroused by any remote excitement or foreign danger; and when the lord Bovis brought his intelligence and dwelt upon the necessity of sending forth a strong army on the instant to quell the insurrection, the dissolute Edeco, who really feared the incorruptible counsellor whom he could not emulate, slyly suggested to Roderick to send Bovis himself. The king, not less pleased to be rid of one whose counsels were sometimes too free and too just to be always welcome, caught readily at the suggestion, and commissioned him accordingly. The willing subject accepted the appointment with alacrity, and proceeded to prepare himself for his new duties. At leaving his master he barely said:

"I will strive honestly to win the victory for thee, oh Roderick! though I fear me it will not much avail thee, since thy courtiers are too apt to lose what thy soldiers win. If thou wilt make Edeco curtail his silks in the matter of tails and tassels when I am gone, he will of a surety prove himself a better man, and to thee a better subject."

"Thou art but a wild animal, my lord Bovis, and I heed thee not. Go to—measure thy garments as thou fanciest them; thy dull sense would strive in vain to take the complexion or conceive the fitness of mine."

Roderick laughed as the two thus jibed each other; but when the lord Bovis had gone, he felt, in truth, that one was wanting in his court, whose absence—as he was alike singular in honesty and wisdom—was more immediately felt than that of any other. But his mind, bent as it was upon the one object of his desires, was rather pleased that the severely virtuous Bovis had withdrawn. He felt as if a great restraint were taken away; and assured that he had provided against the pressing dangers, he once more gave a loose to his passions. With the aid of Edeco whose management had been begun from the moment that count Julian had taken his departure, he soon paved the way for the commission of the heinous crime which he meditated. In the meantime the unconscious Cava, sad and lonely, retired, whenever the opportunity was allowed her, to the solitary places of the garden, where, in secret, she wept for her lover, and meditated upon the fortune which separated them. She little knew that even then—more venturous for her love than ever he had been for his throne and people—the sad Egiza, was compassing the walls which contained her, and, with heedless and daring footstep, was actually treading the labyrinthine groves of the royal garden. There were others as little conscious of this fact as herself, to whom its knowledge might not have been so agreeable.

In a remote chamber of the palace, Roderick and Edeco conferred together upon the base purpose of the tyrant.

"Is all secure?" demanded the former.

"Security itself, cannot be more so, oh king!" was the reply of the creature.

"Thou hast sent the guards to the northern wall?"

"I have, oh Roderick! Thy clamorous summons might bring them to your wish, but they are else beyond ear-shot."

"'T is well—and she, the bird—where didst thou leave her?"

"In the far quarter of the garden close to the eastern waterfall; she sits upon a rock that lies below it; yet the trees fence her in thickly, so that, though she can hear the fall, she yet sees it not. Thou mayst approach, unheard, and look upon her."

"How looks she, Edeco?"

"As some desolate dove whom the fowler has just robbed of its mate. She murmurs little, but you may sometimes catch the burden of a deep sigh, with which the rude waterfall has no sympathy, and half drowns with its noisy clamor. Were it not, oh Roderick! that this show of sorrow adds to the loveliness of her charms, I should deem it but wise in thee to forbear until she hath caught a truer feeling of this garden's pleasure. Her lip would be sweeter, if, like the buds which bloom around her, it smiled when it was pressed, though even its present sadness would seem to increase its sweets."

"Lead me to see her, Edeco, where I may enshroud myself safely and be awhile unseen," said Roderick, whose prurient imagination had been greatly awakened by what his favorite had said. Edeco led the way, and with cautious footsteps the king followed him to a spot, where, hidden from sight, yet able to see his victim, he looked down upon her where she sat in the pleasant shade.

"Leave me now," said Roderick in a whisper. "Leave me, Edeco, yet see that thou keep at hand to hear my summons, only, and to restrain the approach of others. Should the queen awaken—thou knowest."

Edeco well understood the directions which Roderick did not conceive it necessary to conclude, and retired with an assurance of obedience, upon which the tyrant well knew, from past experience, that he might rely with safety. Alone he surveyed his victim, until passion grew strong within him from long forbearance. He descended from the little eminence, the shrubbery of which had concealed him, and suddenly stood before her.

She started, with looks full of surprise, but without distrust.

"Ha! the king!" was the unintended exclamation.

"Your slave, fair Cava. I am no king to you. The name is something formal—something cold. You will affright me from you if you use it."

"What should I say, my lord: I know not else?" returned the maiden with a simplicity which added to her charms in the sight of one who, among the beauties of his court, was accustomed to see but little of such a quality.

"Call me by any name but that—make your own choice to name me, and I shall be well content. I am sick of being be-kinged, fair Cava; and from the lips of those I love, it vexes me to hear such stiff discourse. My courtiers 'king' me, ever. Do they need service, bounty or station, they approach me thus. 'T is still 'Oh! king'—'my gracious lord and master'—'bestow me this'—'provide me with this station.' Wonder not then, I sicken of such speech. I would forget the king—the throne—the kingdom. I know them but by toils, by crosses, troubles—by gilded cares, false professions, and heartless attachments. Think it not strange, sweet Cava, if I would have a different language from thy lips; I would not have thee take the abused language of the common crowd who throng about me ever. Mere mighty names but fetter intercourse—make ice of the court atmosphere, dear lady; and to the poor king, flattered by mouth-service, deny the freedom of the meanest bird, that sings when he is saddest. Do not then, Cava, err in the common fashion."

The face of Roderick looked the sentiment admirably which his lips uttered, and the lady Cava fairly pitied the poor king, in her simple ignorance, who thus bewailed the royalty that fettered him in his intercourse with men, and denied him those pleasures of which he envied the humblest of his subjects the possession. Perhaps there may have been some truth in the language, which, nevertheless, he employed only for the purposes of deception; for certainly, the monarch who is an usurper of his station, and whose daily practices are vicious, must live in an atmosphere too artificial and constrained, to suffer him to know things except through a false medium. But, though Cava sufficiently commisserated the speaker to look in his face with an expression of sympathy, she did not suffer herself to employ any other than the most respectful language in her reply.

"Alas, my lord, what language should I use? Are you not the king, and is it not the name by which the good subject alone should know you? My father bade me ever know you by that title, and I feel that I should not speak wisely, oh king! if I did not obey him."

"'T is a good rule, sweet Cava, for the mere subject. Indeed it is needful too, for the protection of our kingly state, that our people should approach us with fitting obeisance; but there are exceptions from this observance, and he or she whom the king favors does wisely to forget the state, and regard the man only. For you, and when with you, sweet Cava, Roderick would fain be no king, but Roderick only."

"But why, my lord, with me—why would you have it so?" replied the simple girl, without any apprehension.

"For the true love I bear you, my sweet Cava. To you, I am no sovereign, I could be none. I am a slave—a subject, when I seek you."

"My lord!" was the exclamation of the bewildered maiden. He smiled at her simplicity, which seemed to fill him with pleasant, but, as it proved, mistaken auguries.

"You do not conceive me, sweetest. It is true, I am your slave, your subject, not your sovereign. The king commands, but Roderick solicits you. He can bestow upon you nothing of half so much value as that which he implores."

"I do not take your meaning, oh king!" was the response of the untutored maid. "I am but a dull maiden of Andalusia—your speech sounds strangely in my ears."

"There is a language, sweet Cava, which I trust you are better taught to understand," exclaimed the king, as he impressed a burning kiss upon her lips, ere she could comprehend his intention.

The deep blush which then overspread her cheeks, her trembling, and startled apprehensiveness of her air and utterance, spoke audibly for her innocence.

"Oh, my lord," she exclaimed in insuppressible emotion, as she started from the seat, and strove to fly. "Oh, my lord, what have you done—what would you do? Spare me! Let me go. It is wrong, oh king! it is wrong. Let me go to the queen."

His arm arrested her, and he drew her back to the seat beside him. She trembled with apprehensions, the source of which were rather in her instincts than in her mind. Her terrors were those of the bosom and not of the brain, and she shivered with the agony which they excited.

"And wherefore leave me, sweet Cava; and what is the wrong of which thou speakest? Those lips—think you that they were bestowed upon you for non-performance? They have their joys, my sweet Cava, and you must learn to use them. Remember, 't is a king that pleads"——

"A man, my lord!" was the quick response, as she availed herself of a distinction which he himself had suggested. "I know you, my lord, as you yourself commanded, but as a man, not as a king."

"As a man, then, Cava—sweet Cava, only as a man would I have you know me. Behold I put by the sovereign—I command no longer. I am at your feet."

And kneeling as he spoke, but still preserving his hold upon her arm, Roderick strove to persuade her to the embrace which, at the same moment he half enforced. She struggled in his grasp, and with a strength beyond his anticipation, arose to her feet, compelling him, by her successful movement, as he still maintained a hold upon her arm, to rise along with her. Her voice acquired strength and volume as his object became less equivocal.

"I pray you, king Roderick, that you wrong not my ears by such discourse. Remember, sire, I am the daughter of count Julian; and the Roman blood, from which I come, will suffer no dishonor."

"These are words, sweet Cava!"——

"But life rests upon words, oh! king; and a goodly name, and a fearless heart which is strong in its innocence, must yet be heedful that words, which are yet mere breath, do not stun what they might not else injure. You do me injury, oh king! and you do yourself wrong. I would esteem you, sir, as the father of your people; and I pray you that you strive not thus, and speak not that which shall rob you of my esteem in this. I pray you let me leave you."

"No—not yet, sweet Cava. Thou shalt not leave me in anger"—

"I am not angry, my lord. It is not meet that one, young and ignorant, like me, should presume on anger, and"——

The king interrupted her.

"Nor yet misapprehend me, sweet Cava. Wherefore thy alarm. What is it, dost thou think, that I purpose? Speak—tell me."

"I know not, indeed, my lord; but I fear that thou hast not purposed rightly," was the bold reply.

"What didst thou fear?" continued Roderick.

"I know not even that, my lord; but the thoughts were strange which have come to me, and such fears trouble me as have not a name in my mind, and cannot have a place upon my lips. I pray you, oh king Roderick! release me—let me now seek the queen."

"Thou shalt be my queen, fair Cava—the queen of my subjects, and of me; and I will love you better, my sweet, than all queens, and subjects beside."

"Oh! my lord speak not thus. You cannot mean it," she replied with looks of fright.

"By Hercules, I do!" replied the king, mistaking the tones for those of doubt.

"If thou art noble, king Roderick, thou wilt release me. If thou wouldst not be held guilty of unmanly violence, thou wilt be silent, thou wilt bid me go from thee, and spare me further cruelty like this."

"Cruelty, sweet Cava! Truly thou dost much mistake my temper, or grievously do I misuse my language. Cruelty! 't is love, I tell thee, sweet. 'T is love I hold for you. Hear me, dear Cava, never yet have mine eyes looked on woman whom they better loved to look upon than thee."

The cheeks of the maiden kindled with a deeper red, and her eye flashed fire, which, had such power been in human eyes, would have annihilated the amorous tyrant.

"Thou errest my lord- thou hast twice erred in thy speech," she scornfully replied.

"As how?" he demanded.

"Thou hast erred to think that thou didst love—still more hast thou erred to think that the love of this lowly heart could be thine. Even were it not that to regard thee with other than such feeling as becomes the subject, would be crime, I freely tell thee, king Roderick, that my love is given to another. I am betrothed to one, I shame not to declare, whom I love above all other men of earth."

"His name!" demanded the king, while a flashing fury mingled with the lustful gaze of his dark and rolling eye.

"Pardon me, oh king! but I may not tell thee!" was the resolute reply.

"Thou shamest to speak his name!" responded Roderick—"some lowly youth I trow. Comes he not from Catalon, fair Cava. Thou canst not love such a creature. 'T is in vain. Those eyes are for the court—those lips, that form—oh Cava! thou shalt love me. I will not suffer thee to throw thyself away on thy poor chief of Catalon. I will not. Such as are not of the court were but too much honored in thy scorn."

There was an increased flush upon the cheek of the maiden as she replied to this speech, so full of mingled taunt and admiration. But her manner was even more cool and firm than before, and her words less tremulously uttered.

"I meet your censure with a smile, not so much for the mistake which finds a birth-place for the man I love, as that you can discern no good in Catalon. I was taught other lessons. Worth and the elements of virtue spring from timely cultivation, never from mere place; nor, as I learn, are they the growth of a particular soil. The Greek was mighty—was the Roman less, or the Goth less than either? There is no chosen land for noble deeds—high virtue, great endeavor, as I hear, though some are still inferior to the rest"——

She paused, as she beheld a smile pass over the lips of the king, who was in truth pleased with the novel directness of her simplicity.

"Forgive me, my lord; but I have spoken too idly. All this you knew before"——

"I marvel, sweet Cava, you are beyond the time. The graybeards lose the palm. The bookmen's lore hath made solid the silver of your tongue; and you speak, even against my will, truths so bewitching that I cannot help but hear."

Her face became even graver in its expression:

"I have been too bold, my lord, to speak thus flippantly. I would retire."

"Not yet, sweet Cava; but a little while. Why wouldst thou leave me? Dost thou doubt my speech? Do I not say I love thee?"

"Thou forgettest, my lord; I said I loved another," was her prompt reply.

"And what of that? Thou shalt love me too, Cava. Thou canst do this; thou canst try."

"No, sire, I may not! I would be his wife—his true wife. I would look him in the face without fear and without deception, and love him only."

"Pshaw! this is idle, Cava; a virtue now-a-days unknown and stale, not common to the court. Thou shalt be the wife of thy chosen, if so ye both will it; but there needs not that thou wilt love him only. Give to thy state some license, and be mine"—

"I pray thee hold, oh king!—speak not of this. I fear what thou wouldst say, and beg thy silence. I would still esteem you, oh king!"

"Why, so you may, sweet Cava: more—you may love me. Yield to my prayer"——

"A slave!" was the only exclamation of the maiden in reply, as she once more strove to withdraw from his grasp.

"A tyrant, rather, my sweet Cava. You know not how I'll love you."

"Without my will, oh king! what am I but a slave?"

"Have thy own will, dear Cava, as thou willest; but I pray thee bend thy sweet will to mine."

"My lord, once more I pray thee release me; let me seek the queen. I have but too long forgotten myself to speak with thee thus. Sire, I am the daughter of count Julian—a Roman born, of Roman blood, oh king! I will not hear you further!"

"Thou shalt, sweet Cava. With gentle force I'll take thee to my arms. Nay, nay, thou canst not fly."

"My lord, beware! I warn thee. If thou dost me wrong, my father's vengeance"——

"Sweet, simple girl! I have no fear, I tell thee. I am all love. My heart has no room in it for fear, unless of thee. I have no fear of man."

"Of Heaven, then!" she cried desperately, as he grasped her arms and drew her toward him with a fierce determination, not the less visible in his eyes than in his action.

"None, none! sweet Cava, if it stands between us."

"Heaven save—Heaven strengthen me!" she cried, as with a violent effort, that seemed to be awarded to her prayers, she broke from his embrace, and bounded down upon the bank. With the speed of wings she darted through one of the little groves, into which Roderick pursued her. Her fleetness surprised him; and he almost began to fear she would still escape him, when her feet stumbled, and she fell upon the ground a little before him.

"Now, Cava, thou art mine! What now shall keep thee from my arms? Who shall arrest me? Nor Heaven nor man shall help thee now! Thou art mine—all mine!"

"Spare me!—oh spare me, king Roderick! If thou hast mercy—if thou art a man, spare me! I am weak—I am alone—I have none to aid me, if thou wrong'st me! Spare the poor maiden, oh Roderick!—the helpless maiden—and I will bless thee, I will pray for thee, for ever."

"Thou pleadest vainly, my beauty, my bird of beauty, my beloved Cava. But I will not harm thee. It is with love—with a warm, fond love, that I seek thee; and as I have not the heart to harm thee, thy fears and thy pleadings are alike idle Thou art mine! Thou art mine!"

CHAPTER VI.

THE exultation of the amorous tyrant, as he beheld the victim almost within his grasp, could not be suppressed, and broke forth into triumphant language, as he bent forward to embrace her shrinking form; but ere his extended hands could grasp the innocent maiden, and even while her long and despairing shriek pierced the dull ears of the slumbering echoes of the garden, a strange figure bounded madly upon the scene, and, rushing with headlong fury from the cover of a neighboring grove, threw himself recklessly between Roderick and the screaming girl. Well might the tyrant give back in amaze, if not in apprehension, before the strange intruder Well might he shiver with horror, as the wild yell of laughter with which the stranger answered his first demand of inquiry, met his ears. Such a spectre had not often startled the inmates of the pleasure-gardens of royalty and voluptuousness. The habit of the monk concealed the person of Egiza; but the cowl was thrown back and the untonsured hair was visible. The long black locks were matted on his brows; the glare from his eyes was that of madness; and the wild laugh which broke fitfully from his lips, mingled at moments with a choking inarticulateness, gave him all the appearance of one who had just escaped from the bonds of the bedlamite. But there was a terrible directness in his eye, as he gazed upon the shrinking tyrant, which, though unlike the capricious and oblique stare of insanity, was not less fearful to the spectator, as it spoke for a fixed resolve in the bosom of the intruder, which might not be quite so readily disarmed and set aside as the wandering purpose of the madman.

"Who art thou? Whence this insolence?" cried the monarch, after the pause of a moment, in which he stopped to catch his breath. The wild and repeated laugh of the intruder, was his only answer; and the ears of Roderick were pierced with the shrill and mingling tenor of pain and pleasure, which the discordant sounds embodied. Even the unhappy Cava, ignorant, in the disguise which enwrapped him, that it was her lover who had come so timely to her relief, shrunk and crawled away along the bank where she had fallen, as the strange sounds smote so unusually upon her senses. But she was not long ignorant of the truth. Enraged by the intrusion, the disappointment, and the seeming defiance of the monk, he repeated his demand, in tones which showed the aroused tyrant, with whom further trifling would be dangerous.

"Who art thou?" he cried. The answer was immediate:

"Thy foe! Ho! monster, have I tracked thee to thy den? Have I followed thee through thy hellish purposes? Have I come in time to save?"——

And as he uttered these words, he turned a look of painful inquiry upon the shivering, shrinking, but now fully conscious Cava. She clasped her hands as she beheld him, and heard his words; and the smile which rested upon her lips, sad and uncertain as it was, was yet such as to reassure him on the subject of his fearful doubts.

"Or to avenge?" he continued fiercely, after the brief pause, in which he had turned his glance upon her. "Ay, to avenge!—not thee, my Cava, not thee only—though that were enough to drain all the blood from his accursed heart; but the blood of the now sacred in heaven—the wrongs of the great and the good, whom he hath doomed to the scaffold, to chains, to blindness, and (worst doom of all) to banishment. Hear me, father!—hear me, Iberia!—hear me, Heaven!—I avenge ye all! Thou shalt perish, tyrant! The tiger has been followed to his den. There is no outlet. Thy guards are far: I left them on the outer wall, to the east. The dagger is upon thy throat: there is nothing left thee but to die."

And, as he spoke these words, with an utterance not less rapid than his action, he leaped upon Roderick, and dashed him to the earth. With uplifted dagger he aimed at his throat, and although the arm of the tyrant, quick, strong, and ready, parried, and for the moment put aside the stroke, it was evident to him that he could not long avoid his fate. At that instant he found an ally where he little looked for one. Cava sprang to her feet, and rushing to the combatants, grasped the uplifted arm of Egiza with both her hands, and the blow swerved harmlessly aside from the throat, into which otherwise it had been unerringly driven.

"Spare him, spare him! Slay him not, I pray thee. However much he may merit death, let not his blood be upon thy hands."

"What! dost thou plead for him who would have wronged thee?" cried the desperate Egiza. "Whence comes this unnatural mercy? Cava! woman! wouldst thou have me hold thee guilty? Fond to him, thou art false to me. Away! Take thy arms from my neck. If thou beggest for him I'll no longer deem thee honest."

"Thou dost me wrong. Oh! believe me," cried the wounded maiden; "I am true to thee, as ever was woman yet to the faith which she had plighted. He would have wronged me, but he hath not; and I would not that his blood, or any blood, should rest upon thy hands."

"False and foolish mercy! I may not yield to thee, my Cava, since I should but give freedom to the ferocious wolf, again to prey upon my fellow men. Let the tyrant perish, that our people may live. Unloose my arm!—give way!"

"Spare him, spare him!" were her appealing words; but he listened to without heeding them.

"Spare him!" he cried. "What, for further wrong—for other tyrannies—for more lust and bloodshed? Thou art not wise to ask it, my Cava—neither for thyself nor me. Seest thou not that if he live, thou art lost—I am lost—and life, and all that is worth living for, is lost to us. No! I cannot spare him. I love thee too well, my Cava, to heed thy prayer. He shall die!"

Meanwhile, Roderick struggled manfully to escape from the knee of his enemy, which was pressed down upon his breast; but he struggled in vain. The arm of the desperate Egiza threw off the hold of Cava, and a moment after the uplifted dagger, which had been shaken in the face of Roderick during this brief conference, was driven forward, with an unrelenting force and a true aim, at the throat of the victim. But, even then, when the king deemed the struggle over, the doom spoken, and his death certain, he was rescued. A stronger arm than that of Cava, arrested the swift-descending weapon from behind, and forced it from the hand of Egiza. Ere he could turn to meet his assailants, Edeco and the guard of the tyrant had grappled him on every side. They had come opportunely to the rescue of their master. Another moment, and they had been too late. But the fiend whom Roderick served had not yet deserted him; and the unfortunate Egiza, in a single moment, found the position of himself and the tyrant reversed. The guards secured him with a grasp, from which all his efforts—and they were Herculean—failed utterly to extricate him; and the bitterness of his captivity, under existing circumstances, came to his mind in its fullest force, with an almost instinct consciousness.

Roderick rose silently from the earth, as soon as his enemy was taken from his bosom. A grim smile rested upon his lips, as he surveyed his assailant, whom yet he knew not. His eye glanced from the prisoner to the maiden, with looks of inquiry.

"Who art thou?" at length he demanded of the former.

"I have answered thee," said Egiza; "I am thy foe. I have no other name for thee. Thou shalt know me by no other."

"The thong shall force it from thy lips!" exclaimed the king. "Thine eyes shall pay for the insolence of thy tongue. Away with him!" he exclaimed to the guards. Cava sank at his feet.

"I kneel to thee, Roderick," she cried; "thou wouldst have wronged me; I kneel to thee—I forgive thee the wrong; but let him go free—let us both go free."

"Plead not for me, Cava!" said the fearless prisoner. "Thou wrongest both of us to bend the knee to such a monster. Alas! but for thy erring pity, we had not needed thy prayer to our freedom; my dagger had freed us—avenging our own and our country's wrongs at the same moment."

But Cava continued to kneel and to implore the king. He answered her only by demanding, with impatient and furious gesticulation, the secret which Egiza had withheld.

"His name!—his name!"

But Cava well knew that the discovery of her lover's secret would be the signal for his instant and cruel death. With eyes upon the earth and folded hands, she replied mournfully to the demand of the tyrant:

"I may not tell thee, since he hath denied."

"He dies! Away with him to prison!" cried Roderick.

Her shrieks filled the air, but did not move the tyrant. He motioned the guards straightway to remove the prisoner; but the timid maiden had grown fearless for herself, as she witnessed the danger of her lover, and strong in the desperation which her want of strength occasioned her. She threw herself between the king and his victim—she made her way to the prisoner, through the guards which environed him, and, heedless of the reproach which at another time and under other circumstances she would have expected naturally to follow such an act, she threw herself upon the bosom of Egiza, and wept and implored by turns.

"Nay, dearest!" exclaimed the captive, who realized his situation perfectly, and well knew that Roderick was not to be moved by any such exhibition. "This is but weakness. Show thyself firm, and fear nothing. Thy prayers avail not with the tyrant: he hears them but to scorn. I would not have him behold thy sufferings. I would not that he should find pleasure in thy tears."

"Remove her, Edeco; separate them," said the king. "As for the traitor, away with him to his dungeon, and see that he be well secured. I must have time to meditate a fitting punishment for one so insolent."

The commands of Roderick were peremptory; and, not often accustomed to dispute them, the mercenaries were sufficiently prompt in their execution. They seized upon the prisoner with unscrupulous force. With a resolve not less unyielding, though of softer seeming, the fantastic Edeco laid his hands upon the maiden. Her shrieks denoted her agony, though they failed to serve her will.

"You shall not separate us!" she cried, wildly. "You will not—you cannot!" she said, imploringly, as she heard the commands of Roderick, and beheld the obedience expressed in the eyes and in the action of his creatures.

"He is my lord—my betrothed—my husband. We must, we will go together—to the prison, to the scaffold, any where; but you shall not part us—you shall not tear us asunder!"

A bitter smile passed over the face of Roderick, as he heard these words. They were so much poison to his soul. He waved his hand impatiently to the guards. The maiden would have still implored him, but Egiza interrupted her.

"You plead to him in vain, my Cava. He hath neither truth nor mercy in his heart. Go plead to stocks and stones, ere you waste breath on such as he. The wolf shall have an ear to supplication when he hath none—ay, weep with pity when both his eyes are dry. Plead no more, Cava, I pray you plead no more. You wrong your noble nature, when you bend it to ask grace from the unworthy. You debase the creature for whom you pray, when you plead for him to the base."

"You are proud in stomach, sirrah; but the scourge shall teach you a becoming humility!" said Roderick. "Away with him!" he cried to the guards; and they could easily see how greatly he was enraged, as his words were always few in his anger.

"Ye will not!" exclaimed Cava, now addressing herself vainly to the guards; "Ye will not! Surely ye have wives, and daughters! You, my lord!—you!"

Edeco laughed and simpered when the appeal was made to him, and his fore-finger was employed in re-twisting the floating locks on his temples, which in the confusion had become somewhat deranged.

"I thank you," he said, effeminately; "but I have never been so afflicted. It is toil enough, sweet lady, to serve and succor my neighbors. I would not emulate their virtues. They all have wives and daughters."

The occult meaning of this speech was not perceptible to the unsophisticated sense of Cava; but she understood enough from the licentious looks and puerile air of the fopling, to know that he was incapable of feeling her afflictions. She continued her appeal to Roderick and his guards alternately, and with all the earnestness of a devoted heart and a warmly excited spirit; but the wrath of the tyrant was immovable, and as for the guards, a moment of calm reflection would have taught the unhappy maiden that they were incapable of one sentiment of generous pity while in the service of such a master. Little did they heed her prayers or agonies. They obeyed the harsh and repeated commands of Roderick, and with ruthless violence tore her from the bosom to which she had not ceased to cling with a most convulsive effort; and she only ceased to scream and struggle in the utter exhaustion of her nature. She fell back in a swoon within the arms of Edeco; and Roderick, as he beheld her condition, made a sign to the servile creature, which he seemed readily to understand, and at once proceeded to obey. The gesture of the king had not been unseen by Egiza; and the agony of his soul may be better understood than recorded, as his mind conjectured its base and sinister import. Was it indeed true, that he, so lately the arbiter of the tyrant's fate, was now so soon, so suddenly the victim of his will? Could it be, that she, the innocent and blessed idol of his affection, was in the grasp of one whose voluptuous inclinations had already been made so fearfully manifest? And could he not protect, and save, and avenge her? The thought, the conviction, was maddening. He strove with his captors; he shook them with a giant's strength from his bosom, but they clung to him again and again; and, writhing and striving all the while, he beheld the maiden at length borne away from his sight to the secret places of the usurper's lust, and he had no power to arrest her progress, or weapon to avenge her fate. His head dropped upon his bosom in his despair, and he had no spirit to send back from his lips the scorn which he felt in his soul, as the tyrant, taunting him with the power which he possessed over both himself and the maiden, bade the guards hurry him to the deepest prison in Toledo.

END OF BOOK SECOND

COUNT JULIAN;

OR,

THE LAST DAYS OF THE GOTH.

BOOK THIRD.

CHAPTER I.

In politics individuals represent power rather than possess it, as, in the commercial world, money is the representative of value, without having value itself, only as it answers this purpose. The power of the despot is that of the vices, the passions, the injustice of those over whom he rules. It is not the proof of any uncommon attributes in himself. On the contrary, if it proves any thing, it proves the flexibility of his moral powers, and consequently his real inferiority. He is the creature of the vices and circumstances which he represents, and when he ceases to be so, he is overthrown. The existence of a tyrant proves the necessity for one, since it would be utterly impossible for any individual to enslave a people who are worthy of freedom. Sylla never slaughtered in Rome until every senator had become a tyrant. He could no more have succeeded in the time of Tarquin than could Tarquin himself. The representative of the popular mind, at that time, derived his powers from the popular virtues.

Roderick was the creature of his time. He represented the people over whom he ruled. He embodied their craft, their lust, their faithlessness, their cruelty. He was properly their sovereign, and he was rightly their scourge. He had his uses; and we may not regret that in overthrowing a once mighty empire, the Moors overthrew the dominion of the rankest vice and the most reckless profligacy. It is scarcely possible that they could raise a worse in its stead. Yet Roderick, like Nero, commenced his reign virtuously. He commenced as the avenger of his father's wrongs, and the redresser of those under which his people suffered. But he soon found that, like Nero, he could not rule the people whom he did not represent. He was compelled to adopt their vices to maintain his rule; since, to be moral where all were vicious, were to assert a solitude of distinction which must isolate him from all sympathy, and leave him defenceless to all foes. With a rapid retrogade, which was good worldly policy, he soon, like the Roman monster whom we have quoted in comparison, overtook his subjects, and rapidly passed them in his vices. From excess to excess he pursued his way, until the very shamelessness of his indulgences produced that revulsion of feeling in the popular sentiment which would seem to be the legitimate purpose of the tyrant. Men whose own vices had made them monsters, now paused in their progress, startled into reflection as they beheld the career of a monster whose vicious and foul practices far surpassed their own most corrupt imaginings; and the general insecurity under a sway so reckless, at length produced that individual apprehensiveness which works for virtue, as it prompts the continual fear of punishment. The minds of the Goths were alienated from their monarch, not because of his vices, but because their own were outdone. The resources which he possessed were beyond their rivalry; and as even voluptuousness has its vanity, they were mortified into hatred of those excesses which they otherwise had been glad enough to share. They were now as ripe for insurrection as they had been ready for his rule; and he who had never paused or hesitated in the sacrifice of his victim, was now destined to become one. But he dreamed not of this. The blindness which precedes destruction had fallen upon him; and in the vain plenitude of his power, and in the hardness of his heart, he hurried on, utterly forgetting that he but indicated the power which he fondly imagined to exist within himself. With a blindness of judgment, he determined that the trial of Egiza, whom he did not recognise, should take place in public; and like more modern monarchs, who are but too prone to convert the offices of justice into pompous ceremonials, he resolved that an ostentatious display of power should accompany the sentence of the criminal, and discourage other similar offenders. Had he been a wise tyrant, he would have studiously avoided such a proceeding. He would have strangled the offender in a prison which had neither eye nor ear. He would have quelled inquiry as dangerous, and suppressed those shows, to the popular eye, of power harshly exercised in the sovereign, which are more apt to occasion sympathy than apprehension in the mind of the spectator. . . . .

"Thou hast heard, my lord Oppas," said the priest Romano, entering the private apartments of the archbishop, the morning after the arrest of Egiza; "thou hast heard that a goodly stroke hath been aimed at the bosom of the defier of God."

"Ay, my brother; but I have not heard that the defier of God hath been stricken," replied Oppas.

"Of a truth, he lives, and the avenger hath been foiled," said the priest, with a desponding visage; "but it is something, my father, that the blow should have been stricken, since it showeth that God lacketh not in agents who seek to do his will. If there be one to try, there will be two; and the blow that faileth once, or twice, doth not often fail thrice. There are hands yet which are armed, and hearts which are willing, my father; and let the word be spoken from on high, and the sign be shown, and even the poor and humble Romano will be ready for the work of punishment."

The venerable zealot lifted a dagger from his bosom as he spoke these words, and lord Oppas beheld in the expression of his eye that Romano needed but the promptings of a dream by night to enter the palace of king Roderick and do the work of assassination, if he might, as a good service rendered to the Most High.

"Thou art blessed of Heaven, brother Romano, as thou art so ready to hear and to obey," said Oppas, with a respectful deference of manner. "Thou prayest to know thy labors, and thou seekest to perform them. This is the true servant—and thou wilt not long wait the call to service. It would seem to await thee even now, Romano."

"How?—what mean you, father Oppas? Am I remiss?—am I unmindful? Have I suffered the words of Heaven to fall upon unheeding ears? Say, tell me, my father, that I may hasten to bind up the broken places, and amend the errors of forgetfulness."

"I say not that, my brother," replied the cunning archbishop; "I would not pretend to counsel one whom God hath chosen for his own teachings; but I should rather look to thee for counsel, Romano, and for a direction in the passages which are difficult. Yet is this thought of mine strong within me, that thy labors are at hand. Knowest thou the name of him who hath sought to slay king Roderick?"

"No, father; I know not."

"It is the youth who came with thee into Toledo; he to whom thou gavest the garments."

"God is great! He worketh by mystery and in darkness. Who shall fathom his ways?—who shall declare his purposes? Doth it not seem, father Oppas, that there was a will and a power in this matter that came from above? Wherefore should this youth have come so timely to my aid when Roderick had stricken me down among the hills? Wherefore should he have followed me into Toledo, witless of all things?—for of himself did he say that he he had no call within the city. Why should I give him a garment for his protection?—and how should it be that in the secret gardens of the king, despite of all his guards, he should have made his way, unless the spirit of God had so devised it, and sent him forward to work out his vengeance?"

"It is the thought of wisdom, and the faithful servant, Romano; yet the youth hath failed. The tyrant hath escaped the fatal blow, and the minister of vengeance, whether through his own weakness, or that Heaven would spare its foe for a longer space that its accumulated judgments may be more heavy, is now the captive of king Roderick, reserved in his dungeons for a cruel sentence."

"But will God suffer his servant to perish, father Oppas? I believe it not. He will, I think, work out the youth's deliverance; and the safety of Roderick now is but a blind on his eyes, which shall hood him yet for the executioner. The youth must escape."

"Thou speakest thy own labors, Romano. Is it not clear to thee, even as I said erewhile, that thy tasks were at hand? Thou shalt free this youth; it is thy duty—thy own lips have pronounced it such; and I doubt not that the God who hath decreed thy work will give thee strength and wisdom to perform it. And further to confirm this thought, know that the youth hath been carried to the strong dungeon of Suintila, whose keeper is"——

"Guisenard, the lieutenant!"

"The same—the same!" said Oppas, eagerly.

"Art sure of this, father Oppas?" demanded Romano.

"As that I live, my brother. I have the words of those who beheld him carried thither last night in secret."

"Thou hast spoken rightly, then, my father; the hand of God is in this—for, of a truth, my power is great upon the mind of Guisenard, who comes to my confessional, and who will heed the words of reason from my lips."

"Do I not know this, my brother? Is not thy office plain? What though Jehovah worketh in secret, the fruits of his labors come forth in light. I knew in my secret soul that He would reveal to thee what it is fitting thou shouldst know; that He would point thee to thy tasks, and place thy enemy in thy hands. Thou canst move Guisenard at thy bidding, and he will deliver up the unholy trust of the tyrant, when thou shalt show to his sense that it is God's messenger whom he would keep in bondage, waiting for a cruel death. Yet, my brother, though we obey the will of God, we are not to be heedless of the wants of man. When Guisenard shall free the prisoner, it will need that he should fly himself, since the wilful tyrant, upon whose head Jehovah would accumulate sins that his doom should be the heavier, would punish the soldier whose fidelity to Holy Church would be falsehood to him. Guisenard must fly when he has released the youth; and thou shalt provide him the means of flight, and give him direction for a journey to the Asturias, where the young prince Pelayo even now gathers an army. Take this purse—it is filled, and will speed him on his way. Perchance, too, it will prove an argument to his mind, persuading him to compliance with thy demand. The ignorant mortal will heed such argument when better ones perchance would fail. It is our pride and pleasure, Romano, that we seek the will of God, and perform our labors for his love, regardless of all other reward,"

Romano took the purse, which was well filled with gold, with the air and manner of one who scorned what he was yet compelled to conceal with care. He readily recognized the force of the archbishop's suggestion, though he despised the agent he was required to use.

While they conferred, a royal messenger summoned the archbishop to the palace, where, in the hall of audience, it was decreed that the examination of Egiza should take place. A few words more to Romano, and lord Oppas left him to find his way from a back and private entrance, while he went forth with his train, through the great gate of his own residence.

CHAPTER II.

It was not until the archbishop reached the court of the palace that he knew the business upon which he had been summoned. When he was told its purport, his apprehensions began to be greatly aroused. He dreaded lest a discovery of Egiza's secret would lead to a suspicion of his own. Could they do less than suspect the uncle, if they could convict the nephew? The probabilities were manifestly against it. The affair looked inauspicious. It was only by a course of the most daring effrontery and admirable hypocrisy that Oppas had escaped proscription when Roderick came into power. It was only by joining in the denunciations against the powers that had been, and emulating the truckling servility of those who threw themselves in the path and at the feet of the newly-risen, that Oppas had preserved his station as the head of the Gothic church. A policy to which Roderick had now become somewhat indifferent, had prompted him to receive professions from and give credit for sincerity to all those who were allied to the nobility of the nation, or were connected with that more insolent aristocracy which assumed the powers and wore the garb of the established religion. Oppas was a superior politician to Roderick, and well understood the motives which operated upon the latter in his favor. He now as readily conceived that the rashness and self-conceit of the despot would make him less heedful than before how he offended the class of which he was a leading member. Such were his apprehensions that, could he have left the court in secresy, he would have done so, and at once fled, with all his personal retainers, to join the young prince Pelayo, in the Asturian mountains. But this could not be, and he prepared, with his utmost coolness and address, to meet events and baffle their dangers as he might.

The first nobleman whom the archbishop encountered as he entered the court of the palace, contributed to increase his alarm. This person was one of the most respectable among those of the old nobles who yet remained within the pale of the court. He well knew the doubtful character of that loyalty which the archbishop professed; and, with a smile of particular meaning, he thus addressed him:

"What! does the young head still linger upon the old shoulders? Is the old fox to be caught at last? You are scarcely wise, my lord Oppas. I had not thought it of you. I had thought, by this time, to have heard that you were far on your way to the Pyrennees, and rallying the insurgents who are said to lurk in that neighborhood. Were I in your case, and had I half the sagacity which fame ascribes to you, I am sure such would have been my speed, and such the direction which I should have taken."

The archbishop affected a surprise which he did not feel.

"What mean you, my lord Gerontius? What case is this, which so alarms you for my safety; and what have I to fear, that I should fly?"

The composure of his manner was admirable as he spoke these words.

"What! you have not heard?" said the other, quickly. "But I must not so far question your precautions. You surely know of the attempt which has been made upon the life of king Roderick."

"Of a truth, I know that," replied the archbishop; "but how does this concern me in especial, and why should I fly?"

"You know that the assassin is a monk?"

"I knew not that. I hear that he is a mere youth, but nothing more. Is he in truth a monk?"

"Ay, of the Caulian schools—so his garb speaks him; and the king is sworn to rouse you all for it. He couples it with the insolence of the mad priest Romano—and him he couples with the drones that he drove out from the House of Hercules—and these he couples with the whole brotherhood—and the whole brotherhood with the archbishop—and the archbishop with the pope—and the pope with the devil; and to the devil, if I rightly understand, he is bent to send you all, or such, at least, as he can lay sudden hands upon. This is the common bruit through the city; and I held it matter of course that you should have heard it, having, as I well know, in your own keeping such superior sources of general intelligence. You may conceive now why it is that I wondered, knowing your prudence, yet seeing you here?"

There was nothing grateful in this speech of the old noble; but Oppas received it calmly.

"Truly you surprise, if you do not alarm me, my lord Gerontius, These tidings are new to me, and strange. I had no knowledge that the assassin was a monk—still less did I deem it probable that our order, which has always been the readiest to maintain the power of king Roderick, should fall under suspicion of this nature. Nor can I think now that there is any reason in this rumor. Of whom did you receive it?"

"Of whom? What a question! Why, from all the mouths of the court, every prop and pillar of which has its twain. The common tongue is the universal one; and man never lacks language when he speaks evil of his fellow. I heard it from Gunderic, the big-bellied, who puffed and blowed, while telling it, to his own exhaustion and the disquiet of my nostrils: from Sisibert, who apes Edeco, and breathes nothing but scent and sentiment, and mortally hates sense: from Chilibert, the sleepy, who proved the importance, not to say the truth—so far as he believed it to be true, by never once yawning during his narrative: and, to speak guardedly, from a dozen others, of as long tongue and as little authority."

"Your own manner, my lord," said the archbishop, smiling as he spoke, "tells me what regard you yourself give to this story. I may well be indifferent to the clamor of the city, when you speak of it so lightly."

"Nay, do not deceive yourself, my lord bishop, nor let my manner deceive you. I have learned to smile at most matters, but I do not smile at this. Of a truth, I do believe that there is something in it. I have reason to know that Roderick looks suspiciously upon your fraternity, and I bid you be on your guard. I would not that all our nobles should suffer from a misplaced reliance on a monarch who is but too apt to forget an old service, as he is perpetually called upon to remember a new favorite. But, no more. The guards approach. Be cool, Oppas; for the step of Roderick is hasty and his cheeks are flushed. They come."

The advice of the nobleman was not lost upon Oppas, though it was scarcely needed by so old a politician. The guards of Roderick now filled the chamber, and the despot only lingered at the threshold of the hall, uttering some hasty commands to one of his attendants. The nobles began to gather; and in the pause which ensued before the entrance of the king, the archbishop had composed and arranged his thoughts for the approaching trial.

He had need of all his faculties for this event; and those who had heard of the uttered hostility of the king toward the priesthood beheld with surprise his composed demeanor, and wondered at his presence. He knew, much better than they, the imminent danger in which he stood, as he better knew the person of the criminal, with whom his own conscience more perfectly identified him, than could any vague suspicion of the tyrant, based simply upon the garb worn by Egiza. Could the prince keep his own secret, Oppas felt that he himself might escape; for Egiza had been little known in Toledo, and seldom or never seen by those who held the confidential places around Roderick's person. The dread of the lord Oppas was that the prince, hopeless of favor from Roderick, and desperate with hate, might declare himself in defiance; and this done, he well knew that not even his sacred profession could save him from crimination with his nephew, particularly as, from the nature of the disguise worn by the latter, it must appear to the jealous tyrant that his attempt had been distinctly authorized by the priesthood, if not by himself. These thoughts rapidly passed through his mind during the interim which followed the conversation with the lord Gerontius, and before the entrance of the king. It would be idle to deny that his apprehensions were great, since he rested his hope upon one or two contingencies, together with own presence of mind, and watchful use of circumstances as they arose. But he took his seat, seemingly with little concern, at the head of the board and near the throne, where it had ever been his custom to sit; and neither in look, word, manner, nor in the assertion of his state, did he in the slightest particular relax from the dignity which belonged to him as a man, and that which he asserted for his sacred office. The seats around him were rapidly filled up; and if the men of note in that assembly were few—if the essence of character and talent in those who composed the king's council was such as to accord meetly with the degraded spirit and vicious debasement of the kingdom, there was certainly nothing wanting in external show, in rich dresses, the glitter of jewelry and flowing trains, to make up for the lack of better attributes, or at least to reconcile the mere spectator to their loss. The Goths affected the pomp of the Romans and the effeminate voluptuousness of the Greeks; and, for their useless glitter and vain display, they were but too ready to yield up the more substantial qualities of hardy valor and national simplicity. It was thus that the court, on the present occasion, fatigued rather than won the eye with its overloaded splendors; and the profusion of wealth which it displayed but poorly supplied the place of good taste and propriety. Even the guards of Roderick, with their tawdry jackets of purple silk, edged with gold fillagree, and their long spears, the iron heads of which were softened with a deep gilding, presented but indifferent substitutes for those rough warriors who had made the Romans pass under the yoke, and had carried their arms without stop or impediment from the Danube to the Atlantic ocean. The national character was changed. The reputation of their forefathers was no longer a source of pride to those who affected superior refinements; and one of the follies of Roderick, which provoked the sarcasm of the neighboring Moors, was in the assumption of the empty title, along with the idle glitter, of 'King of the Romans;' as if the spirit of the Cæsars dwelt in the frame of the licentious and arrogant Goth.

The entrance of Roderick was the signal for obeisance and servility. He entered with a quick, sudden step, which, though hurried, did not prevent him from frequently pausing to dart hasty and inquiring looks into the faces of all around him Once or twice he paused and seemed disposed to speak to one or more persons upon whom he looked, but as if quelling the desire, or unable through excess of passion to indulge it, he hurried on toward the throne until his eye caught that of the archbishop. As it did so, the king paused, with a convulsive movement. His arm seemed to twich and jerk with the angry feeling in his bosom; but he remained where he was at the moment, and his brow collected over his eye, while it darted forth a light like fire upon Oppas, as if it intended to consume him. The archbishop met his glance without blenching. He knew that this was one of the tyrant's tests. He was wont to say that "he could look down treason, and drive, with a glance of his own, that of his enemy to the ground." But it failed to have this effect on the present occasion. The eye of Oppas was as true to his purpose as was that of Roderick; and, while all in the assembly looked alternately from the king to the archbishop, the former turned away with a ferocious scowl from gazing upon his victim, to dart angry glances upon the watchful assembly. If his eye failed to terrify that of the stern archbishop, it was more successful in controlling those of the spectators. Their acknowledgements of its power were instantaneous. Every face was bent downward in humility, and the vanity of the despot was satisfied with this tacit acknowledgment of his superiority. He proceeded to the throne, threw himself into the seat, and for a few moments a dead silence reigned throughout the apartment. At length, with a voice hoarse and loud, Roderick broke the silence by addressing his parasite Edeco, who stood beside him.

"Edeco!"

With a servile gesture and a fawning smile the favorite approached and bent himself before his master. A brief pause ensued, when Roderick continued:

"Edeco!—But no, no. Thou art not the man. Thou hast counsel fit for other moods, and lighter matters. I would that lord Bovis were here! I could trust him, head and heart I could trust him!"

These words, spoken aloud, fully declared the disquiet of the tyrant. He seemed vexed and bewildered; then, as if resolved, he motioned Edeco back, and, again fixing his eye upon the archbishop, thus abruptly addressed him:

"So, ho! my lord Oppas! You are not content to rule in the church; you would sway the state. It is not enough that you claim an entire disposition of souls; you would usurp that of bodies also. You are choice in your victims. The blood of kings and princes must stain your altars, and you dispatch your assassins to the very palace of your master. But you have dared too much for safety, as you have done too little for success. The church shall not save you; and the insolent head of it, who sits in Rome and sends out his murderous decrees, as if he were God himself, to all parts of the earth—he shall not save you; even if he shall have power to save himself, which is doubtful. I will march troops upon Rome itself, but I will have justice; and his treasury shall pay my soldiers for the toil of his punishment."

A shout rent the air from the armed band around, as Roderick finished his furious tirade. He looked round approvingly upon them, and then his eye rested upon Oppas. The archbishop, seemingly unmoved, replied to him respectfully.

"If I say to thee, oh king! that thy language surprises even if it does not confound me, I shall but say what is the truth. That thou hast the power to punish me for offences, real and imaginary, I nothing question. That thou hast power to extort tribute from the iron keys of St. Peter, I do not deny thee; for God, of his own foresight and for his own purposes, not unfrequently suffers injustice to prevail for a season upon earth, and the axe of the executioner to be stained with the best blood of his saints. This is no new thing in the history of the church's trials, and the apostles have testified to its truth. I look not now to find the princes of the earth perfected in holiness and slow to injustice; and I were but a poor servant of my master, if I were not at all times ready to seal with my blood the faith which I profess. If it be, oh king! that thy anger is against the church, of which I am a most unworthy son, then must I submit to thy decree without murmuring. Yet may I implore of thee to know of what offence I am guilty, and what is thy complaint against the holy father?"

The air of the lord Oppas was that of a saint, so meek, so uncomplaining, so resigned to his fate in consideration of his faith. To a temper like that of Roderick, such a deportment was irritating in the last degree; nor did it lessen his anger to listen to the ready acknowledgment of his power which the archbishop had adroitly given in his reply.

"Now, by Hercules! this exceeds belief. What! thou art ignorant, my lord Oppas? Thou knowest nothing of the assassin? Thou hast not heard of the villain who would have slain thy sovereign, when it is the common speech of Toledo?"

"I have not said this, oh king! Of a truth, I know that such is the common speech of Toledo; but I know nothing of the facts," was the response of the archbishop; to which the answer of Roderick was instantaneous:

"Who said thou didst not know? my lord Oppas. I knew thou didst. But thou dost not justice to thy knowledge. Thou knowest more than the common speech of Toledo; thou knowest the assassin—thou hadst knowledge of his mission. Wilt thou dare deny that?"

"If thou commandest me to speak, oh king! I do deny that I had knowledge of the assassin, as such."

"But thou knowest him?" exclaimed the king, eagerly.

"That I know not," replied the wily archbishop; "for, as yet, I have not seen him. It may be that he is known to me. I will not say."

"He is—he must be! He wears thy accursed garments—he comes of thy own black brood—he ministers to thy church!" exclaimed the fierce monarch. "But I will set him before thee; ye shall see and speak with each other; and I trust to hear the truth—for as surely as yonder streams the blessed sun upon the marble of this floor, so certainly shall the blood of one, or both, or all of you, stream in atonement for this crime, which I hold to have come from your secret counsels together."

"Let it be, oh Roderick! as thou hast said!" exclaimed the archbishop, confidently. "Let the criminal be set before us; if he be of the church, it may be that I shall know him; yet, if he be, I trust to show that the crime he purposed was the meditation of his own heart, and came from no counsels of mine, or of the holy brotherhood."

The king gave a signal to Edeco, who disappeared.

"Holy brotherhood!" exclaimed Roderick, in scorn; "I know your holiness, my lord Oppas, and the holiness of the brotherhood; and, as you know it also, it makes not in your favor, in my mind, that you should so reverently speak of it. But here comes Edeco. Look, my lord bishop, for the prisoner cometh. See that you forget not your friends; see that your faith holds firm, and denies not the knowledge of a brother."

This was the moment of trial for the archbishop, and he addressed all his energies to meet it—for all eyes were upon him as he gazed. In boldness only—in the utmost confidence—could he hope to avoid suspicion. A moment's pause, or hesitation—an averted look, an agitating apprehension, he well knew—as he was closely watched by the monarch and by many who would have been but too happy to avail themselves of his fall to omit noticing his confusion—would confirm the suspicions of Roderick—and his resolution was taken. Rising, as the guards appeared with the prisoner, he himself addressed them:

"Bring forward the assassin, that I may look upon him! You shall see, oh king! that I dread not the contact with this man, which is to confound me—satisfied as I am that I know him not as an assassin, even though I may have knowledge of him as a priest."

The unhappy Egiza, still clothed in the monkish habiliments of Romano, was brought forward accordingly. He had heard the words of the archbishop—and, indeed, they were intended quite as much for his ears as for those of the king. They gave him a clue to the position in which Oppas stood, and taught him the danger of his uncle—not on the score of his relationship, but as he was a member of the same religious fraternity. This was enough for the prince. His resolve was taken; and had he not already determined upon answering nothing that could lead to a discovery of his secret, this would have made him do so. He met the eye of the archbishop with as much indifference as he could command.

"My son, who art thou?" demanded Oppas.

The youth paused a moment ere he replied, as if uncertain whether to do so or not. He then spoke:

"Who are you, that ask?"

"Slave!" cried the furious Roderick, half rising from his throne, and grasping a javelin; "Speak, slave! and answer, or thy tongue shall be torn from thy jaws by the roots!"

"Thou wilt have less answer then than now," was the calm reply; "and wilt add another proof to the folly, not less than the tyranny of thy sway. Art thou answered?"

A dozen violent hands were laid upon the criminal as he uttered himself thus; and this violence on the part of his subjects disarmed that of the despot. He did not like to behold so much of ready impulse, even though in defence of his own authority, on the part of those whom he only required to obey; and to the surprise and consternation of the forward courtiers, his rebuke was by no means gentle.

"How now, my lords; wherefore this violence? Unhand the man, I say. Ye are too bold. Think you if I had needed that weapon should be used, I should ask for yours? Am I so feeble of arm that ye come thus to my aid ere I summon you? Had I needed this free service, and were there danger in the deed, ye had not been so quick of action. I should have waited for you long, and called for ye in vain. Ye had been more ready to help the foe, than the monarch who claimed your rightful service and needed your succor. Give back, and let the slave answer freely. If he is ready to abide the axe-man, he hath a right to speak. He hath but little time for insolence, and I am curious to learn his phrase. You have more matter for his ear, my lord Oppas. Speak to him freely, else you greatly disparage the brotherhood."

"I know nothing of the man, oh Roderick! and wist not what to ask of him," said the archbishop. The king scrutinized him as he spoke this denial, but he detected nothing in the inflexible features of the speaker to give the least color to his suspicions.

"Then I will question him myself!" he exclaimed, turning from his unsatisfactory examination of the archbishop's face, to one equally unsatisfactory and much more annoying, which he bestowed upon that of the prisoner. After a few seconds, during which he gazed at Egiza as though he would read the very thoughts of his secret soul, he abruptly asked:

"Who are you?"

"A man—your foe!" was the reply.

"We shall try your manhood, slave; for your enmity we care not. We shall subdue both. But ere your limbs writhe under the torture, be wise and answer. What name bear you?—whence come you? Speak—unfold the truth, and rely upon our mercy to save, where strict justice would have us destroy."

The prisoner replied, without a moment's pause:

"I fear not your torture, and your mercy I despise—for I believe not in your assurances. I have no name—I am without a country. There is one question you have not asked, which I might yet answer."

"What question?" demanded the king.

"You seem not curious to know wherefore I strove to slay you—wherefore I invaded your gardens of infamy and aimed my dagger at your heart! Why is this indifference?"

"Insolent! Wherefore should I demand that which is so evident. Hast thou not the garments of the monk upon thee? Art thou not one of the creatures that fattened at the public charge in the House of Hercules? Answer, slave! Wert thou not sent upon thy base mission by this same priest? Did not thy charge come from the lord Oppas?"

"No!—thou knowest, Roderick, that it did not. Thou well knowest the motive of my hatred, and the cause which moved me to aim my dagger at thy life. It was not for the church, not for the priest, not for any sect, not for my own ambition, that I strove to slay thee; but for humanity, for virtue, for innocence. Before thy court, in the presence of the aged and the noble whom I see around thee, will I declare the occasion of my attempt upon thee; and if all honorable feeling be not gone from the court—if there be husbands and fathers among them, to whom the virtue of the wife or the daughter is dear, they will rise against thee as with one spirit, and strike at thy heart with a dagger as keen and much more fortunate than mine."

The fury of Roderick could scarcely be restrained, and he was about to rise, and would probably have hurled the javelin, which he now clutched in his convulsive fingers, at the bosom of Egiza, but for the archbishop, who beheld, as he thought, a fitting moment to interpose. He saw that the suspicions of the king—if, indeed, he had ever, in reality, entertained them—were, in great part, diverted from himself by the fearlessness of the prisoner; and he now only feared that the provocation given by the prince, would be such as might prompt Roderick to inflict upon him a sudden death. This he aimed to avert by a new proposition.

"The prisoner," he said, "oh king! declares that he hath neither name or country; but, as I must profess myself deeply interested in the habit which he wears, will it be permitted me, Roderick, to propose to him a few questions in private, in order that I may learn from him the motive for a course which is so very strange and criminal."

"Ha!—to counsel him to further insolence!" cried Roderick, his jealousy of the priest reawakening. "No, my lord Oppas, no! Let him speak without counsel, as I shall look for you to speak. Ye are traitors, both; and I will trust ye not from my sight together."

"I ask it not, king Roderick; in your sight let me speak to this man—but let the guards be withdrawn. I care not what ye do with him: I am prepared for all that you may think fit to do with me: but, as a servant of the church, I would examine him who wears its garments, that I may the better learn the source of his iniquity, and move his conscience to atonement. What should you fear? He cannot escape, nor can I. Your guards are around us—your eye is upon us; you but suffer the criminal to make his confession, if it pleases him, in secret."

"Ay, to thee. He has already made it, I doubt not; but as his doom is fixed, which all your pleading and all his confession may never change, take the privilege which you pray for. Let the guards fall back, Edeco, and suffer the holy brothers to speak together!"

The archbishop did not seem to heed the sneer with which the indulgence was granted; he was only too well satisfied to avail himself of the privilege. Approaching Egiza, with a slow and dignified manner, which was carefully studied, as he well knew that it was closely observed, he at once addressed himself to the leading object which he had in view.

"He has no guess of your secret, Egiza," said Oppas, in the lowest tones; "suffer it not to escape you. You will be doomed to death, and I myself will propose your sentence, the better to avoid suspicion; but fear nothing, I have already taken order for your rescue, and to-night you will hear of me in your dungeon from one on whom you may rely. He will bear a token from me, and you will go with him; but ask him nothing—and be sure you tell him nothing. Be of good cheer—bear with the tyrant as you may, but provoke him not; his day will soon be ended—he is on the precipice. Let us but escape this danger, and we triumph."

"But the lady Cava?" said the prince, in similar tones, overlooking the present difficulty in his way, and only solicitous for her whom he loved; "tell me of her, my father; say that she is safe, that all is well with her, that she is out of the clutches of this monster, and—in honor."

"She is with the queen," said Oppas, evasively.

"Speed—send a letter to her father, if thou canst, for I dread to think of the doom which is before her."

"Let us make thee free to-night, Egiza, and thou canst do more than this—thou canst free her. But, meanwhile, say nothing to chafe the tyrant who has thee in his grasp. Be not afraid when thou hearest me declare thy doom, for, of a surety, I have but this one mode to escape suspicion. Reply to him in a subdued spirit, lest, in his anger, he command the torture for thee."

The youth shuddered, and replied:

"I will try; but I fear me, I should curse the tyrant, though my last breath lingered at his will. Do what thou canst, my father; I leave it all to thee."

The voice of Roderick arrested their conference, but not before the main points of it, as the archbishop had desired, were sufficiently discussed.

"Well, my lord Oppas, to what condition of mind have you brought your worthy brother? Methinks you have had sufficient time to hear his secrets—ay, and to unfold your own. To what doth he confess?"

"He will confess nothing, oh king! neither his name nor the place from which he comes. He is obdurate: I know him not."

"What!—he will not say to you that his brothers of the House of Hercules sent him to avenge their wrongs? He wears their garb; he might reveal to you, having, I doubt not, so much of your lordship's sympathy. But I have an argument—nay, two of them—which shall make him wiser. What ho, there! guards, advance the prisoner. Hearken, slave!—you shall have your life—nay, your freedom—if you will confess the truth. Say that you were sent by these priests, who style themselves of Hercules, and I give you your life. Be wise; for as I have good cause to suspect their fidelity toward our government, I am willing to reward in the most generous manner the person who shall prove to my conviction their almost known treason."

"I were guilty of falsehood, were I to say so. Thou, Roderick, well knowest the cause for which I set upon thee; and to silence the further wrong which thy speech would cast upon innocent men, I will declare all the circumstances which led to my assault."

But Roderick had no wish that the truth should be spoken. It was to suppress the truth that he suggested to the prisoner what his confession should be, and offered him his life—an offer which he meant not to comply with—in compensation for the lie. The game of the tyrant was well understood by all parties. The resolution of Egiza enraged him, and he ordered him to the torture. Fortunately for the youth, the guards announced the approach of the queen. Roderick scowled fearfully, as he heard the announcement. He knew the gentleness of Egilona, and readily divined that, having heard that he sat in judgment upon a criminal, she came—as was frequently the case—to intercede between the judge and his victim, and soften the severities of punishment. Way was made for her train, and she entered the hall of state with the wonted ceremonials. Roderick deigned not to rise at her approach, and she sat down on the seat below him, unnoticed. But the effect of her presence was obvious to all. As if he had given no order for the torture of the prisoner, the king, assuming a milder tone and manner, addressed the lord Oppas:

"The prisoner, my lord bishop, is well tutored. To whom he owes the counsel which makes him thus obdurate, is a matter beyond my judgment, although not beyond my suspicion. You have heard his crime—a crime which, were the criminal a noble of this land, would call for his head. But, as the offender is of the church, a priest, and one who, had he been successful, might have become a saint, the offence, perchance, in thy mind will seem light, and worthy of no such punishment. Give me to know thy thought."

The reply of the archbishop was calmly but gravely uttered, and without a moment's hesitation.

"His offence, oh king! I hold to be of a most damnable kind; and whether the offender be priest or noble, its punishment should be the same. If I am to say—as it would seem to be your desire, oh king! that I should—what the punishment of the criminal should be, I would say death by the axe, as in the case of all similar offenders."

"Ha!" exclaimed the king, who evidently anticipated no such response. Suspecting the seeming monk before him of a connection with the brotherhood whose habit he wore, he looked to hear from the archbishop some exhortation to mercy—some appeal from justice to humanity. Surprised and disappointed, he turned upon the speaker and scanned him with looks of the keenest inquiry.

"Truly!" he exclaimed, after a brief pause, and a laugh of mingled scorn and good nature, "truly, my lord bishop, thou art less tender of thy fellowship than I had looked to find thee. This fellow should be an Arian, a schismatic, a backslider from the square law and the round, since thou shufflest him down the wind with so little concern. Wilt thou mutter for him a prayer, my lord bishop? Doth it come within thy charity to say masses for a soul whose carcass thou art so ready to resign? If it does, go to thy beads at once, and quickly, for thy decree will I adopt. The assassin dies within an hour."

The eye of the unhappy Egiza turned involuntarily upon that of the archbishop The suddenness of the sentence—the brief period of life which it allotted him—cutting him off, as it did, from all hope of assistance such as the archbishop had promised him—brought to his bosom, in that moment, all the sense and bitterness of death, in the conviction of its now unerring certainty. So young—so full of hope—so full of love, and the warm current of a generous affection—to be torn away from all—from youth, from life, from love!—the thought was agony; and the thrill which went through his veins, from the full heart which it convulsed, though he strove to subdue his emotions, or at least to keep them from exposure, was yet perceptible to the keen gray eye of the archbishop, though the latter did not seem to watch him. His overhanging and long eye-brows shaded from others the anxious yet assuring glance which he gave to the prisoner, the moment after the utterance of his doom by the king. That doom, though undisputed, was yet to be modified. The archbishop was not disposed to yield the struggle here. Himself seemingly secure, he was collected enough to preserve his composure throughout the scene; and with that temperate manner, which had, more than any thing beside, availed for his safety in the trial through which he had gone, he replied to the last remarks of Roderick, by seizing upon one part of his speech which furnished a natural opening for a plea in mitigation of the sentence.

"King Roderick little knows the servant of Christ, if he thinks that his prayer can be withheld from the criminal because he belongs not to the true church. Our mission is for such as he. To save the sinner—to turn him from his path of darkness into one of light, is the office of the priest; and these offices are more than ever needed for such as are double offenders—offenders against heaven's laws and the laws of man. But of little avail would be our prayers for the criminal, if he be not suffered to pray for himself. I trust, oh king! that it is not your will that the unhappy man before you should so suddenly be hurried from the presence of his mortal into that of his Eternal Judge; since such a judgment would be little else than hurrying his sinful soul into the deeps of eternal damnation."

The gentle Egilona, for whose ears much of this speech was intended, was silent no longer. She rose from her seat, which was at the feet of the tyrant, and knelt humbly before him.

"Surely, surely, my lord, you will hearken to these words of the lord Oppas?" said she.

"And wherefore? Let the dog die—let him twice, ay, thrice perish! It is his punishment I seek," exclaimed the king.

"But not in his sins, oh Roderick!—not in his sins! Let him repent of these—give him time for prayer, for penitence—that, in the blood of the Redeemer, he may find purification. I ask not that he may be spared; for the dreadful crime of which he would have been guilty, if his cruel desire could have been accomplished, deserves a cruel death. Yet, as his crime was mortal, let not his punishment extend beyond the boundaries of this narrow life. At least, though you deny life to his enjoyment, deny not salvation to his hope."

Thus implored the queenly woman, and the gentle wife. The archbishop knew that he had said enough, and prudently forebore to urge further suggestion. What, indeed, could he have added to solicitations urged by beauty, by beauty in tears, in homage, mingled with religious feeling, and enlivened by personal and devoted love. Roderick refused at first, chafed and chided next, and at length yielded. The prisoner was remanded to his dungeon, and five days were allowed to him to reconcile himself with heaven. . . . .

The departure of the king and his train, was the signal for respiration on the part of the archbishop. He had passed through a narrow and perilous strait, and he now breathed freely. During the whole conference, and while the danger impended, he had preserved a calm serenity of countenance, which nothing seemed to affect; so that, whether guilty, and meriting punishment, or innocent, and likely to suffer from injustice, he still secured the admiration of those who looked upon him But now he trembled. The color fled from his cheeks, as the guards withdrew in attendance upon the tyrant; his knees grew weak, and he looked around upon the noblemen who lingered in the hall with timidity and distrust. The involuntary sigh that then escaped from his lips, drew the lord Gerontius to his side. The old nobleman approached him with congratulations which were not less sincere than earnest.

"Your head was fairly within the jaws of the wolf, my lord Oppas; and I looked every moment to see them close upon it. That they did not is the more wonderful, as they evidently desired to do so. Can you conceive what is your offence, my lord; for it certainly is not that which is alleged. Methinks the king well enough knows the motive of the monk, who, it seems, is the father-confessor of the lady Cava, left with her by count Julian. Such was the speech of one at my side while the trial was in progress."

"Of that I know not," replied Oppas. "He would confess nothing to me. My offence against the king, I readily conjecture to lie in the shallowness of the royal treasury, and the supposed fulness of that of Holy Church. Another day will show."

"Such was my thought—my fear, I should rather say—for my suit at court will then be sped much more suddenly than I desire," said lord Gerontius, with a graver countenance.

"What suit?" demanded Oppas.

"One that I fear to urge—a suit for money. I need certain sums—which I ad vanced to help Roderick to the throne—to keep my estates from the Jews. They are hovering like kites around me, and await but to see what face I wear on my return from court to pounce down upon their prey."

"What favor has been shown you by the king for your services?" inquired the archbishop.

"Favor! Why, yes, 't is a favor that I am yet neither banished nor beheaded. These seem to be the sort of favors with which old service has been requited; and I tremble, therefore, but to speak of mine. The lords Aser and Gnotho—who, in all Spain, toiled so faithfully and gave so freely to make Roderick what he is? Yet are they banished, and without receiving one 'L'ovogild'* of all their expenditures, in return. You may imagine, therefore, with what fears I should demand my just dues, and how greatly my apprehensions should, of reason, be increased when you tell me that the royal treasury is low. I think to go back to my province in despair, without praying for those kingly favors, which mercy may commute to banishment or beheading—the latter being the greatest mercy, when the Jews are already in possession of the body."

The archbishop had some sympathies in readiness for the knight.

"If my treasury is to fill the royal coffers, it will be a merit that I pay some of the royal debts. You will not regret to give me the lien upon your estates, my lord, which the avaricious Jews now hold. Believe me, your indulgence will be much greater."

"Regret! Ah, my lord Oppas, you bind me to you for ever, if you save for me the old dwelling of my fathers."

He would have spoken his acknowledgments at greater length, but the archbishop interrupted him:

"Come and sup with me to-night, my lord Gerontius, and I will then provide you with the money necessary to free your estates from incumbrance. Yet say not

* The first gold coins of the Goths were struck by king Leovogild, from whom they took their name.

where you go, and let your acknowledgments of service be locked up in your bosom. I shall expect you."

The archbishop had secured another ally.

CHAPTER III.

That night the lord Oppas received his visiter with a judicious show of satisfaction, and they supped together without other company. With a delicacy which had its additional effect upon Gerontius, he obtained from him a knowledge of his debts, the non-payment of which worked a forfeiture of his estates; and, without a word, he placed in the possession of the latter a casket containing a sufficient supply of money to meet his responsibilities. The nobleman was loud in his acknowledgments, the utterance of which the archbishop gently discouraged.

"I have saved you, my lord Gerontius," said he, "as I would look for you to save me, should it so chance that I might need your aid; and as men who regard each other rightly, and have common interests growing out of common danger, should always be prepared to serve one another. These are not times, my lord Gerontius, when wise men should pause to give help, seeing good men struggling with the waters. It may be that you shall soon repay me for this small succor by a greater benefit, and one more valued and valuable; but whether you do or not, it gives me pleasure to make you a debtor to my friendship, by so small a service."

"I do not esteem it a small service," said the grateful Gerontius, "and I shall rejoice in the opportunity which shall enable me to requite thee. It is not now that we may command money, either from the prince because of past service, or the nobleman because of ancient fellowship. You shall not suffer loss of this money, my lord Oppas; for now that your generosity hath enabled me to set at defiance the hungry vultures that hang over my estates, I shall be the better enabled to linger about the court, and secure the favorable moment for urging my plea to Roderick."

The archbishop interrupted the speaker.

"Do not deceive thyself; thou waitest in vain for a favorable moment to urge thy plea for money. The monarch who is a debtor, like Roderick, yields no such time to the creditor. Thou wilt but incur danger without profit, to press thy demand for money at any season upon him."

"What, then! am I to lose my substance, and behold him who possesses it bestowing it upon such worthless minions as Edeco?" exclaimed the indignant Gerontius, in reply.

"Even so; and congratulate thyself that the monarch is not more conscientious. Were he less reckless than he is, he would extinguish the debt by taking thy head as a traitor to the realm. Thy very application for the claim, would be a sufficient argument to prove thee so."

"And thou thinkest, my lord Oppas, that I shall never get this money from king Roderick?"

"Of a truth, I do," was the reply.

"Take back thy casket; I will owe thee nothing which I may never pay. My only hope to return your loan is in the late justice of the king."

"No! keep the casket; it is thine, Gerontius, whether thou repayest me or not," said Oppas. "If thou takest it not, it will only add to the already large sums which Roderick has taken from his people, and which he will never return."

"How! What mean you?" said the other.

"Roderick claims a greater reward for indulgencies than ever did the priesthood," responded the archbishop, with a smile. "I said to thee this morning, ere we separated, that the wrath of the king rose from the shallowness of his own and the supposed overfulness of the church's coffers, rather than from any belief in his mind that I was a party with the assassin who aimed to take his life. I discovered that while the trial was in progress. An hour after I had reached my palace, comes Edoco to me with a warning that by noon the next day the king would expect supplies from the church to meet the expenses of the war against Pelayo and the rebels in the Asturias. Thou seest my treasury will be his ere noon to-morrow; and he must have all, else my escape were for a brief season only. That casket were but a trifle taken from the mass; it would add little to my loss—it will be the safety of thy all to thee."

"And yet, my lord Oppas," said Gerontius, "though there be good reason in what you say, yet I am greatly loath to lose these monies which the king had of me; not so much, indeed, because I need their use, as that I chafe at such injustice. I am scarce a man when I dare not demand a right."

"Methinks," said Oppas, with a smile, "methinks thou art extravagant, Gerontius, in thy desires. Who claims to be a man now-a-days, in Iberia? Who is he that clamors for his right? Thou hast lived too long in the country; and unless thou learnest wisdom quickly, thy head will be of little use to thee after a week's wear in Toledo. Take the casket, put it in thy bosom, and let it be of service to thee—it will be of none to me after to-morrow. Release thyself from the Jews, and beware how thou speakest of thy claim to Roderick."

"What! wouldst thou have me yield it utterly?"

"No. Yet speak not of it in what thou sayest to the king. Go to him—lest he think it suspicious that, having a claim, thou shouldst not place thyself in the way for its payment. Solicit from him some goodly office, the rewards of which shall come from the people and not from the royal treasury. To such office he will readily appoint thee; for a royal officer of the Goth is now little else than a collector for the royal treasury."

"But what office could I seek for? I know nothing of such toils. My youth, thou knowest, has been passed among warriors, and in strife with the wild Basques and the impetuous Franks. I am a soldier, and better know the weapon than the pen. In truth, my lord bishop, to confess a truth, what with imperfect eye-sight, and a heavy hand, I am fain to content myself with signing the blessed cross where my name should be written."

The archbishop did not smile at the tacit confession of that ignorance which was common among the nobles of the time, but, placing his hand upon that of Gerontius, he said:

"Dost thou think I would have thee a scrivener? No! Thou lovest command in war, my lord Gerontius. What sayest thou to the military command in thy province? Go to Roderick—solicit that command—but solicit it as an humble and true liege, who, if he has lent his sovereign the money which has made him such, is too wise to remember it."

Gerontius pledged himself to adopt the advice of Oppas, and lured on by the artful conversation of the archbishop, he indulged in a freedom of remark hostile to the king, which put him completely in the power of the former. But neither in word nor gesture did Oppas suffer him to perceive that he was conscious of his indiscretion. So far, the object for which the archbishop had toiled was gained, and he had no desire to alarm the fears of his companion. He had gained an ally, who, in the possession of power, he trusted to mould to his own desires. It may be well in this place to add that his schemes were all successful. Roderick was not unwilling to receive Gerontius with favoring regard, when he asked for nothing from the royal coffers. His application for office was heard with favor, and the military government of his province bestowed upon him, with the right to fleece the people at pleasure, risking nothing more than the forfeiture of his treasure and his post, whenever the royal necessities should be such as to persuade the king that his coffers were sufficiently full to supply them.

When Gerontius had retired, his place was supplied by the fanatic Romano, to whom Oppas reported such portions of the day's proceedings as he deemed it proper to unfold. He took especial care in the narrative not to forget the demand which Roderick had made upon the treasury of the church.

"The gold and silver devoted to pious uses," said he, with a sigh, "will he consume, my brother, in his sinful pleasures. The creatures of his lust will receive them; and that which has been consecrated to God, and to the benefit of his ministers, will be assigned by the lawless tyrant to the reward of all manner of sinfulness and shame."

The features of Romano glowed with a savage joy, as he replied:

"But they shall bring death among his pleasures, and they shall turn his sinful joy into the bitterness of despair. I see the hand and the handwriting, my father—the hour is nigh; and the hour that they drink from the vessels of gold and silver which belong to the Lord, in that hour shall the tyrant die."

The countenance of the archbishop was full of heedful reverence, as he gazed upon the enthusiastic speaker; but he said nothing.

"Ay, my father, I see it and I know it," continued the other. "This youth hath not been spared by the tyrant, but that Heaven hath willed him to the execution of its vengeance. He hath failed in his blow, but he shall not always fail. The spirit moves me to release him, and I am strong to do it. This night will I see Guisenard, who hath him in keeping, and as he hath a becoming reverence for holy things, I doubt not to move him to a knowledge of his sin, in binding him whom God would loose, and in keeping back the hand which God hath commanded to strike."

"Yet should he be stubborn, Romano—should he plead service to Roderick, forgetful of the duty which he owes to his Maker, as it is but too much the practice with the guilty worldling to plead—what then wilt thou do, my brother?"

"He will not plead thus, my father; Guisenard is humble, and followeth closely the commands of his father-in-God. Let one but show him the error of his way—let one but show him that in this deed he keepeth in bonds the special messenger of Heaven"——

"But," said the archbishop, interrupting, "if he should not so readily understand; for he cannot hope to be blessed with the direct revelation which has been made to thee"——

"I fear not that, my father," replied the sanguine zealot—"and even should he deny me, I fear not that God will work the way out of bondage for His servant, even as His angel wrought the deliverance of the holy Peter whom the bonds of impious Herod had fettered fast in his dungeons, and guarded by his soldiers."

"Alas! my brother; but these are not the days of miracle. God trusts now to the faith of his people—to their zeal in his cause, and when this fails, the victim perishes—and it is well then that the victim should perish, since the lukewarmness of the worshippers merits no such benefactor. We must toil for the prisoner, my brother, nor wait the coming of that blessed angel who set Peter free from the bonds of Herod; and in working out this holy design, my brother, the end will sanctify the necessary means, when all others shall fail thee. The purse I gave thee hath an argument for the worldling which shall persuade him when light from Heaven would fail to enlighten his mind; and though I trust that Guisenard will heed thy counsel, yet thou shouldst not forget to employ the lure of gold, should the pure silver of thy heavenly eloquence fail to reach his soul—which it were unreasonable to think, unless, like the master whom he serves, the Lord hath hardened his heart, as he hardened that of Pharaoh, for his destruction."

"I will use the gold," said the other.

"Ay, my brother; thou art chosen for thy work, and thou art bound to its performance. There must be no idle scruples—no tender misgivings, unworthy of thy strength, and ungracious in the sight of God, as they would seem to censure His justice or His judgment. If the Lord hath assigned to this prisoner the holy task of freeing his people from the bondage of the Egyptians, and if he hath assigned to thee the no less heavy task of setting the youth free to this service, thou must do it at every hazard."

"I will do it!" said the zealot, with uplifted hands, and eyes that streamed with a fluid fire and rayed out through his long eyelashes with a light like that of wild insanity.

"Thou wilt try, I well know, my brother—thou wilt try thy pleadings—thy eloquence shall seek to awaken and fill his mind, and move his heart to humanity; thou wilt then try the gold which I have given thee, and then"——

"What then? my father," said Romano, seemingly uncertain what to do in the event of a failure of those influences upon which he so much relied, and which were, as yet, the only influences which his mind had proposed to itself.

"Ay, what then, Romano; for the difficulty and the trial now begin. It were easy for any man to seek to move a jailer by prayers and by the offer of gold to set free the prisoner whom he hath in bonds. It is for the chosen servant of Heaven to do more than this; for he is chosen that he may succeed. What, then, if his prayers fail—if the stubborn jailer be insensible to the wisdom and the plea, and scorn the temptation of gold and silver—shall the apostle forbear his office? Of a truth, no! His task has then begun. What, oh my brother! should be thy performance, if the Lord commissioned thee to take from me the power which I hold among our people? Wouldst thou not strive to do it, by thy prayers, by thy pleadings, by the doom which thou wouldst rightly denounce upon me from Heaven? But if these were unheeded by me—if I scorned thy holy commission, and defied thy threats—if, like Pharaoh, or Holofernes,"——

"Ah, my father, wherefore dost thou ask? Dost thou think me blind to the duties which are before me? Believe me, I am ready. I see. I shall free this captive from his bonds, as the Lord hath appointed. I am chosen for the work, and I shrink not from it. Count it done, my father—count it done, ere three nights shall pass away. I go, even now, to Guisenard. I trust to move him as from his own heart; for I have long esteemed him good, as I know him to be guiltless of wilful wrong. I will plead with him strongly, even according to the best of my poor ability—and the gold will I give him, the better to help him in his flight to the Asturias. Should he not yield to me, and take counsel from Heaven's will—— But, I will not think it. He will hear, he will yield, my father—the Lord will move him; and should he not"——

The fanatic paused, covered his face with both hands, and remained silent for a few seconds in this position. Then, suddenly recovering from his musing, he earnestly grasped the hand of the archbishop, and with increasing wildness concluded thus:

"The Lord hath strengthened me. I see the path which is before me, and I glory in my tasks. Oh! my father, it is a blessed feeling when we can throw aside these frail and foolish attachments which bind us to earth—which bind us in love even of its vices, its weaknesses, its impiety. The laborer in the vineyard of God hath need to discard all these enslaving affections. We are never free until we can cast off those earthly ties which conflict with our duties, and keep us down from that heaven to which we aspire."

But little further conversation passed between them. When the fanatic had gone, the archbishop seemed exhausted. He threw himself along upon a cluster of cushions, and lay for some moments seemingly in deep thought, or stupor, with his face covered by his hands. The path was tangled and intricate before him, and he had need of reflection. Besides, the day's perils had almost enfeebled him. He had escaped them; but how many were gathering in the vista, now momently opening before his view! Should he escape them also? Should he triumph in the completion of his grasping aims—in the attainment of his objects of ambition? What, in truth, were those objects? Was he indeed struggling only for his nephews; or, with a more patriotic spirit still, for the rescue of his country from the iron domination of her oppressor? Neither! The purpose of his mind may best be understood by a reference to those dishonorable acts and reckless crimes which he meditated even now, and which he had already practiced and committed. The strong and deep passions of the man gave double energy to the goadings of ambition, and hopes and desires which he had never yet breathed to mortal were ever present to his thought, and ever foremost in all the promptings of his soul. His soliloquy now, as he rose from the cushions and paced hurriedly the lonely chamber in which he slept, may give us glimpses of that dark policy the fruits only of which we have been permitted to see before.

"A little while, a little while, Roderick, and if thy nature be not changed, and if the stars fight not against me, thy sway shall be humbled. Let thy lusts but prevail with Cava, and thou makest an enemy in Julian who shall hurl thee from the throne and from life. Let the fierce soldier but bring his army to this city, and the game is then mine own. He hath but the soldiers who keep with him at Ceuta—and these the conflict with Roderick shall greatly lessen. It is then for me to bring the discontents whom I have made, and the desperates whom I have bought, to bear upon the strife. My power will decide the scale; and as it is for me to decide, so will it be for me to sway. Then shall I triumph—not with thy kingdom only, thou sodden and blinded tyrant, but with possessions which thy vain heart hath too little known to prize. What hadst thou to do with so pure a spirit, so high, yet gentle a soul, as inhabits in the bosom of Egilona? What had she to do with thee? She could not, she cannot love thee. Alas! the shame that thy foul and common touch, thy free intercourse and debasing converse, should have taken from her perfection, as they have made it subservient to thee!"

The archbishop paused, and moving to the lattice, gazed forth long and anxiously, but in utter silence, upon the lights that still shone from the chambers of the royal palace. It was late in the night when he sought his couch, and then his slumbers were broken, and troubled with annoying dreams.

CHAPTER IV.

MEANWHILE, what of the unfortunate Egiza? He was hurried back to his strong prison in despair. He had seen enough to know that his uncle was himself in danger, and under suspicion; and as he knew not what course the judgment of Roderick had taken in reference to him, he with reason questioned his ability to effect his rescue, as Oppas had promised him in their brief interview. We shall not attempt to describe his feelings and his fears. The anxiety, the apprehension, the despair—not for himself, nor for his own life, but for her honor and her safety, who was far more than life to him. He threw himself upon the floor of his narrow cell, when the keeper had retired, and wept scalding tears. In this position the keeper found him, when he brought him his evening repast. The man seemed to regard with a feeling of compassion the desponding captive before him; and, indeed, a something of respect, almost amounting to reverence, marked his language and manner while addressing him—arising, probably, from the belief that his prisoner was a monk, as his garb denoted.

"Arise, father, arise and eat," said Guisenard; "you are feeble; your limbs lack the sustenance of food. Here is that which shall revive you."

"I need it not," replied Egiza, faintly; "take it away; I shall not want it. Let me sleep."

The reply, though not churlish, was abrupt, and uttered in a manner which was intended to discourage all further solicitation. The keeper did not urge the youth but placed the food on a little table beside him, and was about to withdraw in silence; but his heart seemed touched by the evident self-abandonment of his prisoner, and as he looked upon his face and watched the noble and delicate features which the strifes of manhood had not yet seamed with callous furrows, a stronger sentiment of commiseration penetrated his bosom.

"Father," said he, "your food is beside you; though you need it not now, perhaps hunger will come upon you before you sleep; and you will be better able to meet the trials which are before you, if your body take its needful support. The water-jug is in the niche where it is cool. Is there aught that I can serve you in ere I retire?"

The youth barely raised his head as he replied:

"Nothing—I thank you. I need nothing but sleep. I would sleep, since I may not strive; I would forget, where to remember is to madden. Leave me."

The keeper obeyed him, but much he wondered at the deep sorrow which the seeming monk expressed—so unseemly in one so young, and so inconsistent with the ferocious criminal who had aimed his bloody knife at the bosom of his sovereign. Guisenard was a worthy man, devout without rage, and executing his trust with punctilious exactitude, yet without severity. He left his prisoner with a mind troubled with the thought of that strange inconsistency with which he had been so struck, between the show of human feeling in the assassin and the deed of wanton malice which he had striven to commit. His own thoughts in no way helped him to reconcile the discrepancy, and he unfolded them to his young wife, as they sat down to their own evening repast, in the corner of the prison which had been assigned them as their dwelling. But Amreeta was as little skilled in the elucidation of such mysteries as he, and she diverted all thought of the captive from his mind, by placing their young boy—the sole and lovely pledge of their union—upon his knee. He danced the urchin in air, kissed his rosy and full cheeks, and forgot, in that happy moment, all thoughts and things but such as belonged to the devoted father While thus he toyed, a signal at the portal demanded his attention. He put down the boy, and admitted Romano. He stooped for the blessing of the father, and then led him to the table from which he had just risen. Fresh viands were placed before the zealot, but he declined to eat.

"Give me but bread, bread and water," he said; "this dainty food is ungracious, and of hurt to him who labors for eternal love. My daughter, thou art blessed; and the boy"——

"Is also blessed, my father, for see the health upon his cheeks—how they glow, and how his eyes kindle; and he never cries, my father—he is the meekest, most patient child"——

"Stay, Amreeta—thou art too proud of thy firstborn," said Guisenard, while a fond and approving smile played upon his lips. "Stay thy idle self-flattery, for thy praise of the boy is but praise of thyself. Is thy child healthier, or lovelier, or better than that of any mother?—will not all speak like thee?"

"Ay, but scarcely with so much truth," said the confident mother.

"Thou speakest truly, dame," said Romano, gently; "many mothers may make a boast, like thee, but few with so much truth. Thou art blessed in thy firstborn, who is lovely beyond compare, and possessed of no less strength and health than loveliness; but let us pray thee to make thy boast with humility—for the vain of heart and the strong in confidence but provoke the wrath of Heaven, which comes like the tempest suddenly at midnight. The bloom upon those cheeks which is now a glory in thine eyes, may be pale like death ere the morning."

The fond mother involuntarily drew the child away from the hands of the priest, as if the certainty of evil lay in the bare possibility which he had suggested. Romano smiled, but proceeded:

"Be hopeful, but not proud of thy child, my daughter—for the hope which looks to the favor of Heaven for its fruition, is a direct admission of its power, and such admission must ever secure its grace. Thy son is the gift of God: let thy charge of him be such that in years to come he may be worthy of God's giving. Train not thy child as if he were thy toy, thy plaything, but as if he were an immortal soul, worthy of the favor of a God, yet not secure from the dreadful slavery of the devil. My son,"—turning to Guisenard—"I would speak to thee alone."

The keeper gave a nod to Amreeta, who, taking her child in her arms, was about to leave the apartment, but, with a sudden impulse, she knelt before the priest, and lifting the infant towards him, she implored his blessing. His hand rested a moment upon her head in benediction, his lips moved, but the prayer which he spoke was inaudible to mortal ears. He felt the beauty of the scene.

When Amreeta had retired, Romano abruptly addressed Guisenard in the following manner:

"Of what secret crime hast thou been guilty, oh my son! unknown to and unabsolved by me, for which the Lord has singled thee out for such a heavy weight of punishment?"

"How!—what mean you, my father?" replied the pious keeper, in unqualified alarm.

"Thou hast confessed to me thy frequent sins and errors," continued the priest, "and thy penance has been slight and easily borne. Thy confessions were only of light offences, and such as were readily removed by due atonement and the endurance of thy penance with a right spirit of humility and an uncomplaining temper What heinous crime is it thou hast withheld from my ears? Why is it that our Heavenly Father hath chosen thee for this terrible judgment?"

The consternation of Guisenard underwent due increase as he heard these words, particularly as the air and manner of the priest was grave and solemn, and adapted fitly to the singular language which he employed. He dreaded that some terrible calamity indeed impended over his head, and looked every moment to behold the cloud part and see himself sink beneath the rushing bolt. Ere he could demand an explanation, the priest proceeded:

"Thou hast in thy custody a prisoner, newly brought to thee by Edeco?"

"I have, my father," was the reply.

"Wherefore was he not despatched to the other prisons, by the city barriers?—why was he sent here to thee, my son?"

"Nay, I know not, my father, unless it be that as this prison is in the heart of Toledo, it is deemed more secure than all the rest. Thou knowest that the prisoner is doomed to death—that he hath sought to do murder, even upon the person of the sovereign."

"Thou speakest idle things, my son, and I fear that thou hast grievously sinned, as a just God has willed that thou shouldst be chosen to be the keeper of this prisoner whom thou holdest in bonds, and of whom thou speakest most ignorantly This prison is more secure than all the rest, thou sayest—as if any one were secure when the will of God ordains that the chain shall be broken, that the wall shall part and the captive be free to walk forth, even as did holy Saint Peter over the prostrate bodies of his guards. This prisoner is doomed, thou sayest—as if man could doom and execute when the succor of God is nigh, like a spear that never bends and a shield that never breaks, to resist the doom, and to destroy the evil judge. And shalt thou call this holy man a murderer, whom God hath commissioned to destroy? It were truly an impious speech, my son, and thy penance should be great for its utterance."

"I know not, my father," said Guisenard, after a brief pause; "I know nothing of the matter of which thou speakest. I am in charge as the keeper of this prison, under king Roderick, and it is my duty to keep well and securely the captive whom he sends here in trust. It is not for me to question the decrees of my sovereign, or to say which I shall heed and which I shall reject. My head were scarce certain upon my shoulders were I to determine thus."

"Oh, blind and self-sufficient as thou art!" exclaimed the priest; "thou who darest not set thy judgment against the will of an earthly prince, yet art not too fearful to defy that of the Prince of Heaven! I tell thee, my son, that it is God's messenger that thou keepest in bondage—it is the executioner of His wrath that thou keepest from the performance of his proper duties."

"Truly, my father, I should be grievously sad to think that I should do anything which should be displeasing in the eye of Heaven; and if it were a thing apparent to my mind that the execution of my earthly trusts, as I have been taught to perform them duly, were unseemly in the eyes of God, I would fly from the commission of such an evil as I would fly from the sword and the pestilence. But I cannot think it evil to obey the king who rules in the nation—nor can I think it evil to detain under the command of the proper laws, the person of one who hath striven to murder, in defiance equally of the commandments of Heaven and the laws of earth. Much do I pity the unhappy man who is sent to me for keeping. He is but young to suffer death."

"And thinkest thou, vain man, and self-deceiving as thou art, thinkest thou that he will suffer—that the Almighty Father will leave his servant to perish? Thinkest thou that He will not break his bonds, and open a way for him through the walls of his dungeon, scorning your bolts, and heeding none of your common ways of outlet? He will—look to it—He will; and, if it be that thou shalt not heed the counsel which I give thee—if, in thy obstinacy and pride of place, thou wilt not undo thy bolts and bid the man of God depart in peace, then shall the doom fall on thy head also; for what saith the Lord?—'the chains of the captive shall fall from his limbs, he shall walk erect in the open places, and his guards shall be slain by a sword that is secret.' "

"I hear thee in sorrow, my father. What thou sayest to me is beyond my comprehension and knowledge. I know not that this man is the man of God—I cannot think it; else would he come not with the commission to slay."

"As if God slew not his thousands when it needed—as if he smote not in the high places, in the strength of the palace, in the thick of the host, by hands seen and hands unseen, by day and by night," exclaimed Romano, with impetuous and loud accents.

"I know it, my father; and such I hold to be often the design and the deed of the Lord. But how are we to know the executioner who is sent, from him who, with a bad heart, hath deputed himself for murder? If it be that what thou sayest is to be the rule of common judgment, then would no murderer suffer harm, and then no good man could walk in peace and security. If it be that this man is of God, and from God, then will God work out his deliverance without aid from me"——

"He will! He will! vain officer, He will!" replied Romano, interrupting the speaker. "Fear not that the Lord will not work out his deliverance, and without heeding either thy help or mine. He hath divine agents which are ready to perform when human agents fear to do, or fail Him. But, out of my love for thee, Guisenard, would I have moved thee to this service, because I would not see thee come to harm. Thou shouldst free this holy man, and thou shouldst follow him. Alas! my son, thy thought, I fear me, is too much upon the lowly cares and devouring wants of this earth."

"Of a truth, father, I love the earth, and I love this life, for there are many things in it to command my love; but I love it not to sin for it; and greatly, to my poor mind, should I sin, if, heedless of the trust which is given to me by my superiors, I set this man free, again to murder."

"Thy superiors! Thy superior is God; Him shouldst thou obey. But let me to see thy captive, Guisenard; let me mingle my prayers with those of the holy man in bondage. Would that his bonds were mine, so that I wore the favor which he wears, and which is the free gift of the Father."

Guisenard freely complied with the request of the priest, with whose enthusiasm he seemed to be familiar. He led the way to the cell, and left Romano with the prisoner

---

CHAPTER V.

Sleep, in the dungeon of Egiza, had kindly come to the relief of its inmate Care, fatigue, pain, had produced their united and natural effect upon him, and, in spite of thought, he slept. But he slept not soundly. The jarring and sliding of the bolts aroused him; and, in the dim light, uncertain of the character of his visiter, and thinking only of enemies, he at once apprehended that the executioner sent by Roderick was at hand. He started to his feet, resolved to provoke, by a violent resistance, a more summary death than that of the axe; but, in the next moment, he felt how idle was the resolve, since he was weaponless. The anguish of that conviction who shall describe? The consciousness that he lay, like one bound hand

and foot, having neither the power to fight nor to fly, at the mercy of his enemy, was humbling and maddening at the same moment. To strive to the last, opposing blow to blow and skill to skill, would, to the desperate mind, be a rapture of itself, and would effectually soften, if it did not disarm, death of all its terrors. But to die without stroke or struggle—to await the blow, effortless, yet anxious—the mind toiling, yet with a body unperforming, though writhing—is to die of a shame, and an agony, having stings far beyond those of death. These stings were in the mind of Egiza, as he felt the helplessness of his situation. But his confidence was not entirely subdued.

"I have limbs, I have strength, I am still a man!" he exclaimed aloud; "and I am unbound!"

With these words, he rushed toward the entrance, where the outline of the intruding person was dimly perceptible. The words of Romano reached the ear of the captive, ere he approached him, and before he could strike the idle but premeditated blow.

"Ay, brother; and thou shalt have freedom!" exclaimed the monk.

The progress of the prisoner was arrested; his clenched fingers relaxed, his hands fell at his sides.

"Who art thou?" he demanded, abruptly. "I thought that thou wert my executioner."

"No, my brother; I am the poor monk who provided thee with thy garments; and I come from the Lord, to strengthen thee with hope, so that thy triumph over thy enemies may be complete."

As Egiza heard these words, his thought was of the promise of the archbishop Oppas.

"He hath not, then, deserted me!" he exclaimed.

"Deserted thee, holy brother! the thought was sinful. Never yet did He desert those who put their trust in His word. He sends me now upon the work of thy deliverance from the Amalekite; and though the path is dim before me, and scales upon my vision still intercept the light that is to guide us forth, yet do I nothing fear that the gates shall be opened wide, and thy deliverance be as sudden as it is certain. It may be that, for the more effectual revelation of His power, He may delay thy release until the latest moment—ay, until the very moment which the Belshazzar of this land hath decreed for thy destruction. He will set at defiance the decree; He will defeat the bloody and unrighteous judge; He will give thee vengeance upon thy enemies."

In the feverish state of Egiza's mind, such language did not seem exaggerated. He regarded the monk truly as a fanatic, and as one in the employ of the archbishop; but he did not for a moment conjecture the sacred light in which he himself appeared to his companion. Had he done so, he might have felt and spoken in tones of much greater hesitation and humility, nor shown that composed and sternly elevated mood which came rather from a despair of all help than a confidence in any heavenly interposition. The monk, on the other hand, ascribed to this latter cause, the firm tones, the fearless defiance, the reckless hardihood of the captive's demeanor. He beheld in his, one who had the very words of the Deity for his assurance, and who, however he may have doubted his own security for an instant, was too much filled with sanctity and preternatural strength, to remain doubtful for any longer period. His deportment toward the youth was that of one who stood in the presence of a superior intelligence. He regarded Egiza as upon that higher eminence of divine favor to which his own eyes were turned in hope and holy expectation. So adroitly had the suggestions of the archbishop been insinuated, which appealed to the monomaniacal tendencies of the fanatic, that he had ceased, after the first moment of their utterance, to regard the speaker except as a humble agent for transmitting them from the divine source of all intelligence to himself. Holding Egiza as one to whom he was a chosen auxiliar, the escape of the former and the successful prosecution of his divine mission were, of consequence, paramount aims with himself, through which alone his ambitious desires could be realized. The rescue of the youth was, therefore, his greatest object. For this he was not merely ready to suggest plans, and to undergo toils, but to destroy all who stood in his path, and to pour out his own blood with as little scruple. The madness which reconciled an otherwise correct mind, and a heart rather gentle than otherwise, to such extremes, was at the same time potent enough to color objects and arguments with the same false and morbid complexion. Then it was that the merely human fears and feelings which Egiza uttered before him, were all tinctured with a most heavenly coloring. The vehemence of the youth was zeal for his Master; his despondency a noble humanity, which had been the true cause of the Deity's selection of him; and the fear of death, which had moved him to the first show which the captive had made of violence toward him when entering his dungeon, only sprung from a desire to perform his work ere he departed for his reward.

"Thou hast well rebuked my impatience, holy father," replied Egiza, referring to the supposed eulogy which the monk had passed upon the lord Oppas; "thou hast only done him justice. He hath been a true friend to me ever, when other friends failed me; and I look not to find him forget his promise."

"He spoke to thee, then, my brother. He promised thee; with His own lips He spoke to and promised thee!" exclaimed, rather than demanded, the excited enthusiast.

"Ay, this very day, with his own lips, he promised to send one to me on whom I might rely."

"And I am he! Oh, Blessed among the blessed! the Glory where all is glorious! Supreme Father! Divine Principle, which is every where, carrying life and light, doing wonders without ceasing! wherefore is it that the poor worm is so honored with Thy grace? what am I, that Thou shouldst lift me to Thy holy work? what are my poor prayers, that Thou shouldst heed them—or my vain wishes, that Thou shouldst hearken to them? Lord! give me strength and grace, that I prove not unmindful of Thy service. Strengthen me, oh Redeemer! that I fall not back—that I yield not to the Tempter, whether on the right side or on the left, but pursuing the steady light of Thy holy will—which burneth for ever before my eyes, in the sunshine and in the storm—that I toil on without ceasing, nor weary in the well-doing which I have begun! Oh my brother!" he exclaimed, now addressing the wondering Egiza; "Oh, my brother! favored and blessed among men! I joy with a full heart that I have been chosen to minister to thy release. Thou shalt go forth from these feeble walls; they shall not restrain thee. I see thy deliverance with my soul, even as I shall see it with mine eyes; for though the keeper hath once denied me to let thee go free, yet do I not despair that he will relent, that he will yield to my prayers, that he will give heed to my warnings, and let thee forth in safety, ere the doom fall upon him also, even as it shall fall upon the hardened heart of the Pharaoh who enslaveth this nation."

"He hath denied thee? Thou hast sought him, my father?" said the prisoner, to whom the latter part only of the zealot's ravings had been comprehensible.

"He hath, my brother," was the reply; "but Guisenard is a worthy man, who meaneth well, and whom I have long tutored. He hath a love and reverence for me which shall, I trust, move him to my wishes. I have other arguments in store for him which must prove triumphant over his rebellious heart, though he fear not the displeasure of Heaven. He will"——

"Hast thou gold?" demanded Egiza, interrupting him. "The man who would scorn all your arguments and mine, would yield to the reason which is in gold, my father. Has not the lord Oppas given thee gold for this purpose?"

"Of a truth, he has; bnt I had forgotten!" The zealot took a heavy purse from his garment, as he replied; "but how couldst thou know that, my brother, unless Heaven had opened thine eyes to a divine perfection of sight?"

"'T is but reason, my father, that the lord Oppas should avail himself of an influence having a power upon most men, in these corrupt and dishonest times," replied Egiza.

"'T is a divine instinct, my brother, which makes thee to know it. It must be that Heaven intends that this gold—as it were to mortify the poor vanity of my mind which made me to think that my frail arguments could move thy close and stubborn keeper—is the power which, under God's permission, shall alone set thee free. Let me go, my brother, that I may make trial of it upon Guisenard," replied Romano.

"It will do more than all thy arguments, holy father," said the melancholy captive, whose words were nevertheless held to be oracular. "I doubt not that it will be received as reason, when thy promise of Heaven, and thy threats of its wrath, would only be heard with laughter or defiance."

"It must be so, my brother," replied the monk; "and yet Guisenard hath ever been a dutiful believer, and a man humble in carriage as in desire. I will speed to him at once, and make the trial of this yellow temptation; for, as God wills that it should be tried, it is holy; and the Power that created may well use, for His own glory, the thing of His creation."

He was about to depart, when Egiza arrested him:

"Ere thou goest, my father, hast thou not with thee some weapon—some instrument which shall guard life or give death. If thou hast, give it me: if thou hast not, bid the lord Oppas provide thee with one, which thou shalt bring me."

"He hath already done so, my brother; but I had forgotten. But thou knowest, thou seest all things. I go to plead with Guisenard."

He gave a dagger to Egiza, and with a few words of respectful benediction, as if receiving the blessing which he bestowed, he turned away and would have left him; but when he sought egress from the apartment, he found that the door had been cautiously fastened upon him also, by the watchful Guisenard.

In the first moment of this discovery, distrusting all men, and inferring danger from all circumstances, the gloomy Egiza apprehended that the agency of the monk, as an emissary of the archbishop, had been discovered, and that the plan for his escape was thus defeated for ever."

"They have listened—they have heard us, my father; they keep watch over us both."

"Fear nothing, my brother," replied the sanguine Romano, whom no misfortune seemed to discourage; "the Lord is our strength and our redeemer; He will not deliver us to our foes. Of a certainty, he will shield thee and give thee release, my brother; though I—poor and feeble worm that I am, whom He hath only too much honored already—should be left behind to perish. But I will call to the keeper, who will give us speech, and show wherefore he hath thus closed the bar upon us. Guisenard!"

The priest called aloud, while, with the handle of his dagger, Egiza beat upon the door within.

"At least!" exclaimed the latter, exultingly, while waving the glittering instrument in the dim chamber in which it was yet distinctly visible; "at least, I have a sharp weapon which will help me in the struggle. I shall not perish like a chained beast, whom the sportsman may strike at pleasure, and without fear. If I must perish, I will perish like a strong man, and some among my enemies shall perish likewise."

But there was no cause of present apprehension. The jailer came to the relief of Romano, whom he quickly permitted to come forth, apologizing gently for the detention which he said had been unavoidable, as he had been summoned to other duties in a distant part of the prison. How strong was the disposition, at that moment, on the part of Egiza, to rush forth also, and to rely upon the strong arm for his release! But prudence got the better of the ill-advised suggestion. He knew that there were other and bolted doors through which he must pass; and when he gazed upon the keeper, and measured his vigorous frame with his eye, he felt that nothing but entire imbecility of soul on the part of the latter could possibly enable him to succeed. He resolved patiently to wait events, relying on his uncle, and the zealous Romano, whom he saw depart with anxiety and regret.

Romano retired with Guisenard to the apartments of the latter; but brief time for conference was allowed them. A heavy summons at the main portal of the prison, announced the arrival of others destined for its occupation; and he signified to the monk the necessity for his leaving.

"It is already beyond the hour, my father; and if the espatorio should hear of this irregularity, it would go hard with me—it might be the means of losing me my office."

"Beware!" exclaimed Romano, anxiously, when he found all his persuasion of no avail in obtaining permission to continue the conference longer; "beware that the love of thine office does not make thee forget thy love to God, and thy proper performance before him. To be the officer of Roderick should not be a desire so great with thee as to be the servant of Jesus; and in fulfilling thy trust to the one, and that one the wrong-doer, I warn thee that thou mayst do grievous offence to the other—and He thy Saviour or thy Destroyer, as thou thyself only shall by thy acts determine."

The keeper heard him respectfully, but insisted on the performance of his duties to his earthly sovereign.

"Another time, my father," said he, impatiently; "I will hear thee. To-morrow and to-morrow night; any time before the hour set for extinguishing the lights and closing the gate."

Romano prepared to depart, as Guisenard hurried him. The necessity for doing so seemed to become more and more evident every moment, as the thundering at the outer entrance grew more and more violent. But the zealot was not content to acknowledge this necessity, and murmured to the last. He was a little pacified, however, as, ere he went, the keeper begged for his blessing.

"I give it thee, my son, with the hope that this night the spirit of the Lord shall come upon thee, and that thou mayst have a better knowledge of what thou hast to perform; for, in truth, the peril is at hand, and as thou standest as one in a dangerous place, to whom a step to the right or the left may prove fatal, I pray that thou mayst have a blessed counsel from Heaven, teaching thee to hearken to those who know the path of safety, and are ready to guide thee in it. I bless thee, my son, and I pray that thou mayst be blessed with the divine counsels which we all need, and thou more greatly than any, in the work which is before thee."

"Amen! my father," replied Guisenard, with reverence, as they parted.

Stimulated by the religious fury which filled his bosom, Romano had no desire for sleep; and, though the hour was late, yet trusting to find Oppas still up, or most probably not giving the doubt a thought, he proceeded to the archbishop's palace. He had been waited for. The latter was too deeply interested in the subject of the monk's mission to resign himself to sleep while the labors of the priest were yet unconsummated; and his anxiety to hear, though suppressed by the stronger policy which governed him, was scarcely less active than was that of Romano for speech. It will not need that we should dwell upon their conference. It is sufficient to say that the archbishop, still aiming at an entire control over the mind of the zealot, furnished new arguments and repeated old ones in a novel form, calculated to inflame his fanaticism, and prevent its rage from subsiding. The religion of the zealot is most commonly the vanity of a strong but unequal intellect, of a mind in which the faculties are not equally balanced—some few, and those, perhaps, the most selfish (such as the imaginative) being too greatly in the ascendant to forbear tyrannizing over the rest; and whether the man in whom this occurs be of the religion of Jove or Brahma, of Manco Capac or Mahomet, the mere principles of his professed faith will have but little influence in modifying the madness under which he moves. Any religion would serve equally well, in the hands of a cunning prompter, to impel such a person to the foulest crime, who, in its commission, would never for a moment question in their own minds, or suffer others to question, the great service they were rendering to God.

The archbishop was a prompter cunning after this fashion. Cunning, not wisdom, was the art which he employed. The distinction between these two powers is not sufficiently dwelt upon. The former pursues an object, whether it be good or evil, without scrupling to employ in its pursuit every agent that may serve it, whether right or wrong. Wisdom has but one single aim, and that is right; and she employs but one set of agents, and those are all right. We should have reason always to suspect the propriety of employing any other, since, when was it ever known that the powers of evil came freely to work for the principle of good? Truth is always single; and if we kept this fact continually in mind, truth would be a common virtue of the household, which is now a mystery.

But power and perverse passions were the objects for which the archbishop toiled, not virtue; and the practice of fraud and subtlety, from having been employed by him for the attainment of these objects, became objects of themselves in time, and he derived pleasure from their practice. The pursuit of mischief called for his ingenuity, and the love of the curious and the ingenious is a natural love of man. Had Oppas not aimed at power—had he not craved the satisfaction of passions which, in his instance, were denied—he would still have practiced the cunning with which he controlled and prompted Romano, for a pleasure of its own. But in their use, the creature which they moved was suffered to behold none of the secret springs. The art concealed itself, and the heedless fanatic assumed to himself, as innate discoveries, the various plans and purposes, every one of which the other had insinuated. Not a word spoken by Oppas was without its signification; and when, that night, Romano left him, he went forth, ready, as the minister of Heaven's wrath, to commit any crime that might tend to bring about the purpose which he had constantly in view

That night and the ensuing day was a weary and a painful time to the prisoner. The keeper, Guisenard, came more than once to speak with him. The manner of this man was kind, and in his language he strove to be consoling. He evidently pitied Egiza on account of his youth, and much he wondered that one wearing the holy garments of the priesthood should have been prompted to the attempt at crime which had been charged against him. He was led to think, from the interest which Romano had taken in him, that there must be some mistake in the matter; and this led him to yield sundry little indulgencies to Egiza, which were not often bestowed upon convicts. Water was furnished him for his ablutions, a mirror, and a light; and when he came to the cell and sat down with the prisoner, Egiza thought he could see in his features the evidence of that natural spirit of benevolence which had shown itself in conduct very different from that usually of persons in his occupation. Guisenard even brought his son into the cell with him, and in the display which he made of a father's tenderness, his features grew still more softened to the eye of the prisoner.

"Thou hast friends?" asked the jailer.

"I know not!" was the gloomy reply.

"Thy father lives—or thy mother?"

"No! thank Heaven!"

"What! dost thou rejoice," exclaimed the other, half revoltingly, "that they are no more?"

"No! I rejoice that they live not to share with me the terrors of this place—of their son's shame, and the cruel doom before him."

"And why didst thou provoke that doom, my father? Why—if thou hadst a terror of this death which is before thee, and of the shame that comes with it—why didst thou risk the foul crime for which thou art to suffer?"

"Foul! dost thou call it?" said Egiza, sternly.

"Ay, foul! What other name, my father, for the deed of the assassin? I had thought that in the solitude of thy dungeon, and the impartial current of thy serious thoughts, thou too wouldst esteem that to be foul which nothing but the greatest provocation could excuse, and which I hold in thee to be the fruit of a sudden impulse."

"And so it was! But the impulse was that of justice, sir keeper! and my sorrow is that my blow was defeated that would have hurled the base tyrant from life, and to his deserved hell, in the same instant; for I would have stricken him while in the full fury of his sin!"

"It is a bad thought, and it were a very cruel deed, my father; and it were God's providence that thou didst not strike surely!" said the keeper.

"It was a most unhappy fortune for this accursed land that I failed in the blow, and that the slaves of the tyrant set upon me. Hear me, sir keeper; thou art wedded, thou hast a child—I see in the dim light of this dungeon that it is lovely. Is the child of our sex? or of that weaker and fairer, more dependent and suffering, and therefore dearer sex, which lies at the mercy of man, and, failing in his protection, is lost! lost! dreadfully and deplorably lost for ever! Is thy child a girl?"

"No, my father!" replied the keeper, startled by the vehemence of the speaker, and clasping the little one closer in his arm as he spoke; "he is a boy."

"Thou hast reason thank Heaven, and bless his mother, that gave thee not a woman child! Else, like me, thou mightst have stood to see her a victim, or struggled vainly to protect her from the brutal lusts of the tyrant, and perchance of his slaves. Leave me, sir keeper! leave me! Look not upon me, I pray thee! I am cursed!"

The tide of thought was overpowering, and for a moment reason seemed to be swept away by its impetuous torrent from the brain of Egiza. He threw himself upon his face on the stony floor, and shivered and writhed as if wrung by convulsions. The child screamed, terrified by the vehement action of the prisoner. The keeper, to quiet him, withdrew in silence; but he felt more commiseration for the speaker, and more horror at his approaching doom, than he had conceived it possible for him to have felt for any criminal, before this revelation reached his ears

CHAPTER VI.

THAT night, the food given to Egiza was from the table of Guisenard, and far superior in quality to that provided for the prisoners. But he touched it not, though the keeper in person entreated him to eat. He neither looked upon the food nor the keeper, but with a moody spirit he turned his face upon the wall, and answered in monosyllables only to the salutations of Guisenard. From this mood, the good-natured keeper strove, but vainly, to turn the current of his thoughts. He spoke of many things, of passing events which he thought might interest him; and at length he referred to the subject of his assault upon the king: but on this, Egiza sternly silenced him.

"Enough!" said he, "Enough that I failed in the blow; that I could not save. I would pray now to forget."

When Guisenard was about to leave him, the better feelings of the prince predominated, and he came forward, and with gentle accents prayed the keeper's forgiveness for any harshness of speech which he might have employed:

"But, in truth," he said, "I am too wretched to respect any, even those who love me. I know not what I say."

He requested Guisenard to lead the monk Romano to his cell, whenever he should come, and the jailer then retired, more than ever impressed with sympathy for his suffering prisoner.

When Romano came, he proceeded as usual to the private part of the prison, in which the keeper dwelt, and partook of his evening meal, along with the family, as if he were one of them. Guisenard had much to say of his prisoner, in whom he had become interested; and Romano was not slow to encourage the favorable impressions which the mind of the latter had received. But vainly did the enthusiast strive to fill the more human understanding of the keeper with his own elevated fancies. He could not be persuaded that Egiza had striven to slay the king as the special agent of the Deity. He had seen enough in his interview with the prisoner, the particulars of which we have briefly recorded, to know that passions and feelings of earth prompted the blow of the avenger, even as they had prompted the criminal excesses of the king which had provoked it. The efforts of Romano, therefore, to inspire a reverential regard for the convict in the bosom of Guisenard, failed entirely; and he smiled only at the bigotry of the monk, in which he could not participate, to the great annoyance and the unsuppressed displeasure of the latter.

"Thou art blind, my son—be not wilful," said he, in tones of mingled entreaty and rebuke. "It is for the ignorant to be humble. They should hearken to the words and obey the directions of those who are blessed with a better vision. Thou seest nothing in this holy man, but a goodly youth who hath been wronged in his earthly possessions, and has sought, with the base frenzy of a feeble spirit, to revenge himself after the fashion of earth upon the wrong-doer. Alas! that the noble self-sacrifice of the martyr should go unheeded thus among men! How many are the holy spirits, suffering for God and for the truth, whom the blindness of men hath thus deprived of the glory which is of right their due! But they can not do injustice always; and eternity heals the wrong as it overturns the vain and capricious powers of time. It is fortunate that tyrants can only kill: they can not hurt They rend the body with their powers of torture, but the soul—the soul, my son—that smiles at the sacrifice, and rejoices at the place of human punishment, as at a sure token of eternal reward. Their revenge is the revenge of virtue; and that consists in the great final triumph of the truth. If they rejoice to behold the tyrant writhing in the unquenchable flame, which his own hellish heart hath kindled, it is not because they would witness his suffering—except that in his suffering the truth proves itself triumphant and makes itself secure. This holy man had no purpose in his effort to destroy Roderick, except to rescue the church, and to vindicate the superiority of God. He strove not, as thou idly thinkest, to revenge a personal wrong, and to appease a merely human feeling. He hath been commissioned for higher objects, and by a higher power; and the justification which thou wouldst make for him, in the deed which he aimed at, is only truly human, as it derived its perfect sanction from the countenance and direction of God. There is no justification for crime, unless such justification come from the express will of Heaven; and man may shed no blood, and take no life, unless it be for the salvation of Holy Church, and for the protection of that sacred principle of truth, which is beyond all value, which the recklessness of the tyrant who should be cut off, would otherwise endanger. Look, then, upon this holy messenger in his proper light, Guisenard, ere thou suffer from the anger of the Lord, with him against whom the decree hath gone forth. I see it written in letters of fire upon the wall—'Roderick is devoted!' I hear it spoken in tones of thunder! Now, even now, I hear it! Hark!" And he paused, with uplifted finger, and looked up, as if listening to some passing sounds. "Dost thou not hear?" he continued.

"No, my father, I hear nothing," replied Guisenard.

"Alas, my son! thou art deaf as well as blind. I tremble for thee, Guisenard, unless the Lord suddenly and of his free grace touch thy senses with a keen perception. Thou seest not the writing which flames before me. Thou hearest not the deep voice which rolls along these thick walls, and says, plainly to my ears—'The wrath of the Lord is on its way, winged with red lightning and confounding thunder. Roderick, thy kingdom is taken from thee! The Mede is at thy gate—the Persian is on thy throne!' I hear these words, and I tremble. Thou hearest not, Guisenard—and Roderick heareth not; but though ye hear not, ye shall both tremble. I would not have you perish, Guisenard, with this evil-minded and devoted king, for whom the two-edged sword of doom is even now whetted. Provoke not the wrath of the Destroyer, but yield thyself to His will, and let His people go. Say to the prisoner, whom thou hast in bonds—which God will burst in his own good time to thy confusion, if thou heed not the words which I say to thee—say to him, 'Depart in peace, and the blessings of God go with thee.' Say to him thus, this night, this hour, my son, if thou wouldst have the blessings of eternal favor upon thy head."

"If I would have Roderick take my head, thou surely meanest, holy father. I were but a rash man to risk such danger for any person, however holy and praiseworthy his life, who was not of kin or connexion with me; and still more to risk the lives of my wife and little one: for, of a surety, the king would devote us all to that fate from which thou wouldst have me release the prisoner."

"He would not—he dare not!" exclaimed the monk, vehemently. "Terribly would the wrath of God avenge thee, my son, upon the head of thy impious murderer!"

"Perhaps, father, perhaps; but I love not vengeance, and thy own teaching makes it unholy. I would rather not provoke the wrath of Roderick, to my own undoing, since the vengeance of the Lord upon him, for the murder of myself and mine, would be of little account to me, after my own blood were shed," replied the jailer, with a more worldly, and perhaps more natural sort of calculation than comported with the superhuman imagination of Romano.

The indignation of the fanatic seemed almost unbounded, as he exclaimed:

"Oh, thou of little faith!—thoub lind, yet unbelieving; who canst not see of thyself, yet will not trust to the guidance of the Lord! Dost thou think that He would suffer thee to perish, if thou servest Him? When hath He ever failed those who put their trust in Him? Thou canst not show me! Yield to His desires and thou art safe; but put thy trust in princes of the earth, and I tell thee, Guisenard, thou shalt perish! Save this holy man, and, if thou heedst my words, the vengeance of Roderick can not touch thee. Thou shalt fly with him thou savest!"

"What! to be hunted by the soldiers of the king through all places, wild and strange, and among all sorts of men, more savage than the hills they live among! No, no, my father!—such were a folly in any man; and a greater folly in him who hath a young wife and an infant child to provide for. It behoveth such, as thou hast often tutored me, to be contented in their places, to be patient of their trials, and bear up meekly under the toils which are put upon them."

"Alas! my son, that thou shouldst take the sacred councils of the church for their perversion. True, I have taught thee these things; but I have nowhere taught thee to minister to tyranny, to yield to the exactions of vice, to make thyself the bondman of sin and injustice. If thou servest this tyrant in his tyranny, thou art also the tyrant—for a tyrant is a thing made up of yielding instruments and directing vices. If the tools were not there for the artisan, vainly would his hands strive in the erection of the palace or the prison. If the slaves were not ductile to the desires of the master, vainly would he strive to slaughter in his hate, and debase and dishonor in his lust. If there were no ready men like thee to keep the keys of the dungeon, the good man would not often be torn from the blessed sunshine of Heaven, and the sweeter sunshine of life and freedom. Roderick has no strength save from thee and such as thee. Thou makest his strength, my son, but thou canst not sustain it. Thou tellest me that his soldiers will hunt thee, among the savage hills and in the secret places; and I tell thee—for the spirit of prophecy is come upon me, even as it came upon Saul, so that men wondered—I tell thee that the hour is at hand when Roderick shall have no soldiers to pursue either thee, or thine, or others. But a little while—but a few more hours of mortal time—a few more blessed and lifting thoughts, and this worm, whose very power is come from corruption, and who rules like death in the rottenness of humanity, shall perish, and be cast out from among men, and they who bow down to him now, in fear if not in honor, shall turn away from his loathsome carcase in a worse fear, and with a bitter sorrow for their past servitude. It is against this shame that I would warn thee—it is from this doom that I would save thee, Let the holy man go free; and do thou and thine fly with him to the hills, in fear of the wrath which is to come. Fear not, I tell thee, the wrath and the soldiers of Roderick. Ere long his wrath shall turn into trembling, and his soldiers shall perish in battle or fly to the mountains, as I now counsel thee to fly Let me not pray to thee or counsel thee in vain."

"And even were I to escape his wrath, and the soldiers who would pursue us," replied Guisenard, who seemed to take no note of Romano's prophecy, "what then should keep us from starvation? I know those hills and secret places, and if they do yield a shelter, it is like that of the house of famine, which all men are glad to shun. I should be forced to descend the hills to the cities for food, lest my wife and young one famish; and that were delivering myself at once to the sword from which I had fled so vainly."

"Mark how the providence of God pursues thee, my son," answered the zealot, drawing from his cassock the full purse of gold which the archbishop Oppas had given him; "Behold, this is the lucre which thou art loth to resign. It is in such as this that Roderick rewards thee, as the minister of his tyranny and crime. The Lord is heedful of thy safety; and that thou mayst lack no reason to follow the safe course upon which I would set thee, that gold—the slave of God, not less than of man—the gift of the church, I bring to thee, so that in flight thou mayst not suffer from want, neither thou nor thy child. Take it; it is thine, my son. Go, set thy prisoner free."

The single-minded keeper paused for an instant, ere he replied; but not in doubt, or deliberation. A feeling of surprise overcame him, and, though he had already regarded Romano with the most respectful and reverential feeling, he now looked upon him with a sentiment of distrust if not dislike. At length he replied:

"Take back thy gold, my father; if thy pleadings availed not to move me, if my own sorrow for the poor youth availed not, I were base indeed to let thy gold do more than these. Take it back, father Romano; I sorrow that it should be brought to me in temptation, and I doubly sorrow that thou shouldst bring it. For thee, I would do much; but that which I would not do for love of thee or pity for him, I would not do for the criminal love of gold—nay, scarcely in the fear of immediate death!"

"In the fear of death then be it, my son Guisenard; for, of a surety, God will punish thee with death and with judgment, if thou wilt not let His servant go," answered Romano.

"Be it so, then, my father! I believe thou meanest me well; but I feel that I am right now, and I fear that following thy counsels I might be wrong. In God is my trust, and if I err, He, who sees my heart, knows that I err not through a love of error, or a selfish love of life."

"But, my son,"——

Romano would have spoken further, but the keeper interrupted him:

"Thou wouldst see the prisoner, my father. He desires—I had almost forgotten it—he desires to have counsel with thee, and he prayed me that thou mightst seek his cell soon after thy coming. The hour is late; if thou wouldst see him to-night, thou must hasten, for we have but little time ere the outer porch of the prison must be fastened."

Without waiting for any reply, which the monk nevertheless made, the keeper led the way to the cell of Egiza.

"Alas!" exclaimed Romano, "wherefore wouldst thou close the outer porch of this dungeon, which can not long confine this holy man? If the outer porch of thy heart were open, my son, thou wouldst be rescued, not less than he. But it availeth not to speak, when the neck is stiffened, when the heart is hardened, when the victim is chosen. Yet I would that it were not so. Guisenard! Guisenard! my son! thou hast listened to me always, and heard my words with a becoming reverence. Let them not fall upon thine ears unheeded now. Give ear in season, and take the promise and the security of safety from my lips. I would save thee, my son, from the bolt that is threatening. I warn thee; I pray thee! Wherefore wouldst thou perish?"

The keeper was firm, though gentle, in his reply:

"Wherefore, my father, wouldst thou urge me further?"

"I would save thee! Deny me not! Say that thou wilt free the prisoner and live!"

"Nay, father Romano, no more of this! I have already answered thee!"

"God have mercy upon thee, then, Guisenard; thou art in His hands only. Lead on!"

These words were uttered by the fanatic in the solemn manner of a judge consigning a prisoner to his final doom. They were not without their effect upon the keeper, though not in the slightest degree to weaken his resolution. He felt a momentary chill about his heart, but he replied, unshrinkingly:

"So be it, my father. I commend myself and mine, in hope and confidence, to God. The cell is open, father."

Romano entered, and the door was closed upon him instantly. He was alone with the prisoner.

CHAPTER VII.

"Brother, dost thou sleep?" said Romano, advancing toward the unhappy captive.

"No, father; I longed for thy coming too anxiously to sleep. What tidings dost thou bring me? May I hope? What says the keeper?"

"God has hardened his heart, my son, even as he hardened the heart of Pharaoh, that he may the more certainly perish. He denies to let thee go."

"He denies me! Didst thou offer him the gold, my father?"

"I did; but he refused it!"

"Then all is lost!—life, love, vengeance!—all! all! This, this is bitterness! God be with me!—God strengthen me to the last, and save where I can not!"

With these words, he fell upon his face in all the self-abandonment of despair. The monk knelt down by his side, and his hand rested upon the head of Egiza.

"No, my brother; all is not lost. Despair not; the dawn is a sister of the dark. The day is breaking before my vision, and I bring succour to thee from God. What though man denies thee, and in his fear or in his hate, his selfishness or his scorn, he shrinks from thee in the hour of thy trial, and with a weakness like that of the blessed Peter—which, at moments, is too strong for the purest faith—yet will He who moves man at his pleasure, strengthen thee and save. He will save thee now, according to the promise made to thee even in the presence of thy human judge; He sends me to save thee, and I am ready for my commission. Rise, rise, my brother; lift up thy head and hear the counsels with which Heaven hath inspired me."

Much wondering at the manner of the monk, and anxiously curious to hear what was to effect every thing, at a moment when he was the most hopeless of all things, Egiza arose from the floor on which he had lain, and stood in silent attention. Romano did not suffer any time to elapse before he proceeded thus:

"Thou hast the weapon of death, my brother, which I gave thee. Thou wilt not fear to use it when thou hast a commission from Heaven for its use, and when it is in the name and on the behoof of God that thou wilt strike."

"What mean you, my father?" replied Egiza, in some surprise. "Upon whom should I use it; whom should I strike? If it be the tyrant, believe me, thou canst not put me upon a task which shall prove more grateful to a famished spirit."

"Ay, and that task shalt thou have also; but it is not now the tyrant that thou wilt have to strike. It is one of those who toil for him—one of his arms, his creatures. It may be that thou wilt have to execute many such, ere thou executest at full the vengeance of the Lord. Thine arm may grow weary of mowing where the tares are thick, yet must thou not grow weary in spirit where the service is so sweet to the soul. The servants of the tyrant are tyrants also, since in upholding his wrong they are also wrong-doers. It is one of these that thou must gird up thy loins to slay. The victim is chosen for the sacrifice, and the Lord will deliver him into thy hands."

"Of whom dost thou speak, my father?" demanded Egiza.

"Of whom but Guisenard, thy keeper? Hath not the Lord shown him to your eyes, and taught thee in a vision what thou shalt do to him? I have been more favored, my son; I have seen, and thy labors are clear before thee. Thou hast the weapon of death, and the victim will soon be ready. When I summon him to let me go forth from thy prison, then shalt thou rush out upon him. In the dim light of the long passage, it will not be easy for him to mark the difference of thy form and features from mine, since our habits are the same; and this will enable thee to encounter with him before he can apprehend thy purpose. Thou wilt then smite him down, in the name of the Lord; and Heaven give thee strength, my son, so that thy hand shall fail not in the holy performance."

The astonishment of Egiza may be more readily imagined than described. He found it impossible to reconcile the continued and devout references of the monk to the Deity, and the bloody suggestion, which he uttered as if under Heaven's own promptings. There was no tremor in Romano's voice as he made a proposal so full of horror, such as would most probably affect the voice of almost any criminal, however hardened he may have been in the practice of crime. There was no husky hesitation in his accents, nor were the tones more than advisedly suppressed in which he spoke. On the contrary, if there was any thing to affect the calm evenness of its utterance, it was something like exultation, as if assured that the approval of the hearer would follow the counsel given, as certainly as that of God would follow the execution of the deed. The wonder of the captive rendered him almost speechless. He had no knowledge of the madness which preyed upon, and prompted the movements of Romano's mind; aud the steady composure of his voice and manner, drove all idea of insanity from his thought. While, therefore, he paused in wonder, the monk grew somewhat impatient.

"Thou hast heard me, brother?" said he.

"Ay; and thou wouldst have me strike the keeper. It is that."

"Even so!" replied the monk; "there is no course else; it is the will of God."

"Thou hast tried the gold, thou sayest?"

"I have, my brother."

"And he refused it?"

"Ay, in the hardness of his heart he rejected the rich gold of the church's coffers, and the richer gold of its counsels and its prayers. The church hath no further need of the soul which hath heard its counsels and its prayers with scorn," said the stern fanatic.

The thoughts of Egiza were wild and various. He had no hope but from this man, who had evidently been sènt by his uncle; and all means had been tried (so he said) but the one, the thought of which had filled his bosom with so much horror. The hope of life, of freedom, and revenge, made him pause; and the strife within his mind, as he endeavored to deliberate, was almost torture. However, his better spirit prevailed.

"This man," he said, as if musing, "this man hath come to me in my dungeon—he hath sat with me, and sought to cheer me—he hath spared no kind offices which would give relief—and shall I slay him now?"

"Ay, slay him even as the Lord hath appointed; for hath He not declared that all the means shall fail thee but this. Hath He not hardened this man's heart, that he might perish? There is but one way, and that is the appointed. Vainly, my son, wouldst thou seek for another; and it were an arraigning of Heaven's justice wert thou so to seek. It is decreed that this man is to die, and that through his death shalt thou seek for thine own safety. Thou must do it."

"He hath a wife, too, my father; perchance a young and lovely woman."

"A most blessed woman is Amreeta. God will provide for her; He tempereth the wind to the shorn lamb, and the birds shall bring tribute to the widow."

"And the sweet child, my father! He brought the child to my cell, and dearly did he seem to love it!"

"Of a truth, he does, my son; and the child is one most lovely and winning of love. And it is wonderful to me that the unhappy father, having the double blessing of a fond wife and a beloved child, should so run counter to the wishes of the Lord, through whom alone come these blessings, and by whom they may be taken away. Oh! that he were wise for life. Oh! that he were wise for his own happiness and safety. But he is not. The Lord would have gathered him, even as a hen gathereth her chickens; but he would not, and the doom is gone forth against him. He must die."

"No! my father," exclaimed Egiza, firmly; "he must live! I can not strike that man, though it be save my own life. He hath been kind to me, when kindness was service; he hath spoken gentlest words to me, and I know he is pained in soul that I am doomed to suffer. I can not hurt him; my heart refuses—my hand would fail me at the stroke; I would perish rather."

"Thou must not perish, my brother, for the Lord hath need of thee; nor do I censure thee for a shrinking spirit, since I now see that God hath designed thee for another work than this. It is enough service for thee to slay the greater tyrant. To other hands may fitly be given the toil and the glory of the smaller sacrifice. Father! be with me, and make me strong! I see the duty which is before me, and I gird up my loins and nerve me to the task! Brother! this dagger is not for thee; give it me!"

Egiza had not heeded the speech of the monk. The last words, however, met his ears and he freely resigned the weapon which he had determined not to use. With the handle of it Romano beat upon the door, and summoned the keeper with a loud voice. When he heard the steps of Guisenard he became silent for a moment, but his lips were moved in prayer.

"Pray for me, my brother; thou who art so near to God, will do well to pray for me now. Pray that I be endowed with the needful strength to execute the purposes of Heaven."

While he spoke, the door was opened, and the monk immediately emerged from the apartment; the door was shut instantly, and it was only as the retreating footsteps ceased to be heard by the prisoner, that he began to meditate upon the conduct of Romano, and to conjecture a sinister import in the language which he had employed. His heart misgave him as he mused on his last words, and he reproached himself for having yielded up the dagger; but such reflections came too late. The keeper was beyond the reach of his voice, and he waited in painful anticipation of events which his imagination but partially conceived. He did not wait long.

With all the solemn devotedness of spirit, such as might be supposed to have filled and governed the patriarchs of old, when they imagined themselves to be called by Heaven to the performance of new and trying labors, Romano prepared himself for those tasks which he fancied were assigned to his hands by the direct mandate of the Lord. He yielded but little, if any thing, to the seeming necessity for circumlocution and subterfuge which one about to do that in which he looked to meet with resistance wonld find it prudent to employ; and the very dagger which Egiza had given him, was not placed within the concealing folds of his garment until he was in the passage with Guisenard, nor was it then placed there with the view to its concealment. He deemed no such precaution necessary, as he did not doubt, in his own language, that "the Lord had delivered up the victim for the sacrifice," and nothing could avail for his safety, when He willed it otherwise. The passage was long and dark, nor did the doubtful lantern which the keeper carried tend very much to enliven its gloom. The light which it gave seemed only to guide their feet, step by step, to the entrance of the prison; and the impatience of Romano to execute his commission did not allow him to delay his performance until they had reached that point. When about midway, he abruptly stopped, and placed himself directly in front of Guisenard. The latter spoke in surprise:.

"What mean you, father? Come, hasten, for Amreeta awaits us. She has prepared some fruits"——

"Fruits!" exclaimed Romano, "fruits! It is thus that we dream of life in the midst of death! It is thus that we talk of indulgence when the scourge hangs over our heads! It is no time for us to think of fruits, my son; no time for me—still less for thee. Hear me, Guisenard! I come to thee with a message from the Lord. He hath seen thy blindness—He hath heard thy wilfulness. Once, twice, thrice, already, hath He sent me to thee, praying thee—for thine own sake, and for His service—to let His servant go. Once more He sends me to thee with this prayer; nor with a prayer only, but with a warning also. Undo thy bolts, Guisenard, throw open thy doors, and bid the holy man of God depart in peace, ere the wrath of Heaven fall upon thee and blight thee into blisters. He who keepeth the apostle of the Lord in bondage, keepeth a fire which shall consume, a storm which shall rend him—a pestilence which shall make him a damned and loathsome thing for ever. God hath blessed thee, Guisenard, and thou hast much to live for. He hath blessed thee, as He now sends thee counsel whereby thou mayst disarm His anger and secure His favor. But His further blessings shall depend on thee. Wilt thou let His servant go?'

"Alas! my father, why wilt thou press this matter upon me? Have I not said to thee, I can not? Greatly should I grieve to bring upon me either the wrath of God or thy reproof; but I can not think that because I keep the prisoner who was alloted to my keeping by the espatorio, safely as I am bidden, that I should vex Heaven, as I certainly would not displeasure thee. I am sorry for this unhappy youth, who hath surely suffered wrong; but I dare not let him go."

"Thou art not sorry!—thou dost not think that he hath suffered wrong!" cried Romano, "else thy plainest sense of merely human justice would have thee set him free! But I argue and plead with thee no more. It is in the name of the Righteous Judge and the Relentless Executioner, that I now speak!"

"Nay, father, let us in; Amreeta waits for us."

And the keeper would have led the way on, as he spoke, but Romano caught his arm and detained him, while he replied.

"She must wait, and thou must wait, Guisenard, while the judgment of God is spoken. Hear me, my son. The bolt of Heaven is uplifted—the doom is ready to fall, and thou hast but one more moment left thee for grace! Once more, Guisenard, I demand of thee, in the name of the Mighty One of Israel, wilt thou let His servant go?"

"No, my father! I"——

The words were arrested. The blow was as sudden as light—or as the heavenly vengeance which the fanatic Romano insisted that it was. The dagger was buried deep, by a nervous hand, in the bosom of the keeper; and the words of the murderer that followed it were as stern as if heavenly vengeance and heavenly power to execute its vengeance were both equally in the possession of the speaker.

"I pleaded to thee, I prayed thee, I counselled thee, and gave thee warning: but thou wast blind with a wilful blindness, and I now thrust thee out among the lost ones!"

The blow was a fatal one. The words of the wounded man were few, and betrayed the paralyzing effect of the stroke he had received.

"Ah! you, father! Ah! my Amreeta!—my boy—my boy!"

He grasped the arm of Romano a moment after, with both his hands, the lantern yet swinging upon one of them; but his strength was not sufficient to restrain that of the assassin. Romano drew forth the steel, and the whole frame of Guisenard quivered like a fringe tree shaken in the sudden wind of September. He gasped the prayer for mercy which he could not speak, and by the light of the lantern he saw the gleaming rust of the steel, as it was driven a second time toward his heart. His prayer was not heard—it did not stay the blow; again the steel was buried, and this time broken in his bosom. He fell upon his face without a groan, crushing the lantern and extinguishing the light beneath him as he fell.

In the deep silence which followed, the hands of the wild fanatic were uplifted in prayerful acknowledgment to Heaven; and through the dense gloom that was around and above him, he distinctly beheld an eye like an emerald, peering out in glory and approbation through the pitchy darkness of the night and place. He stooped to the body a moment after, and dispossessed it of the massive bunch of keys which hung at the keeper's girdle. Then moving back firmly and without swerving, yet with no other light than that of his zeal, and as if he were really governed and guided by the divine instinct which he assumed to himself, he proceeded directly to the cell of the prisoner, without faltering once in his attempt to find it. A moment sufficed to set the captive free.

"What hast thou done, my father?" asked Egiza, as he came forth from his dungeon.

"As I was commanded. Praise be to the Father, and to the Son, for they have broken thy bonds, my brother; they have freed thee, and sent thee forth upon thy goodly work."

"But the keeper?" exclaimed Egiza, in doubt and apprehension.

"Stay!—he lies before thee; step this way, or thou wilt tread upon him!" said Romano.

"Thou hast not slain him!" cried the prisoner, as he started back in horror.

"Yea; I smote him, as I was commanded, so that he died. Follow me; the way is dark, but the eyes of God are upon us, and all will be light ere long."

They had now reached a spot where the passage opened into another, which led to the apartments occupied by the keeper's family. When there, they heard a voice gently calling:

"Guisenard! Guisenard!"

The tones were those of Amreeta—of the widow, fond and happy in her ignorance, whom a few hours, perhaps moments, would awaken from her dream of joy to the reality of her loneliness and the anguish of her despair. The heart of Egiza felt chill within him as he heard these tones, and he reproached himself for all the misery which he knew must follow the discovery of the truth.

"Let us hasten, father!" he said, hurrying forward as if to escape from the reproaches which every sound of the widow's voice carried to his inmost soul.

"It is Amreeta, the wife of Guisenard," said the priest, as he drew forth the key which was to undo the gate before them. "Wilful man!" he continued, as if in reflection to himself, "but for his devoted blindness—but that he was bowed down to the footstool of this accursed Pharaoh—he had still been happy with his young and gentle wife, and the sweet boy which she brought him."

"No more, no more, father! I pray thee, no more!" cried Egiza, in tones of agonizing reflection. "Let us speed—let us fly from this place; I would not hear her voice again! Quick, my father; thrust back the bolt; let us feel the cool air, or I faint."

"The gate is wide, my brother. God hath delivered thee in safety; to Him be all the glory and the praise. I have been but a humble instrument in His hands; even as this iron instrument hath been in mine. Thou art free. The walls of the pagan Scipio are before thee; the palace of the accursed Roderick on the left. A light thou seest is burning in his chamber; but how soon, my brother, will all be dark in that palace! It is with thee alone, my brother, thou knowest; and I crave not for thy secret."

"I am free!" exclaimed Egiza, not seeming to hear the monk, while the sweat poured freely down his forehead and his neck. "I am free, father, and I thank thee for thy service—though I would"——

He was about to say, "though I would not that thou shouldst have paid so dear a ransom for me"—but he forbore, since it would have seemed ungracious for him to have done so; and he now began to discover the madness under which his companion labored.

"Thank me not, holy father," replied the priest; "it is my joy to serve the Lord, and to help him whom the Lord honoreth. Thou little knowest how my heart rejoices that I have been permitted to do for thee so much. Tell me what more I may do for thee, and increase the happiness which is now living in my soul."

"Lead me to the lord Oppas!" was the reply, and they trod the streets in silence; Egiza filled with thoughts and feelings that troubled and rebuked him; while Romano, his hands reeking with blood, felt nothing but a holy fervor, which increased with every moment of his internal self-contemplation.

END OF BOOK THIRD.

BOOK FOURTH.

CHAPTER I.

THE historians have described Egilona, the queen of Roderick, in brilliant colors of romance. Poetry, indeed, would fail to make her lovelier than she appears in the pages of history. Living at a period and in a country in which so little was the regard paid to virtue that vice deigned not even to wear the garments of hypocrisy, and all was gross and audacious in the vulgar and vicious indulgences of court and people, Egilona not merely maintained the dignity of the queen, but the unapproachable purity of a faithful wife and a superior woman. In her presence licentiousness was rebuked and quieted; and Roderick himself, though not sufficiently refined in his nature, to accommodate himself to those restraints which he esteemed in her, yet felt their influences upon him sufficiently to forbear in many cases where his tumultuous passions and indomitable pride would otherwise have prompted him to brave the eye of the public, and prove his vices to be not less audacious than they were gross and selfish. Add to this, that Egilona did not merely maintain her virtue, but, subsequently, her religion also. Her piety was exemplary; and, though she became the spoil of the Moorish conqueror, she yielded nothing of her faith; but, with a womanly tenacity, when she had become the wife of the misbeliever, after the death of Roderick, she exacted such concessions from her Moorish lord to the Christian forms of worship, that she is supposed by many to have converted him. One of her arts to compel at least his external acknowledgment to the images of the Saviour and the Virgin, is worth recording. She had the doors of her apartments in which she kept them, made so low that he was always compelled to stoop upon entering. "She was," says Rasis, the Moor, "a right worthy dame, right beautiful, and of a great lineage." When Bilazin, the Moor, the son of Muza, whose captive she had become, proposed to her to become one of his wives—his law allowing him seven—she replied: "Sir, offer me no violence, but let me live as a Christian;" and he married her; and, through her influence, his sway over the Christians became mild and gentle as her own character, and the faith which she professed.

But we anticipate. These are events which belong to other chronicles. At this time, the lovely Egilona dreamed not, any more than her vicious lord, of the trials which were before them, and the destiny which was to abase the latter, and change, if it did not abase, her own fortunes. She was a Christian, but not a prophet; and meekly regarding present events, she had but very little solicitude about the future.

When, in the fierceness of his merriest mood—having extorted from the archbishop a large amount of the money of the church—Roderick informed her of what he had done, her reproaches were fearlessly uttered. She had beheld with pain the treatment which the lord Oppas had undergone at the trial of Egiza, as she neither suspected nor believed in any connection between the former and the meditated crime of the latter. Her gentle nature even prompted her to plead, as we have seen, for the indulgence of time which had been granted to the criminal; and though she did not pray for his pardon—for she regarded his crime with too much religious not less than personal horror to prompt her to such an extreme of charity—yet her pleadings had not been spared to procure for him every indulgence which might have been supposed not inconsistent with the doom before him. That he was spared the torture, might even be ascribed to her presence at the trial; for Roderick's curiosity to ascertain the secret of the person who had braved him, was only restrained by the dread that she might hear that from the lips of the prisoner which, licentious as the monarch was, he would willingly have kept from her knowledge, though perhaps indifferent to its exposure to all beside. Feeling as she did toward the Christian faith and toward its professors, her sympathy took an active direction when she heard from Roderick of his morning spoliations. She well knew that any effort to make her rapacious lord disgorge his plunder would be made in vain; and resolute to do all in her power to amend the injustice and atone for the wrong, she sent for the archbishop to her private apartments. To these apartments Oppas had never come without experiencing a strange mingling of painful and pleasurable sentiments; and even now, with mingled doubts and hopes, and not untroubled by goading fears, he prepared to obey the summons with sensations which he loved too well entirely to suppress. He had the passions of the man, which his profession could not quell; he had the tastes of a courtier, and more than a courtier's ambition; and, in the beauty of Egilona and we may add in her very virtue, there was a hopeful prompter to his passion, which encouraged him to dream of enjoyments not merely inconsistent with the profession which he taught, but hostile to the very virtue which he so much admired. When the command was brought him to wait upon the queen, his heart bounded within him, his pulse beat with increased quickness, and he felt the warm glow rise to his cheek from the over-full fountain within his bosom. With a feeling and a thought rather of the vain boy than of the religious and venerable man, he proceeded to make his toilet with the care of one about to go before a person in whose eyes he desired to seem well; and never did youthful lover arrange his dress with more precise and elaborate care than did the archbishop. The imposing garb of the church accorded well with his strong and majestic figure; and as the lord Oppas moved before the polished steel plate which reflected back his person and brought it distinctly out, as if it had been chiseled in the blue metal of Damascus, his eye remarked with unconcealed satisfaction the vigorous and stately tread of his person—the manly and muscular fulness of every limb, seeming more like that of a warrior king preparing with heavy mace for approaching battle than that of the humble servant of God, solicitous of favor only in the eyes of a Supreme Master. For a moment, while engaged in this survey of his own person, such seemed to be his thought. He paused before the mirror, and his right arm was involuntarily extended. He would have grasped the sceptre at that moment, and his conscious soul seemed to bound and pant with the haughty and the fond idea.

"Will it be?" he said, musingly; "Will it be? Will it *not* be?" he exclaimed with more energy; "Or do I but dream? Is the strife—is the hope—is the toil that I have had, for nothing? Will the proud boy, Pelayo, triumph without my aid, and requite my assistance but in the idle acknowledgment, which is the common recompense! No! These serve not me! I labor not for him; nor yet for the lovesick and feeble Egiza. They think me their ally—their willing friend—their creature. Fools! they are mine. The hour is ripening—the church is strengthening amongst the people, and, if the pope will but heed my prayer, it shall have its own armies! And who shall lead those armies? Who?"

His question was answered by himself, as, lifting the crosier from the table, he bore it aloft with his extended arm, as if that moment he grasped the mace of the soldier rather than the sign of peace; and his eye gleamed with the fierce desire of battle which was working in his soul, as the strong thirst of his ambition led him to regard this theatre as that which was preliminary and essential to his full and complete success.

"Ay, the crosier shall become a sword—and the sword"——

The archbishop paused. He did not venture to conclude the sentence, even to himself. The sceptre was still something of which he might dream, but not speak. There were still uncertainties to overcome, and seas to cross, and church prejudices and popular prejudices to be worked down, by the gradual attrition of events, before the cowled head could surrender to the Gothic horns. The laurels alone could conceal the shaven crown, and make it worthy of the coronet he coveted; and these were yet to be gathered on the field of strife. These thoughts, and the doubts that came with them, oppressed him, and he turned away to the contemplation of other objects. His toilet was completed, and, bidding his groom provide for him a favorite steed, he set forth on his way to the palace.

CHAPTER II.

To his surprise the archbishop met king Roderick, just as he was about to enter the apartments of the queen. To his greater surprise yet, the king smiled upon him, and spoke in language not merely of condescension but of regard; as if he had lost entirely from his memory the transactions of the morning. Such are the caprices of tyranny. Indeed, it is the caprices of tyranny which make it tyranny. It is the alternations of power which occasionally soothe and soften its own terrors, that prompt to continued obedience in that spirit which, in the people, would otherwise discard their shackles. Were it not for the hope of amendment, which the insidious smile, the bland indulgence, and the cunningly conceived promises hold forth, resentment would soon correct wrong, and suffering rise into rebellion, and exact justice on fearful terms of rebuke from the reckless oppressor. The successful tyrant is the judicious thunderer.

But such was not Roderick. He loved too much to hear the sounds of his own thunder. He was too fond of witnessing the exhibitions of his own power, and of having it beheld by others; and in this, in great part, lay the secret of his downfall His bland benignity of manner, on meeting with Oppas, was not the result of any thoughtful policy It was simply in his change of mood that he smiled. Besides, he had gained one, if not all, of his objects. He had extorted the wealth, to obtain which his anger had been admirably pretended; and with one whose profligacies demanded continual supplies of money, the attainment of so large an amount as had been furnished by Oppas, was a sufficient occasion for good humor. A moment's reflection soon taught this to the archbishop, and he too smiled—and, with more of policy than Roderick, he too appeared to discard from his thought the scene of the morning, which had been so full of peril to him. A few words were exchanged between them, and the king, having bid the archbishop attendance at council on the ensuing day, left him to bestow his offices upon the queen.

A single maid was in attendance upon Egilona, and her she dismissed upon the entrance of Oppas. She sat upon a raised cushion of rich velvet, which lay on the floor; and her eyes, when lifted upon the appearance of the archbishop, were full of tears. She motioned him to approach, and he sat down before her on the edge of the cushion. In silence she sat for some moments, and her beautiful eyes were fixed upon the faint but lovely rays of the evening sun that streamed through the lattice. She seemed to derive an interest from the survey of their flickering and uncertain hues, which every moment of the sun's decline would necessarily divert from their place, and diminish, as well in quantity as in richness. After a few moments, consumed in this manner, she spoke—her thoughts still given to the beautiful objects on which she had been gazing.

"My father, I have been thinking sadly, as I gazed upon yon streaming light of the declining sun, how the bright things and hopes of life escape from us; how we see and touch and taste, only to lose for ever; and the thought has occasioned in me a sort of wonder that we should so blindly and so earnestly pursue visions which are so deceptive. When I first gazed upon those bright colors, that are sliding further and further from me at every moment, they appeared like a broad wing of purple all over the spot where now thou sittest, and even to my feet. I could have laid my hand upon them where I am sitting. They are now beyond my reach; and though I rise and pursue—yea, though I grasp them—in a little while and they will flee from my sight, as certainly as they do from my grasp."

"Yes, my daughter; but the morning restores them to both touch and sight," said the archbishop.

"Alas! father; but with the morning there is a change upon the sunlight and upon me. The beams are not the same, nor do they rest upon the same spot; and a like change is in the eyes that survey them. In a little while, and their beams will fall upon me coldly: in a few seasons, and I shall behold them in hues less rich and in rays less vivid than I see them now. The sense will be dim, and my heart will not leap, as it was wont, to go forth in the sunlight and be a partaker of the air. I feel already a forecast of the change which is to come, and, in my thought, I begin to perceive the gloomy shadow which time is about to cast upon my person."

"Wherefore, my daughter, should such thoughts of sadness come to thee?" replied the archbishop. "Why shouldst thou speak of time—of the chill and darkness of age? Thou art but young, my daughter."

"Ay, father; but so is the flower which is cut down in the morning," was the quick reply.

"True, my daughter; but thy hope is greater than that of the flower," returned Oppas.

"Yes, father, if I hope according to the truth. But if my hope be but of this life—which, alas! it too greatly is—then have I no better hope than the flower, and I have a fear which affects it not. This is the sorrow which troubles me, my father. I yearn for earthly joys, for earthly treasures—and sometimes forget those higher and better desires which should fill the heart of the true Christian. I would confess to thee, my father; but not as I have confessed to thee. I would tell thee of thoughts and desires which haunt my soul, and which yet have no name within my bosom. This is the evil which afflicts me. I feel that there are thoughts that trouble me, and hopes which keep me from the due consideration of holy things; yet am I without the form of speech which should enable me to bring these thoughts to thy understanding, and help thee to discourse with me upon them for my absolution. Wherefore should this be so, my father? Canst thou help me in any way by thy counsel?"

"Thy case is that of thousands, my daughter, and there is no misfortune in it; for as light often cometh out of the womb of darkness, so does strength come out of despondency, and hope from humiliation. The state of man on the earth is one of continual strife, and chiefly with his own passions and vain desires. It is in his conquest over these that he acquires that proper grace which fits him for the unselfish and God-loving abodes of heaven. Thy study must be to overcome these vain desires, these earthly longings—to bring thyself to a proper and careful thought of thy destiny."

"Ah, my father, it is this which I would know. What is that destiny?" asked Egilona.

"The answer is easy, my daughter. Thy destiny is to live: thy destiny is life immortal—eternal! It is the difficulty to realize this wondrous truth which carries down thousands and thousands of sinful people to depravity in this life, and dreadful despair in that which is to come. If thou, or any of us, my daughter, would have it as a present and continual thought in our minds that the time which we are spending upon earth is a probationary time, and that we do not begin to live until we begin to live for ever, how little to thee would seem all the longings which beset the vain hearts of those who strive and struggle for evermore, like the fly against the light, for their own destruction. How idle and worthless would be that striving for wealth, for the glitter and the gain, which dazzle the poor insect of humanity and tempt him, in his miserable weakness, to all manner of mean and sinful doings and all forms of injustice. To unlearn pride and the falsehood which is born with us, is to open our eyes to a perception of the truth. Humility is the first lesson, penitence the next, and love the last. Love, the prompter, becomes the consoler, and finally the rewarder. And it is for thee, having thy destiny of eternal life clear to thy mind before thee, to resolve whether it shall be a life crowned and made for ever happy with eternal love, or wretched with a hate not less enduring. Confess to me, my daughter, the sins and the sinful thoughts which trouble thee; this is the task which humility puts upon thee. Be penitent, and consolation flows, and eternal love and life are thine own."

"I will try, my father, and may the blessed Virgin give me strength to know and to name my infirmities, that I may have the consolation which I seek. But first, my father, let me strive to do justice and to amend, in what I can, the wrong which has been done to thee and to holy church."

"What mean you, my daughter?" demanded the archbishop.

She did not immediately reply; but, rising from the cushion, she went to a richly wrought cabinet of Mosaic which stood in the apartment, and returned almost instantly, bringing with her sundry caskets of royal gems and female ornaments of great value, apart from their exquisite workmanship. These, the tributes of Roderick, her relatives, her courtiers, and of her own purchase, she placed in the hands of the archbishop.

"Take these, father, they are of great value in men's eyes—they are also of great value in mine. Many of them are gifts from my lord, when, perchance, he loved me better than he loves me now. Many of them came to me from the kindest of mothers, and some I have bought, in my own lavishness, from the rich Jew, Ben-hazin, of Tangier. I give it now to the church, that I may restore thee something of thy loss, and, as it were, divest myself of some of the shows of that idle vanity of earth, which it may be afflicts my thoughts and keeps them from making them selves entire and single when I would throw myself at the feet of the Lord. Take them, my father; wherefore wouldst thou refuse?"

"Thou hast spoken of my losses, and of the losses of the church, my daughter. What is the meaning of thy speech?"

"Alas! father, wherefore wouldst thou have my lips utter that which is so much a shame to my heart to feel? Do I not know that my lord, king Roderick, whom I love not the less that I do not approve in this—do I not know that he hath dispossessed thee of the monies and the jewels of the church—that he hath taken from the altar of God the tribute put there by His worshippers, and hath thus despoiled the penitents, whose gifts they were, of the goodly shows of that penitence which was to work for their salvation. I trust in the Virgin that they will not suffer harm therefrom, and I would fain replace, or restore their holy offerings with my own, which though less sacred, my father, as they are not yet consecrated to godly purposes, are yet I believe of great worth to make good to thee those which thou hast lost."

"I did not think, my daughter, that thou knewest of this unholy spoliation. It was my thought that king Roderick esteemed thee too devout a worshipper to venture heedlessly upon letting thee know of this sacrilege. Alas! my daughter, though the rich offerings which thou now puttest into my hands may well replace in temporary value those of which the altar hath been dispossessed, I know not what atonement will purge the heedless offender of this most heinous sin. It will be a curse and a"——

"Stay!" she exclaimed, "stay, father; speak nothing, I pray, I beseech you, of the curses of the church. These would I disarm—these would I avert from my lord's head. He hath been sinful, I know—greatly sinful; but not in wilfulness, my father. Evil men have been his counsellors, not his own thoughts: and it is my hope that he will of his own resolution do the church justice for this wrong. I have spoken with my lord, my father, to this end; and I have also shown to him how greatly it did pain me to hear the violence of his speech this day to yourself, my father. I told him (though it would not need that I should show to him that which his own sense would more readily perceive than could mine offer, would he but calmly think ere he moved in performance) of the grievous sin to speak in such a fashion to one so much his senior in years, and so made sacred as it were from assail, wearing the very livery of God himself. Thus did I declare to him of my thought but a little while before you came, and I am fond to think that he will repent him of his sin, and make due atonement which shall be grateful no less in Heaven's sight, my father, than in thine. Be sure, my father, that if prayer of mine be blessed, he shall not fail in this atonement."

"Thou art thyself blessed, Egilona, blessed among women!" exclaimed the archbishop, while his hand rested upon her head; and he paused after he spoke these words, and his lip quivered, and there was a tremulousness in his voice which her ear detected, but the sources of which, in the innocence of her pure heart, she did not dream. She knew not that in that moment when his lips pronounced a seeming benediction, that the blood was bounding in his veins with the pulse of a wild and merely human passion. She had no thought that when his hand rested on the long and beautifully dark hair, that gathered in thick volumes and fell down upon her snowy shoulders, that his mind was even then dwelling only upon those feminine charms which were before him, and was as utterly foreign to the subjects on which both of them had spoken, as were her own thoughts from every thing like guilt. And when his fingers, relaxing as it were with the relaxing thought, glided from her head and rested momentarily upon her bare and beautifully rounded shoulders, little did she for a moment imagine that she—kneeling and wlth clasped hands, saint-like in soul as in posture—that she had imparted the flame which was then scarcely suppressible in the bosom of him before whom she bowed. She did not look up, else it must have been that his passion would have been seen by her eyes, glaring forth from his. There, indeed, it had utterance beyond the intelligence of words; though it might have been, had she not then spoken, that the full soul would have forced the unwilling tongue of the archbishop into speech, in defiance of all his efforts to prevent it. But the pure, subdued, and gentle tones of Egilona were as a spell upon the troubled waters of his soul. He trembled as he heard them, and he listened breathlessly.

"Bless me not, father; I am not worthy of your blessing. I feel that I am not. I feel strange thoughts, and I have longed to ask of you counsel, and have your guidance in doubt. I will confess to you, my father, that I have sinned grievously since I received your blessing last. I have been angry, and have spoken harshly to Gerdovia, one of my ladies, using wicked words, and employing ungentle threats to compel her better service. But there is a sin in my soul, father, which is even greater than this, and greatly do I tremble, father, lest thou shouldst deem it beyond grace of pardon. Know then, my father—alas! the sin—know that there is a damsel lately come to the court, named the lady Cava, the daughter of count Julian, of Consuegra, who is gone to Ceuta. She is a damsel lovely to the sight and winning in the eyes of man. Her father gave her to my charge, and she has been a dweller with us in our garden of the Tagus, where I made her an attendant upon my person. But, my father, a discontent soon arose within my bosom, and a strange apprehension, when I saw the eyes of my lord, king Roderick, gazing frequently and fondly upon her. Then it was, father, that I envied her the possession of those charms which God had given her"——

"'T was a false judgment that made thee do this," exclaimed the archbishop, interrupting the speaker quickly, "for of a truth thy loveliness is far beyond hers She is beautiful, I freely say; but her beauty is that of the thoughtless and immature girl, while thine is the beauty of soul and person, alike, of the highly taught and the reflecting woman; and the loveliness of thine eye and countenance, speak not for themselves merely, but for a rich and flowing fountain which thou hast within thy bosom of noble spirit and commanding thought. Thou, Egilona"——

"Nay, father! thou hast enough said for my humbling," were the words of the queen, mistaking or seeming to mistake, utterly, the purpose of the archbishop. "I know that it was a foolish vanity in me to think of my own poor beauties, if such they may be called, in opposition to the lady Cava's; but truth it is, I thought of them with envy—ay, with hate, when I beheld the eyes of my lord follow her, and heard his soft words in her ear."

"And thou heardst him then?" exclaimed the archbishop eagerly.

"Alas! for me, my father, I heard him speak in praise of those beauties which I envied, and my heart sickened within me; and in the madness of my spirit, my father, I privily left my chamber and watched my lord, as he pursued his steps toward the apartment of the lady Cava, having in my heart a vexing hope and a dreadful fear all the while, that he meditated an evil thing in his mind."

"And thou sawest him in her chamber, my daughter!" exclaimed the archbishop, his hands trembling even while they contracted themselves more closely upon the neck of Egilona.

"Alas! my father, how shall I tell thee? But even to the entrance of her apartment did I, like a thief in the night-time, follow my lord, and know not where my evil spirit might not have carried me, but that the lord Edeco then appeared, and, with a guilty dread lest I should be seen of my lord, I fled back to my own chamber, where I could not sleep. The evil spirit was still within my heart—it is now there, my father, filling me with all vexing thoughts, and making me sin hourly, as it brings me bitter and strange thoughts and wishes that I know are sinful."

"Thou sawest him to her chamber, thou sayest?" exclaimed the archbishop, musingly.

"Alas! my father, though I shame to say it, of a truth I did," answered the fair penitent.

"Unhappy man! foolish as false! to fly from beauties so superior—to scorn a heart so much more worthy, and to yield himself up to crime for a silly girl, and one scarcely ripe to the knowledge of affection!"

Such were the exclamations of the archbishop. Egilona seemed to hear him with surprise. Entirely absorbed with the conviction of her own errors, she had given no thought to those of her husband.

"Speakest thou of my lord, my father?" she asked, when the archbishop had concluded.

"Ay, Egilona, of that sinful, that soulless man, who seems madly bent on wronging the good, and the holy—he who despoils the church, who despoils the innocent, and who wrongs thee. It is of him that I speak."

"Nay, father, but thou shouldst not. It is of my sin that I would have thee speak to me. It is for thy counsel, not for the reproof of my lord, that I come to thee. I would have thee chide the evil spirit from my heart, and teach me the better way and the better thoughts of good. Do this, my father, I pray thee; but say nothing of my lord."

"Alas! my daughter, the sin that makes us sin is a sin to be chided also. Hath not the wrong of thy lord led thee to wrong; and is not one evil the fruitful parent of the other? The axe should be laid at the root, if we would deny that the branches should bear. Was it not the voice of Roderick that prompted thee to the error thou hast committed?"

"Alas! my father, I fear that the error was but too strong in mine own heart—for, to tell thee a truth, I had strange thoughts and unkind suspicions of my lord, ere this, and of the lady Cava."

"And wilt thou tell me, my daughter, that thou hadst them unjustly? Alas! no. The errors of the king Roderick are but too commonly in the mouths of the whole court"——

"But not mine, my father. It is not Egilona who will or should speak thus of her lord; and I would pray thee for that counsel which should strengthen me even against the thought."

"And this I cannot give thee, my daughter," answered the archbishop, quickly "Thou art commanded to hate the vice and to fly from the vicious. The Lord himself hath commanded, and the hate which in thy heart has taken the place of love for king Roderick"——

"Nay, father, that were a dreadful sin. Thou dost me wrong. Evil is in my heart, I know—this I have confessed to thee already—but no hate. I hate nought that has life, not even things that crawl, the poisonous reptiles that crawl and sting, not even these do I hate"——

"The lady Cava!" exclaimed the archbishop.

"Ah! father, thy words crush me; but think not that I hate the maiden—I fear her, I fear her charms!"

"Thou hatest them, Egilona."

"Father, forgive me; I fear I do hate them—I envy them!"

"My daughter, let thyself see. Blind not the judgment and good sense which is growing within thee. Why shouldst thou hate the lady Cava, or her charms? they wrong thee not. The wrong is that of Roderick, not of the poor maiden whom he seeks. Wilt thou do another wrong, in the maintenance of his? Wilt thou revile the poor victim, because thou art wedded to the criminal? Alas! for thee, my daughter; thy gifts to the church are unavailing—thy prayers are unavailing; for how canst thou look to the blessed Virgin to uphold thee, and intercede in thy behalf, when thou givest countenance to him who wrongs the Virgin? Take back thy offerings to the altar; they are not worthy of a place before it, nor can they be consecrated and made holy when they are the tributes of a heart that is obstinate in its sin, and pleadest in its defence.

Egilona sank in terror at the feet of the archbishop, as she heard this threatening language.

"Crush me not, holy father!" she exclaimed; "crush me not; I am but a poor, weak, sinful woman, and I would be a loving and devoted wife."

"But thou canst not. If thou lovest sin, thou partakest of the sin; and thy best confession before Heaven, will be that in which thou declarest thy readiness to cut off and cast away thy right hand if it offend thee. Tell me then, my daughter, the truth. The truth alone shall save thee, if it should condemn thee; for though of the truth thou mayest be convicted of the sin, yet is the truth itself a virtue which shall prove a fitting foil to the sin. Thou hast, I know thou hast, a becoming fear of vice, and thou dreadest its presence; thou hast hated it also—thou shouldst, thou dost hate it. Say, Egilona, when thou hast beheld thy lord, king Roderick, sinfully inclining to other women, and forgetting thee whom it is his solemn and sworn duty to remember, has not thy heart grown cold toward him"——

"Never, oh, never!—as I live, never!"

Her ready response interrupted and, as it seemed, somewhat disappointed the archbishop.

"Nay, be not too fast—be not rash, my daughter. The church esteems it no sin if thou fall off in thy regards from those whom thou findst vicious—if thou art cold to those whom thou didst once love, perhaps, whenever thou seest them unworthy Nay, it esteems it a virtue so to become."

"Alas! father, this virtue is not mine. Though Roderick has of late forgotten me, and his neglect has given me many hours of weariness and weeping, yet have I loved him not less in my soul because of his desertion. Even when I beheld him heedless of my regards, and following after the beguiling charms and arts of other women—nay, when I beheld him as I thought, seeking himself to beguile the unwary virgin—yet did I rather envy those he sought, than anger with him for his wanderings. I have been ever fond of him, and true to him, my father, though, before thee and Heaven, I fear that he hath almost utterly forgotten me. He cares not for my love."

There was no satisfaction in the countenance of the archbishop as he heard this reply. His looks were full of disappointment, and he half withdrew his united hands from their clasping folds upon her neck, as he spoke thus:

"But there have been moments, my daughter—nay, there have, there must have been—when, seeing him thus wanton, thou too hast sighed, my daughter, for a like freedom and like indulgencies. There have been noble gentlemen of the court whom thine eyes have looked upon with pleasure, nay with desire."

"Never! oh, never! my father. The Virgin keep me from so sad a fault."

"Bethink thee, my daughter, thou art not infallible. We are are all weak, and to be weak, indeed, is only to have an opportunity to approve our virtue. I mean not to reproach thee with any sin beyond the passing thought, the momentary desire, the lust in thy soul, which thou didst suppress—perchance, the very moment in which it came to thee. This, indeed, is thy nature—the erring nature of thy sex; and not to know such feeling, such desire, is to differ from thy nature, and to be superior to all of thy sex. It is expected from thee, this weakness. It is thy strength, when thy virtue is strong for its subduing. Such has been thy case, my daughter; nay think, ere thou denyest it. The church is indulgent, my daughter, and its censures are only given to concealment and perverse devotion to sin, not to free confession, not to the sinner who tears open the dark shadows with which Satan would hide the corruption of the heart, and begs for the friendly knife of the soul's physician to cut away without sparing the callous and the leprous spots thereof. Confess freely, my daughter; thou hast desired, thou hast sighed for other regards than those of thy lord."

"Never, never!—as I live, never!"

"Of a surety, thou hast seen many noble gentlemen, who well merit the love of woman?"

"Truly, father, I believe it; I think there are many such."

"And thou hast seen such?"

"I doubt not—I believe it, father."

"And hast thou not remarked that there were many having the graceful demeanor and the manly beauty of thy lord, who were yet more regardful of the love which they had won; did such not seem to thee at the moment, persons to love and desire? Didst thou never, in thy thought, and without thy wilful resolve, make such comparison in thy passing mind? Hast thou not remarked other noble dames, blessed with the affections of such lords, yet more honored than thee, in their constancy? Bethink thee, Egilona, ere thou speakest; I know it must have been."

Again did the hands of the archbishop unite in a fond and fervent pressure upon the neck of the devotee, as he listened for her answer. But he heard nothing that he longed to hear, and his hands were as quickly withdrawn as placed, in the mortification of his spirit.

"Of a truth, father, as I kneel before Heaven and thee, I think never! It is true, I have regarded other noble gentlemen with esteem, and some with admiration, but not one with a feeling inconsistent with that which I owe to my lord, king Roderick It is true, I have beheld with sorrow and with deep affliction the neglect of my lord and his pursuit of other women, but even when I suffered and sorrowed the most, by reason of neglect or injustice, I never once held it fitting that I should anger with him, and never did it seem to me that I could love him less. So far from this, though it may seem strange to thy understanding, as it hath been a passing mystery to mine, I feel that I have even loved him the most at moments when I have believed him least worthy of my esteem, and as most ungrateful to my love. I know not what this may mean, unless it is the will of Heaven, by which to show to woman, who is the weaker and the humbler object, that, as she is dependent, she must be dutiful; and as the love, which to her is the very breath of life, is so capricious and so little likely to be secure, even where it is proffered by men in other respects the noblest and the truest, so is it the more necessary that she should be unshaken in her constancy, that her faith may work in behalf of him she loves, and for the salvation which were else for ever forfeit. It was by love and self-sacrifice that the blessed Jesus died for the race of man, which fought against His holy and saving labor; and the love of woman were of little worth, if she were not ready for the same sacrifice, should it need, for him that she is bound to—even though he slight her homage and prove faithless to her love. I rank the love of man, my father, with that blessed sunshine which I watched when first thou camest. We have not heeded it while we have spoken, and lo! where is it now? See, but a few scattered rays rest upon the orange-leaves which twinkle before the lattice, and now they are dark in their own deep hue, for the beams are departed. Are not these beautiful things that fleet from our affections and our eyes so fast, are they not blessed monitors to prepare us for our departure, and to lift our thoughts from a too devoted love for any of the vanities and seeming joys of earth?"

"Ay, my daughter, and from its affections, also, where they chime not with the blessed precepts of divine grace and truth. Shouldst thou become enamored of that sunbeam so that its absence gave thee pain, thou wouldst be guilty of an error, and the penalty would be hourly pressing itself upon thee. Still more heavy would be the penalty, if thou didst love a light which came to thee from the infernal abodes of the damned. Shalt thou, my daughter, love vices which have a like origin; thou shouldst"——

What more the archbishop said, or would have said, was lost in a new and unlooked for interruption. While he spoke, a sudden clamor arose from another part of the palace. Shriek upon shriek, in the voice of a woman, rang through the apartment, rapidly repeated and increasing in loudness with every instant. The tramp of feet, as if in flight and pursuit, followed each interval between the cries; and while they wondered at the uproar, the sounds approached, and in a few moments after the door was thrown open and the lovely Cava, her hair dishevelled and floating in the air, her whole features convulsed, her eyes red, full of tears, and almost bursting from their sockets, burst into the chamber, and rushing forward, fell, rather threw herself, at the feet of the queen. Her cries all the while continued, without intermission.

"Leave me, father," said Egilona, rising and motioning the archbishop; "leave me for awhile. I will again send for thee."

The archbishop instantly withdrew, bearing with him the rich offering which the queen had made to the church, and she was left alone with the beautiful woman whose fatal charms, destructive to their owner, had brought scarcely less misery to the queenly Egilona.

CHAPTER III.

A MOMENT only had elapsed after the departure of the archbishop, when Roderick came to the door of the queen's chamber. His appearance was the signal for the renewal of those piercing shrieks with which the flying Cava had startled the palace, and which, in the presence of Egilona, had been changed into a long unbroken sobbing.

"Save me! save me!" she screamed in terror, the moment that her eyes beheld the face of the king. "Save me, dear lady! I pray thee save me from that bad man!"

"Man, dost thou say, maiden?" said Egilona. "It is my lord, king Roderick, whom thou beholdest. Dost thou not know him?"

"Too well, too well! Save me, I pray thee! Hide me from him! Hide me in the earth! Let him not approach me!"

Roderick was about to enter and to speak, when the wild paroxysm of Cava was renewed. Her terror became extreme, and rushing in the opposite direction from the door where the king stood, she dashed herself against the unyielding wall as if she would have found an escape through it, though at the hazard of her life. Her terror seemed to increase as she found her flight prevented, and, sinking to the floor, in a series of hysterical paroxysms, she shrieked and gibbered like an idiot, dumb with fright, her hands extended toward the entrance and waving away the intruder. This was no time for explanation; and, venting his anger in muttered curses, which Egilona heard imperfectly, he left his victim to the considerate humanity of his wife. Nor did the noble woman who, in that bitter moment, in the despair of the young maiden before her, beheld the full realization of her fears, suffer her own sense of injury to make her heedless of her who had been, however unwillingly, the cause of it all. Her humanity and religion were triumphant over her woman pride. Gentleness was her instinct; and, sighing bitterly, she proceeded to soothe the terror and condole with, if she could not alleviate, the sorrows of the maiden. Tenderly lifting her from the floor where she had fallen, she bore her to the cushions, and proceeded to a cabinet from which she took some bottles of reviving cordials and perfumes. With these she bathed the temples of Cava, who, meantime, spoke nothing, or single words only, but who maintained, all the while, with few and those brief intervals, a most distressful sobbing.

"Poor maiden!" murmured Egilona, as she performed these kind offices—"Poor maiden! would that I had never seen thee, ere I had seen thee thus. Would thou hadst still kept with thy father, in his secluded hills, where thou hadst peace—and innocence. Alas! how will my lord look upon his face? How shall I surrender thee to him? What shall I say, in discharge of his fond trust—in fulfilment of my rash promise? Oh Roderick, Roderick! what a ruin hast thou made!"

Cava shuddered in the arms of the queen. She had heard the tones of condolence, she had distinguished some of the words, and when Egilona paused, and the warm tears fell fast and thick from her eyes upon the cheek and bosom of her she sustained, the poor girl turned herself so as to look up into the face of the queen, and with broken words she thanked her for the sympathy she gave.

"But!" she exclaimed, wildly and passionately, a moment after, "speak nothing of my father. No! no! I never more shall see him. I dare not! He will spurn me from him; he would slay me with the sudden blow!"

"Nay, speak not thus, sweet Cava; be not thus passionate. Why shouldst thou not see him? Thou dost him wrong. He will not hurt thee."

"Ah, madam, thou knowest not!" exclaimed the shuddering victim—"thou knowest not, and I cannot tell thee. I have not the words—I have not the strength. But thy lord—the king—Roderick—to whom, as to a father, did my own father give me in trust—he"——

She threw herself from the arms of Egilona, and her face lay prone upon the floor, which was wet with her gushing tears. The queen strove in vain to pacify her.

"I was not guilty!" she exclaimed, in continuation; "Oh! believe me. They blinded me, and the strength of men was upon me. Hadst thou, oh! hadst thou kept me to thyself, in thy apartments, nor sent me to that far, fearful chamber!"

"Would that I had!" exclaimed the queen, fervently. Cava continued:

"I cried to thee, my lady, I cried to thee in my terror and my pain, till my breath left me. I cried to thee with all my strength, but thou didst not come. Why didst thou not come; why didst thou not save me?"

"Alas, my poor maiden! but I heard thee not. I would freely have died to save thee."

"I called upon God, too, and he did not hear me. Upon my father; oh! that he had heard—that he had dreamed of this! I had been safe! But all deserted me—

none came; and I am—oh God! oh father!—I am what I dare not name, and what will kill me. Would he had slain me! Would that Roderick had put a keen knife into my heart, ere I had seen this day—ere he had done me this wrong! But it is not too late. I can die—I can die! *He* shall not see my face! I shall not look upon *him* in my shame!"

Raving thus with the fever of mind and body both, she started at these words from the floor where she lay, and looked wildly around her.

"What wouldst thou, Cava?" demanded the queen.

The poor girl did not immediately answer. Her eyes seemed to search over the apartment; then, as if disappointed, she sank forward again upon the floor, exclaiming, as she did so, in reply:

"Death! death! I would have death: I must! It will hide my shame; it will give me quiet; it will stop this fire in my brain; it will save me from my father—my proud, poor father."

"And wherefore, dear Cava, dost thou fear to see thy father? He will not chide thee; thou art not guilty."

"I am! I am!" she vehemently exclaimed; "I am guilty of life. The life of woman is her purity. She is guilty if she survives it. Canst thou not help me? Oh, my lady, my royal mistress! be my friend; give me help; let me have death. Give me some weapon whose keen, quick stroke will release me from this dreadful agony. Give it me, I pray thee, that I may die ere I see my father."

"Speak not thus, my dear Cava; but pray to Heaven rather for strength, for peace, for resignation," said the queen.

"Ay, it is well!" exclaimed Cava, now sitting up, and speaking not merely in tones of firmness but of vehemence; "it is well for thee, Egilona, to counsel me to resignation, when thy lord hath destroyed me for ever! Thy counsel of resignation to me is but a counsel of submission; but I warn thee that my submission will work wo to thy lord. I will die—I know that; I cannot live—I must not; I will perish, ere my father shall behold me; but he shall hear of my wrongs, and he shall avenge them! I will not perish in silence, though I perish in secret My prayers, ere I die, shall move the winds of heaven, if other messengers be denied me, to bear the tidings of this wrong to my noble father. He will avenge me terribly upon thy lord; he may not be counselled to submission to such foul dishonor."

It would be needless to linger upon this painful scene. Words would inadequately express the anguish of the unfortunate Cava. She was a maniac for the time; and it was only by sheer exhaustion of the animal faculties, that she was quieted at last. In the pause of her passion, the queen summoned her attendants, and they bore her unresistingly to her chamber; but as the fatal apartment in which she had suffered the dreadful wrong which had debased her pride and shaken her reason, opened upon her, the paroxysms of her frenzy were renewed. The excitement of her mind gave new powers to her body; and of a sudden, with one piercing shriek, which rang through the vaulted passages, she broke away from the grasp of those who attended her. With a flight which seemed that of a bird, and a footstep whose fleetness set all pursuit at defiance, once more she hurried along the course which she had taken when flying from her destroyer. Once more she would have rushed into the presence of Egilona, whom she had just left, when, at the entrance of the queen's apartment, she met the cruel Roderick himself. The sight was like a sudden blow from a steel-gloved hand upon the poor maniac. Her hands were thrown up in horror and affright, and she sank to the floor with one deep exclamation of dread and disgust, which smote to the heart of the tyrant. The attendants seized upon her senseless person, and conveyed her now without difficulty to the chamber whence she had fled, and in which the kind providence of the queen had commanded that two of them should remain with her. Nor did Egilona content herself with this degree of care. She visited the unhappy victim in her chamber, and with a humility which was not without its effect upon Cava, she bore with all those bitter reproaches, which, in her despair and agony, the latter did not scruple to utter. The blow which had destroyed the maiden, had also been a cruel blow to her; yet never did Christian meekness and Christain hope more admirably sustain, even while they subdued her high and holy spirit. She herself spoke no word injurious to her lord, though she spoke to Cava in tones and language of sympathy and encouragement, befitting the ears of one who had so grievously suffered; and when, at length, in stupor rather than sleep, the poor maiden lay before her with closed eyes and in utter silence, never did sinner pray more fervently or plead with more humility for grace from heaven on the sufferer, than did the wife of him who had been the parent of all the suffering. Nor should it subtract from the power of her prayer, that she mingled with it a humble petition for mercy on the wrong-doer. Her love, like the heaven to which she sent her entreaties, was boundless; and in her charity, while she wept the crime, she could yet hope foi that indulgence for the criminal which the interests of her own heart, if not the merits of his for whom she prayed, imperatively demanded.

CHAPTER IV.

The unhappy Cava slept; but her spirit was awake, and her dreams were full of the liveliest images of horror. The events of the day were renewed by her aroused fancies in the night; and her sudden shrieks, as she started from her rest, broke the slumbers of the maidens who were alloted to sleep with her. They quieted her with difficulty; and, finding that she was watched and guarded as it were, her anguish put on the aspects of a sullen stupor. She gave no seeming heed to those about her, or to the pressing and cureless thought, but appeared now satisfied to endure the sorrow which she could no longer avert. The hours were passed in a slow silence on her part, though her attendants in many ways strove to attract her attention and enlist her interest. They spoke in light tones and in playful language in her hearing; but that which they meant as music was only so much discord to her soul. Like one sinking into stone, she sat in a gloomy indifference before them. They brought her music, and the gay seguadille—a dance originally Roman, but mingled in Iberia with certain Moorish movements; they danced before her with the grace peculiar to the Spaniard; but they failed to awaken her regard or affect the dull, immoveable features of the mourner. She ate, as if in compliance with a customary habit, and not with appetite; and consciousness seemed almost to have left her, until late in the day ensuing her wrong, when Roderick presumed once more to appear before his victim. With his presence, life seemed once more to awaken. Her consciousness came back to her in a renewal of her wo, though not with such an exhibition of it as before. She did not shriek—she uttered no moan. Her heart seemed to have acquired undue and unnatural strength; and though she turned from the presence which was no less dreadful than hateful to her soul, and fixed her gaze in mute deliberation upon the stony wall of her chamber, her wo was no less apparent to the intruder in its dumb aspect, than when, with hair disheveled and voice screaming as she fled, she had made her escape from his fierce embrace. He motioned to the attendants to leave the apartment, and she saw them do so without seeking to arrest them. This appeared a favorable indication to the mind of the lustful monarch. He approached her where she sat, and kneeled down beside her. She started to her feet, and retreated slowly to the opposite end the room; and when he rose to follow her, and looked upon her face, all passion was checked and chilled within him. Her looks wore that expression of indescribable despair which says, more emphatically than language, that hope is for ever gone. Her eyes were luminous, but stationary. They gazed fixedly upon him, and no single revolution of their orbs took place while he watched her. Her lips were rigidly closed together; and when they separated to admit her speech, her teeth remained fast clenched below. Her voice was hollow, like that of one perishing with hunger in the deep abyss of some dismal cavern; and every word which she uttered went into his soul like a keen iron He trembled while he heard her.

"My lord, approach me not. If you do, you approach one who is wedded to and resolved for death. The power of death is even now upon me. I feel it in me; in my veins—in my head—in my heart. If this may not disarm your cruel lust, may God have mercy on me—I can do no more. You have already doomed me. Be satisfied, and leave me to die. It will not be long; and I would be at peace—such peace as you have left me—until that moment. Be merciful; let me not pray to you in vain. Be merciful, and spare me from any farther violence."

"And why do you fear violence at my hands, fair Cava?" replied the monarch, in tones in which respect and appetite were strangely mingled. He approached as he spoke. She waved him back, while she replied:

"Why do I fear violence at the hands of him whose brutal power hath destroyed me? Why does the mother clasp the shivering infant to her bosom, when she hears the tramp of the wild beast which hath devoured its brother? But you mistake me, king Roderick; I do not fear your violence. You cannot harm me now. You cannot—you dare not again seize me, with foul thoughts, in your polluting embrace. I am secure from that in your fears, in your apprehensions, and these spare mine own. You would as soon clasp the decaying bones of the already buried, as clasp me. In the death which is now feeding on me, and which you must behold in these eyes, I am secure. It is your touch from which I would fly; it is your presence that I would not behold; it is your voice which I would not hear."

"So stern, so cruel to me, fair Cava; whose only error was in loving thee too much," said the monarch.

"Thou love!" she exclaimed; "oh God! how are thy blessings and thy benefits profaned! Love cherishes, but thou hast destroyed. In thy selfish and sinful lusts, king Roderick, thou hast blasted as sweet a hope as ever blossomed in poor maiden's heart. For the pleasure of thy foul passion—the passion of an hour—thou hast taken from me life and love, and all that I have lived for, and all that I could love; and now I crave but one mercy at thy hands—that, as with thy unmanly violence thou hast degraded me from hope, and deprived me of the love which honored and would have blessed me, thou wilt employ another violence, in compliance with my prayer—the only one which I make to thee—and rid me of life also. Do so, king Roderick; and if I cannot bless thee, I will at least thank thee for the kind though destroying blow."

"Alas! Cava, wherefore dost thou urge me thus? Why wilt thou not be happy, as I implore thee? Thou art not the beloved of a poor hilding—of a trader to

Tangier and the Pillars, that needest to be virtuous. Thy state gives thee a certain freedom which thou wert not wise not to use. Wouldst thou be unlike the other dames of the court, many of whom would joy at thy fortune? Remember, it is a king who implores thee, fair Cava; he can make thee a princess, before whom even Egilona herself shall bow. He can deck thee with jewels, and honor thee with a service which shall vex into jealous fever the proudest damsels of the court."

"Thou knowest me not, king Roderick. These things have no power upon my thoughts. I seek for no admiration which shall beget envy in others; nor would I trench upon one smallest right of that noble lady, Egilona. But why do I speak to thee thus? Thou canst not persuade me, king Roderick; thou mayst trample me into submission by thy brutal strength; thou mayst misuse this frail body by cruel and unmanly violence; but it is my joy that thou canst not move my spirit; thou canst not persuade my mind by any temptation which thou showest me. If it has seemed meet with God to deny me the strength to resist thine, at least He hath not denied me the resolution of soul to reject thy prayers and scorn the arts and temptations with which thou wouldst bring me to thy purpose. This is my consolation now; that I have not yielded, though I have suffered—that I have not been guilty of wrong in the wrongs which I have borne. It will be this only which gives me strength to hope that I may see and speak but once with my father ere I perish."

"Ha! dost thou hope thus, Cava; dost thou hope to speak with thy father of thy wrong? Wherefore this? Of what avail will it be to thee that thou shouldst have speech with him? What wouldst thou say to him, to please him or to help thyself."

"I would have vengeance, Roderick! a vengeance as fearful as the wrong I have borne; and for this reason would I see and speak with my father. It is my only prayer, ere I die, that he may hear from my lips, or gather, if I have not that privilege, the tidings from some swift messenger, of thy brutal rage and the disgrace which thou hast cast upon his blood. He will not sleep ere he avenge it. He will not sell thee his honor for the baubles in thy gift. I know him, and thou knowst him well; and when he shall hear of the shame of his daughter, beware his wrath! it will sweep and rend thee, king Roderick, as even now—better heedful of his trust than thou of thine—he rends the armies of the invading Moor, which beset thy coast."

"But thou shalt not see him, fair Cava; thou shalt not reveal this madness to his ears; nor shall he have idle knowledge of thy secret. Thou wert too bold to declare thy purpose. These walls shall circumscribe thee till thou growest wiser. When thou shalt meet my love with a gentler temper, thou shalt have freedom—but not till then. Nor shalt thou have cause of anger with me the while. I will woo thee, fair Cava, as I have wooed no woman yet. I will minister to thee in a thousand forms of love, and thou shalt not withstand me. Wherefore wouldst thou withstand my love? What is this demure virtue which thou affectest? A bond and a fetter, fit only for the cold hearts whose icy temper is proof against all pleasant warmth. Such is no heart of thine. Thine shalt melt to mine. Thou shalt smile where thou frownest now; and, forgetting the idle rules of that freezing chastity which unloved maidens fitly boast, thou shalt meet my spirit with one no less fond and apprehensive of its joys. Such is my hope, sweet Cava; and in this hope I will keep thee in bonds until the season of its spring. When, like the bird which has grown familiar with his wires, thou singest a sweet song of content in mine ear, then will I withdraw the bolt, and give thee the freedom which thou wilt not use. Meanwhile, sweetest Cava, give ear to reason, and bend thy heart, stern and stubborn though it be, to the fond pleading and the single truth of mine."

"King Roderick, I trust thou wilt not keep me from my father," said the forlorn woman.

"Will I not! Believe me, but I will. I am doubly sworn to it now, since thou hast forewarned me of thy purpose. My love for thee is enough to make me resolute in this; and while thou threatenest, a prudent caution prompts me no less to the same resolve. Thou art my prisoner, sweet Cava; but like a choice bird, of mellowest note and loveliest plumage, thou shalt be so tended that thou shalt not feel thy bondage, nor behold the wires which restrain thee. Ere many days, thou wilt forget thy cage, and begin thy song of gladness as before."

"If thou hast so resolved, king Roderick, I have not the strength to break my bonds, nor the wing to fly them; but I may at least be permitted to hope that I bear my bondage in solitude. I will bear thy restraints, if thou come not nigh. I will be submiss, so that thou come not near to compel it. But I warn thee, king, that though I have not the strength to break thy chain, nor the wing to fly from thy prison, yet I despair not of escape from thee, and I feel that vengeance is sure. I know that I will break through these vain restraints of thy power, and I trust in Heaven's justice to avenge my wrong."

"I fear it not, sweet Cava; and thy threats, not less than thy hopes, are idle and fruitless. The walls are thick, and my guards fill the garden. How canst thou escape?"

She moved a step toward him, ere she replied; then, in solemn accents, which he felt even while he flouted them, she spoke:

"By a stronger arm than thine—by Death! I tell thee, king Roderick, that she, the pale maiden, who was given to thee in trust—having youth, and beauty, and a heart which was gushing with warm hope and the innocentest love, but whom in thy wanton cruelty thou hast dishonored and destroyed—will escape thee by death. It comes—slowly, perchance, but surely; and I feel that it is at hand Ere three days, I tell thee, thou wilt hear, when thou least thinkest to hear, or it may be when thou least thinkest of her—that she is free. They will tell thee, while the untasted wine is at thy lips, that Cava, thy victim, is dead—that she fears thee no longer, as she fears thee now. Thou wilt hear; and, haughty as thou art, thou wilt tremble."

He did tremble, though he ceased not to speak boldly, and in accents persuading her to guilt. But she answered him no more. She turned from his presence, and gave no reply to his solicitations, even if she heard them. After fruitless efforts, as well of argument as of entreaty, he resolved for the present to forbear her presence, trusting that time and subduing circumstances might change her temper, and soften that stern resolve of character, which it had not been his lot, in that licentious court which he ruled, to encounter often—and which, indeed, from the gentleness of Cava's demeanor heretofore, and the pliant softness of her manner, would have seemed as foreign to her character as it was singular in his sight. Her character had undergone a most unexpected change. She was no longer timid, shrieking, and apprehensive. She was strong in her despair, resolute from the dreadful cruelty to which she had been subjected, and totally unapprehensive, as she had already suffered the worst of injuries. When Egilona visited her, which she did soon after the departure of Roderick, she found her as calm as the immoveable rock, and seemingly as insensible.

CHAPTER V.

THE desires of the archbishop were in some measure gratified, though the interview with Egilona had been productive of but very partial gratification to his personal feelings. The treasure which he had received from the queen, compensated in great part for that of which Roderick had despoiled him; and the discovery he had made, while in attendance, and which abridged the interview, had its advantages, and furnished the argument which he had long desired by which to move count Julian to his purpose. To effect this object, what did it matter to him that the girl was destroyed? What was her virtue, her peace of mind, her happiness in this life and the next, to his ambition? Had there been thousands, instead of one, whose sacrifice were essential to his projects, he would not have scrupled to have required it; though the temporary and uncertain dominion of a few short years over a vicious and changing people, was the sole reward as it was the sole stimulant to such a grievous sin.

The shrieks of Cava, her flight and dishevelled appearance, as, rushing from the brutal embrace of Roderick, she sought the presence and protection of the queen, revealed the catastrophe to the archbishop. When he reached his own palace, he proceeded to avail himself of his knowledge. In his private chamber, he prepared the billet which follows:

"TO JULIAN, COUNT OF CONSUEGRA, IN COMMAND AT CEUTA, ETC.

"It is in the mouths of many that Julian left his daughter, Cava, at the court of king Roderick, as he well knew the surpassing beauty of her charms, and as well the fierce passion of the king for such loveliness as hers. That he hath not erred in his expectations, is no less the rumor of the court. Cava, it is said, hath been distinguished by the king's eye; and the bruit is, that, though she hath lost in virtue, yet will the gain of Julian in high station be proportionate to her loss and great beyond his desire. Yet, though this be the speech of many who have integrity and speak not often idly, there are some who remember of the noble blood and proper pride of the Julian family, who, though they cannot gainsay the tidings of king Roderick's favor and of the frailty of the lady Cava, are yet unwilling to yield faith so readily to that which reports the willing pliance of Julian to his own dishonor. One of these, in his sorrow and his doubt, hath written these presents. He asks not for reply, since the deeds of the father, hereafter to be shown, will testify how far he hath been a party to the ruin of his child."

This done, he called a trusty courier, to whom he gave instructions to proceed to the command of count Julian, at Ceuta, to whom he should contrive the delivery of the letter without being seen to do so. The characters of the writing were disguised, and there was no signature. He well knew that with a man of the high spirit and proud sense of honor of count Julian, it needed not a name to prompt him to action in a matter of such painful moment; yet the courier had his instructions to wait, observe, and, if need be, to act discretionally upon the movements of Julian, with authority from the archbishop to declare himself as the bearer of the letter, and to reveal its author, should events seem favorable to that course

CHAPTER VI.

A DAY passed, and the night following came the release of Egiza from his dungeon. His escape from his pursuers has been noted, and we have seen his safe arrival with Romano at the palace of the archbishop. His appearance was productive of no little anxiety to the latter, who felt that he was hourly accumulating new toils around himself, from which nothing but the strong hand and the rapid progress of desired events could give him extrication. To his nephew, he spoke freely of his fears.

"You must fly. There is no shelter for you here. Your escape, and the death of Guisenard, will rouse the rage of the tyrant even more greatly than before, and he will hunt you in every suspected quarter. My palace will be one of the first places of suspicion, and you must fly from it this very night."

"God will keep his own!" exclaimed Romano; "let the holy man resolve for himself, my father. He hath slain the jailer, and he hath confounded the pursuers; and he will write the doom upon the walls, yea, in the very face of this Belshazzar; and the Lord will be his keeper, and he will suffer no harm. Praise be to the Lord!"

The zealot continued to murmur to himself in broken prayers and praises, but the archbishop gave them little heed; and though his conduct awakened the wonder of the prince, yet he was too much filled with his own troubles of mind to dwell long upon those of another. His reply to Oppas revealed the deep anxiety which possessed his soul.

"Tell me not of flight, uncle; tell me of nothing but the maiden. What of Cava? Speak!—answer me that."

Romano looked up with some bewilderment. Oppas had his own reasons for concealment of the truth. He replied, evasively:

"Indeed, my son, I know nothing."

"Speak not to me of flight, then. I leave not Toledo till I see her and know all, and hear from her own lips whether I dare continue to look upon her with hope, or"——

He paused and clasped his burning brow with his hands for a moment; then starting suddenly, he was about to depart.

"Whither wouldst thou go?" demanded the archbishop.

"I know not; I am blind—I am without thought or direction," was the desperate reply.

"Nay, then, my son," said the archbishop, placing his hand tenderly upon the shoulder of the youth, "let me counsel thee."

"Restrain him not, father!" exclaimed Romano; "he does the will of a greater than thou. The spirit of the Lord is upon him, and His hand shall guide his footsteps. How hath He led him in safety, to the discomfiture of the pursuers. The fierce man, thirsting for his blood, stood up in the way of the Lord, and I smote him—even under the fifth rib I smote him, as the Lord had commanded."

"I must go, uncle," said Egiza to the archbishop, in a whisper. "I cannot remain here in safety, and I would not wish to do so. I must seek the palace gardens this night, since I may best penetrate them now undiscovered by the guards. But I would not have this strange priest to follow or go with me. Thou must divert his thought—his attention. Do not suffer him to pursue me."

This did not appear so easy a matter. The zealot seemed to consider himself the special attendant of the man of God; and when Egiza rose, he rose also—when he moved, he followed him—and when he spoke, the look of Romano denoted the watchful regard which he gave to every syllable that was uttered. But the ready thought of Oppas relieved the prince of his difficulty.

"Command him as thou wilt, my son," he replied to Egiza, in the same subdued tones; "he will obey thee. Speak to him with authority; it will the more insure thee his regard to what thou sayest, for he holds himself, by divine command, to be thy follower and servant."

"I will then bid him remain with thee," said the prince.

"By no means, since it may be that he has been seen in thy prison, and the murder of the keeper may be traced home to him. If he be found here, suspicion necessarily touches me, and it behoves me at this moment to be doubly cautious. Send him rather beyond the walls: stay, come with me while I will find thee a commission for him. But bid him await thy return here."

This dialogue was conducted in a whisper. Egiza, as the archbishop counselled him, bade the zealot await his return. He folded his hands upon his breast, and bowed reverently as he promised to obey.

"As thou wilt, holy brother. To move or to rest, to strike or to spare, even as thou commandest, am I resolved and ready. They serve not the Lord who serve Him not according as He wills, and not as they will themselves; and the self-willed and the stiff-necked He smiteth with the sword. Ay, He smiteth him with a sword in the moment of his presumption, and his pride is sorely humbled. I will await thee, holy brother, even as thou commandest; the will of God be done."

The archbishop, regarding the famished and enfeebled looks of the zealot, inquired if he needed not food.

"Food! holy father; no! This earthly tabernacle hath need of little, and that little I already have. My food is the contemplation of the Lord's glories, His mysterious ways, and His almighty providence In my fastings I have heavenly manna. The bread which supports me is His blessed love; the drink which refreshes me is the blood of His atoning grace. Shall I hunger after earthly and low meats, when such food as this is spread before me? I were most unwise to do so; and the taste were perverse which could endure the common viands of mortal desire, after such blessed refreshment."

"But thou wilt grow weak and weary, my brother, unless thou wilt partake of this mortal diet. Thy limbs are feeble now—thy face is thin and wan"——

"Feeble, my father! dost thou say? Alas! thou art blind to say so. The strength is great within me. Thou knowest not the power, under the Father, of these poor limbs. I smote him—thou shouldst have seen me smite him; though he had eaten of flesh, and was strong among men, after the common thinking of mankind—yet I smote him, even as the butcher felleth the ox, with a single blow did I smite him to the earth. Yet had he eaten in my sight—he and his wife! May the blessing and the bounty of the Lord be upon her and the child!"——

Egiza shuddered and turned away with a strange sickness, as he listened to these words. But the fanatic proceeded:

"He had eaten and drunken of earthly food, and he fancied that he was strong. He refused the Lord—he defied His power—and he perished. But I, who had not eaten, holy father—if thou wilt believe me—I, who had eaten but of the bitter root, and drank but of the simple water, for days and weeks—I, whom they call feeble and thin—with the blessing and strength of the Lord, I smote this strong man who had fed upon flesh daily, and he fell like an infant before my blow. Vainly did he strive; for though he lifted his arm to avert the blow, and would have grasped my throat with his extended fingers, yet the arm was palsied and the fingers were stiff, and they could not seize the flesh upon which they rested. Wonderful, wonderful is the Lord! He is a God doing wonders!"

The madness of the zealot was evidently increasing in even degree with his fast increasing feebleness; and anxious though Egiza was to obtain intelligence of Cava, and thinking indeed of little else, he could not forbear to linger and to listen to the peculiar idiosyncrasy which Romano's words developed. He little knew how completely his madness had been the result of that artful management of his uncle, of which he, too, had been, in another respect, the equally unconscious victim.

CHAPTER VII.

They left Romano, and proceeded to confer in another apartment. Here they resolved that the fanatic should be sent upon some business of fancied importance out of Toledo. This charge the archbishop assumed to himself—Egiza being required simply to instruct the priest to obey him, as if he himself commanded in each particular. The prince then demanded a dagger from his uncle, which he received, and hiding it in his bosom, he prepared to take his departure. When they returned to the room in which Romano had been left, they found him lying upon his face. He was faint with exhaustion; and though he seemed conscious of their presence and care, he did not at the moment give any evidence that he understood their words. The archbishop commanded that wine should be brought and poured into his mouth This revived him. A little food was brought at the same time, and an effort was made to force or persuade him to eat. But it was not successful. They poured a small quantity of wine down his throat, and a temporary reanimation of his frame was the consequence. Meanwhile, Egiza, taking advantage of the circumstances, left the palace; and though the eyes of Romano beheld his flight, and gleamed with disquiet and dissatisfaction as they beheld, yet his limbs refused their office. Their strength, of which he had boasted but a little while before, was seemingly all departed. It had been overtasked by the labors put upon it; and the probability is that the hallucinations of his mind had been in great part the result of his ascetic life and unnatural abstinence. He nevertheless pushed aside the attendants who administered to him, pointed to the door through which Egiza had fled, and strove to rise and pursue. But he could not; he sank back with a deep sigh and lay motionless on the floor. The archbishop at first thought that life had departed; but when he placed his hand upon the body, it shrank from his touch, and the next moment Romano raised himself to a sitting posture.

"The holy brother, my father? Where hath he gone? Shall I not see him? Hath he left me no tasks?"

"He hath, Romano; these will I deliver to thee in season."

The eye of the fanatic brightened, and a smile of pleasure rested upon his thin and pallid lip.

"Give them to me now, my father!" he exclaimed, striving desperately to rise to his feet.

"Nay, not yet," said the archbishop, persuasively. "There is yet time. To-morrow"——

"There is no to-morrow for me, my father. The Lord hath called me. I heard His voice but now, calling unto me, and I sank down in a swoon while I heard it. What the holy brother hath left for me to do, that must I do quickly. I have little time; keep it not from me; let me not go before my tasks be ended, and the good work done, which hath been left to me."

"Thou hast done thy work; thou hast been the faithful steward, and mayst go without fear to thy account."

"Said *he* so?" eagerly demanded the dying man. "Did he tell thee this, my father?"

The archbishop nodded in affirmation. Romano clasped his hands, and the muttered prayer and thankfulness of his lips were audible, though indistinctly syllabled, and the tear stood in his eye—the bright drop of a most pious gratitude—in proof of the delight which this intelligence gave him.

"Now am I ready to depart!" he exclaimed. "The day is done—the night is coming on—the weary shall rest....... Yet, father," he continued, rising and resting his form upon his elbow; "yet, father, if thou wilt believe me, I had nearly faltered—nearly sank back from the blessed heights—when the promised land lay before me. What a moment of blindness was that, my father!"

"What moment, Romano?"

"When I faltered."

"And when was that, my brother?" inquired the archbishop; not so much with a desire to know as to amuse and satisfy the mind of the dying man.

"When the Lord bade me strike. Then, then, I bethought me of the long communion I had had with Guisenard, ere he had sworn himself God's enemy and the oppressor of the brethren; and I bethought me of his wife, who is young and passing lovely. Many a time had I broken and blessed the bread in their habitation. Alas! that it was God's pleasure that I should do otherwise. This was my weakness, father; when I thought too much upon these things. I had almost stumbled, and fell back from the service; but I grew strong, when the keeper bade me sup with him. I smote him ere the speech was over; but I had almost missed, I had almost lost for ever the blessed crown which is before my hope in this hour. And there was yet one more trial to my soul, my father—one more trial, when the piercing shriek of the woman came to my ear, as we fled. Hush! hark! I hear it now!—now!—now!"

He clapped his hands upon his ears, shrieked loudly himself, then with one convulsive effort fell over upon the floor, still and lifeless as the man he had slain in his madness.

CHAPTER VIII.

The archbishop was confounded. He had not expected a death so singular and so sudden. He saw, from the moment of Romano's return with the fugitive, that the tenure of his life was slight as the solitary fibre from which the indefatigable spider depends with all his fortunes; but he looked to see him linger on while the quick and animating spirit of his phrensy was still within his bosom to sustain it. Such might have been the case, had any new duty been assigned him by Egiza, as the Messenger of Heaven. The pious fury which had sustained him so long without food, would have sustained him to the end. But the body—the frail garment of mortality—was, in his instance, upheld and warmed and invigorated by the moving principle of mind, wrought upon by the highest of all mortal powers, religious zeal, and concentrating every faculty of thought and feeling upon a given object. This object consummated, the chords were naturally and necessarily relaxed. The steward had fulfilled his trusts; to employ his own words, and at the same time afford the proper clue to his sudden death—the duties of life were fairly over, and the laborer had gone to his reward.

It was fortunate that, at the moment of Romano's demise, the archbishop was alone. Though confounded by the event, he did not forget his customary policy. He carefully closed the door of the apartment, secured the key, and leaving the body where it ceased to live, he retired to his own apartment. Here he deliberated upon what he should do in the present difficulties. It was manifestly necessary that the corpse should be removed. If, in the search which he knew would be made after the fugitives, it should be found in his dwelling, the suspicions which must follow in the mind of Roderick would be difficult to parry, and, as he well knew the scorn if not hatred which the latter entertained towards the priest—a scorn that only foi bore injury as it too little esteemed the object, or was governed by a policy that feared to break utterly with a powerful priesthood—he dreaded lest Roderick should identify him and his feelings with those of the deceased. This was a well-grounded fear, and it called for especial caution on his part, not merely to avoid the hostility of the despot, but to disarm those suspicions which might otherwise stand greatly in the way of his farther projects. It was his policy, not merely to avoid all question of his fidelity, but particularly to inspire the king with confidence in it. He aimed at the employment and direction of Roderick's power, not less than the aggrandisement and promotion of his own; and this could only be secured by a policy as tortuous and refined as his desires seemed to be ultimate and difficult. But the removal of the corpse of the fanatic was absolutely and immediately necessary. This was resolved upon; and the mind of Oppas, while he resolved, conceived a project in which boldness seemed the fruit of necessity. He gave orders to his servants to retire to their offices for the night, while he prepared to undress himself alone. This done, he arranged a habit which he wore only upon occasions of similar necessity, and which effectually disguised his person. Having put on this dress, he waited patiently the progress of the night. When the hour had become sufficiently late, he descended without a light to the apartment in which he had left the body of the monk, and with ease raised it upon his shoulder. The burden was slight. The miserable ascetic, to whose wretched system of life the irregularity of his mind and exhaustion of frame, might be ascribed equally, was a mere skeleton, and the powerful limbs of the archbishop, better calculated for the fatigues of the field than the humbling devotions of the cloister, bore the corpse as if it were unfelt. Cautiously moving through the apartments, Oppas made his way without interruption into the outer court of his dwelling, and paused under its archways, until he could note the appearance of the street. Finding all quiet, he emerged from his place of concealment, and went resolutely forward in the direction of the royal palace, which rose before his eyes at a little distance. He had not gone far when he beheld the shadow of a mule, and a man lying beside him, seemingly asleep, against one of the columns of the public aqueduct. He laid the corpse down upon the ground, and went forward to reconnoitre the spot. The man slept soundly. He was a water-carrier, and only waited thus the coming of morning to commence his duties. The goat-skins in which he carried the water, lay about and beneath him; and the patient mule, as if long accustomed to his present station, stood by, entirely untethered, and yet immovable. Having satisfied himself that he might pass unnoticed, the archbishop hastened back, and resumed his burden. He passed the aqueduct, and the sleeping man, in safety, and approached the palace. When he came in front of it, he paused abruptly, and sank behind one of the rude stone abutments of the fabric A soldier paced along sluggishly, before the court, and was then approaching. The apprehension of the archbishop was, that he might walk the whole length of the palace, and if he did he could scarce escape detection. To be discovered, was to lose everything, and the resolve of the stern churchman was as fierce as it was ready. He felt for the handle of his dagger in his bosom, made it easy to his grasp, determined, if he came nigh, to stab him to the heart. But he was spared such a cruel alternative. The soldier sauntered but a little distance in front of the court, then wheeled about, and proceeded in the same listless manner toward the opposite tower. With the change in his movement, the archbishop resumed his own, and reaching the entrance of the palace unobserved; immediately darted beneath the arches. It was here that he resolved to leave his burden; and with something of tenderness toward the corpse, he placed it directly before the massive gate which opened upon the great hall of the royal dwelling. This done, he hurried away. With cautious steps he moved onward until he had got fairly beyond the reach of the guard, when he resumed the unruffled and composed gait of one who had no motive for flight or fear. He reached his own habitation without any adventure, and slept, in an hour after, as composedly as if nothing had occurred.

CHAPTER IX.

Meanwhile, the hapless Egiza, was pursuing his own lonely pilgrimage to the gardens of the royal palace. He had once before scaled the walls, high and huge, which the tyrant had raised as a barrier, to keep away the intrusive footstep and the curious eye from the scene of his lustful and luxurious pleasures. There was no reason why he should not scale them again. He went forward, approached the walls, and prepared to do so; but while his hand grasped the rugged projection of the wall, and ere he sprang upward, he heard a murmur, and the tread of a footstep within. He paused and listened; the sounds at length died away, and with a reckless spirit, seizing the protruding rock, and swinging upward with elastic muscle, he planted his foot firmly upon a strong knob, that bulged out midway upon the wall, and, in another instant, looked down upon the lonely maze of grove and garden, that spread themselves out before his eye, in the spacious courts within. All was silent at that moment in the scene before him. The moon was just rising, and brought with her from the east a gentle breeze, that, as it came subdued among the flowers, was rather a melodious breathing than a zephyr. The deep leaves of the olive lay here and there like glittering specks of water before his eye, as they gave a plane surface to her rising glance; and the vine spreading with dark purple clusters, in a wanton maze that clasped even the tops of the gigantic oak-tree, and bound them in many places to the wall itself, upon which he leaned, and over it wandered with unrestrained luxuriance, made a roof to the verdant neighborhood, which rendered it a spot as secret and secure as it seemed sacred to the generous nature to which it owed so much. How beautiful was the night, even to his gaze! He had a soul open to such influences, and it was a source of frequent sarcasm, if not censure, on the part of his brother Pelayo, that he could dream away the hours in slumbrous groves, as idle as the birds that fill them. "At our birth," Pelayo was wont to say; "at our birth, Egiza had all the ballad minstrelsy," and the phrase denoted truly the pliant spirit of the now hapless youth to all gentle and natural influences. Though miserable, he could not even now reject the sentiment of loveliness which filled his soul, at the various pictures which lay before him The moonlight, rising over the gloomy towers of the palace, stole through the thinly scattered leaves and the open boughs, and lay, here and there, like so many silvery gems, mottling the dusky ground; while, on the thicker foliage, her glances rested as upon a plate of green and polished metal, which reflected back a loveliness that was even richer than that they received. A light more subdued, and therefore sweeter than that of day, played fantastically upon the gloomy towers of the palace, and the solemn crags of rock which furnished a natural wall to one portion of the garden, through the ledges of which the interrupted Tagus went slightly murmuring. Dark hollows in the rocks, and among the courts of the palace, where the light did not come, stood like so many lurking shadows, crouching for concealment. Upon those towers the eyes of Egiza were riveted in mournful anxiety. What were their secrets? How anxiously did he desire, yet how greatly did he dread to know what they could unfold. To think only, was to suffer a misery too acute for his endurance; and he was about to rise upon the top of the wall, and descend to its inner base, when a slight rustling in the leaves below warned him to use greater caution. He drew back and listened quietly, though with unspeakable impatience, for other sounds, while his eye peered watchfully over the wall. In a few moments a soldier emerged from the chesnut-grove, which lay at a little distance off, the thick foliage and massive limbs of which had entirely concealed him, and the glittering shaft of his silver-headed pike waved as he paced along within a few feet only of the eye of the fugitive. He could have grasped it with a sudden effort, and had there been but one soldier, and no other mode of entrance into the garden, he would not have scrupled an instant to have done so. But in another moment a second soldier made his appearance from an opposite point, and the two moved off together in the direction of one of the towers of the palace, to the guard of which they seemed to have been assigned. Egiza readily saw the risk and danger of descending from the spot at which he stood. While he gazed and listened, his eye turned on the wall which lay by the Tagus, and partly within its waters, the murmuring sounds of which had guided his ears, and insensibly attracted his sight; and he saw that the region of the garden upon which he looked lay in greater depth of shade than any other. He readily conceived that in this quarter the grounds would not be so well guarded as that lying toward the city, and the thought which prompted him to seek an entrance in that direction was instantly acted upon. He leaped once more to the ground outside the wall, hurried around the heavy blocks of palace and prison, which lay between him and the river, and soon reached its margin. A little farther observation only was necessary; to enable him to see that it was easy to enter from this quarter. The majestic river floated on calmly beside him, but as it shallowed to its shores in little rivulets, and broke upon the rock of wall that divided it from the garden, where its murmurs made a fitting music for the triumphant and stately march of the stream which went on so unheedingly, he felt that he could wade easily to the ledges that lay at the foot of the wall, and he then thought that with the assistance of the shrubbery that grew thickly, even amid the shallows, he might readily effect his ascent. He pressed forward unheeding the depth of water, though, in some of the hollows of the stream, he found himself up to his waist. Passing over the rocks, which were scattered thickly about, he soon reached the base of the wall, and paused for momentary rest and observation. He sat upon a stone the while, which was covered with moss; around him the bushes were thickly waving, and from a cleft in a larger rock, which rose beside him, a ragged tree had shot upward, crooked and imperfect in its growth, but nevertheless admirably calculated to serve his purposes. Of this tree he availed himself to rise to the wall, and then his task was easy. The groves within were of a density which guaranteed security from all passing scrutiny, and no stir or sound below him indicated the presence of the jealous sentinel. Seizing upon the broad and massive limbs of a huge chesnut-tree which grew near an angle of the wall, he descended by its trunk, and once more found himself within the same inclosure with the beloved object of his affections and his fears.

END OF BOOK FOURTH.

BOOK FIFTH.

CHAPTER I.

Meanwhile, what of the unhappy Cava? We left her abandoned to despair, and eagerly desirous of that fate which, she predicted to her seducer, was approaching fast. The encouragement which she gave to her grief was calculated to contribute to the fulfilment of the prediction. Yet she had uttered no sorrow. She now poured forth no clamorous shriek, such as had startled the echoes of the palace when first king Roderick had committed his brutal violence. She was now silent in her wo, but it was the deadlier and deeper from its suppression. She sat apart from those who watched her, while her face wore all the rigidity of marble. Her ear seemed obtuse; she grew indifferent to what they spoke, and almost unconscious of their voices. When her eyes were uplifted they did not seem noteful of the objects upon which they were fixed. There was a glazed and death-like lustre in their expression, as if the tears had become frozen in the orb, and preserved its glow while utterly defeating its capacity to see.

Vainly did the maidens seek to interest, or, at least, to attract her attention. They tried the arts of music upon her, but in vain—they moved her not. They engaged in curious games beneath her eyes, but she took no heed of their progress; and they won and lost—exclaimed with disappointment and victory, without being able to secure a smile or a word from her for whose attention they toiled. At length the queen came to their assistance, and, dismissing them, she sought, and with more success, to attain their object. The victim turned her eyes with consciousness, and teeming with expression, upon her who was only less injured than herself. There was sympathy between them—the sympathy of a mutual suffering. The wrong which had destroyed the one, had gone like a burning arrow into the bosom of the other; and though Egilona had no reproaches for her husband, she was yet just enough to know how much he deserved them.

"I have a prayer to thee, Egilona," said Cava to the queen, as the latter concluded a kind wish to be allowed to serve her; "and thou mayest greatly serve me. Wilt thou do it—wilt thou grant to the poor Cava the only prayer that she will ever make to mortal again? Say, dear lady, that thou wilt—say, and I will bless thee, if, indeed, blessing from my lips be not hurtful to the pure like thee."

"Oh! speak not thus, my Cava—thou art pure, and blessed in thy purity. Give me to know thy wish, and I will endeavor to deserve and to secure thy blessing."

"But thou hast not said—thou dost not say," exclaimed Cava, with much anxiety, "that thou will grant me what I pray for. Tell me that thou wilt, ere I name it to thee, since it were vain to say to thee my desire and have it denied."

"If it be not wrong—if it be not of hurt to king Roderick, Cava, I will surely do what thou askest of me," replied the queen.

"Alas! if it be not of hurt to him who hath been of such grievous hurt to me! Well, even thus, Egilona, even thus will I pray thee. It is not of hurt to him—it is nothing—nothing in thy eyes or in his, but much in mine, which I now implore at thy hands. Say, then, that thou wilt yield thee to my prayer."

"Speak, Cava—tell me thy wish," said the queen, kindly, "and if it be as thou sayest—of no hurt to my lord, and in itself not wrong—I promise thee to do as thou wishest."

"Bless thee, bless thee! Thou wilt hear and judge for thyself. Thou wilt see that I ask nothing which should be hurtful to any; but, as one whose hours are numbered—who looks not to live many days—bring me pen and paper—I would record my last thoughts and wishes for the eye of one who should know them all."

"Ah! then thou wouldst write, Cava. Thou shalt have what thou prayest for. But thou speakest idly. Thy hours shall be long and happy; thou shalt live, and be blest with a devoted love"——

"Oh! vain, vain and cruel, Egilona, is the speech which thou utterest in my ears. Thou knowst that I cannot live—that I dare not live—that, as I have lost that which secures respect to life, and a proper love to woman, I have nothing left me now but to die. Do not, then, utter such words in my ears; thou knowest that they are idle, and thy own heart, to which I leave it, will tell thee that I cannot live—that I must die, or live as one utterly shameless in the world, as I am now utterly without hope of happiness in it. Jeer me not, then, with such idle fancies; and as for the devoted love"——

She paused; a shuddering went through her whole frame as she thought upon Egiza, and a worse bitterness than death was at that moment in her heart. Egilona felt that the poor victim had soothly spoken, and she resorted to other modes of consolation. These were not found so easily; and the hapless woman smiled with all the sadness of despair, as she listened to the fruitless efforts of the amiable queen. These she heard with patience to the end; and when the arguments of the speaker were exhausted, she quietly reminded her of her promise. Egilona rose, and was about to go forth in search of the things required, when Cava, seeming to recollect a forgotten thought, stayed her departure.

"Yet, my lady!" she exclaimed, "I would not that it should be known what thou bringest me. Fold it in thy shawl; let them not see it; let him—thy lord—let him not see it, above all, nor know what thou doest. He may else deny thee."

"Nay, wherefore doest think so, Cava? He will not deny thee. Thou doest him wrong."

"Do I?" exclaimed Cava, mournfully. "It may be; but I think it not. I would only be secure of having what I seek, and I would, therefore, have thee cautious; indeed, I would not that it should be known to other than thyself. Promise me, dear lady, that thou wilt be secret."

The queen promised her and departed, wondering at the suspicious nature which this last desire implied. But Cava was more sagacious than her mistress. She could better conceive the policy of Roderick; and she applied to the only person whom he had not thought it necessary to counsel in reference to his victim.

CHAPTER II.

Egilona brought her the parchment and the pen, which she carefully concealed from sight. The first moment in which Cava found herself alone she proceeded to make use of them. The fruits of her industry were the two following letters, addressed, one to Egiza, and the other to her father:

"Egiza—my lord, that should have been, had our hopes been blessed—farewell, farewell for ever. Hold me as one dead to thee, even if I be not dead to life. There is an impassable gulf between us. I cannot love thee, lest I should debase thee by affections which can never more be hallowed. I cannot keep thy love, since such cannot belong or be given to those who are degraded. I cannot look upon thee, even if I live, since I feel my shame, and should dread to meet with favor in thy eyes. Yet, for the love which thou didst bear me, give me thy pity now; let thy prayers go up for one who has not so much sinned as suffered sin—whose weakness of body, not whose willingness of mind, has given her up—a most unhappy woman—to the brutal rage of a tyrant. I can speak no more. My cheeks, which have been cold and pale, like the unfeeling marble, now burn me as I write thee. I dare not say what I have suffered—thou wilt scarce dare to conceive it. Yet, think only that I I am lost to thee, to hope, to life, to myself, for ever, for ever, and thou wilt know cannot tell thee. Once more, my lord—my noble lord—once more I implore thy pity and thy prayers for the wretched Cava."

This letter was not written without many efforts. The tears, shed freely now, which had been so long congealed in their fountains, stained the sheet. Her hand trembled, and when she had finished, her nerves seemed about to withdraw from her all sustaining strength. When a little composed, she wrote to her father, and though with as many tears, yet with far less effort and emotion. A sterner spirit seemed to pervade her soul, and as she had prayed to her lover for pity only, she now prayed to her father for revenge.

"Would it had pleased the Almighty!"—It was thus that she began an epistle which brought desolation upon the land, and watered every foot of its soil with the noblest and best blood of the people—"Would it had pleased the Almighty, my dearest father, that the ground had opened and swallowed me up, rather than that I had ever live to see myself reduced to this wretched necessity of writing to give you the knowledge of a disgrace which will cause an eternal disquiet in your bosom. The innumerable tears which have blotted, and almost effaced this whole letter, will let you understand the violence I do myself in writing you such unwelcome news. But I apprehend, that, if I should defer it one single moment, I might leave room to doubt whether, at the time when my body was defiled, my soul was not likewise stained with an indelible blemish. Who can ever put an end to our misfortunes except you repair the insult which has been done us? Shall we stay till time makes public what is, at present, a secret—when we shall be cursed with an opprobious name, more insulting than death itself? Oh! wretched and most deplorable destiny! In a word, my dear father, your daughter—your blood—this branch of the royal Gothic stock, who, like an innocent lamb, was recommended to the care of a ravenous wolf, has been violated by king Roderick. If you forget not what you owe to your illustrious blood, you will revenge the affront offered it, by destroying the tyrant who has so basely stained it. Remember that you are count Julian, and that I am Cava, your only daughter."

These letters she concealed, having first made duplicates—the better to secure the certainty of having one or other reach their destination. At this time she knew of no means of transmitting them. She had not thought much upon this difficulty. Her first object had been to procure the means of writing that which she well knew she would not be suffered verbally to communicate to either of those for whom her letters were prepared, and which, indeed, she very much doubted her ability to speak. This accomplished, her next thought was upon the mode of sending them. She had some trinkets—some rich gems, which had been employed in decorating that person whose charms they could not enhance, and which ceased, indeed, to maintain their value in such connection. It was by means of these trinkets that she hoped to effect her object. She had learned enough of the mercenary character of all around her to believe that she could readily bribe one of the maids about her to execute her desires. But while she reflected upon this part of her purpose, a dreadful thought came to her mind. The address upon the letter to Egiza lay before her eyes, and she shivered as she demanded of herself where he should be found. The dreadful doom to which she had been subjected, terrible and trying as it was, had too completely occupied her thoughts to suffer her to think of him. Where was he? she now demanded. Did he live? Had he not also fallen a victim to the ferocity of that tyrant whose unscrupulous lusts had destroyed her. With this apprehension she fell upon her knees—then upon her face, and long and fervent was the fond prayer for his succour and release which she poured forth to the ever-present God. Her prayer was heard, and the boon accorded to her. That very night Egiza was released from his prison, and was, though she knew it not, a close watcher, from the thick groves which concealed him, of those towers which still held her as a prisoner.

CHAPTER III.

The appearance of Romano's body at the gate of the palace, produced an astonishing sensation when it met the eyes of the populace on the ensuing morning. It was beheld by the water-carriers first, and they proclaimed it throughout the city. The soldiers on duty about the palace, dared not remove it, until commanded by their officers, and the citizens in the meantime collected from far and near to behold it. The fanatic was well known, and greatly esteemed throughout Toledo. By many among the lower orders, he was regarded as a saint; and the rigid and ascetic life which he invariably led, at a time and in a region where none were abstinent, and few moderate or just—these qualities in the deceased, had commended him to the favorable consideration of many who were not low; as it is not unfrequently the case that we admire the virtues in another, which we dare not ourselves practice, and which we admire probably for that very reason. The venerable features of Romano commanded respect, apart from his known character; and as the head keeper of the famous House of Hercules, he was regarded as one endowed with a sanctity beyond any of his fellows. When, too, it was recollected how grossly he had been spurned by Roderick, there seemed a solemn meaning in the fact of his having come to the door of the despot, in order to breathe his last; and this thought took various shapes at the expense of Roderick, as the crowd momently increased to survey the body, until they looked up and around them in anticipation, while they spoke freely of the judgments which were to follow.

By the time the sun had fairly risen, the crowd had increased to such an extent as to alarm the apprehension of the soldiers. Their murmurs were audibly uttered, and now and then a sentence from some hasty speaker, betrayed a spirit of insolence, which was very apt in those days to draw down summary punishment upon the heads of the populace. They all remembered the virtue of Romano, and the transition was easy from the virtues of the deceased to the vices of him who was supposed to have destroyed him. One of the speakers, a sturdy Gallician, endowed with all the pugnacity which distinguished his fierce tribe, was the first to approach the body of the deceased priest, and kneeling down reverently before it, to breathe forth his maledictions freely upon those, whoever they might be, whose cruelty had reduced it to its present condition. The language which he employed offended the jealous soldier who stood by, and with all the contemptuous insolence which marked the deportment of the military in that period toward the inferior and laboring population, he threatened to apply the staff of his spear to the speaker if he did not instantly depart. This threat aroused the other, who, in an instant stood upon his feet, and looked, if he did not threaten, defiance. His eye flashed fire, and his lips were compressed, while it could be seen that the short stick which he carried in his hand, and which was simply the handle for his panniers, was grasped firmly, as if about to be employed as a weapon of strife. His look and attitude irritated, if it did not alarm the soldier.

"Wouldst thou bite, dog?" he exclaimed. "Hence—get back to thy brethren! Begone, ere it be worse for thee!"

As he said these words, he advanced, and, with the point of his spear, pricked the Gallician in his side. To the surprise of the solders, no less than of the populace, the stick of the latter was raised instantly, and with one blow he shattered the spear of the soldier, breaking it completely in twain, just where the iron head was fastened upon the wood, and leaving nothing but the pole in the hands of his assailant. This daring act of insubordination was beheld with astonishment by the crowd, who, for a few seconds after, preserved a profound silence, awaiting the issue, for they looked every moment to see the bold Gallician hewn down by the approaching comrades of the soldier; but when they beheld the stupid wonder with which the latter stood, looking alternately at his broken spear and at his sturdy opponent, a unanimous and spontaneous shout, which made the area reëcho again, attested the delight which the circumstance afforded them. They had too frequently suffered under the insolence of the soldiery, which they dared not resent, not to rejoice in any rebuke which should give them that revenge which they had never dared of themselves to take; and shout succeeded to shout, and clamor to clamor, increasing rapidly, and stimulating momently that sentiment of new-born courage in the mob which came to them like a draught of intoxicating enjoyment. The clamor aroused the rage of the soldier, who instantly rushed upon the Gallician. Their weapons were more nearly equal now than before; and the short stick of the latter, while it effectually parried the thrusts of the soldier's staff—for he still used it as a spear—rang about his head with a quickness which he found it impossible to parry. A sharp stroke sent him reeling backward, and the Gallician pressed upon him. Luckily, at this time, several of the guards rushing from other sections of the court, came to his assistance, and the sturdy Gallicean, still waving his stick in triumph, gave back slowly before them, until he was sheltered in the crowd, which received him with joyful acclamations.

Their clamors chafed the soldiery, already irritated by the defeat of their comrade. They collected together, and resolved not merely to disperse but to chastise the populace. This, however, was no easy matter. The guards were few; but accustomed to strike without being resisted, they did not count the difference of numbers, and resolutely determined upon having satisfaction for the insult, which they had received. Besides, it was necessary that they should preserve the silence, not less than the security of the palace; and such now was the excited feeling of the mob, that their clamors increased with every moment of delay. The whole front of the court was covered with them; and their heads and hands swayed about with the increasing swell, like the waves of a broken sea. They were unarmed however, with the exception of a few staves and sticks, and the short knife—the handle and blade being both of steel—which the natives generally carried. These, unless the owners of them were determined upon extremes, could not have opposed effectually the small but drilled band of armed men that now advanced in a close body, compact as a wedge, upon the mass; and this determination was, as yet, lacking in the hearts of the greater number of that mighty but undecided mass. As those in front beheld the approaching soldiers, they turned, with one or two exceptions, to fly; but the crowd behind them, still increasing, and as yet ignorant of the danger of those within, opposed an effectual obstacle to their flight. The soldiers pressed upon them with a haste of step and a ferocity of demeanor which proved them to be quite in earnest, and rendered it necessary that those in danger should do what they could in the emergency to avoid or avert it. A few fell to supplications; but the greater number were silent and sullen—and one or two, the more resolute among them, already grasped the handles of their knives. At this moment the Gallician, who had been completely hidden in the crowd, was seen bustling forward to the front; and this temerity in seeking the danger which all others were disposed to fly, was hailed with murmurs of applause from many around him. But there was one in that numerous assembly—but one—who sought to restrain the fierce mountaineer. That was a female, a young girl, not more than fifteen, whose dark sparkling eye was now bright with tears of gathering apprehension. She grasped the arm of the Gallician, which was lifted high above the heads of the crowd, and bore aloft in its yellow hand a thick Gothic curtal-axe, which waved threateningly conspicuous in the eyes of all. Her words at the same time, pleadingly soft, were still audible to all around.

"Do not, do not, dear Toro!—remember our poor mother!—come with me, brother—she is waiting for us by the fountain, and if thou shouldst come to harm, what will become of her?—what will become of me? Do not go forward—thy life is precious—and see, where the guards come. Stay, stay!—go back with me, brother—help me out of the crowd."

"Unloose me, Toly!—let my arm go," cried the impatient brother, as he still pressed forward to the front, bearing the girl along with him, who clung resolutely to his arm, while she pleaded for his retreat.

"Be not rash, dear brother. Toro, Toro!—our mother, dear Toro!—she waits."

At this moment the charge of the guards was made, and the bristling line of pikes, bearing down upon the indecisive crowd, produced a terrible uproar and confusion in front. The assailed and unarmed line, thus exposed unwillingly, and unavoidably now, to the assailants, reeled back in consternation upon the dense and mighty mass, which was still gathering behind them, and while some fell, struggling and kicking confusedly upon the ground where they lay, others, with a supernatural exercise of physical energy, the result of their sudden and great terror, pressed their way farther back among the crowd, ever turning those immediately in the path, and bearing those along in their flight who yet seemed resolute to go forward. Of this number, was our bold Gallician. Vainly did he strive to resist the rush; for though possessed of immense strength for one of his size, it proved unequal to the task of opposing the impetuous progress of those whom the pressing terror was impelling in blind confusion. Hoarsely he cried aloud to them with bitter reproaches, while with arms and knees, and full and forward chest, he threw himself in the way of one after another of the fugitives. Meanwhile, the soldiers, provoked by a brutal indifference to the cruelty of such an assault, continued to thrust among the crowd with their spears, wounding severely and indiscriminately the miserable wretches who offered no resistance. But they urged the fugitives too fast, and the peasants, goaded, beyond patience, and unable to escape, like the trampled worm, turned at length upon their enemies. The Gallician beheld the awakening spirit of his brethren with delight, and with a joy which was absolutely furious; he shouted to them in brief, stern, quick cries, bidding them do as they beheld him do, and promising them success, if they would but show a proper courage. With an unscrupulous effort, which was almost violence, he broke away from the grasp of his sister, who still implored him with lifted hands to desist, and hurried forward. The young maiden strove to follow him, and though swayed about with every movement of the striving bodies around her, she contrived to keep him in sight. A spear was levelled at his throat the moment he appeared in front, which he parried first and then grasped with a prompt and efficient hand. In the next instant his axe clove the head of the soldier, whom, with a jerk upon the spear, he had drawn within reach of the blow, and he fell dead without a groan.

There was a dreadful pause after this had been done, but it lasted for an instant only. The soldiers, furious at what they saw, now turned their entire rage upon the Gallician, who was conspicuous in front, and he must have perished but that the blood dripping from his axe, which he bore within sight of the multitude, had a powerful effect upon them. They saw it on every side, and from the remotest members of the mass, a shout—the shout of a common appetite, of the ferce instinct of destruction—arose terribly on the air. The language of that shout was a stimulant to the mob, and it had an appalling meaning to the soldiers. They were now conscious, for the first time, that the mere pressure of the human mass in front of them, must be fatal, and they sought to amend their error. They now aimed to retire, until they could recruit themselves from the guards who filled the various stations in the palace and the neighboring gardens; but their movement had still farther the effect of inspiring the multitude. The members in the back ground, now farily conscious of what was going on within, and at the same time secure themselves, gave full exercise to their curiosity, and pressed forward, urging those within more densely between the walls of the court, and more immediately upon the soldiers. The latter sounded their trumpets of alarm; and a moment's consideration then came to the fierce Gallician. He now saw the beginning of the end, for which, in the first movements of his impulse, he had not prepared. He had struck at first, because of the personal indignity to which he had been subjected—he had armed himself and reappeared, because he perceived that his fellows were about to suffer for his offence; but it was only when he had advanced nearly to the front, that he knew of the presence of his sister. Taking advantage of the pause in the strife, occasioned by the falling back of the guards toward the inner court of the palace, he endeavored to bear the girl to a place of safety; he had already got his arm about her waist, and had lifted her from the ground, intending to bear her if practicable, through the crowd, when a hollow and deep voice from the midst of the mass attracted the general regard.

"Saint Romano! Saint Romano! my brethren!" was the sudden cry. Every eye was turned now upon the body of the fanatic, which lay upon the steps of the portal, leading to the inner courts, and to which the backward steps of the guard were turned.

"Shall we leave the blessed remains for his murderers to trample, my brethren?" continued the mighty voice.

"No, no, no!" was the cry from a thousand tongues.

"Saint Romano—the body of the saint is ours—let us bear it to the sanctuary of the Holy Church. Come, all ye who would be blessed, come! Give your hands to the labor, and let us bear the holy corpse of the saint to the bosom of the Holy Church!"

Such was the cry from hundreds. The deep voice from the bosom of the multitude was heard again, and its summons was potential.

"Saint Romano, the blessed martyr—whoso shall touch of his body, shall have eternal life."

This was enough. The enthusiasm became a fury, and from the farthest groups of the mob, to which this adjuration had extended, all strove in the effort to obtain possession or at least a touch of those holy remains which were to work out their deliverance and salvation. A common rage was in every countenance—eyes were kindled with hope, hearts beating with excitement and anticipation, while the compressed lips of all forbid the utterance of that breath, every particle of which seemed essential to the desired object. One short, one mixed cry, in which the unanimous motive was clearly uttered, was all; and the silence which followed it, was like a spell. There was something terrible in the sight of thousands, thus striving and toiling forward, in one direction, with one aim, with all their strength, and their souls evidently going with their efforts, yet in such profound silence.

The rush of the mighty mass was irresistible. Vainly did the fearless and strong Gallician, sustaining his lovely and terrified sister in his arms, endeavor to stem the torrent, and maintain his ground. His teeth were shut together—his axe lifted to threaten—his whole frame thrown forward—his head thrust down, like that of a wild-bull when he meets the sudden hunter, resolute to rend the approaching enemy; but in vain. Vainly would the advancing individual, whom thus he threatened, have sought to turn aside and avoid him. He was but one of the thousand wedges of the impelling mass behind. The study Toro was drawn forward and compelled to join in the rush; but he still bore his trembling and panting sister aloft, unhurt, though terrified in the last degree, by the pressure of the crowd and the madness of its every movement. The guards turned at the entrance of the court, and presented their spears immediately over the corpse of the newly created saint. But of what avail were such weapons, or weapons of any sort, in opposing men on the eve of salvation? The spears were dashed aside, and even where they took effect upon the body of one or other of the mob, the individual only thrust himself still more impetuously upon the shaft, which was buried in his body, willing to perish, if he could only fall upon the miserable but worshipped remains which lay before him

The efforts of the guards were unavailing. Indeed, they were utterly surprised by this unwonted outbreak of the people, and they were divested, in consequence, of half their accustomed confidence. They were borne back from the body of the fanatic, over whch their spears had been crossed, and, separated in the rush from one another, broken and disordered, they fled tumultously through the passage leading to the inner court, and sought safety by the most dastardly flight from a pursuit which they thought would have been continued. It was here that they should have made their stand. The passage was narrow, and might have been maintained by their small number against thousands. But they had been completely terrified by the sudden, unusual, and unlooked for exhibition of the popular rage, and they fled, without being conscious, for several minutes, that they were not pursued.

CHAPTER IV.

The only object of the mob had been obtained. In all their rage they had never contemplated an assault upon the palace of their tyrant. This may have been the desire of some, but the great mass, as yet, were in possession of too few thoughts, to dream that they had other rights than those of service, and other hopes than those of animal indulgence in this life, and vague ideas (scarcely less animal in their promise,) of salvation in the next. Religious frenzy had drawn them forward, and having the sacred remains in their possession, for which they had ventured life, and the touch of which was to give them life eternal, they were satisfied with their achievement. The corpse was lifted from the ground; and when it appeared in the arms of those who had the felicity first to lay hands upon it, conspicuous to the eyes of all, and over the heads of the mob, their shrieks of fury were changed to shouts of congratulation. From hand to hand the sacred remains were borne aloft by the populace, its course altered momently in compliance with the will of the boldest or the pressure of the strongest handed. Now it was hurried in one quarter, now in another; and in their enthusiasm, grasping it from every direction, it was in great danger of being torn in pieces. Some leaped above the heads of the mass, pitching forward recklessly in their efforts to touch at least the garment which it wore. Mothers lifted up their infants as the carcass was hurried by, that the unconscious babes might obtain the valuable pressure for which they could make no effort; and in the madness of the moment, fierce men strove with one another, even to blows, for that contact with the object of their common veneration from which so much was hoped.

But the Gallician, Toro, beheld their fanaticism with scorn. He had been busy, from the moment of the flight of the soldiers, in the effort to extricate his sister from the press of the crowd. To this object he had devoted all his strength; but he had striven idly. The impetuous torrent bore him from side to side, with his precious burden, until his strength was almost exhausted. In vain did he seek to command attention by his voice. There were none to listen. None gave heed to any object except the poor remains of a man, a victim to madness like their own, whom, in their folly, they had sanctified.

"Accursed fools!" exclaimed the Gallicean; "they will waste time with their plaything, until the guards collect and crush them."

His speech was uttered sufficiently loud for all to hear, who stood around him. Indeed, he addressed words to the same effect to many. But groans of devotion and shrieks of delight, drowned his voice and defied his arguments; and panting and striving, at least to preserve his position, and protect Toly against their pressure, he was compelled to abide the progress of events, and wait patiently until their madness should have found its termination in their general physical exhaustion. Meanwhile, the crowd pressed to and fro upon him, and he was compelled to resort with every moment to stern words and sharp strokes, to secure his place. The terrors of his sister were duly increased as she beheld the increasing violence of her brother. He could scarce forbear the use of his curtal-axe, when some zealot, more furious or less heedful than the rest, encroached upon the little space which he maintained as a sort of boundary in front of him; and to the howling of this or that devotee, he had bitter words and fierce execrations. Toly dreaded lest the harsh language of her brother should provoke retort, and probably violence; but he had no such fear.

"Nay, they do not hear me," he would reply to her exhortations; "they are too mad to hear—they are deaf and stupid; and even if they did hear, I care not. A set of cowards—the base scum; if they had but the proper spirit, we should have torn down these walls and left not one stone of the palace upon another. The place was ours—had they but gone forward, it would have been done, and we should have had our revenge. Now, it is hopeless. They will waste all their strength upon the body, or upon one another, and by noon they will fly like hares from the dog, if they see but a single one of the soldiers, whom they have just now driven. Ay, roar fool!" he exclaimed, as one ragged wretch rushed by him, with a wild shout, hurrying toward the group over whose heads at that moment the corpse of Romano was in progress—"roar and howl—'t is all that you are fit for. The prick of a spear-head, and the stripes of a green thong, are your proper counsellors. They only keep you right, and send you forward, and keep your brute madness in check!"

"Oh, Toro! do not speak thus, or speak not so loud," said Toly. "If they hear they will strike—they will hurt you."

"Let them try—the curs—let them try!" and the Gallician waved his axe, while, as if to prove his scorn, he thrust forth his foot as one of the group rushed by him, and the fellow tumbled over the obstruction and went forward at full length to the ground. The fierce laugh of the Gallician followed his fall, and afforded the injured man but an equivocal atonement for the wanton indignity which he had suffered; but, when he rose and looked upon the offender, he saw enough in his countenance to satisfy him that he was not the sort of man whom he could trifle with. Hurrying on, therefore, the fellow joined the crowd—while Toro, the offender, turning to his sister, with a laugh, exclaimed:

"You see, Toly, what spiritless wretches these are—how worthless. I only wonder that they pressed the soldiers as they did. Indeed, they never would have done so of themselves. The pressure came from those without. They were in no danger, and they knew it; and they were not unwilling to have their sport at the expense of those within. The fiends light on them; but I fear that they will make us suffer yet. I would, that you were out, Toly. Why did you follow me?"

The girl pressed his arm, but said nothing. At that moment a dreadful shout rang through the crowd.

"Raise me, Toro, and I can see, and tell you," said Toly to her brother, while he was vainly striving, on tip-toe, to look over the waving, rolling and reeling heads of the dense mass before him. He did so, and the cry of the girl was immediate.

"It is a woman, Toro!" she exclaimed. "They have raised her up—fie—fie—her neck is bare, and yet she does not heed it. She scrambles among the people—they tear her clothes—they will kill her, Toro—they pull her about so. No—they seem to carry her forward. How she screams and laughs. Ah! I see—I see"——

"What, Toly?"

"The body of the holy man, brother. It is that which she strives at. She clambers over their heads, I know not how; and yet they pull her back—some pull her back—some push her forward. Hark! hear how she screams. She has nearly reached the body. Now, now—she grasps—she siezes it by one arm. She falls—they have let her down—no! they lift her again, and oh! Toro, how they have torn her clothes. Take me down, brother, I must not look—I would not see It is too ugly."

Toro gently let the maiden down, while, mounting upon a small rock, he strove to behold the scene which she had witnessed and in part described. The woman of whom his sister had spoken, was still in sight—a virago, evidently, of immense strength and size. By dint of violent exertions, she had forced her way among the men; now on equal terms struggling with them upon the ground, and now rising above their heads, sometimes with their help, but most frequently in defiance of their opposition. She had at length succeeded in grasping one arm of the sainted Romano. To this she clung, while those in possession of the body tugged a different way. At length she fell to the ground, but this did not have the effect of making her relax her hold. On the contrary, it not only gave to her increased powers for retaining it, but enabled others around her to seize upon the same unconscious limb, and to unite their strength with hers in opposition to the equally determined fanatics who had possession of the body. The tide of numbers swayed to and fro, under this conflict. Shouts and screams filled the air from both parties, as they severally gained or lost an advantage in the strife. Almost naked to the waist, the fierce woman still struggled and fought, with all the vigor and more than the madness of the men around her. The fury of a tigress seemed to fill her bosom, and now she raved and now she swore, while, in her efforts, she did not scruple to seize, even with her teeth, the arm of one of those who drew in the same direction upon the lifeless and yielding limb. Piece by piece the sleeve that covered it was torn away, and the withered and yellow flesh was left in her tenacious grasp. She held on to her prize as if life and immortality were hers in consequence. Nor was the hold of those in possession of the body less unyielding. They strove with redoubled efforts to bear away their relic entire. Wherever a hand could secure a hold, it was taken; and those who could not, grasped firmly upon the more fortunate arms which did. At length the joints yielded—they twisted the fibres which secured the shoulders—then tugging with diligent ferocity on both sides, they wrenched the arm from the socket, and the flesh and fibres were separated and torn in fragments, like decayed and worthless rags. A wild shout of delirious triumph rent the air, and in the same moment the ragged and bleeding limb was seen waving in the eyes of thousands, above their heads, in the hands of the fierce and triumphant virago. She was alone in the possession of the prize. The men who had joined with her in the struggle had relaxed and withdrawn their grasp, when the limb separated. A feeling of natural horror ran through every bosom, even among those who had been most active in the strife. But she suffered from no such sentiments. Her shrieks were preëminent above the clamors of the crowd, and the Gallician shuddered as he beheld her, armed with the yellow, meagre, yet blood-dripping limb, forcing a passage through the crowd by the sheer force of that terror which its approach seemed to inspire. His feelings of disgust would not permit him to look longer, and with a shiver he descended from his perch, and clasped the frail form of the young girl beside him to his bosom, with an increased apprehension, which the spectacle he had witnessed was well calculated to occasion.

"Oh, Toly! what would I not give if you were free from this press!" he exclaimed, as he put his arm fondly about her waist.

"Do try, Toro, and get me out. Our poor mother will fear that harm has come to both of us, unless we go to her directly."

Toro looked about him with many anxious doubts.

"Harm will come to us," he muttered to himself, "unless we can get out now. We have little time left us."

"What say you, Toro?"

"Nothing, Toly—only follow me. That mad woman has left an opening, and if we could only reach it, we should be safe. Follow me closely. Grasp my doublet thus, and keep close. I will get you out, if the strength of a man may do it."

He placed the skirt of his doublet in her hand, and resolutely pushing among the crowd, he led the way, and Toly, trembling at every movement, clung close, and strove to follow him through the opening which, by sheer resolve of temper and strength of arm, her brother sought to make.

CHAPTER V.

But their progress was necessary slow and scarcely perceptible. They had not proceeded ten paces when a sudden clamor was heard—the clamor and the clash of arms, the unfolding of heavy gates, and the rapid tread of approaching soldiers. The inner court gates had been thrown wide open, and the Gallician augured from this that the guards were about to return, mounted on horseback for the strife. With the thoughts of the plunging of horses among the unarmed and crowded population, he turned quickly and caught up his sister in his arms.

"What is that, brother?—is there danger?" she demanded, trembling with new terrors as she looked upon his countenance, where ferocity began to be qualified by apprehension and anxiety.

"Ay, Toly—a little, but not for you, Toly. You shall be safe."

She clung to him as she cried:

"Yes, Toro, you can save me, I know. You are strong enough—as strong as any of these men. But, make haste, Toro, for I fear the crowd, and they squeeze me dreadfully now."

He set his teeth firmly and made no answer as he struggled forward with his burthen, but he muttered to himself while he did it, and, to the quick ear of Toly, his mutterings were half audible.

"I will try to save you, Toly—with my own life will I try. I am strong, true, as any one of these, but not as all."

"Oh, Toro! what is it you say? Can you not save me? Haste, brother! remember our poor mother—let them not crush me thus. Save me! save me!"

The breathing of Toro was suppressed awhile. He strove with the right arm extended, and bearing the girl in the other, to force the passage. While he strove, one of the flying crowd who was behind him, grappled his shoulder with the same object. The fierce Gallician turned and smote him in the mouth with the handle of his axe which he still held firmly, as a weapon might soon become imperatively necessary. The fellow gave back in terror, and Toro resumed his flight. A woman lay struggling under his feet—the terrors of the girl within his arms made him reckless, and the bosom of the fallen and writhing victim became his stepping stone, as it had already been that of hundreds. He pressed onward, certainly but slowly, and began to hope; but, looking over the track before him, the entire area was still covered with dense and struggling masses. He was almost spent. The sweat trickled from his brow, and the weight grew almost insupportable upon his arm.

"Oh, Toly!" he exclaimed, in mournful accents, which reproached her more painfully than stern language could have done—"oh, Toly! why did you follow me!"

"Forgive me, brother," she whispered, rather than spoke—"forgive me—I was a foolish child—forgive me and save me! Save me, Toro, this time, and I will never vex you again. I will try and do everything for you, Toro. I will never marry—no! not even if Diego should ask me—if you will only save me."

He kissed her—amid the crowd, none of whom beheld it—he kissed her, while he murmured, resolutely but sadly:

"Ay, Toly! if I die for it, I will save you. Be of heart, and let us try once more. The Blessed Mother be with us—we will try once more."

CHAPTER VI.

MEANWHILE the crowd became conscious of the approaching danger. They regarded no longer the body of the fanatic, which fared more fortunately than the living thousands over whose heads it was hustled. It was borne in triumph out of the mass, and was received by those who remained on the outside, and who bore it away in triumph, to be hoarded up with other relics equally valuable and equally maddening to the minds of thousands as well in that as in times more remote. The escape of the living in that dense mass was not so readily effected; and, pressed on every hand, in a court which was narrow in proportion to its great length, having no guidance but the individual impulses which drove each other in a different direction, and to the obstruction of one another, they struggled vainly for escape. Confused by their fears and mutually baffled by their various impulses, when the alarm was given from within of the approaching soldiers, they grew blind with very terror. Shouts and shrieks of fear filled the area where they struggled, and falling upon each other in heaps in their vain efforts at flight, they presented no obstruction to those who sought their destruction.

The sound of a single trumpet silenced the clamors of the mob with increasing terrors. Toro, the Gallician, still maintaining his burden, with failing limbs but with unrelaxing resolution, with writhing neck, and eyes cast for a moment behind him, sought to discern the condition of things among the enemies at whose mercy he well knew the wild, thoughtless, yet cowardly wretches were, who strove with contrary minds at a single and common object. That one look was all that was allowed him. In that glance he beheld Roderick himself rushing forth, mounted, at the head of the guards, part of which were also on horseback, and attended by Edeco and a few other noblemen. The king was in armor, but without his helmet. His armor seemed to have been put on hurriedly, and his weapons seized in haste. The Gallician saw that his features were full of fury. Indeed, it would be an idle attempt to depict the anger of one like Roderick, the spoiled child of fortune, and for so long a time accustomed to the most complete exercise of his own will, and the most brutal disregard to the rights, not less than to the will, of all others. It was absolutely fearful even to the eyes of one, like the Gallician, so entirely indifferent to all the minor influences of fear. His eyes glared like those of the wild-boar, whom the spear of the hunter hath pierced at the very entrance of the den where his young are hidden. His cheeks were the color of a bright and sudden flame—his hair floated wildly above his head, and its raven hue still more contributed to give an air of fierce resolution to the almost scarlet terrors of his face. While Toro gazed, he instinctively pressed forward; he saw that though there were numbers still between the tyrant and himself, on whom his vengeance must first be wreaked, he was yet conscious that these would offer but a brief obstruction to the passage of men on horseback. To throw a greater number between was an object therefore, but this was the object of hundreds, who were not, like himself, incumbered with a burden, the weight of which, if it did not enfeeble the mind, increased its anxiety, and oppressed it with apprehension that weighed it down, even more effectually than its physical pressure did his body. The prayers and pleadings of the poor girl—her entire dependence upon the strength and resolution of her brother, greatly increased both, and never did man yet labor more desperately, and strive with less fear and more zeal to achieve his object, and secure the saftey of the beloved one and the depending.

Help, Holy Mother!" he prayed inwardly—"help, Holy Mother!—give me strength—thy blessed favor upon the young girl, not yet fifteen—a pure virgin, who keeps thy thoughts in her mind, as, when she is at home in her chamber, she hath thy image for ever before her eye. Be thy white arms of blessedness about her neck, so that she be saved to our mother, and if it please thee, serenest Virgin, I will return to the strife, and fight for thy grace and honor. Be with her, Mother of God, and help us forth from these numbers!"

He did not pray only. He struggled bravely; but the Virgin did not heed his prayer. The density was greater than ever, and in the next moment, Roderick charged headlong, followed by his nobles and guards, upon the terrified and shrieking populace. However provoked it may have been at first, nothing could have been more wanton or unprovoked than this movement now. The people were only turbulent in flight. They were seeking, on all hands, to effect their escape, and would have been glad to disappear, and would soon have dispersed, had sufficient time been allowed them. But this would have been no gratification to the reckless and remorseless tyrant, to whom the unnecessary display of his power, in its most cruel forms, was the highest pleasure. He had no thought, no mercy, for the thoughtless and unreckoning wretches who were then scrambling forward in the very attitudes —those of flight and fear—which would rather have called for the smile and forbearance of the wise and merciful ruler, than his blows and fury. He charged upon them as they flew—he smote recklessly on all hands, and looked not to see whether his weapon descended upon the head of the resisting or trembling man—whether he struck the wildest of his own sex, or the weakest and gentlest woman. His example was closely followed by his soldiers, and for a few seconds their horses trampled and their weapons mangled none but unresisting and screaming fugitives.

But this could not last for ever. The sheer physical impracticability of flight where such numbers struggled, was, of itself, sufficient reason why those should turn to defend themselves who could no longer hope to fly. They did so with their staves and sticks, and such rude instruments as they had seized in their haste. At first they did not aim at anything more than to parry the thrusts of the soldiery; but this show of defence was soon changed into positive conflict, by the ill-judged haste and ill-reasoning anger of the king. He could not brook to see the base plebeians striving even to protect themselves from harm, and with increased impetuosity charging them himself, he bade those who followed him do likewise. They needed no second exhortation—they rushed on with a fury kindred to that which now filled the bosom of their savage master, and only paused in their brutal melee, when it became necessary, for the slaughter of more victims, that they should tear away their pikes from the writhing bodies, to which they had already given the fatal and the final strokes.

The madness of despair seized upon the crowd, and they grappled the spearmen about their necks while engaged in this bloody work. Roderick, shouting the war-cry of the Goth, plunged amid the thickest of the fray, cleaving down with his heavy-handled sword, all who stood before him. The rising hoofs of his steed hung over the heads of the brave Gallician and his trembling sister. The madness which filled the crowd wrought with redoubled violence upon him. With a mighty strength he raised her above the crowd, and throwing her forward, by this means increasing the space between the poor girl and the ferocious monarch, he stood alone, and more ready and resolute to confront his fury. As the hoofs of the steed descended, he leaped aside and boldly grasped the bridle with his hand. His swarthy cheek grew purple with his rage—his coal-black eye looked the anger which the words from his lips expressed and as Roderick beheld the look, the action, and the general manner of the Gallician, he could not but see in him one who would not scruple, if it needed, to strike even at the bosom of royalty itself. The thought enraged him, and rising on his stirrups, he waved his sword above the head of poor Toro, resolved that the descending blow should cleave him in twain.

"Ha! slave!" he exclaimed twice, as he struck. He struck heavily, but the blow descended upon a head which it could not harm—the steel was buried in the skull of one whom he had slain before. The agile Gallician, as he saw the meditated stroke, swinging upon the bridle of the steed which he had grasped, threw himself completely under the animal's neck, and out of the way of the impending blow. In the next instant, and ere the tyrant could recover his weapon, the sharp knife of Toro was driven up to the handle in the bosom of the plunging animal. He bounded forward among the crowd, uttered one wild snort of fear, and struggling and plunging with his fearless rider, he sank dead, while the populace, unable to escape, closed around him.

"Toly! Toly!" cried the Gallician, in a piercing voice of terror.

A faint cry came to his ears in return—a suffocating cry, and he shivered, though he rushed forward as he heard:

"Toro! oh, dear Toro!" said the gasping accents.

"Here Toly! I come—I come!"

"Come!" was the faint and scarcely intelligible word with which she replied. He leaped with an agonizing apprehension over the heads of those who stood between him and the spot from whence the sounds arose—he dashed aside the peering heads of the curious and the trembling, and paused in doubt, for he knew not where to turn. The hoarse voice of Roderick was heard at the place where his steed had plunged and fallen; and then, once more, the faint accents came to his ears, seemingly from the same quarter:

"Come, Toro! come!"

He rushed forward, though the enemy was there. He could see the form of Roderick rising—he could hear his furious language—and his uplifted sword was visible to his eyes; yet he hurried toward him. The faint voice of his sister was again heard in a feeble scream, which at length died away in a murmur. He leaped on the dead horse—her face was barely visible beneath it. Her eyes were closing, but a faint light was perceptible to his beneath the shutting lids. She seemed to recognize him, and the lids partly receded, while she looked upon him. In another instant they were shut for ever.

CHAPTER VII.

He stooped to the body. He strove to drag the crushed and mangled remains of the girl from beneath the carcass, but he could not, and he trembled—for the heart of man never believes in the utter insensibility of that which it loves—lest he should hurt the innocent, of whom, in life, he had regarded the lightest curl of hair with a fondness which would have prompted him to risk life freely in its protection from the slightest harm or the most casual indignity. He shrunk back from the task—

the terrible truth came upon him in frenzy—the sister of his boyhood—the child whom he had loved almost alone of all the world—the favorite of his aged mother, and his own, she was dead—and such a death! Crushed, trampled down, and mangled beneath furious and flying men, and the hoofs of the agonized war-horse, himself stricken with death, and by his arm. He sank down beside the body—lifted the long and raven locks which were dabbled and clotted with her own blood, and gazed upon the terrible spectacle for an instant in speechless horror. Shrieking and shouting he started to his feet. Fury was in his soul, and he panted for revenge. What then was the uplifted sword of the tyrant—what the pikes of the soldiers! He felt them in his flesh; but there was a deeper wound within his soul which made him indifferent to their tortures. He rushed fearlessly upon the king, and defied his weapon. Fired with his spirit, and unable to fly, the populace gathered around him, and answered his shouts with their own. The uplifted arm of Roderick was grappled by one from behind, and his balanced weapon shone idly in the air. It was not suffered to descend. Toro rushed upon him while in that situation. Already his knife glared in the eyes of the monarch—another moment and it would have been buried in his heart; but with the desperateness of his situation came increased powers of body and resolve of mind to the beleaguered king. He dropped his sword which had thus been made useless, and shaking off the assailant who held his arm, he grasped that of the fierce Gallician. Vindictive and maddened as he was, his strength was not equal to that of Roderick, and though the latter could neither overthrow him, nor wrest from him his knife, yet was it equally impracticable for him to inflict any injury with it upon his regal opponent. Thus they stood—thus they strove, like two angry demons, contending fearfully, yet in vain, while all were striving around them. But though Toro could do no harm to his foe, his grasp kept him in a situation which momently exposed him to the assaults of others, and but for the desperate devotion of his guards, Roderick must then have perished. But they clung to him in his peril with a fidelity worthy a far nobler service. They fought and fell—the plebeian knife was drenched in their blood, without discouraging those who yet survived. They girded their master to the last—presenting their weapons like men, and unsparing of their own bosoms while seeking to cover his. One of them grappled Toro and sought to tear him from his hold; but he, in turn, was seized by one of the populace, and fell a victim to his boldness. The crisis was momently becoming more fearful to the environed monarch. His guards were diminishing—the mob growing proportionably strong, and from their obvious advantage, more and more resolute and wild. A shudder, but not of fear, convulsed the frame of Roderick, as he became conscious of this fact. To die thus ignobly—in such a strife—bound like a slave—without arms—without even a breathing field and room to struggle; this was not merely to die, but to die shamefully. Toro felt his convulsion, though it lasted but for an instant, while he grappled him.

"Ha! tyrant! dost thou tremble! Thou hast slain the weak and the innocent—the trembling innocent; who could not help themselves, nor hurt thee! Yet thou tremblest!"

"Not with the fear of thee or them, slave!" was the fearless reply of the monarch, as he strove with renewed but unsuccessful efforts, to extricate himself from the iron grasp which the Gallician had taken. Toro with clenched teeth replied:

"Slave though I be, it will not be long ere I am thy master—master of thy life. Look, tyrant! they come. Ho! men! slaves and knaves, hasten! Here is work for you. Ha! ha! ha! Dost see them—dost see them? Look! they hasten. What though I strike thee not myself; yet I bind thee for the knife! Ho! there! Will you not strike?"

A gigantic serf from the mountains of Asturia sprang forward, and vainly did the presented spear of one of the soldiers seek to arrest his progress. An unarmed peasant of Andalusia threw himself forward upon the extended shaft, and it snapped like a brittle reed beneath his weight. The arm of the Asturian was lifted; his knife pointed to the king's bosom, and no seeming hope of his escaped remained. But nothing daunted, though weaponless, motionless, and at the mercy of the peasant, the king abated none of his fearless spirit. Gazing steadfastly at the enemy, he exclaimed with a stern voice:

"Slave! wouldst thou strike thy sovereign? I am Roderick the Goth."

The very name of his victim appalled the executioner. The mark was too high for the soul of the peasant, and he sank back among the crowd, with more terror than had troubled the bosom of him whom he had threatened.

The peril was passed. That moment saved Roderick. A new ally came to his aid. Shouts rang from the scattered soldiers, who still fought, though feebly, with different bodies of the populace, unable to help their master, or to extricate themselves. The shouts went warm and cheering to the almost hopeless monarch. He turned a quick, momentary glance around him, and beheld charging horsemen. The sight had its effect, though of a different nature upon the Gallician. Vainly now did Toro strive to use his knife. The king was invigorated by hope, and his enemy strove without success. The horseman came on rapidly to the charge, and taken in the rear, the populace were seized with consternation. They were beaten down on every side. Two hundred armed and well mounted warriors were upon them, hewing fiercely among the undaunted and half-exhausted peasants. A voice from his new allies came to the ears of Roderick, and it no less astounded than cheered him. It was the voice of one upon whom of late he had not counted. It was the archbishop Oppas, who came to his rescue, heading his own retainers.

"Rid me of this knave, my lord Oppas, and name thy own reward!" cried the king, as the archbishop approached him. Toro released his hold upon the king, in order to encounter the new comer; but Roderick relaxed not his. He held the arm of the Gallician, while the huge mace of the archbishop descended thrice upon his head. The second blow had slain him, and the brother lay in death by the mangled remains of the hapless maiden whom he did not desire to survive. The fight was ended with the blow; but Toro was not the only sacrifice to the fury which he had helped to provoke. Nearly three hundred serfs perished, along with a goodly number of the soldiers by whose arms they fell. Yet, among the carcases that strewed that unhappy field of blood, they found not that of Romano. Devotion had achieved its object, and the sacred bones had been carried to a place of safety and concealment, long ere the strife had ended.

CHAPTER VIII.

This scene of tumult and terror which we have endeavored, though feebly, to describe, though seemingly irrelevant to the progress of our narrative, was yet not without its influence in favor of one of its chief personages. It gave an opportunity to Egiza to emerge from his place of concealment, and advance boldly through the garden to the rear of the palace, before the courts of which the strife was still going on. He heard the clamor, he beheld the rapid progress of the guards, as, in obedience to the prevailing necessity, they were drawn from their several stations, in order to make head against the insurgents; and, though he had not the least idea of the cause of such commotion, he readily divined that it arose from some outbreak of the popular spirit. As the guards left the garden, he approached the palace, and giving no heed, and scarcely an ear, to the loud shouting and fierce cries in front, he was only solicitous to seek and see the one ruling object of his thoughts and his affections. Not with such a spirit as this would his brother, the single-minded Pelayo, have welcomed such a commotion. He would have hailed it as the beginning of a strife in which he was secure of triumph. To rouse the spirit of the populace against their tyrant had been the labor and the wish of both. It had been a tedious labor, and it seemed almost to be a hopeless desire. They had toiled long, and with results which imperfectly corresponded with their efforts. But here the work was executed to their hands. The people were awake, aroused, angry, and in arms. They needed nothing but a leader, and in him they would have found one who would not so soon have suffered the fire of so noble a spirit to have been so shamefully extinguished. Quick to see the opportunity, prompt to secure it, the energies of Pelayo would have annihilated Roderick by a concentrated movement of his entire masses upon the conspicuous tyrant long before any succour could have reached him. A far different spirit controlled the movement of Egiza. Though brave enough, with his foe immediately before him, he lacked that sleepless energy of character which would have prompted him to go in search of his foe, and enable him to seize upon all events calculated to bring about the issue which he desired. He did not think, as he beheld the rush and consternation of the guards, that their panic declared the situation of their master, or if he did, he did not further deliberate upon the application of this panic to the noble purposes of his people's liberty, for which he had set forth with Pelayo, and for the security of which the latter was still nobly striving. Feeble and vascillating, with a heart filled with a softer fire than that of freedom, and a spirit which was too selfishly devoted ever to serve a nation in its hour of danger, the hapless prince, ignorant as yet that all was lost, or worse than lost, for which he had striven, hurried on without interruption to the foot of the tower in which Cava was a prisoner. Had he known her fate for whom he toiled, his feet had taken a different direction. He would then have done for personal vengeance what Pelayo had done for his people.

Let us return to the inmates of the palace. The clamor which had aroused Roderick, and challenged his presence in the fearful melee which we have witnessed had drawn the queen and her handmaids to the massy towers which looked upon the area, where, watching and trembling, they saw a part of that commotion on the termination of which depended their own fates. The defeat of Roderick would have been a signal for their own destruction, since the infuriated populace, it was but reasonable to believe, would have ravaged the palace, where they well knew there was so much treasure to reward plunder, and so much that was tempting to the lustful and licentious. Their apprehensions came not to Cava. She knew, indeed, that strife was going on. Perhaps, too, there were moments when she thought that there might be danger—that death might follow to thousands from that strife; and that she, too, might fall the victim of the unsparing sword. But the fear of death was no longer a fear in the bosom of the once timid Cava. She had resolved upon death. It was life only that had fears—it was life only that teemed with terrors. She dreaded that her living eye should again encounter those of the beloved and the venerated. She dreaded to see her father—she shuddered when she thought that she might again behold her lover. And yet, when she thought of his danger, and of the fierce tyrant in whose presence she believed him to be; when she thought upon the cruel death which awaited him—which, perhaps, had already befallen him—her love grew predominant, and, for a while, she trembled for him with an anxiety that almost wrought a forgetfulness of her own despair. How glad would she be to die for him—to arrest the cruel blow—to brave the deadly rage of the tyrant. She sank upon her knees as she thought upon his dangers. She strove to pray, but she could not. The moment that she demanded the Almighty presence, she flelt that His eye looked upon her shame; she felt that it was a God of vengeance and not one of mercy to whom her spirit, in its fervent mood, could properly address itself. Her prayer took a different direction. She no longer prayed for the safety of her lover; she prayed rather for his death.

"If he love me—if he hold in his heart, oh! blessed Mother of God!" she cried, with hands and eyes uplifted to the "Mother of Grief," who looked down from the gloomy walls upon her—"if he hold in his heart but half the love for me which I have in mine, then grant that the axe has fallen upon his neck; that he may no longer see—that he may never hear my shame, till, like himself, I shall cease to look upon earth, and hear its cruel sounds—till, like himself, with thy mediation, Blessed Mother, and the mercy of thy Son, I am a dweller in a better world, where lust is shut out, and where the tyrant may not come."

Even while she prayed thus, a voice—a gentle, but quick and anxious voice—reached her ears from below. She trembled in every limb as she heard it. Too well she knew that voice. Its tones, gentle and soliciting, rebuked her for her prayer. She had prayed for his death; dared she now look upon his face?—dared she encounter that eye which she had just now desired should be sealed for ever in the eternal night of death? She dared not—yet she must. She had not wished to see him; she had feared this interview—yet he had come opportunely. Her revenge was in her thoughts, and she felt that she could not die until her father knew her wrong. This passion strengthened her, and, with an apprehensive thought that was like an instinct, she had planned her purpose ere she rose from her knees to approach the window looking out upon the garden whence the sound arose. meanwhfle, the appealing tones once more reached her ears, and she heard the rustling of the boughs beneath. He had climbed one of the trees of the garden, almost immediately below the window,' and its thick umbrage half screened him from her sight, while effectually hiding him from all scrutiny of others, had there been any, from below. She brushed the tears from her eyes ere she sought the window. It was now her object to conceal all traces of her suffering—all such traces, at least, as should speak for her peculiar injuries. She did so. Her voice was bland, musical, and if not lively, at least not sad, when she replied to his first inquiries.

"Cava, sweet Cava!" he exclaimed; "you are safe, well, unharmed?" was his first anxious question; and it spoke and demanded volumes in answer She did not answer it—not then, at least.

"Nay, heed me not, Egiza; speak for yourself; tell me, are you safe? Are you secure from danger? Has the tyrant freed you. Are you not pursued?"

"I am safe, dearest—safe, as you behold me; but I am not freed, and may be pursued I am a fugitive, and must fly soon and far. But of me—nothing. Tell me, my own love—say to me, Cava—give me a sign—a look; wave but your handkerchief to tell me that you are mine—solely mine; that you are not"——

The waving of the handkerchief interrupted his speech. Well did she understand the import of his interrogation. Grateful, indeed, was she that he had suggested a form of reply which would obviate the necessity for speech. A nice delicacy had prompted him to this, and she had seized upon it with avidity. The falsehood may be forgiven; she prayed fervently that it might; she did not intend to deceive him long, and the pang was great at her heart that she was compelled to do so even for a moment. A brief time was consumed by him in congratulations; and he then urged upon her to join him in flight. But the bolts were closed without; the walls of her chamber were high, and the means of her descent wanting. Nor would she have assented, even were flight possible. She had other purposes, and she proceeded to their execution.

"I cannot join you now, Egiza; but I will shortly prepare to do so. Meanwhile, my lord, I pray you to receive this letter. Convey it with instant dispatch to my father—nay, you need not go yourself, but send it by some trusty hand. This done, come instantly to me, and I will then join you, at the foot of this tower."

She threw him the epistle prepared for her father, which we have already read. He descended from the tree, and picked it from the ground where it had fallen.

"I go, dearest Cava; yet greatly do I dread to leave you. I fear"——

"Fear nothing!" she replied, in tones of solemnity, very unlike those which she had employed in the brief interview preceding, and which brought an instant feeling of disquiet to his heart.

"How, dearest?" he exclaimed. "What is my security—what is thine, against this tyrant? Do I not leave you in his power—in the walls of his accursed palace? And is there not everything to fear from his still more accursed lust?"

"No, nothing!" she replied, in tones of reassuring confidence—"be sure, my lord, I have nothing to fear; you know not how strong I have become since we were torn asunder. I have a talisman which will shield me from all further wrong. I am safe from him—from all—from everything, save thy hate, thy scorn, Egiza, thy loathing! Tell me, am I safe from that, Egiza? Wilt thou love me—wilt thou promise to love me ever, my lord? Say that thou wilt ere thou leavest me."

"How, my Cava—wherefore this—what mean thy words? *I* scorn—*I* loathe thee, dearest? Wherefore should I? Wherefore shouldst thou fear such injustice at my hands? Believe me, sweetest Cava, I love thee; I shall ever love thee; I cannot help but love thee!"

"Bless thee, my lord—Heaven bless thee, that thou sayest so; yet would I have thee swear it; swear it by the Holy Mother ere thou leavest me; swear it, and come then, when thou hast dispatched the mission to my father—come quickly and receive me. I will then be all thine—in life, in death, for ever more—thine, and thine only!"

"By the Holy Mother—by the Blessed Jesus, I do swear it, my Cava; and if I speak thee falsely in this, may I perish!"

"Thanks, thanks! Fly now," she exclaimed—"fly now, my lord; thou wilt find me at thy coming."

He kissed his united hands to her, and turned away to leave the garden. Her eye watched him in his progress till the folding umbrage concealed him from her sight, She then turned within the apartment, and once more addressed herself to prayer before the image of the Virgin, whom she implored for strength with all the solicitude of one about to set forth upon a journey of great toil and greater peril.

CHAPTER IX.

BUOYANT, with a lightness of spirit which for many days before he had not felt, Egiza rapidly made his way across the garden. There was no obstruction to his progress. The guards as we have already seen were all withdrawn, to engage in the strife in the palace court in front, and were not yet permitted to return. Indeed, the strife, or rather the slaughter, was not yet over. The fierce Roderick had not yet glutted his vengeance, nor appeased his anger. The mere dispersion of the fugitives was not enough for a mood so sanguinary as that which marked his character; and long after opposition had ceased that day, did his keen sword drink of the blood of those who were neither bold enough to fight nor swift enough to fly. Murder succeeded to strife, and drunk with gore, and wanton in due degree with the absence of opposition, his features and his deeds, not more deadly than before, were yet more fearfully foul. The sanguinary career of the tyrant was scarcely over, when Egiza emerged from the garden. He had made the same cautious circuit of the ground in effecting his departure, as he had chosen at his first entrance; and the way was long, before he could compass the extensive courts and wings of the palace, spreading up as they did, even from the golden bedded river to the opening valley within which, and immediately contiguous, the city stood. What a sight then met his eye! Trails of blood marked the ground around him, and denoted the flight of the wounded fugitives. Faint cries of flight echoed along the distant hills, and indicated the apprehensions of those who still fled, or the agonies of those whom the murderers had overtaken. Hurrying groups, in which women were quite as numerous as men, having reached a supposed perch of safety, on the hill tops, paused to survey the bloody scene from which they had just escaped; and the immediate field of battle was now absolutely bare of all those who yet lived, either for pursuit or flight. None but the dead were there—the piled bodies, crushed, mangled and trampled down—with faces lifted to the sun, as if challenging compassion and Heaven's vengeance—alone testified to the cruel horrors of the strife in which they had perished.

The whole scene struck Egiza with no less surprise than horror. When had these deeds been done? What was the occasion? Who had been the parties? He now remembered the shouts and clamors which he had heard, as he was about to enter the garden. He had also seen the departure of the guards from the enclosure toward the courts in front; and to their absence he well knew he was to attribute the impunity with which he had penetrated to the tower, in which Cava was confined; but so completely had his soul and thought been given up to her—so entirely had her situation and supposed danger, absorbed all other objects in his mind, that the battle in the courts in front, if waged immediately beneath his eye, would, it is more than probable, have called for as little of his regard as did the various circumstances which had challenged, without heed, his consideration. He looked now with horror and sufficient consciousness upon the bloody prospect before him. While he gazed he heard the cries of the returning soldiers, and, following the lead of one who seemed a spectator like himself, he turned aside for security into a little recess formed by two jutting walls of one wing of the very prison from which he had escaped the night before. The propinquity of this prison annoyed him, and he would have left it, but that the soldiery was at hand. He heard their shouts, and looking forth cautiously, caught a glimpse of his uncle, the lord Oppas, at their head. The mystery of the connection was doubly increased as he surveyed the archbishop—armed in mail from top to toe, and carrying a mace, which had evidently done fearful execution in the conflict. How could he have fought? was the question with Egiza—not for Roderick? and if he fought against him, was he not a conquerer? He rode as such, in full armor, unrestrained, and a goodly troop, wearing his household badge, were following at his heels. The joyous thought came to his mind that Roderick was no more—that Oppas had headed the successful insurrection, and that the path of safety and happiness, henceforward, lay open to himself and Cava. The dream was dissipated in a moment after, when Roderick, unhurt, and with weapon bare, came bounding furiously forward to the side of the archbishop. The vindictive fire still blazed in his dark eye, and overspread his fierce features and crimson face. His arm not less than his weapon, had been literally drenched in blood, and the dark stains extended beyond his elbows. His helmet was off—lost in the melee—and the black hair was, in many places, dyed with the same bloody tokens of the recent strife, while his hoarse voice shouting his approbation to lord Oppas, proclaimed him sufficiently the victor. With a countenance in which exultation and ferocity were mingled pretty equally, he looked round upon the field which was every where marked with the trophies of the strife; and his ferocity was increased, and his exultation somewhat diminished, as he beheld how many of his own guards were mingled with the carcasses of the unhappy peasantry, whom he had slaughtered. His jealous eye looked round greedily, as if to see that there were no other victims yet to strike, and bitter was the fury which he expressed to Oppas, when he remarked that one-third of the number of his guards had perished in the conflict, being nearly half the number of the half-armed peasantry whom they had slain.

"The base curs, but they shall pay for this!" he exclaimed. "By saint Jupiter, but they shall! I will have a bonfire of these carcasses, by the light of which I will hang up an hundred of their brethren. But for you, my lord Oppas, I had perished by the hand of that villian mule-driver—his knife was at my throat, and the hand which held him back from the stroke, was well nigh palsied ere you came. I have done you wrong, my lord bishop—I will do you right. You shall not say that the king of the Romans is ungrateful, though truly you may complain that he hath been unjust. I have been deceived, my lord bishop. Busy and jealous spirits were about me, counselling me against thee, and proclaiming thee a traitor, along with that outlawed brood of Witiza. I have erred, my lord bishop—the Goth has erred. He can say no more."

He extended his bloody hand as he spoke, and the wily archbishop grasped it with an air of mingled gladness and humility, as he replied:

"Nor need you to have said thus much, oh Roderick! I feared not that I should have justice in season, at thy hands. Well I knew, that busy tongues had done me wrong to thy ears—and deeply did I feel the severity which followed it. But I am more than gratified now, since thou hast permitted me to think that I have rendered thee a service in a moment of necessity."

"A service!" exclaimed the king. "By Hercules, I tell thee thou hast saved my life. My blood, ere this, hadst thou not put in when thou didst, had reddened the knife of that infernal mule-driver. Nay, never mince the matter—I tell thee, it is so. My hand that grappled his lifted arm, and stayed the stroke, was failing me—numbed, almost paralysed with the long strain upon it. I feel it now, to my elbow. I had not counted the holy twelve, ere it had utterly given way, when thou camest to my help. I owe thee a life, my lord bishop—a life, which I might have lost, while my lieutenant Edeco, here, was adjusting his gorget."

A smile of bitter scorn played upon the lips of the king, as, looking round upon Edeco, he uttered these words. In nowise discomposed, the latter casually responded:

"Not so, oh Roderick! and I marvel that thou shouldst mistake the yellow fingers of the Bascon, who made free with my poor throat, for those of your espatorio. I owe the bishop a life also, oh king; since the good onslaught, which saved you from the muleteer, gave me pleasant release from the most cruelly oppressive fingers that ever yet troubled my gorget. A fellow bearing your badge, my lord Oppas, clove the Bascon's skull, and not till then, would he be pursuaded to release my throat. I would I knew the fellow, that I might pay him the value of a life"

"Let the sum be small—a leovogild, or so," was the half-scornful, half-playful reply of Roderick. "For," he continued, "hadst thou counted it at more thyself, thou surely hadst striven for it better, I saw not thy strokes—I heard not even thy shouts, which should have cheered our men. My own voice grew hoarse in its labors to remedy the lack of thine."

"And wouldst thou have had me, oh Roderick! mingle sounds so unseemly? What ear would have noted the war-cry of the espatorio, when it was ringing with that of the king. But I did cry aloud, oh Roderick—I had need to do so, for the knaves pressed me sorely, and never did I behold men hang back more lazily than ours. I had need to cry aloud and spare not, and, but for thy own shouts, oh king! thou must have heard me."

"Ay, methinks I did hear certain clamorous entreaties for mercy, which seemed to come from the quarter where thou sayest thou fought. The voice was small and soothing—it had an air of the chamber, Edeco, which was marvellously like to thine."

"By the ghost of Cæsar, king Roderick!" cried the courtier, with a greater degree of earnestness than was his wont, "but thou dost me wrong. I struck many and weighty blows—I fought like a true man—and my cry was not for mercy, but for vengeance and battle. Would I cry for mercy to such dripping knaves? Would I take life at their hands? By my beard, no!"

"A brief oath!" cried the king, laughing—"and a carefully trimmed one. Thou hast brought thy credit to a narrow point, Edeco, and a little of the oil of beasts, such as they sell to thee at such cost from Tangier, will make all smooth to thy conscience."

The popinjay stroked complacently the inverted pyramid of bristles that depended from his chin; and smiling good humoredly, but contemptuously, the king turned from his favorite to the archbishop. The contrast between the two, forced itself at this moment more than ever before his consideration. The sleek effeminacy, and loose, voluptuous air of one, compared unfavorably with the lofty, inflexible demeanor, the fearless manhood, the erect carriage, and the almost barbarian simplicity and sternness of look, which distinguished the archbishop. He was clothed in a suit of full armor, plaited but plain, of bright steel; and the heavy mace, which he bore, of the same metal, covered with blood-stains, which were not yet dry, carried with it indubitable testimony that he who bore it was not merely a carpet-knight. Admirably did the war habit which he wore, become lord Oppas; and we may add, studiously and with the most elaborate care had it been chosen by the wearer. He was not insensible to the fine symmetry, the superior manhood, and the noble carriage of his person—and the very opportunity of appearing in the splendid military costume of that age, was to him a matter of infinite gratification. Yet did he conceal this little vanity of heart, by a careful sobriety of countenance, and a reverential form of speech. While he fought manfully, he deplored war; and only recognised its propriety in regard of the leading necessity, which left no other alternative between that and greater immoralities.

"By my faith, lord Oppas, but you are a warrior!" cried the king, as he surveyed him. "The coat of mail better fits your limbs than the surplice; and the mace in thy hands is a far more imposing object than the crosier. I will look me out a husband for the church, who bears himself less vigorously in fight than thou! What sayest thou, Edeco, if I wed thee to the Gothic church? She is a rich damsel —indulgent, too, to the select; thou will have infinite time for thy caparison, and thy privileges—but let my lord Oppas tell thee of them. He shall be eloquent, if I err not, in his speech of them; and let him tell thee but half, I look to have thee don the cassock with impatient haste, and hurry with even greater speed to the confessional. Ha! my lord bishop, have I touched thee, ha! But for thy privileges—nay, I know it—but for thy privileges, thou hadst been a warrior—thou hadst striken heads, rather than hearts; and I will wager an Andalusian damsel against one of thy golden candlesticks that thou hadst done more good in quelling rebellious men, than thou hast ever done, in censuring dreaming women. Ha! wilt thou wager, my lord bishop. If thou wilt"——

Egiza heard nothing more, and the sentence was concluded by a burst of broken laughter from the king, which seemed to follow some reply of Edeco. The cavalcade were now passing the open court, in one of the recesses of which the prince found shelter. He concealed himself, as they now passed, behind one of the massive projecting buttresses of the wall; while the stranger, who had likewise sought concealment in the same area, sank behind a corresponding projection of the wall opposite. It was then, while the tyrant and his train were passing; while the tramp of the heavy horsemen, and the clattering of armor, and the confused hum of voices were in his ears—even then, audible beyond all other sounds, and mingling with them strongly and painfully, came to the senses of the prince a stifled moan, followed by bitter and broken accents, from the bottom of the recess behind him. The voice was that of a woman, and he turned involuntarily at the sound. He was surprised and startled. Such had been his hurry and excitement upon first seeking the shelter of the court, which was deep and spacious, that he had failed to see that it was already occupied in front. He now started, and shuddered with horror at the cruel picture which he had not marked before. An old woman sat upon the ground, with a young girl and a youth before her, both of whom were dead. The head of the former rested upon her lap—a hand of the latter was clasped in one of her own. This she let fall, as the train of the tyrant came in sight, and her withered arms were lifted to Heaven in imprecation as it passed. The bitter words which she uttered were partly audible to Egiza, but not to those in whose denunciation they were uttered. Few were the words, yet dreadful was the curse which she uttered in that moment. With laughter on his lips Roderick passed by, unconscious of, and indifferent to, the miseries which he had brought upon the land; but the wretched and desolate woman cursed him not the less, as she saw that he heard her not. Her appeal was to Heaven, and through Heaven's judgment only could she hope to have her imprecation descend upon the head of him who had despoiled her of her children. She was the mother of the fearless Toro, and the gentle girl, his sister, for whose safety he had striven so unsuccessfully, and for whom, indeed, he had perished. Had it not been necessary for her extrication, he had not remained in the crowd. She had unwisely followed him, and the anguish which he suffered, even ere she had fallen a victim in the strife, and the apprehensions which he felt on her account, were more painful to his heart, than any blow which he suffered in his person. But they neither suffered now; and the soldiers who slew, and the tyrant who permitted and provoked the slaughter, passed on without emotion to the proud palace and the pampering feast. Little thought had they of the thousands whose humble cottages they had that day filled with misery and death. Few were the reflections, and slight the commiseration, which, in that period, the prince gave to his people. Man had not then risen to command the rights of humanity. His rights then were those of service, not sympathy. He had limbs and sinews, could procure arms, and possessed a valor which feared not to grapple with the forest lion; but he lacked the few crowning thoughts, which could concentrate his own powers and those of his kindred in a common cause. Barbarians are individuals—not men. They feel a common necessity, but they lack a common purpose. Could the brave Toro have been heard, when he spoke of the common danger; could he have been followed, when his hand pointed out the common direction, which their own safety counselled them to take, his own cottage, and those of hundreds besides, had not been desolate that night. But the Avenger was at hand, and the imprecation of the aged woman had not been spoken idly. The blood of the murdered had gone up to Heaven, and rang in thunder-tones through the eternal vaults. Even then the bolt was aimed at the offender, and the Angel of Divine Wrath stood with unfolded wing at the eternal portals, waiting but the fiat which should send him forth on his work of annihilation.

CHAPTER X.

Egiza had not beheld the efforts of the Gallician in the strife in which he perished; he had not seen his fiery energies striving to the last, for the rescue first, and finally for the avenging of his innocent sister. He felt, consequently, but little or none of that interest in the fortunes of the group which a previous knowledge of events must have inspired. But there was still enough that was painfully picturesque in the situation to rivet his regard. It had been a scene for the patriot painter, seeking to leave a record of the fruits of despotism, which should be an argument to all succeeding ages. When the cavalcade of Roderick had gone by, and it was safe for him to emerge from the buttress, in the rear of which he stood, he hurried with a painful sort of curiosity to the back part of the recess, where the group found shelter, anxious to learn the particulars of their history, the catastrophe of which, so far, was amply delivered in the two silent forms now lying beside their lonely mother. The man who had found a similar cover with himself, on the approach of Roderick's party, behind another buttress of the walls, as if moved by a like curiosity, followed his steps—and they both stood, but without speech, in the presence of the woman. She looked up after a pause of a few brief moments, in which her lips had moved, though in the utterance of no distinguishable words.

"What come ye for?" she demanded; "ye can do them no more hurt. Feel them, they move not—they have no more life. But this morning the boy brought me water. Look now!" She raised his head as she spoke, and let it fall suddenly upon her lap. The blood and matter oozed out from the cloven skull as she did so, and lay in clotted masses upon her garments; but she seemed not to heed; while, lifting the head of the girl with more of tenderness, she subjected it to a like test, and allowed it to fall with its own unresisted weight upon the lap beside that of her brother.

"Is't not enough?" she demanded. "Would you give them more blows? You may, but they cannot feel them. Go, take away your bloody axes from my sight. You would not strike the dead. No, take them away."

"We have no axes, good mother. You mistake us," said the prince. "We are not soldiers—our hands have not done this."

"I see them—think you to hide them from me? But I care not—I fear them not. Perhaps, it is me that you would strike now. Toro said you would. He always said that the soldiers would as soon strike a woman as a man, and perhaps sooner, since then they had not so much to fear in return. But you may strike—strike, only give me time to say a prayer, and perhaps a curse. I would curse—it is easier to curse than to pray, when one's children are murdered. Toro, I will curse for you first, and the curse shall be upon the Gothic men! For you Toly, I will curse all the Gothic women!—let the devils hear!—let them come out of the tombs and hear, for I would give them work. Are you not a Goth?" she suddenly exclaimed to Egiza; but without waiting for his reply she continued, and her features assumed a horrible and ghastly expression of rage as she spoke, as if they had been those of one long familiar with curses, and thrice blasted of Heaven. "Go! I curse you with many deaths!—with the death of all that love you!—with the death of all that you love!—may you eat of your own hearts, bloody Goths that ye are! Go to Roderick your master, and may ye perish like him! I curse ye all, for ye have cursed me!"

"But we are not Goths. I, at least, am not a Goth!" was the exclamation of Egiza.

"Nor I, mother!" hurriedly repeated the stranger, as if to divert the curse of the desolate woman.

"It matters not!" she exclaimed. "If ye are not Goths, what are ye? Ye are not men, or ye had not suffered these things. Ye are the base slaves of the Goth—that serve his sway, and do his bidding; and I curse ye—with a worse curse than I have for him! Had ye been men, ye would have fought like Toro; and then he had lived, and Toly had lived, and I had been happy with my children; but now I have none. Do ye not hear? Go! I give ye curses for company to travel with! Leave me now, or handle your axes! I care not how soon you strike!"

She drew the dead bodies at the same moment in a fervent embrace to her bosom, and looked not up once at the spectators, nor uttered another word to them, while they remained. The scene was too painful for contemplation, and they simultaneously turned away from it. When they had reached the outer wall of the court, Egiza remarked more narrowly the person of his companion, and beheld with some satisfaction that he wore upon his bosom the leathern pocket, or pannier, which was the certain sign of the courier. This discovery delighted him.

"You are a courier?" he said.

"I am, father," was the reply; and it reminded Egiza, that he wore the habit of the Caulian friars.

"I would employ you then," said Egiza. "I would have you ride with all speed to the fortress of count Julian at Algeziras, and it may be that you will have to pass to Ceuta. Bear this letter to the lieutenant in safety, and your reward shall be suitable to your labor. He is a generous prince; you will not speed in vain; and, in earnest that you shall not, here are ten leovogilds! Will you speed on this journey?"

The man closed with him instantly, and received the money.

"What time will it be before you start?—I would have you proceed quickly," was the farther address of the prince.

"I will but pause to bait my horse," was the reply. "An hour will find me on my way to Algeziras."

"Enough! Thou wilt deliver the missive into no hand but that of count Julian; he will reward thee for greater trouble in so doing."

"I believe it, father. His hand shall take it from my own. The blessed Virgin hear me as I promise, and help me as I perform. Father, your blessing."

The courier knelt to Egiza before he could interrupt him; and the latter, deeming it better to maintain his assumed, than risk the exposure of his real character, without scruple conferred the blessing which was solicited; an offence, for which he prayed forgiveness from Heaven, the moment that he was alone. Speeding the courier upon his way, he hurried back in the direction of the royal garden, where the woman of his heart awaited him.

CHAPTER XI.

SHE awaited him, but how! Little did he imagine the sort of reception which he was to have, as he hastened, with a buoyant heart, to the spot where she had pledged herself to meet him. Little did he dream that all the toils which he had undergone, and all the sacrifices which he had made, for the single object of his devotion, were undergone and performed without avail. He was now to experience the just reward of his narrow selfishness. Heedless of what was due to his people, to justice, to freedom, and to his father's memory, he had been meanly solicitous of his own enjoyment, without any of the cares of life; and to secure this object, he had basely shuffled off all the solemn responsibilities of his birth, as a prince and citizen, alike. He was now about to be taught the noble truth that the cause of liberty is the common cause of man; and that no station can be secure, whether high or humble—no happiness certain, whether lofty or unpretending, in any land where injustice remains unpunished, and where tyranny is suffered to obtain a foothold.

With the last lingering look upon her lover, as he left her to seek the courier who was to convey the letter to her father, the unhappy Cava had addressed herself to prayer. That parting with Egiza was the last—such was her resolve; and, strive as she might, she felt that she could not pray. A dark shadow waved its arms constantly between her eyes and the image of the Virgin. The features seemed to contract, and the brow to frown upon her. The benevolence which had looked forth upon her from the maternal eyes had departed, and she felt that she had sinned in her resolve, and was about to do a farther and a greater sin in its execution. The tears ran down her cheeks as she prayed for mercy—for indulgence; but the frown passed not away from the features to which she looked, and the dark shadow waved its arms more frequently before her eyes, and finally shut out the blessed image entirely from her sight.

"Oh, mother! desert me not," she cried; "desert me not! Thou knowest that I have not sinned in this dreadful suffering; that I strove against the sin; that I called upon thee all the while. I called upon thee, mother, but thou didst not come."

Once more her eyes caught a glimpse of the blessed features, and they seemed to smile upon her; but the prayer of her lips, the next moment, again brought with it a blindness of the sight, as it denoted a greater blindness of the spirit.

"Take pity on me, Mother of God!—pity on the poor handmaiden, who kneels to thee. Be thou before me, oh blessed Mary!—be thou before me at the Burning Throne; soften the eyes that look upon me—plead for me, and win the grace for me in mercy, which, through the intercession of thy son Jesus, thou canst well command. Thou knowest that I cannot live; I cannot live for the scorn of those I love—for those that should have loved me. I cannot meet their eyes. I dare not look upon them. I must die!"

The once gentle features scowled upon her, and a voice at her very heart appeared to say:

"And art thou more bold to meet God, whom thou now seekest willingly to offend? Art thou less ready to look upon man than upon God? Is the Eternal Love nothing to thee; and is the mortal love everything? Foolish and sinful that thou art, seest thou not that what is pure and worthy in the love of earth, is a part of God's love which He resumes at death, and which lives for thee evermore hereafter?

Be not blind to offend God. Live for prayer—live for His love and mercy, if not for the mercy and the love of man."

"Would I could!" exclaimed the desperate woman, as if in reply to this exhortation. "Would I could dare to live, to meet his face, to serve his bidding, to be in his presence ever. But I am not strong enough."

A voice at her ear seemed to her to say:

"Thou art not!" and the shadow swelled and distended as she listened, until her eyes swam in the increasing darkness, and her extended hands grasped the wall below the image of the Virgin, to whom she vainly stretched them for support. The evil prompter had triumphed. The soft features of the Mother of Grief no longer looked forth upon her, or looked forth only in rebuke. She rose from her knees. She hurried to the recess in which she had hidden the letter to Egiza. This she grasped in her hands, as she hurried to the lofty window. She climbed—she stood upon the ledge, another step and she was upon the balustrade, and nothing now remained, but God, between her and the awful precipice. She turned her eyes once more within the room in search of the Virgin, but she saw not even the picture. A hand seemed to grasp her throat. She strove for breath—she was choking with her terrors, but she suppressed them:

"Let me not feel it, mother—my flesh shivers—I would not feel the pain. I am dizzy—I—ah! I reel—I fall—Mother of God—Blessed Mary, help me—stay me—keep me back—I would not perish now—I would live!"

These were her last words as she disappeared from the window. She had repented of her resolve; but too late. Her head was dizzy with her elevation—her knees gave way beneath her—and her last appeal, her last resolution to live, came from the first physical consciousness of her inability any longer to maintain her perilous position. Yet, as if the reluctant repentance was still in season, the cruel pain of the death which she had chosen, was spared her. Ere yet she reached the end of that fearful flight—ere yet her delicate limbs came in contact with the unyielding and cold earth, all consciousness had departed, and she felt nothing after. One part of her prayer seemed to have been heard by the Blessed Spirit to whom she addressed it, and permitted by the indulgent God. She had been spared the pang from which her flesh had shrunk in apprehension, and the earth seemed to have received her as gently as it does the traveller who sinks into a passing slumber by the wayside.

CHAPTER XII.

Thus, like one who slept happily, was she found by Egiza. He had passed the walls in safety. The guards were not returned, or were in very small number within the garden. He reached the appointed spot without interruption. At first, approaching the tower, with eye turned upward to the window at which he had before left her, he saw her not, until his feet were nearly in contact with her garments. Then, he started back with surprise and apprehension. The next glance somewhat reassured him. She seemed to sleep. The features were composed—even placid, and a smile rested upon them. He stooped—his arms encircled her—he was about to press her lips with his own, when he started back, and now trembled with apprehension. A slight stream of blood oozed from the corner of her mouth, and her cheek, which rested upon the grassy bank, as he slightly lifted her form and changed its position, was impressed with the green outlines of its several blades. A slight cry of doubt escaped him, and he called to her with a hurried tremulousness of accent which he vainly strove to overcome.

"Speak to me, Cava—dearest—best beloved—my heart—my life—speak to me—tell me that you are not hurt—that you live—that you will fly with me. Speak to me—it is Egiza, your own Egiza, who implores. Speak! speak!"

He lifted her from the ground—the eyes opened upon him, and glared glassily and cold—the long hair was undone, and the unsupported head distorted the limber neck, as it fell heavily back upon her shoulders.

"God! she *is* dead!" he exclaimed, as he suffered the insensible body to fall from his arms. He knelt like one stupified—aghast, and utterly silent beside her. He could not realize the dreadful truth before him. He could not trust the evidence of those senses which had been impatient to behold a far different prospect. While he gazed astounded, upon the inanimate maiden, he caught a glimpse of the letter in her hand. It had been clenched firmly, and was still held fast. He extricated it from her grasp, and with swimming eyes read the superscription to himself. Convulsively he tore asunder the folds, and read the epistle, which but too plainly announced the wrong which she had suffered, and but too certainly accounted for the manner of her death. Twice he perused it, then crushing it convulsively in his hands, he sank upon the body with a single groan of the intense and otherwise speechless agony of his soul. A cry from above startled him. He looked up, and met the terrified gaze of a group of women. They were those who had been assigned as a watch upon the movements of Cava. They had been led to a brief desertion of their trust, by the clamors of the populace in the courts fronting the palace, and they returned to find their captive free. Their shrieks filled the air, and he heard the clamor of approaching voices. He started to his feet. A new impulse prompted him, and he lifted the insensible victim in his arms. He rushed through the coppice, and with gigantic effort ascended the walls of the garden. The voice of Roderick reached his ears, and with a vindictive fury he felt for the dagger which he had placed within his girdle. It was no longer there. He was unarmed, but desperation filled his soul, and he shouted his defiance aloud. His shouts aroused a soldier who guarded a corner of the walls, and who instantly made toward him. His approach produced no pause in the progress of Egiza, as it occasioned no apprehension in his mind. He dashed forward unhesitatingly, still bearing his insensible burden.

"Stand!" cried the approaching soldier, presenting his spear as he did so. "Stand! or I thrust you to the earth."

"Stand!—yes!—I will stand upon thy carcass, reptile; upon the carcass of thy master! Get from my path, I tell thee!"

"A madman!" exclaimed the soldier involuntarily, but presenting his spear, more in apprehension than resolve. Egiza dashed it aside, and darted upon him, grappling at his throat with the one free arm. The soldier shrank back, but still presenting his spear, it took effect with the next effort which Egiza made—not upon his person, but that of her whom he bore. The spear-head was driven through her breast, and he let her sink to the ground with a feeling of horror, as if a new crime had been committed. Then, having both arms freed, he sprang upon the now unarmed guardsman, whose weapon remained fixed in Cava's drapery, and from which he vainly strove to wrest it. Before he could succeed he was grappled in the arms of the furious prince, whom no effort at this moment could possibly resist. In a moment he had lifted the clinging and struggling soldier from the ground—in another he had hurled him from the wall and into the garden, where, maimed and lacerated, he lay writhing fruitlessly, among the thick plants and shrubbery. Egiza paused not to behold him, but seizing once more upon the dead body of Cava, he hurried forward with insane agility, seeking to gáin that portion of the garden-wall where it had a natural and easy descent, by means of the tall trees which grew there upon the loose rocks by the side of the river. Ere he could effect his object the alarm was given behind him, and the guards were in full pursuit. There was but little time for hesitation, and, when it became clear to him, as it soon did, that he could not reach the point proposed before his pursuers were upon him, without a thought of the desperation of such a deed, gathering the body up more firmly in his grasp, he leaped from the lofty point of the wall upon which he stood, boldly into the deep and boiling river which hurried on beneath it. A cry something between a shout and a shriek rose from the soldiers that pursued, who had reached the surface of the wall in sufficient time to behold the desperate deed, and to note its consequences. Roderick, too, appeared upon the wall, followed by the archbishop Oppas, a moment after, and their eyes were intently fixed upon the yet bubbling spot upon the waters, where the fugitive with his unconscious prize had descended. He arose but the spectators were more conscious than himself. In the concussion which followed his contact with the waters, the body of Cava had been torn from his grasp, and his arms were struck out upon the stream rather in search of her than in support of himself.

"Shoot! shoot!—is there not a bowman among you to send a shaft through yon sturdy traitor?" was the cry of Roderick to the soldiers One of them advanced, armed with the required instrument, and the aim was already taken, when the arm of the soldier was arrested by the archbishop.

"Why do ye stay the shaft, my lord Oppas?" demanded the king, who beheld the interruption. "Let the knave shoot, and be sure of the traitor."

"See, oh king! he hath disappeared!" was the reply—a reply uttered with a calm ease of voice and manner, which had not been attained but with a wondrous effort. The lord Oppas knew his nephew, his favorite nephew—and, selfish though he might be in his ambitious projects, he was not utterly insensible to the ties of kindred, and to the once noble promise of the youth whom he now saw perishing. He turned away from the prospect, and ceased to look. The tyrant gazed again and again upon the surface of the stream, which hurried on with indifference to its eternity,the ocean; and the rapidity with which strong life may be abridged, was forced upon his thought at that moment more emphatically than by the repeated murders of his own hand, and those which but a brief hour before he had witnessed and commanded. There, life only had departed—the strong man lay still in his eyes—no longer struggling it is true—but with the massive limbs, and the corded muscle, as if strong to struggle still. Now, not a vestige remained, either of the life that prompted, or the frame that followed its direction. It was something terrible even to the reckless despot, that single instance, not of death only, but seeming annihilation. But he affected not to heed the sight.

"Come, my lord Oppas, let us in—Egilona shall give thee thanks for thy good service, and for her lord's life, which thou hast saved to-day. Nay, look no more. It is all over with the ruffian. Tagus will cast him up ere it gain the ocean, and if it do not, the loss will be to the vulture, and the gain to our nostrils."

"But the maid—the daughter of count Julian?" said the archbishop, in a tone of inquiry.

"Is silent," was the quick reply of the king, who placed his hand familiarly on the churchman's shoulder as he spoke it. "Cava is silent; and so, my lord Oppas must be the friend of Roderick. She stole off with her paramour—do you heed me—and they perished together in their flight. Come, to the queen, to the queen. We are waited for."

In the presence of Egilona, Oppas forgot his nephew—everything, indeed, but her beauties, and the lustful ambition which they had long inspired.

Yet Egiza lived. Without his own consciousness he lived. Borne down by the current beyond the eyes of his enemies, he was rescued from the waters by the timely aid of a fisherman, who dwelt upon the banks, and who, at that fortunate moment, was plying his vocation in his little barque. With a doubtful kindness, the rude man brought him to the shore, restored him to life, and gave him, while he remained feeble, the shelter of his miserable hut. There let us leave him.

END OF BOOK FIFTH.

BOOK SIXTH.

CHAPTER I.

The Arabs of the East, under the Caliph Almanzor, had swept, with the sword of the prophet, the Oriental nations. The progress of conquest had brought them to the shores of the Atlantic, and they already looked forth upon the narrow straits which lie between the Pillars of Hercules, with the impatient yearnings of a desire which was yet beyond their power to satisfy. To overpass this narrow limit, to possess themselves of the fertile regions which lay beyond, was an appetite the more keenly felt in consequence of the obstacles which opposed it. Of the wealth and luxury of the Gothic empire of Spain, they had full assurance; of its feebleness, however, they formed no adequate conjectures. It had been fortunate for Spain, that the defence of Tingitania, or that small portion of Western Africa which still belonged to the empire of Roderick, had been intrusted to a veteran soldier so renowned as Julian of Consuegra. Julian was one of the greatest warriors of his time. With a natural predilection for war, his experience had confirmed the tendencies of his genius. Skilled in all the military arts of the period, he was beloved of the soldiery. Ten thousand well-appointed warriors obeyed his paramount authority; and, placed upon the borders of the kingdom, and constantly threatened by an active and imposing enemy, they had preserved their courage and military vigilance. They suffered from none of those enervating tastes and luxuries which enfeebled, in the heart of the kingdom, the great body of the people to which they belonged. They knew nothing of those vices which disgraced the court, and found their way from that polluted fount, through all the arteries of the social system. They constituted, on the frontiers of Tingitania, a powerful military colony. Their virtues, in times of comparative security, were exercised by the labors of the field, and by those toils of the hunter and the peasant by which men's muscles are rendered equally enduring and elastic. A hardy simplicity of character made them heedless of luxuries, and the occasional demands of war had no other effect than to increase the charm of their rude mode of life, when a return of peace or quiet enabled them temporarily to enjoy it. Count Julian, whom, for many years, they had known as their only leader, was, in some sort, their patriarch. He regarded his followers with the friendly interest of one who had always secured their fidelity; and his frankness of manner, great bravery, and the even measure with which he administered justice among them, left him without a competitor in their confidence and affections. They knew little of the Gothic kingdom—nothing of Roderick or his predecessor; had little interest in the internal affairs of the empire, and, as has been already in part intimated in our history, would have been much more ready to follow their immediate military leader, at the expression of his bare will, as absolute subjects, than they would have been to throw up their caps in acknowledging the elevation to the throne of the sovereign born in the purple! That such, indeed, had not been the case on the ascent of Roderick, was due rather to the loyalty, or, it may be, to the prudence of Julian, than to any notion which his followers entertained of what was due to legitimacy.

Contending with such a people only, the Arabs, whose otherwise victorious arms had borne the crescent of Mahomet over the proudest cities of the East, could form but an imperfect idea of the nation at large, whose interests they maintained in Tingitania. Reasoning from what they knew, of the valor of these men of the frontier, they might very well entertain serious doubts of ever gaining foothold upon the shores of Spain, to which their eager eyes were directed in equal hope and misgiving. But, though this great conquest might yet appear beyond their grasp, the spirit of Moslemism necessarily hurried on its warriors to the complete conquest of Western Africa. The provence of Tingitania was too necessary to the integrity of Almagreb, not to make it desirable that the military colony of Julian should be driven across the straits. However brave and indomitable might be his ten thousand followers, however skilful their commander, it was still beyond reasonable conjecture that they should be able long to hold out against the mighty force which the standard of the prophet could array for the completion of conquests. One hundred thousand veterans were brought together for this purpose. From the seat of the caliphate, at Damascus, Waled Almanzor, otherwise called by the Moslems, the "Sword of God," had issued his command to drive the Gothic Christians unto the waters of the sea. His troops were free to this enterprise. His foes had sunk, in all other regions, before the baleful influence of his prevailing star. Led by Muza Ben Nosier, one of the most remarkable of all the warriors of the early ages, they were drawn together from all parts of Almagreb. A mixed multitude, they sent up to the heavens the separate cries of a thousand tribes of the great desert. A fiery race by nature, the fanatic tenets of the prophet had given to their mood an intensity which, like the famous artificial fire of the Greeks, was only heightened by the effort to extinguish it. Impatient of opposition, as special instruments of eternal truth and vengeance, they held life cheap in comparison with conquest. To perish in the prosecution of their holy war, was to secure immunity for their sins and salvation for their souls; and the pangs of a violent death, in this life, were more than compensated by the glowing descriptions of sensual happiness, by which their prophet proposed to reward them in their transition to the next. Light and vigorous, fearless and full of faith, skilled in the use of their weapons, and rendered more so by actual conflict with a thousand various tribes, they threw themselves forward upon the Goths of Tingitania, with the reckless hardihood of men who had nothing to lose but all to gain, even from the worst issues and results of battle.

Their great leader was a warrior after their own hearts. Muza Ben Nosier, when summoned by the caliph to the command of Almagreb, was in his seventieth year; but he had lost in age but little of the vigor and elasticity of youth. In several respects he had undergone no change from the character which he had borne in youth. Time, which subdues the blood in other veins, seemed only to have given a fresh impetus to his. He was still the fiery warrior which he had been when he went forth a humble follower in the armies of Mahomet. Religious fanaticism had added to the force and fervor of his temper; and success, which, after a certain space, seems to satisfy the cravings of most warriors, contributed only to the increase of his desires in this respect. Fierce, yet cool and calm in his deportment—vindictive and deceitful—impetuous in battle, but a most subtle politician—Muza was altogether one of the most remarkable men of modern periods. That he was selfish, mercenary, bloodthirsty and unjust, is probably natural enough to such a person. This, perhaps, is to be understood as inevitable from his successful leadership of such people as those who followed him to battle. There were veterans under him not less remarkable—one of whom will become even more conspicuous than himself, in the progress of this narrative.

The opening of the year seven hundred and ten, was an eventful period in the fortunes of Gothic Spain. It found the fortresses of the Goths in Tingitania, everywhere menaced by the power of the Moslems. Musa Ben Nosier led the assault upon that of Ceuta, the most powerful, defended by Count Julian in person. The forces of the latter, in Africa, were, as already said, about ten thousand men. Those of the Arabs are said to have defied computation. The more cautious estimates of the historian have placed them, however, at no less than ten times that number. Confident in his strength and superiority, assured by continual success, Musa Ben Nosier, disdaining the slow processes of siege, at once led his formidable array against the Gothic towers. The genius of Mahommedanism has always preferred to make its conquests by storm. From the rise of morn to the set of sun, his fierce and active followers flung themselves with desperate hardihood against the ramparts of Ceuta. They asked for no forbearance—they yielded none. The assailant who looks not to his own danger, is not easily defeated. The swarthy sons of the desert had never yet taken counsel from defeat. They disdained the cold considerations of prudence. They went forward to conquer; and death, in this desire, was still a conquest, sufficiently precious to reconcile them to all the danger. But, in this instance, their fiery valor was in vain. The Goths of the frontier were worthy of the old Romans, from whom it was their boast to have sprung. They were a stern and stubborn people. If they lacked the peculiar fire of the Arab, they had a patient doggedness of resolve which more than compensated for the deficiency. If they were less lithe and active, they were more firm; and, with a power of resistance such as the sullen rock opposes to the billows, on the edges of their own empire. The children of the desert thus flung themselves upon the walls of Ceuta, only to recoil, like broken billows of the sea, from the fast-rooted Pillars of Hercules. Their fury, their numbers, their fanaticism; their rage of conquest, their scorn of death; the wild cries with which they went into battle, the stormy clamor of the cymbal and barbaric drum—were all fruitless. They were driven back, baffled and dispirited, from the Gothic fortress; and, as they fled in confusion, Julian sallied forth, and a terrible slaugher ensued among the flying columns. For once the Moslem despaired of his prophet. The spell of his invincibility seemed broken. His progress was fatally arrested, and even Muza, the fierce, the proud, the fanatic, trembled with the conviction, that, in his defeat, the waves of Moslem conquest were to be stayed for ever. Sore in spirit, discomfited, confounded, he sought the shelter of his camp, and, in resolute seclusion from all his followers, declared to them the depth of his affliction and disgrace.

Far different was the feeling within the walls of Ceuta. A natural, and not unbecoming exultation filled the bosom of Count Julian. His followers gloried in their successes, and boasted of their exploits. Gothic Tingitania rang with the shouts of triumph, and the name of Julian was thrice honored with the grateful applauses of his people. Gay lights shone from the house-tops, bonfires blazed in the streets. Merry strains went up from terrace and balcony, and, in the general impulse of rejoicing, beauty and innocence forgot that there were Moslem spoilers in the land. If ever heart was satisfied with itself, it was that of Julian. He sat within his chamber, meditating the victory which he had won, and the farther duties which yet remained to his valor to perform. He thought with pride of the applauses which he should win from Spain—the thanks of his sovereign, the shouts of his people, of which these, that occasionally ascended to his ears, were so many faint but expressive harbingers. Even at that moment the messenger was in the court below, bearing the fatal missive from the dishonored Cava.

"In no hand but that of Julian of Consuegra, can I place the letter."

Such was the answer of the courier to the attendant.

"Follow me."

He did so, and stood in the presence of the warrior.

"From whence?" demanded the latter.

"From Spain—from the city of Toledo. I bring a letter from one who bade me haste, and find my reward from Count Julian. The grass has not grown beneath my feet."

"'Tis well," said Julian, slowly receiving the letter. Then addressing the attendant: "Take him hence, and see him fed and comforted. Yet stay—remain! From whom got you this missive?"

"I know not well. He was a Cambrian friar."

"An evil race, methinks—a restless, troublesome——! The writing would seem to be that of Cava!—of my child!"

Julian went aside, and with the letter still unopened within his grasp, trode slowly the apartment. Pausing at the side opposite that where the messenger stood, he contemplated the superscription of the letter with signs of emotion.

"I know not why, but something disturbs me. I feel a vague sense of evil. This is the writing of my child, but how unlike! The line is uneven—the words are interrupted. She writes not usually thus—and to me! The child has suffered—she is sick! Jesu grant it be not worse! But this is a sorry weakness!"

He unfolded the missive as he spoke—drew near one of the cressets which burned against the wall, and proceeded to read. On a sudden his cheek paled, then flushed—a convulsion passed over his countenance and shook his frame. He looked round him, and exclaimed:

"Ha! stay! where is this villain courier?"

Then, as his eye found him—the object which it sought—he crumpled the scrawl in his hand, bounded forward, and before the astonished messenger was conscious of his movements, he had grappled him about the neck. A simple effort sufficed to bring him to the floor. The serf was as an infant in the clutches of the strong man. He gasped—he could not speak—while the terrified attendant looked on aghast, with horror and surprise. The scene lasted but an instant only. As suddenly as he had taken hold upon his victim, did Julian release him from his grasp. He rose slowly to an erect position, and, while the big veins stood out, cord-like, upon his forehead, and big drops of sweat rose upon his brow, he moved backward a few steps, seemingly, in the effort to recover himself. The courier partly rose also, but, as if still apprehensive of danger, crouched once more upon the floor.

"Rise!" said Julian.

The man obeyed him in silence.

"Hither—to me!"

He betrayed some reluctance to obey the farther command.

"Fear nothing! Nay, even though you prove false, fear nothing. Hither!"

The tones were hollow and strange. They did not assure the trembling messenger, but he dared not hesitate. He approached; and, seizing one of the lights that stood at hand, Julian thrust it close beside the countenance of the man, and steadily gazed upon his features. The scrutiny lasted but an instant.

"He is, indeed, nothing but a courier. Take him hence."

When he was gone, Julian once more unfolded the fatal letter, which had been crushed in his grasp even before he had finished its perusal. Once more he took it to the light, and with desperate determination proceeded to make himself master of its contents. He did so. His hands fell at his side. The cruel paper escaped his grasp. His eyes were lifted up in agony to heaven, and then closed as if in the pangs of a deatn spasm. With the single words—

"My child! my child!"—

He sunk, in a convulsion, upon the floor of the aparment.

CHAPTER II.

Terrible indeed was the shock to the unhappy father. A man of intense passions, of indomitable pride, of exquisite sensibility—for all these may, and do, frequently exist together—thus dishonored by his sovereign at the very moment when he was most exultant in the consciousness of having achieved for the kingdom of that monarch one of the most important victories,—the revulsion of feeling was actually so great as to choke, for the moment, all the most vital faculties of his physical and mental nature. For more than two hours he lay unnoticed in his swoon. His officers and followers were too busy without, in attendance upon their duties, or in the enjoyment of those sports and revels which grew naturally out of their recent triumph, to know any thing of the suffering of the strong man within. It was by the slow recovery of his unassisted faculties, that he finally became relieved from this situation. His eyes opened upon the scene around him. The cressets were still burning upon the wall. The fatal letter of Cava lay beside him. His convulsion had served in some degree to obliterate the impression of his misery. He had but a vague, confused sense of suffering—an imperfect memory of a terrible wo—dark, fathomless, eternal. But the sight of the scrawl, as he half rose from the floor, restored his more perfect consciousness. He grasped it convulsively.

"It is no dream!" he exclaimed; "the truth is here—the cruel, horrible truth! God of heaven, have I been reserved for this!"

He took the paper in his grasp. Once more he crumpled it in his hand, as if to stifle its cruel tidings. Once more he unfolded it, and drew near to the lights. As he read, the strong man grew once more convulsed with his agony. But, this time, the pressure upon the heart and brain was somewhat lessened by the big drops which gushed out of his burning eyes.

"My child! my poor child! why hast thou been abandoned of heaven? Why was thy innocence no surety—no safeguard? Oh! brutal, bloody tyrant! Oh! dark, viperous wretch! insatiable for spoil—heedless of honor and of virtue! But I will set my foot upon thy neck! I will rend thee as the tiger rends the lamb! I will gloat upon thy agonies in death! My child, my child! thou shalt not pray vainly for the vengeance which is thy due!"

He strode the chamber with irregular but heavy steps, the letter clasped in his hands—then, closing and lifting them to heaven, he paused.

"I must return to Spain—I must rescue the poor child from his grasp. I must do this with the smile of one who knows no injury—who feels no hurt. I am desolate at Ceuta—thus will I declare myself. I need my child, my comforter, at Ceuta. On this plea will I get her from his arms—and then! oh! then——"

Voices were heard before the entrance. He paused, the door was unclosed, and one of his officers appeared conducting a stranger.

"Who is this? Who art thou?"

The stranger answered:

"Let this man retire; then will I speak."

"Be it so. Speak! Who art thou?"

The officer disappeared, The stranger advanced.

"Look on me. Thou knowest me."

"No! I know thee not."

"'Tis well."

The stranger was of graceful and becoming form, and bore himself with an air of natural majesty. The tones of his voice were sweet, but solemn. His garments were those of a monk, but they were rent and stained by travel and exposure. Julian perused him for a moment with an indifferent eye, which showed no sign of recognition.

"Thou knowest me not; yet thou shouldst know me. I am Egiza, son to Witiza!"

"Ha! thou art he who sought my daughter to wife? Coward that thou art, loving this unhappy maiden—thou in Spain, breathing the same atmosphere with her—thou hast yet suffered her to fall a victim to this brutal tyrant. Methinks, hadst thou but half manhood, didst thou cherish but a tittle of the passion which thou didst profess, thy arm could have saved her from this cruel, killing wrong. Thou wouldst have been taught by quickest instincts the moment of her danger; thou wouldst have been nigh and powerful to save her when she cried aloud for help. Methinks I hear her now—that voice! that innocent, entreating voice—it is ringing in mine ears! Hark! dost thou not hear? 'Save me! father! dear father! Wilt thou not save me from this monster!'"

Julian assumed the attitude of one who listens—his finger uplifted—his head thrown forward—his air that of one absorbed in attention. But he maintained the attitude for an instant only. He turned abruptly upon his visitor:

"Thou didst not help! Perchance thou couldst not. Well, what brings thee hither now?"

"To aid thee."

"In what do I need thy help?"

"In vengeance!"

"Ha! true! There is *that* yet for us. But we must pluck the victim from the monster—the lamb from the wolf! My child, still precious though dishonored, flies to my love from the arms of this monster. We must smile for this! Put on the lamb, approach meekly, play the hypocrite; and only show the teeth when the precious innocent is safe from harm. Thou lovest her—thou hast loved her, young man. I repent me that I did not yield her to thy love. But I nothing dreamed of this. How should I dream of such indignity to child of mine! That this reckless king should dare so high—should so presume on brutal appetite—should—— But this avails us nothing. Thou wouldst aid me—we would have our revenge. Well, it shall be so. I must first remove my child from the embraces of this Roderick."

"This is already done!"

"Ha! thou hast saved her?"

"She is saved!"

"How? Here?"

"In death? The beautiful Cava is no more among the living, unless it be with the angelic hosts of heaven!"

"God! I thank thee! This one pang is spared me, that her blood crimsons not these hands. Dear child! may the blessed have thee in keeping! Thou art with thy mother, in heaven; Frandina, Cava—he who loved ye, and loved ye only, stands alone on earth. He hath now but one work before him, and that must be accomplished."

A brief period was employed by the wretched sire in giving utterance to that natur?' ebullition of passion which the terrible event occasioned in his soul; and he then succeeded in so far subduing the expression of his agony, as to listen to a long and painful narrative which Egiza had to relate. This over, Count Julian summoned his attendants. A stern composure settled upon his features as they made their appearance; and, commanding them to prepare an apartment for his guest, he proceeded to shut himself in from every eye.

"Leave me, now," he said in subdued accents. "I cannot hide the agony which rends me, and it suits not that I should bear, in any presence, the expression of a weakness which befits not my authority. This night for sorrow. When we again meet, young man, it will be for other and sterner feelings. The attendant will lead thee to a chamber. Sleep, if thou canst!"

With a stern gripe of the hand—such a pressure as one gives who feels how inadequate are words to the earnest thoughts which he yet desires to express—he dismissed the young man to the care of the attendant. Then, fastening the door of the apartment, as excluding all further interruption for the night, he yielded himself up to those humiliating contemplations, which must naturally be supposed to oppress a mind and spirit so endowed and so constituted as were his. What were his meditations and what his agonies—in what hopes and memories he found his consolations, if any of these he had—must be left to the farther progress of this narration, and to the lively conjectures of the reader. But, till a late hour of the night, his footsteps might have been heard by the warders who kept watch in the courts below, as he strode, with irregular movement but without pause, in the otherwise silent chamber above.

CHAPTER III.

It was long past midnight when the chamber assigned to Egiza was thrown open by a page and entered by Count Julian, who bore in his own hand the lamp which gave light to the apartment. The young exiled prince, exhausted by anxiety and travel, was sleeping; but his sleep was troubled with fearful and tormenting images. He groaned piteously, and his arms were extended, and his hands closed, with the action of one engaged in a struggle with his direst enemy. Julian, as he beheld this sight, dismissed the attendant, and, setting the light upon the floor, bent over the sleeper. His hands were placed upon his shoulder, and his voice summoned him to rise. There was an impatience in his movement, and in the tones of his utterance, which seemed occasioned by the fact that one, suffering, though perhaps in different degree, from the same cruel affliction with himself, could thus subside into consolatory slumbers. The agony in his own heart taught him to believe that his eyelids would never again be visited by that sweet soother of the wretched and desponding soul.

"Arise, and come with me! Thou hast surely slept enough. It will help thy slumbers hereafter, when thou hearest that we are now on our quest of vengeance. Arise, if thou hast the heart for food like this!"

Egiza was upon his feet in an instant.

"I am ready," was his only answer.

"Give me thy hand!" said Julian, while he extinguished the light. He grasped the wrist of the youth, who felt the fingers of his conductor, like so many icicles, closing upon his own. In this manner they went forward, the youth unknowing whither. In a few moments they found themselves in the court of the citadel and under the full glory of the starlight. The heavens wore an unclouded hue of such sweet serenity, that Egiza looked upward with the momentary flush of one who fancies that pure spirits are gazing down upon him. Julian's eyes were fixed upon the earth. His fingers still grasped the hand of the youth, with a muscular tenacity which only forbore to give pain. They went on in silence until they reached a postern. Here Julian spoke a few words, in low tones, in the ears of a soldier who made way for them as they emerged through the opening. The gates were closed behind them, and as the morning star looked out from his fold they found themselves beyond the walls of Ceuta and on their way to the tents of the Almagreb.

"Whither do we go?" demanded Egiza, somewhat impatient of the silence. His hand had been released by his conductor the moment they were without the fortress.

"What matter?" said the other. "Hast thou anywhere a home? Hast thou a country? Art thou not an exile—a banished man! Is it not permitted to any one to slay thee! What shouldst thou care whether thy feet wander through the courts of Andalusia, or among the wild tents of Tingitania?"

"It is true!" said Egiza, mournfully, and with that seeming lassitude of spirit which was but too apt to control and enfeeble his energies.

"True! ay! But is that good reason why thou shouldst faint? Is it not something to move thee to manhood rather?—to make thee show thy strength, thy resolution—to arm thee with pride and hate—to fill thee with a bitter anxiety for strife—to give thee courage—to show thee where vengeance is to be won, and make thee to laugh at dangers?"

"Thinkst thou that I fear?"

"No. But not to fear is not enough? The common brute opposes a firm front to the danger which assails him in his own jungle, but the nobler nature waits not to be baited in his den. To endure is the mule's courage—to contend is the lion's instinct. The breadth of back and strength of sinew counsels one—the great spirit informs the other. Wouldst thou have vengeance, there must be deeds as well as endurance: a courage to seek and assail, not less than a hardihood to contend with the danger when it comes. I tell thee, man, I am one to pluck down the temple upon my own shoulders, if so be that I can drag my enemy in the same moment beneath the toppling ruins!"

"What meanest thou?"

"I have said to thee—hast thou a country?"

"Have I not answered?—I have none!"

"Nor I! nor I! But yesterday I had a country! Did I not love that country? Witness, ye stars, that have seen my watches for her safety—ye sands, that have beheld my marches and my battles—with what ardor, what constancy, what strength, let the Arab tell you—let all Tingitania, all Spain declare! Over these plains but this day I hurried, smiting, sweeping the swarthy Arab from my path with the unsparing edge of the sword. Look around you: here are the proofs. My foot, even now, is upon an enemy's carcass!"

Egiza recoiled. Such was the fact. The face of the slain man was turned upward, pale and immovable, beneath the light of the stars. Rigid in death, his eyes were yet opened to the heavens, glazed and glittering with a spectral stare, that made the youth for a moment forgetful of his own griefs in the natural horror of his emotions. Before him were numerous proofs of the truth which Julian uttered. Their course lay along the plain of battle. Their feet were momently among the dead. Little heaps lay, at intervals, where the opposing combatants had fallen together; and sometimes the sandals of the prince were held to the earth in the little puddles of congealed, or congealing gore, which, but a few hours past, had warmed som hopeful human heart.

"Ay, here they lie! These are sacrifices, which, but this day, I offered up fo the safety of my country. This hour I have no country! The desert is now mor dear to me than Spain. These Arabs whom I slew—they who survive—are les the foes of Julian than the Goth and the sovereign whom he serves with suc base fidelity."

Stern and solemn was the silence which ensued. Slowly they made their wa among the bodies of the slain. The plain of death was covered with thousand As far as the eye could stretch Egiza could detect the little heaps which, he to well conceived, were raised of stiffened corses that had lately been living hearts. A natural horror kept him silent while they hurried forward. But, indeed, Egiz knew not well what answer to make in the hearing of a passion, such as that o Julian, which seemed so much more intense and overwhelming than his own. H did not conceive the purpose of the other, though he had vague doubts and mi givings of the purport of the journey. But, with that incertitude of charact which distinguishes the feebler moral nature, he did not venture to question i object. He did not demand, as the more determined temper always does, that th blind should be taken from his eyes. The superior will of his conductor effectually cowed and coerced his own. On they went, he following in a silence which, but for the mutual solemnity of their thoughts, would have been humiliating to his mental independence. He was in no mood for speech—and brief, broken exclamations only, now fell from the lips of Julian. Still they trode through ranks of the dead. At length they reached the summit of a hill which they had been gradually ascending. Here the carnage seemed to have been most terrific. Here the pursuit ceased—and the last terrible struggle had been made by the fugitives to unite against their pursuers. Every step was made over bodies of the slain. The light-armed Arab, with his dark eyes glistening in death, lay grappled and stiff in the immovable grasp of the more muscular soldier of the north. The fire seemed to linger still in the eyes of the one, and the fierce muscular compression of strife was still conspicuous in the close pressed lips and frowning forehead of the other. Gazing, even against his will, upon these frightful images, Egiza was not conscious of those farther objects towards which the hand of Julian was outstretched.

"See you not?" said the latter.

The tones of his voice, which were hollow, struck painfully upon the ear of his companion. He looked up. They stood on the summit of the hill, the opposite side of which sank abruptly. The wide spread plain was before them; and, in the distance, a thousand dusky objects were spread out which the inexperienced eye might not define, and scarcely distinguish

"Seest thou?" said Julian.

"What are these?"

"The tents of the Arab!"

"Ha!"

"Within those tents sleep the soldiers of Muza Ben Nosier. But this day my foes, they were driven with shame and bitter discomfiture from before the walls of Ceuta. Now !——"

"What wouldst thou ?"

"Now !—I hold them foes no longer. The savage is the friend of Julian—the Arab, the African, the wolf, sooner than Roderick and Spain. This night I take my place in the tents of the Arab."

"Thou will not yield thy country to the infidel ?"

"I have no country !"

"Why hast thou brought me here ?"

"For vengeance !"

"I will not go with thee !"

"Thou shalt !"

"I will not be a traitor to my country—yield my religion to the infidel—renounce my God !"

"Country—God—religion ! Ha ! ha ! ha ! Why did I cumber myself with this boy ? What ! thou hast a country ? It has given thee a precious shelter ! A God ? He has watched over thee truly with paternal care ! Religion ? Verily ! thou wearest the garments ! Go to ! thou art no man !"

"Show me the way to vengeance upon Roderick, and thou shalt see if I lack manhood."

"And thinkest thou, idle boy, that the arm of Julian would need thy help if fate should give us chance to meet Roderick in combat ? And thinkest thou that such poor revenge as his destruction will satisfy a thirst like mine ?"

"What vengeance wouldst thou have ?"

"Vengeance upon the criminal, be sure ! vengeance upon his creatures—the ministers of his will—those who pander to his lusts, and stimulate his monstrous appetites !"

"I am with thee."

"Nor these alone. I will leave my vengeance as a trophy upon the face of the land over which he sways ! Her blackened cities shall be the monuments of my wrath ? Her smoking turrets shall proclaim my triumph, as, in their pride of place, they beheld the dishonor of my child !. Ages yet to come, which shall hear of the shame of Cava, shall hear, also, of the terrible vengeance of her sire ! The Arab shall be the weapon of my wrath !"

"We part : I go with thee no more !"

"Nay ! nay ! we cannot part ! Thou shalt go with me, thou shalt partake in this glorious consummation. My daughter gave thee her love—I had been better pleased had she chosen a bolder spirit ; but as she loved thee, thou shalt partake of the vengeance to which I dedicate my soul this hour. Spain is no more thy country. Thou art a banished and proscribed man. We cannot conquer Roderick but through the heart of Spain. Come with me, my son. It is not that I seek thy help, or care for what thy arm may do ; but I would have thee share, for my child's sake, the great revenge which is to pacify my heart !"

"I dare not ! True, I have no country, but I will not be a traitor to the country which was once mine !"

"Will not ! Say'st thou, will not ? Say not so. Be not rash—be not erring, my son. Bethink thee ! Be wise—be bold. Be with me the minister of a mighty vengeance." This was said entreatingly and in subdued accents.

"I cannot—I will not—dare not !"

"Will not ? Then thou diest ! Thus I cut asunder all the links which bind me to the soil of Spain !"

Sudden and terrible was the doom that followed. The fierce man smote the unconscious victim to the earth with a single stroke of his dagger. He uttered not a word—not a groan. The weapon had passed into his heart with unerring aim, and the unhappy prince fell on his face, upon a hillock of Gothic and Arabian dead. Julian lifted the dagger aloft in the starlight, as if dedicating it to the service of some observant Fate; then, calmly folding it beneath his vest, he continued his way in the direction of the tents of Muza Ben Nosier.

CHAPTER IV.

We have said that this deed was executed calmly. There is a calm of the passions, when most excited, when most intense, just as there is in the tempest, when all its powers are most awfully arrayed for action. The temperament of Julian was of a sort that, after the first terrible outbreak, appears singularly subdued even in its fiercest rages. It is as if the ordinary exercise of thought and judgement, overthrown by one deep convulsion, no longer provoke, by their unadvised suggestions, any farther struggle with that frenzy which they have already felt so forcibly. Shrinking from the conflict, they leave the torrent unopposed, and though it still rushes headlong with irresistible power, yet its waters, meeting with no obstruction, no opposition, move forward smoothly and with even surface, to the bosom of the mighty deep. Of their volume, of their depth, of the vast troops of terrible forms that glide below, ravenous for prey, the eye sees nothing on the seemingly placid and innocent waves above. There is nothing more awful in the moral world than those mighty passions which thus hurry forward, wearing a surface so deceitful.

Yet Julian was not calm. There was nothing placid in his soul. There, all was confusion and uproar—a conflict which he could not govern—frenzies by which he was mastered—which his thoughts no longer availed him to oppose. It was only to the eye that he was thus subdued. That he felt something of the awful deed which he had just done, may be inferred from the brief sentences which fell from his lips as he proceeded—musings which seemed in some degree designed to lessen the enormity of the offence, by showing how valueless was the previous boon of life of which his sudden stroke had deprived his companion. The stern philosophy which he thus expressed, was found in that fanatic mood which has, in every age, provoked to like performances some of the most remarkable of men.

"Incapable of vengeance, for what should he have lived? If there be no natural passion to be fed—if there be no country to retrieve, no father to protect, no wife to love, no pride to feel, and no revenge to take—there is death only. He could not have lived to hope—he might to shame. It is better thus. Enough, that he stands not in my path—obstructs me not—thwarts not, with his feminine fears, the great work to which, this hour—hear me, ye Arab dead, whom I have stricken!—I dedicate all that is left me of strength, or soul, or passion. Spain! Spain! thou hast looked on the dishonor of my child, and shalt share in the doom to which I devote the tyrant thou hast served. Thou heardst her cries! thou sawest her agonies! thou knowest her shame! Thou shalt know the vengeance of her sire! Come to me, dark spirits of the Moslem and of night. Mohammed!—Lucifer! I summon ye, here upon the field, from which a thousand gloomy ghosts are rising up in your honor—I summon ye to the retribution craved by mine! Take from me these feebler affections which would unman me. Take from me all human thoughts of country, friends, affections—make me what ye would have me—that, working in your cause, I may triumph in my own!"

An awful majesty—the gloomy pride of a satanic spirit—glared from the countenance, and declared itself in the attitude and action of Julian, as thus, in sentences more broken than in our arrangement of them, he devoted himself to the stern deities of hate and vengeance. His form seemed to dilate as if in communion with the invisible world which he thus challenged to the audience. His hand was stretched in threatening to the opposite shores of Spain. His voice was deep and portentous. Terrible, indeed, was the shock which he had received. The mind of power was deranged—the nice adjustment of its capacities was partially lost, but there was still a strange and awful harmony in its action, in obedience to the new and absorbing motive which his spirit had received. It seemed as if the new deities which he invoked had accorded him a nature, in lieu of that nobler one which he had lost, by which his way was shown him—dark and marked by madness as it was—inflexibly to one consistent end and undeviating purpose. It is thus that the intense aim of the monomaniac accords to his moods the semblance of a method, which is wanting to all its purposes but one. The mind of Julian could now grasp but a single object. There was no need for reason—her faculties were suspended. Even as he waved his hands in threatening—even as he invoked his deities of vengeance—a gloomy form, a dusky shadow, with long trailing garments, swept between him and the red orb, on which his eye was unconsciously cast. A shrill gust passed over the bloody plain, and Julian felt that his prayer was answered. The dark and mighty spirits which he had summoned had yielded to his wish. His invocation was heard, his vow sanctioned—his foot was yet to be placed upon the neck of his prostrate country.

He had now no relentings. He hurried toward the tents of the Arab. There they lay, a thousand dusky shapes, with their crescent-summits gently gleaming in the starlight. The horse-tails were waving before each. The great banner of the prophet rose up conspicuous in the centre, just beside the tent of Muza. On its top shone forth a golden emblem of the moon in the first quarter, which, to the eye of the faithful, might naturally seem to ray out with a brightness of its own. Wild and beautiful was the scene, silent and softly peaceful, of that strange and wondrous picture. The camp of the Moslem lay as still, in the serene starlight, as the crowding dead, among whose insensible forms the feet of Julian had passed. But he beheld as little of the splendid beauty of the one scene, as he had done of the terrible features of the other. The eye of his soul was turned within, and there were objects of more startling character there, for his contemplation, than any in the external picture. The hell of a heaven-abandoned heart, conscious of wrong—or it may be unconscious—but going aside from all the social gods which it has been taught to follow and obey, is too much crowded with its own horrors to find any in the external world.

A light from the tent of Muza streamed timidly forth and lay in a long direct line, stretching to the very foot of the great standard of the prophet. At the foot of this standard, Julian of Consuegra came suddenly to a pause. He lingered for a moment. Here his guardian genius made its last stand. Virtue opposed herself, however faintly and feebly, to the haughty strength of her assailant. But her voice had sunk into a whisper. It was not entirely unheard—but it was unheeded. The demon of vengeance mocked her supplications. Hate answered, with terrible strength of utterance, to all the suggestions of love. The dark spirits were about to triumph. One involuntary shudder passed over the form of the apostate, marking the brief conflict between the contending genii. The ties of country were given to the winds. The remembrances of youth—the triumphs of manhood—the honors of a family name—the trophies of reputation—the regard of friends—the tributes of the good and great—all availed nothing in that final struggle. With clenched hands, thrice shaken toward the shores of Spain, Julian advanced firmly to the tent of the Moslem. The die was cast. His form covered the light which guided his footsteps to the entrance. He did not suffer himself to linger, but, with a will becoming more and more obdurate with every moment of delay, he strode with deliberate resolve, and growing erectness, within the concealing folds of the canvas, which, in the same moment was to shut him out from his country and his God.

CHAPTER V.

The night was far advanced when Julian of Consuegra penetrated the tent of the Arabian, Musa Ben Nosier. But the latter did not sleep. He was even then busy with his best consellors, in considering the events of the late battle, its disastrous effects, and in how far it was in his power to repair them. Deep, indeed, was the mortification which he felt at the signal defeat which he had sustained. The Arab warrior was unaccustomed to reverses. Hitherto, his army had swept onwards with the inresistible wing of the tempest. Thousands had perished by the way side, but countless swarms, that seemed never to know decrease, had gone forward, like their own locusts, blackening the face of the land, and leaving but desolation behind them in token of their terrible progress. His sword had indeed seemed to carry with it, as claimed by the Moslem prophet, the irresistible will of the deity. The oriental kingdoms, realms the most powerful in the East, had yielded to his arms. That he should be baffled upon the shores of the Atlantic by the Northern warriors, scarcely numbering one tenth his legions, might well provoke his fiercest passions and prompt the expression of his immitigable rage. Musa Ben Nosier was a man of terrible passions. But he also knew, in some degree, the art of suppressing or silencing their exhibiton. He could enjoy their excitements, yet hide their show. The flame could burn in his bosom—nay, warm it into powerful impulse and decision, yet could he preserve upon his features the aspect of a most placid calm, an indifference amounting to coldness, which effectually baffled the anticipations and judgment of the beholder. He was greatly advanced in years. Seventy summers had passed over his head, yet he looked not less bold, less strong, or less capable of endurance. His beard was thick, and hung down upon his breast, soft, white and flowing, as that of the earliest patriarchs of the East. White as the snows of Caucasus, he had the art of dying it with henna when he came before strangers, by which, as his cheeks were smooth and unwrinkled, the appearance of much age was removed from his face, and the spectator beheld only a great warrior, in whose limbs there was yet the promise of long years of brave achievement. The unexpected entrance of Count Julian surprised him, and the white beard, now loose and untrimmed, betrayed the extreme age of the venerable warrior. He sat upon a divan of oriental richness. His tent declared the vanity and the wonder of his conquests. The shawls and furs of one region, the crimson drapery of another, the gems and jewels of a third—were hung, or strewn about the chamber, in careless profusion. In the centre burned a glorious cresset, whose rim, crowned with precious stones, cast about the apartment a prismatic halo which dazzled the uplooking vision to behold. The caftan of the old warrior was set with jewels. The scymitar which lay upon his lap was surmounted in like manner. A sapphire, whose worth might be that of a princely city, glowed softly upon the front of his turban, from which shot up a single feather of the heron.

Musa Ben Nosier was in council with his best officers. Their personal state was scarcely less imposing than his own. Their conquests over wealthy nations, had led to their adoption, in great degree, of the wealth and and luxuries of which they came into possession; and, indeed, the love of splendor is natural to the simplest tribes of the Orient. Five war-like captains surrounded their chief. They were a hardy and valiant band, with fiery black eyes, swarthy cheeks, and great muscular activity Their words, as they conferred together, were few, but expressive. Their tones were low and earnest. Their countenances denoted depression, but showed nothing of unmanly despondency. They felt their reverses, it is true, and were mortified by them—but these feelings did not lead to any abandonment of hope or resolution. It was of their future hope and resolution that they spoke, when the gigantic form of Julian of Consuegra stood proudly in their midst. His superior height and bulk, the massy vigor of his limbs, his erect majestic frame, fierce commanding eye, might well cause to start the inferior persons—inferior in majesty and bulk at least—by whom he was surrounded. His air was rather that of conquest and defiance, than of friendship or solicitation.

In an instant every form was erect, every eye darkened with indignation, every scymitar flashed in the light of the burning cresset, as if winged for instant execution. Old Musa Ben Nosier was in a moment on his feet, his right foot thrown back, his right arm swung in air, and his keen weapon of Damascus, glittering in a snake like circle behind his own head, ready to descend upon that of the intruder. Scornful and haughty was the smile with which Julian beheld these preparations. His form remained unshaken, erect and unmoved, as at his first entrance. His arms were folded upon his breast with the placid indifference of one who feels that there is nothing now for him to fear.

"What!" he exclaimed, "fear you danger from one man, he weaponless, save with this, and this even now dripping with Christian blood!"

He drew from his breast the dagger with which he had stricken down the young prince, Egiza, to the earth. Thus speaking, he flung the weapon at the feet of the Arab chieftain.

"Behold me!" he exclaimed, "Julian of Consuegra, your enemy—he stands unarmed among ye—strike if ye see fit, and if thus your terrors move ye!"

Musa Ben Nosier lowered his scymitar, and resumed his seat upon the divan—the weapon was again laid across his lap. His followers, at a sign from their chief, forbore their attitudes of defence.

"Why comes Julian of Consuegra to the tents of the faithful?" demanded Musa. "Why comes our enemy to the Arab? Would he have peace with the sons of the prophet?"

"He would *give* it—and more! He would give them victory!"

"Ha! speak on!"

"Julian comes to bring conquest to the tents of the prophet. He comes to yield the keys of Tingitania—nay, more—Musa Ben Nosier shall have possession of those keys which unlock the gates of Spain—which secure the empire of the Goth—the great cities of Roderick—realms of wealth and splendor—territories of pride and numbers—such as the Arab does not dream in all his Mauritanian range—these are gifts which Julian brings to the Arab!"

"Thou canst do this, and wilt?" demanded Musa eagerly.

"I can do this, and will."

"Wherefore? What wouldst thou that Musa Ben Nosier shall do for thee in return?"

"Give me vengeance!"

"Vengeance!"

"Ay! vengeance! the last, the best food to the famishing heart of pride. The blood of the tyrant—the foe! Thou shalt have all Tingitania, all Spain, so that thou shalt help me to my vengeance upon Roderick who sways the realm thereof."

"What hath he done to thee, that thou shouldst hate him thus?"

"What matter that thou shouldst know? Enough that he hath wronged me so that I pant for vengeance—so that I have but one prayer—one passion—and that is for his blood. Let this suffice thee—this is enough for thee to know."

"Nay, by the prophet, but thou errest, Count Julian of Consuegra. We may not trust the enemies of the prophet but for good cause. This day thou fightest like a brave soldier and a faithful, in behalf of thy king and country; this night thou wouldst destroy them both. That thou wast in earnest this day, when thou didst battle under the banners of the cross, thousands of the slain among my people declare from the bed of slaughter where they lie. But that thou art in earnest in what thou sayest to-night, is a matter to be shown by sufficient reason. What has happened to thee since we met in battle but this morning, to make so great a change in thy heart? What have been the tidings of this night, that thou art here with a language which is now so strange?"

Wild and terrible was the meaning in that eye which the Count Julian cast upon the speaker.

"Moor!" said he, "there are some words which the proud heart dreads to speak. There are some truths too terrible for the strongest soul to bear when spoken. Thou art a warrior—thou canst feel what it is to be stricken with dishonor! Ha! thou canst feel shame—thou hast a guess that there are some injuries that stain as well as hurt—that degrade as well as destroy. Wouldst thou have me name my hurt? Wouldst thou have me linger over the words that tell of my dishonor—that show me trampled in the earth, with all that the Christian heart considers holy in the world of his private affections, made loathsome, even when most precious in his eyes?"

"There are offences against the proud heart which it feels shame to declare, even as thou sayest," replied the Arab, gravely.

"Think thou then that mine is the worst of these—that there is none more terrible or humbling to the soul, than is the one which hath driven Julian of Consuegra to thy tents, seeking that vengeance which else he may not compass. He comes to thee with a cry of blood. He will give thee blood. Thy sword shalt grow weary of slaughter in the ranks of the Christian—thy feet shall tread upon their haughtiest necks—thy crescent shall shed its baleful lights from the high turrets which now bear the banner of the cross. These shall be thy triumphs, if thou will lend thyself to mine. Array thy troops with mine at my bidding, and I will lead thee into the very heart of Spain. I will yield that fatal country to the empire of thy Caliph. For me, I have but one prayer—I make but one stipulation—that no weapon in thy array shall dare uplift itself against the heart of Roderick. He shall be my prize and victim only. I claimed his life for my reward. That is the one sole prayer, as it is now the sole object, which dwells in mine!"

"Thou hast said well, and if Musa Ben Nosier, leading the troops of the prophet, could put faith in the words of the infidel——"

"Pshaw! what dost thou heed of these tenets of a national superstition—thine or mine!" was the scornful response of the apostate. "Thou art a man and a warrior. What matter to thee these idle reveries of the dreamer and the woman—these miserable mummeries by which the cunning priesthood fetters the feeble spirit to its own purposes. Thy God shall be mine, if thou wilt. I have a purpose—a conquest—a large human desire, which reigns paramount in my bosom. Thou hast also. Shall these be baffled and set at nought because of a fable. I tell thee, Musa Ben Nosier, if thou hast at heart the triumphs of thy Caliph, as Julian of Consuegra hath those of his revenge, then will thy faith in me carry thee far above the miserable superstitions of those creeds which make the vulgar worship among our mutual people. It is not what I believe, but whether thou believest me! Look I like one who comes hither to deceive? Have I put myself, unweaponed, in thy power, for a falsehood? See'st thou not in these eyes—in this face—hearest thou not in my voice—in these accents—that I am dishonored—wrought by shame to madness—that I am terribly earnest in what I promise—in what I demand? If thou be true to thy Caliph, thou canst not help but give thy faith to my assurance. Thy question is not whether I believe in Jesus or Mahomet, but whether I believe in the tyranny and crimes of Roderick—whether I am sincere and resolute in the burning desire to avenge them."

We need not pursue the details of this conference. Suffice it that Musa Ben Nosier still hesitated. He was a truer worshipper, after his faith and fashion, than Count Julian had ever been with his. He believed that, to the inherent virtues of Mohammedanism, all his successes were fairly to be ascribed; and he looked with real horror upon the apostate when he so coolly declared his indifference equally to all religions. Julian, meanwhile, had withdrawn himself, with averted brow, as if disdaining farther exhortation or argument, to a remote part of the tent; leaving the Arab generals to discuss among themselves what decision to make upon the matter. It does not need that we should inquire how it was that Musa showed himself so cautious in committing his armies to a project which promised so greatly for the success of his cause. It may be that he knew not the extent or the weakness of the empire of Roderick—it may be that he questioned the ability of Julian to convert his forces to the cause of their country's enemy. It was certainly impossible to doubt the terrible sincerity of Julian's hate, gleaming out in his eyes, and articulate in every syllable of his keen and anguished utterance. It did not matter that the Moslem did not feel in the same degree with the Christian warrior the cruelty and shame of the peculiar wrong which had driven him to desperation, and which, by the way, it became necessary for him to declare in language which was humiliatingly distinct. The purity of woman forms but a humble consideration in the eyes of a people who regard her, in the highest point of view, only as a minister to the most sensual appetites of man. Her fidelity, as a creature of the harem, does not necessarily involve a guaranty of her purity as a moral being.

But, while Musa doubted, one of his warriors, who had hitherto observed the most cautious silence, approached and challenged attention. Tall and gaunt, with a face scarred with wounds, and roughened by long exposure to the worst conflicts of the seasons, was the person of this warrior. He was a genuine Arab—one whose soul might be said to live only in arms and the excitement of the strife. His height, like that of Saul, exceeded that of most men; his arms, unequally long, extended almost to his knees. To complete the hardness and severity of this outline, he was wanting an eye, which was stricken out by an hostile lance in one of his numerous battles. He was called for this reason *el Tuerto*, or the One-Eyed; Taric el Tuerto! This man had no pleasures but in war. His affections were set upon his steed and scymitar. He was the perfect master of his weapon; and it was wonderful, even among his brother Arabs, to see with what proficiency he could use the lance in battle. He had been marked from his boyhood as one of whom wonders might yet be known; and there were prophecies among his native people of Damascus, that promised that he should one day become a mighty instrument for conquest in the hands of Mahomet. It may be that this was one of those predictions which lead to their own verification. It may be that, even in this hour, in the tent of Musa, Taric el Tuerto, hearkening to the words of Count Julian, and heeding the reluctance of his general, remembered the early tradition of his youth.

"Why," said he "should you doubt the assurance of the Christian? Is it not a great conquest which he promises? Shall we forego this conquest because of the peril? Is it that we have no soldiers for the adventure? Are lives too precious for the risk? Are the warriors of the prophet too apprehensive of danger, to encounter peril for the promotion of his work? What is the peril? Death? I fear not death! A thousand sons of Ishmael are ready to fall with me in battle. I will take this danger, nothing fearing but that we shall find good friends. Give me but a handful of the forces of Waled, and send me forth with the Count Julian."

The words of the swarthy Arabian were of instant effect.

"If the Christian will swear upon the Koran—if he will forswear the cross, and adopt the crescent?" said Musa.

"Surely!" exclaimed Taric, looking to where Julian stood; "surely if he hath suffered this great wrong—if he hungers for this great revenge—he will not shrink from a trial of which he thinks so lightly."

The flushed features of Julian were turned upon the group. There was a moment's hesitation in his glance; but as he read the expression in their eyes, he strode toward them.

"Behold!" said he, and, as he spoke, his foot trampled heavily upon the cross-hilted dagger which he had previously cast upon the earth. The action was understood.

"It is good!" exclaimed Musa Ben Nosier, and, striking the little gong which stood beside him, he pronounced, in low accents, the single word, "Abul-Cassim!"

The priest made his appearance from a recess in the apartment—a man of venerable aspect, having a benign and gentle countenance. A few words from Musa explained his object. The Arab generals surrounded the apostate. Abul-Cassim advanced, bearing in one hand a splendid copy of the Koran, in the other a small casket of solid silver, in one of the compartments of which was a chafing dish of fiery coals. A rich stand of ebony, cushioned with crimson, was placed before him, upon which the Koran was laid. The casket of silver occupied a ledge or shelf below it. An odorous powder, cast upon the coals, sent up a grateful but somewhat oppressive perfume; and while this was floating in the confined atmosphere of the tent, Abul-Cassim brought forth a chrystal vase filled with the purest water. In this he motioned Julian to lave his fingers.

"This is a wretched mummery!" was the exclamation of the person addressed, but he complied with the requisition. This done, Abul-Cassim laid bare the wrist of the Christian, and, with a sharp instrument which he had previously dipped in some precious ointment, he punctured the skin. Julian submitted with the air of one who himself scorns the performance. The operation consumed but a single instant, and, when it was over, Julian observed, with a feeling of disquiet for which he was scarcely able to account, that a distinct blood-red crescent was visible upon the arm. Instinctively he passed his thumb over the character. The Emir smiled as he did so. It did not lessen the disquiet of the apostate to discover that his involuntary effort to obliterate the foreign and unnatural symbol was wholly fruitless. It was the effect of natural superstition that made him feel, however little of a Christian he had been before, that he was now wholly separated from Christian alliance, and delivered over to the arch enemy of that creed in which his people still believed and trembled. A chapter of the Koran was now read by Abul-Cassim, and Julian of Consuegra was ennobled in the ranks of the Moslem faithful. Did he fancy at that moment the distant shriek which filled the air? Was it, indeed, the last cry of the maternal genius, abandoning her sacred trust forever?

CHAPTER VI.

THE unholy compact was at length accomplished, and Julian of Consuegra, while the star of morning looked pale and ghastly down upon the uncovered faces of the slain, retraced his way over the field of battle to the walls of Ceuta. In the single hour which he had passed in the tents of the Arab, he had completed all the plans by which to render his treachery to his country successful in her overthrow. We need not dilate upon or detail the schemes in this object, devised between himself and Musa Ben Nosier. Let it suffice that the latter wrote to his caliph, Waled Almanzor, in all the exulting spirit of a newly acquired hope. He reminded him of his past conquests, and begged permission to undertake the new. Of this permission he had no doubt, and he suffered none to escape him of the entire success of those designs which he meditated now. The assurances of Julian were such as to remove all his fears of the powers of the Goth—fears which might naturally enough be awakened by the terrible repulse which he had just received before the walls of Ceuta. The apostate count had but too truly shown him the weakness of his country—its wealth, its vices, and the emasculating sloth and luxuries in which all ranks of her people indulged. Her strength lay chiefly in the army of the frontier, and that army, veterans under Julian himself, were, as he truly described them, faithful personal adherents of himself, rather than the subjects of Roderick, or the sons of Spain. The aged, but fiery souled Emir, depicted in his letter to the caliph, the empires already subdued, the spoils already won, and pronounced the treasures and the charms of that now unveiled before his eyes, and ripe for invasion, as superior to them all—equal to Syria in the serenity of its sky and the fertility of its soil; Arabia Felix in its delightful climate; India in its spices and fragrance; Cathay in its precious metals; Hegiaz in its fruits and flowers, and Aden in its majestic cities seated by the sea. Shall such a land, he asked, be left with the unbeliever, when we may so easily subdue it to the sceptre of the faithful. The caliph's reply was immediate and favorable. 'It is the will of Allah!' was his answer; and the legions of Islam, twelve thousand in number, under the conduct of Taric El Tuerto, were put in readiness, with the aid of Julian, to attempt the conquest.

The apostate chieftain was not idle. But his passion did not lessen his policy. He was one of those dark, proud spirits, who, with a soul shaken to the centre by his own great grief, can, after the first terrible convulsions, conceal utterly all outward commotion that is busy still within. Though a man of unbending and sleepless passions, he was yet a politician. From the moment, when at midnight, he left the tents of the Arabian, he devoted himself to the task of winning his soldiers to his purpose. For this purpose his great wealth was distributed among them. What was wealth and treasure to him who had first made the sacrifice of friends and country to the desires of an unsparing vengeance. His officers were already devoted to his will. His soldiers beheld in him their immediate sovereign, and acknowledged, in the long relationship which they had maintained together, a friend and leader, rather than a lord and master. It was not difficult to secure for himself those affections which had long been withdrawn, upon the skirts of Barbary, from any social affiinities with their own people dwelling beyond the straits. Julian was soon sure of his adherents.

He too had his correspondence. He wrote, by a trusty hand, to the Archbishop Oppas, and adroitly insinuated such hopes in the bosom of that subtle priest, as re-awakened in full all of his ambitious projects for the princes, his nephews, and himself. Of the fate of Egiza, Oppas knew nothing. Julian spared him that portion of his knowledge, secret to all but himself, of which he had left such a sudden and bloody record, at midnight, on the battle-field of Ceuta. But the archbishop had learned to base no calculations on the spirit of this feeble prince. His eye had gradually turned to Pelayo, as to the active hope of the royal family which had been deposed; and the letter of Julian had scarcely been received and announced, before his own mission, embodying the new hopes which he had imbibed from Julian, were transmitted to the daring young chief, who continued to bring together a little army in the secure passes of the Asturian mountains. The communication made to Pelayo informed him only of the defect of Julian, with the forces which he held at Ceuta. Of his own alliance with the Arabs, Julian had withheld the information from the archbishop. That was his secret only, for he dreaded lest the religious prejudices of the priest might render him reluctant, even at successful revolution, sustained and brought about by infidel alliance. His caution was unnecessary. Oppas was scarcely less corrigible, in this matter, though a Christian teacher, than himself. To the king—to Roderick, he who had thus driven him to the deepest desperation, and to the commission of the last of crimes—he also wrote. He was able, in this letter—such was the strength of his will, and the intense character of his hatred—to forbear all complaint, and every show of passion. He spoke of his daughter as if he knew not of her death—as if he entertained not the slightest notion of the brutal usage she had endured—and spoke to the tyrant, as if still his warm and confiding adherent. Bitter was the pang of suppression which the apostate felt, as he wrote this fraudulent epistle. Wild was the shudder which shook his frame as he laid his pen aside, and gave freedom to the emotions which he struggled successfully to keep down till the scroll was written. He had his policy in this also. He could tell the monarch of his victory—could dilate on its extent—its advantages, and the security which it had brought. But this security was not yet complete. The Arab was not entirely subdued. He was still in force in the pastural vallies which spread themselves in the sun, sheltered by the distant range of the Atlas mountains; and drawing new warriors to his thinned array from the numerous tribes of the desert, which had been subdued by the sword of Islam. To crush effectually this enemy—to drive him far from the neighborhood of Tingitania, and prevent the accumulation of powers which, at a later period, it might not be so easy to overcome, it was necessary that new succors should be sent to Ceuta. Arms and horses, in particular, were among the desired supplies, and for these Julian wrote to Roderick in language of entreaty, the earnestness of which was well calculated to make itself felt without provoking suspicion. Remembering the awful vision which he had witnessed in the mysterious cavern of Covadonga—the vision of these swarthy invaders, following in the pale light of the baleful crescent—recalling the terrible prediction which he could not drive from his senses, and which told him that, by infidels in this aspect, his sceptre was to be wrested from his hands, the soul of Roderick was startled by its fears, and he readily conceded to so brave a captain as Julian, all that he craved for the defence of the frontier against this greatly threatening foe. In his anxiety and apprehension, he stripped his kingdom of its means of defence, and, even as the apostate count had desired, accumulated, ready for the use of the traitor, the implements of war, and the steeds necessary for a mighty cavalry, conveniently at the foot of the rock of Calpe, one of the great guardian mountains which keep the entrance to the Mediterranean sea.

Circumstances continued to favor the progress of conspiracy. The temporary suspension of hostilities, and the disappearance of the Arabs from the immediate neighborhood of Ceuta, by withdrawing from sight the immediate danger, disarmed the fears of the Gothic monarch. The preparations which he made and the precautions which he had begun to take for the safety of his kingdom were at once suspended, and satisfied with having furnished adequate means for its defence, to the very person whom he had most reason in the world to fear, he again surrendered himself to the heartless dissipation and the unwise tyrannies in which he had so long indulged. But he was soon to waken from his dream of security and the voluptuous languor of that life which had so enslaved his soul and subdued his courage. The preparations of Julian being all complete, he summoned the veteran Taric el Tueito to his side. The banner of the Christian and of Islam waved together in the ghastly starlight, as, darting across the narrow streight that divides the shores of Spain from those of Africa, the prows of the Arabian, which had been silently gathering along the coast preparatory to this event, shot into the dark but sheltering shadows of the great mountain height of Calpe.

"Here," said Julian the Apostate, to the gaunt and fiery veteran, Taric el Tuerto, as they climbed the rugged elevation, and looked down upon the blue waters that lay below sleeping in the serene starlight—"Here did Hercules the mighty set up his pillar. This is the rock of Calpe."

"And here," said the ambitious and impatient Taric—"here will I set up mine, and it shall be a mark forever, high above the sea. Calpe no longer! It is my mountain now—'Gebir al Taric'—the pillar of Taric."

Strange that the exulting and arrogant spirit of the Arabian should, in this moment, have spoken in the voice of prophecy. His pillar has indeed overthrown that of Hercules. To this day, Gibraltar—"Gebir-al-tar"—is the name of the mountain—perpetuating the events of that night of import, and of the confident speech of the Islam chieftain.

CHAPTER VII.

THE troops of the Arabian once safely landed upon the shores of Spain, the resolved spirit of Taric el Tuerto led him to a performance which forced upon his followers the necessity for putting forth all their valor. He secretly set fire to their ships, and when they gazed with appalled hearts upon the terrific spectacle, and demanded to know, how, if the fortune of war should go against them, they were to escape from the country? He answered sternly, "There is no escape for the coward!" When they asked, "Are we never more to behold our homes?" his reply, "Your homes are before you," declared for the presence of a spirit which soon made itself acknowledged by the multitude. The resolve of their leader set their hearts on fire. They felt that they had now to win their country with their swords. Prophecy came to their encouragement. Auguries and miracles declared in their behalf, and for the sacred mission of their leader; and the fearless Taric, no less politic than brave, did not forbear the employment of auxiliary arts, to find a sanction for his own audacity, in provoking the religious and sensual enthusiasm of his followers. But our details must not relate to him. Our eye rests upon the dark and terrible spirit, at whose instigation he lifts the baleful lights of the crescent upon the heights of Calpe. He marks the progress of the Moslem with exultation. He sees in the fierce and single-eyed Arabian, whose fanatic energies have warmed the meanest of his followers with a fiery temper like his own, only the minister of his individual vengeance. Living for this passion only, he sees not the awful vision of his country ruined, which had else harrowed up in humiliating agony every pulse within his bosom; but, as if blinded for the destroyer, and decreed to work in blindness until the terrible destiny to which he is set shall be fulfilled, he rejoices in the progress of the invader over devastated plains and burning cities. That progress was at once begun. The sons of Ismael, impetuous by nature, and urged to superior impulses by the tenets of a faith which found and taught that the scymitar was the true means and medium for spiritual conversion, suffered not the grass to grow beneath the feet of their horses; and no provocation beyond that already flaming and inextinguishable fire within the heart of Julian, was necessary to goad him to activity in the fearful mischief to which he had set his hands. The united forces of the Moslem and the apostate chief were soon in motion, and the astonished Christians of Tarifa were suddenly confounded with the presence of the turbaned enemy, at the very moment when they felt themselves most secure from any danger by the great preparations made for the defence of the kingdom, and the recent great victory of Julian at Cueta. Their hasty levies under Theodomir were driven from the path of the invader, who continued to advance with equal speed and good fortune into the very bowels of the land.

It was in the midst of his most precious luxuries, lapped in profligate ease, abandoned to his insane pleasure, slothfully confident and criminally joyful, that Roderick was surprised with accounts of the invasion of his kingdom. The despatches of Theodomir smote his senses with a terrible sense of apprehension. When he read, in the language of this brave old chieftain, that the Africans were upon him, without ships, and as if descending from the clouds—he recalled once more the fearful vision of the enchanted cavern. His memory took a wild and rapid survey of the events from that period to the present time, and his conscience, not yet utterly crushed and subjugated in his repeated crimes, smote him keenly with the wrongs which he had done to Julian, and the hapless child of that apostate sire. Of that apostacy, to this hour, he yet knew nothing. The deeds of Julian in the foray which he was now making into his motherland, had not yet rendered him conspicuous, as they were destined to do, in the sight of his countrymen; and Roderick, regarding him as the warrior upon whom, over all, the safety of the realm depended, now felt more than ever how cruel had been the recompense which the monarch had bestowed, in requital of the great services of the subject. The defeats of Theodomir, and his appeal for succor, rendered necessary his immediate preparations. Roderick was no imbecile in moments of peril, and he now prepared to act with a decision which was honorable to himself, and not unworthy of the valor of his race. Forty thousand men were summoned to the field, and put under the command of Ataulpho, a prince of the royal blood of the Goths. This prince was brave, and so, perhaps, were the nobles and the soldiers who followed him to battle. But they lacked in military experience—they were without discipline, and the luxuries of all classes of the people had unfitted them for the vigorous duties of the camp. They lacked in that hardy muscle which could best have served them in the field. Ataulpho sought out the invaders with all diligence, nor did they avoid the encounter with an enemy fully twice their number. This inequality of number was more than compensated by the wild enthusiasm of the Arabians, by the vindictive fury of the apostate Christian leader, and by the superior skill and hardihood of their soldiers. The Gothic warriors fought gallantly, for they still cherished a portion of that valor, which, from immemorial time, had conducted their sires through successful conflict. But they strove against the fates. The stars in their courses fought against Roderick as they did against Sisera. In the midst of the conflict, when the troops of Taric were about to recoil from the stern and determined ranks of the Christians, Julian of Consuegra, at the head of a select body of horsemen, charging upon the centre where Ataulpho fought, turned instantly the fortune of the day. Ataulpho fell, but not before the weapon of the apostate. His arm struck no blow in the perilous conflict. His judgment led, his sword pointed out the way to victory, which his soldiers successfully pursued; but he kept his own weapon unstained, reserving his personal valor for a nobler victim. Grimly and coldly did he gaze upon the havoc of the field. His emotions were all still and silent as the storm, when marshalling its tempests for the sea. He beheld, with no exultation, the great banner of the cross go down in dust and blood—beheld, with scarce a mood, whether of pain or pride, the noble features of Ataulpho, as pale and ghastly, smeared with dust and blood, and looking still terrible from the conflict, his head, smitten from the trunk, was lifted high upon a lance in the presence of the triumphant armies. It was necessary that Ataulpho should be slain—that his army should be annihilated—if only that his path should be laid open to his own particular enemy. But not for him to feel emotion of any description, whether of gladness or of grief, but in that one event. The passions of his heart were not now to be awakened until his weapon crossed in mortal conflict with that of Roderick the Goth. He reserved the prowess of his arm—matchless at any weapon—only for this single foe. What to him was the constant progress which the Arabian made? What to him were the armies which he overthrew? save that each advancing step, and each successive victory brought him so much nigher to his enemy. Well he knew that it was not possible for Roderick to forbear much longer to appear at the head of his armies. Shame, and the absolute necessity of addressing all his military skill and valor to the exigency, (and Roderick was not without high reputation for both,) would, he well knew, soon bring the tyrant into the field. But he did not allow for the cowardice of a guilty conscience. From the moment when tidings were brought to Roderick that Count Julian fought with the invader and against his Christian countrymen, he shrunk from the necessity of meeting with the foe. He had no fear of the armies of the Moslem—would probably have joyed in the encounter with the foreign enemy—but his heart failed him when he thought of meeting in battle with the proud and mighty noble whom he had so deeply injured. What were his feelings when the tidings reached him of the successive defeats and destruction of his army—of his kinsman's fate—the slaughter of his bravest leaders, the veterans and the nobles of his kingdom—for it had been the policy of Taric, counselled by Julian, to single out for slaughter the distinguished persons, suffering the hirelings and the common herd to escape with little notice. The infidels in growing numbers overspread the country. Host after host from Africa, hearing of the successes of Taric, followed in his footsteps; and the smokes of their devastation, rising up everywhere from the plains of Sidonia to the fertile waters of the Guadiana, called reproachfully upon the imbecile sovereign to shake off his lethargy, and to lead his mightiest force against the infidel. Nor did they summon him in vain. His old courage was gradually reviving in his heart—

reviving, perhaps, at the instigation of that very fate which required him for the sacrifice. He shook himself free from his nervous apprehensions. The name of Julian lost its terror in his ears. The awful image of the injured father of Cava ceased to look out in characters of fear upon his vision; and a burning desire to resent the insolence of the invader, and revenge the wrongs done to his kingdom, at length drove him into the exercise of energies of a kind which almost compensated for all his previous apathy. His movements were urged with rigor. His troops were assembled with speed. His nobles were summoned to his side. Weapons were brought, armor forged, the various munitions of war sought for in all directions, while his camp witnessed momently the arrival of men, mules and horses, from all quarters of the kingdom. Roderick possessed in himself rare natural resources of strength and providence, of which the slothful career in which he had so long indulged, had not entirely stripped his genius. But his strength lay quite as much in himself as in his armies. The levies thus hastily brought together were not the men with whom to meet the hardy veterans of Julian and Taric. Nor were the nobles on whom he relied, altogether calculated as counsellors or leaders for an exigency so fearful as that which threatened the kingdom. Many came, but few deserved to be chosen. Roderick felt but small confidence in their succor when he looked around him. Many of the nobles gave him, he well knew, but lip service. Many of them had suffered by his injustice—and, upon the rest he could found but few hopes, whether as respects their conduct or their courage. The Archbishop Oppas came with the rest, and was one of the king's most trusty counsellors. His conspiracy had been too cautiously carried on for the suspicions of the tyrant. More than once in danger, he had more than once escaped by the adroitness of his judgment, and, on each occasion, by securing additional holds upon the confidence of the sovereign he was now preparing to betray. It was he, chiefly, who had persuaded Roderick to take the field in person. He exaggerated the strength of the kingdom, the valor of the troops, and the weakness of the invader. He wrote to Julian: "The tiger leaves his jungle. Be you ready with the hunters." And Julian rose when he read the missive, and a convulsion of joy shook his manly frame. A deep red light seemed to kindle in his eye, and there was no more apathy in his movements. He shook his hand slowly and threateningly, as if one even then stood before him. Then he might be heard to mutter, as if to one speaking behind him: "Peace, Frandina, reproach me not! The hour cometh and the victim. Peace, pure and suffering spirit, thy stains shall all be washed away in blood." Then, moving with hasty stride to the tent of Taric, he said to that chieftain whom he wakened from iron slumbers: "Arouse your Arabs, Taric, for the day is reddening in the east. Arouse ye, for, even now, Roderick is setting his army in array, and marches to the banks of the Xeres. It is there that we shall meet him." And, this time, Taric el Tuerto rose with a submissive air, for the command in the eye and the voice of Julian was that of a master, not to be withstood. From that moment the sway was with the great avenger. The troops were marshalled, and Julian of Conseugra led the host, calmly, and with the countenance of one who has already willed that a mighty victory shall follow.

CHAPTER VIII.

Roderick had put forth the most astonishing efforts for bringing together his soldiers for the war; and as the numerous host defiled through the plains of Andalusia, on their way to the seat of conflict, the soul of the tyrant forgot its fears and evil forebodings, exulting in conviction of certain and complete conquest. The host was beyond computation great, no less than fifty thousand horsemen, and a countless multitude of foot covering the plain like an agitated sea. But it was not such a host as the experienced man relies upon, and its very masses were unfriendly to its celerity of progress and the concert of its action. Never had there been in Spain the spectacle of such a multitude, and thus caparisoned. The luxury of the land was more conspicuous than its power. The nobles of the Goth were clad in armor better adapted to the uses of the spectacle and ceremonial than to those of battle—better calculated for the bright eyes of damsels than for the wild buffets of sturdy enemies. Art had expended all its fancies, and wealth all its materials, on this vain foppery; and curiously adorned with gold and precious stones, with drooping plumes and silken scarfs, and surcoats of brocade or velvet richly embroidered, the vain-glorious creatures of the court, prepared to undergo the toils and dangers of the camp and field. They still possessed the spirit and courage of their sires, and this, perhaps, was the redeeming aspect in their progress. They could meet the foe without shrinking, and striking boldly if feebly, could in this manner die, if they could not do, honorably. If the nobility were thus decorated with superfluous trappings, the common multitude were wanting in the absolute necessaries of war. The politic providence of Julian had stripped the kingdom, as we have seen, of the means necessary for arming the people against sudden invasion. Lances and shields, and swords and crossbows, might be seen among them, but without any uniformity of equipment upon which so much of the success of an army, acting in masses, depends in any encounter with a foe. Thousands were provided only with sling and stone, with bill and bludgeon, and the ordinary implements of husbandry. They were without a knowledge of war, and, lacking in discipline and arms, gave little promise of that good service which the sanguine and eager spirit of Roderick anticipated at their hands. They shared in some degree, however, the courage of their monarch, and when he appeared at their head, mounted on his favorite charger, Orelia—a noble form himself, clad in armor of burnished gold, and looking the emblematic hero of his kingdom—their enthusiasm declared itself in a shout which rent the firmament. Their courageous impulse encouraged their sovereign, and making them a speech full of encouragement and of hope, he concluded with commanding their instant march for the Xeres in compliance with the insidious counsel of the Archbishop Oppas. This wily traitor had already contrived to establish secret but regular communications with Count Julian, The latter was punctually apprised of every movement in the camp of Roderick. Similar intelligence was conveyed to the young Prince Pelayo, who was summoned with his little band of partisans to descend from his mountain passes to the famous quarry which the usurper was preparing for the stroke. Pelayo was not made acquainted with all the facts in the history of Julian, which, by this time, were in possession of Oppas. They did not revolt the latter, though he well knew that their revelation would produce such an effect on the gallant and faithful prince, his nephew. To him the story came that Julian had revolted in behalf of Egiza, his brother, or himself, the heirs of their father, unrighteously slain by Roderick. That he should bring among his followers a small force of Arabs whom he had overcome, drawn to his service in Tingitania, offered no reason for suspecting him. Glad of an opportunity at last to cross weapons with the usurper with some prospect of effectual struggle, Pelayo readily put his troops in motion for the purpose of forming a coalition with Julian, against Roderick, before the two armies could possibly meet on the banks of the Xeres. At this place, and in the moment of greatest struggle, even while the battle raged, the treacherous archbishop was to draw off his legions, and crossing to the side of the invaders, return with fatal effect against the ranks which had counted on his strength and assistance. Such was the cunning contrivance by which it was calculated that the overwhelming masses of Roderick—overwhelming in spite of all their inferiority of weapon and discipline—were to be foiled and overthrown. The archbishop headed a select body of soldiers. They were attached to his cause with a sort of personal attachment. His solicitude for a long time had been to bring about this feeling. For this he had spared no means. Cajoling arts, kind offices, and a liberal bounty, had won the hearts of their leaders, while other means of a grosser nature—animal indulgencies and high wages—had effectually won to his purposes the common people. The soldiers led by Pelayo were a hardy tribe of mountaineers, a simple, virtuous race, unaccustomed to luxury, little ambitious, and content with that poverty which they knew how to enjoy, as it seemed to secure them the precious boon of liberty. Pelayo was the very leader for such a people. He loved no silken couch, loathed with a strange dislike the voluptuous effeminacies in which his order were wont to forget themselves and all the virtues of becoming manhood, and, superior to all considerations of self, set before them ever the example of a self-denying spirit, toiling only for the glory and safety of his people. They believed equally in his valor and his virtues. Secure of both in him, he was secure of their loyalty and adherence, and when he bade them descend with him to the conflict with the usurper, they bounded up and went forth as to a festival.

Little did Roderick dream of these dangers. Oppas, with an adroitness which has distinguished the established priesthood in all periods, had wormed himself into full confidence of the usurper. His counsel, urged indirectly, suggested frequently rather than boldly declared, was that which Roderick preferred commonly to the arguments of better men. He encouraged the rapid movements of the usurper against the enemy, before his followers were provided with weapons, and in spite of their obvious want of discipline. His argument was a specious one: "Shall we wait," he asked, "until the force of the Arabs, now small in numbers, shall be increased by countless swarms from the desert? Already they begin to pour in upon us, and we must crush them speedily, if we would not do battle with all Almagreb!" The impetuous nature of Roderick readily sympathized with this seemingly wise but really injudicious counsel, which Oppas rendered more palatable still by insisting upon the great ease with which their myriads could be overthrown. He spoke with scorn of their numbers and their skill, and by adroit flatteries, so wrought upon the spirit of the king that he longed for nothing so much as the encounter with a foe, from whom, according to the voice of prophecy, he had everything to dread. The artifices of Oppas did not stop here. We have already seen in previous pages the glimpses of a passion which he felt—a passion perhaps more criminal than any other that worked within his bosom as it meditated injury to the most unoffending innocence—for the person of the beautiful spouse of the usurper—the meek and gentle Egilona. It was the hope of Oppas to secure this victim in the course of those events which his artful counsel was now hurrying forward. He promptly availed himself of the suggestion of the innocent and dutiful wife, herself, to promote his passionate devices. "Why," said she, "should I not follow my lord in this march of peril? Why should I not be near him in the hour of danger? Too well I know that his fearless spirit will bear him where the strife is thickest—that he will rush to the embrace of war, and grow mad with rapture in the dreadful glory of the flashing spear and scymitar. Verily, it is but meet that I should be near him in this peril, that I may tend upon him should he suffer hurt—which Jesu forbid—dress the wounds of his limbs, and sooth his weariness with my cares, and console him after his toils by the song and story which he so much loves."

"It is thy duty, daughter, that thou shouldst thus attend thy lord. Thy thought becomes thee. It were pitiful if he should be wounded and alone, needing succor and soothing which thou mayst bestow—and thou absent here reposing on thy couch, little heeding of his wants and sorrows."

"Ah! father, I thank thee from the bottom of my heart for this sanction. I have already spoken of it to my lord, but he chides me for the thought. Thou shalt help me in my quest. Thou shalt speak to my lord, and show him what is needful for me to do, and to desire, and what is but right and generous in him to grant. Wilt thou not do this, holy father—I pray thee to serve me in this wise, for well I know that thy counsel is of all others most grateful to my lord."

"Verily, daughter, thou art a pattern of virtue and duty. The sex is honored in thee, and the church glories in thy faith. How rightly dost thou see these things. Where should the wife be, in the peril of her husband, but by his side? I would not have thee share in his danger, for that becomes not thy feebleness of sex; but there are duties in which thou art strong, and these are particularly needed of thee to exercise. Daughter, I will speak to thy lord in thy behalf."

"Oh, father, how shall I thank thee?"

"Thanks, dearest daughter of the church, it needs not. It needs but duty only. Verily, the heavens smile upon thee, and thy virtues will greatly serve against the too erring and too vicious nature of thy lord. Thou art precious, my child, in the sight of heaven. Thou remindest me in thy meekness and loving-kindness of those accepted women which made lovely and secure the tents of the ancient patriarchs. Be thus, ever, my daughter, and the smiles of the Virgin shall give thee countenance and protection in the moment of thy greatest need."

Thus speaking, while the royal lady knelt with uncovered head before him, his paternal hand rested on her neck, and, unconsciously, as it were, glided into her bosom, the heaving billows of which were swelling with a sense of pleasure at the terms of commendation which she heard from one in whom she was accustomed to behold the visible agent, and almost the only means of communication with her Saviour and her God. She felt no distrust of that patriarchal pressure which was yet not without its influence upon other sensibilities than those which belonged to her devotions. How should she dream to find the wolf in the shepherd! The pure heart, unconscious of guilt itself, not easily suspects the secret guilt in the souls and thoughts of others. The meek submissive woman, untrained and inexperienced in the strifes of the brutal world, is slow to fancy cunning or deceit in those minds upon which society itself commands that she shall rely. And thus it was that the pure-souled Egilona knelt before the lascivious and abandoned priest, submissive, while his polluting hands, made authoritative by his patriarchal mission, presumed upon freedoms with the person of the innocent and lovely, which are permitted by heaven to the sacred rites of wedlock only.

Very difficult was it for the bold and impious Oppas to tear himself away from the exercise of his audaciously assumed privileges. She, the meek and virtuous woman, knelt still, immovable as beneath a spell, looking down upon the earth, and submitting, as she fancied, to a benediction which was to secure her the special favor of the Mother of the Lamb. The wolf in sheep's clothing tore himself away at last. His hands lifted her from the ground, and rested still upon her snow-white neck and bosom, while pressing his burning lips upon her cheeks. This was all apostolical only, in the humble and unsuspecting thoughts of the woman—for a purer heart than that of Egilona never beat within mortal breast.

To Roderick, Oppas urged the wishes of Egilona—and his own—but with a different argument. To the fearless man he justified the presence—not of the queen only, but of the court—on the ground that there was no danger. "Shall these infidels thus affright us with their crescents? Are these barbaric drums so terrible in our ears, that we must needs keep them from the ears of our women? Is there no valor among your nobles that they dread lest the ladies whom they serve should see them as they go into conflict. I tell thee, Roderick, if thou wouldst have thy young warriors do famous service, let them be seen of the young maidens of the court." And the subtle priest then made some familiar farm-yard allusions to the effect upon the courage of the male bird, of the presence of the female.

"Verily, my Lord Oppas," said Roderick, with a merry visage, "thou hadst been a better soldier than a priest—albeit, thou hast some of the rarest attributes for the priesthood also. Thou hast a tongue to wheedle Satan himself out of his prey—and, I tell thee, I half suspect thee of a warmer passion for the sex than thou hast for the surplice and the altar. Thou canst not cheat me, lord bishop. I know thee, if the church does not. But thou art right in this. Shall these scurvy sons of Ismael make us afraid? Shall there be no more smiles—no more sunshine because of their moons? By Bacchus, I will it otherwise. Egilona shall be with us and the court. We shall have all the dames of beauty and of grace, to see that we are not wanting in the spirit to defend them. Our young nobles shall do battle in their sight, and well I know there will be no cowardice—no skulking then."

There were other counsels among the veterans, but those of the archbishop prevailed, and when he bore the grateful intelligence to Egilona, his wild passions rejoiced in the renewed exercise of his patriarchal privileges. Once more his lips were pressed upon her cheek and forehead—once more his audacious fingers rested upon her neck, or lifted, in a seemingly wandering mood, the tresses of her silken hair; and evil were the triumphant thoughts which kindled into burning tumult the blood mounting to his brain, as he rushed in imagination over the brief interval between that moment and the day when the woman at his feet was to be widowed by his unbridled passions.

CHAPTER IX.

Of the further details of the conspiracy against the crown of Roderick it does not need that we should now take heed. It will suffice to remember that the conspirators were counselled by shrewd, sagacious heads; men well experienced in such practices, and entirely free from those disquieting morals of patriotism which might have made them scrupulous in such employment. They carried their plans forward so as to include all the probable elements of success—neglected no precautions, and disregarded none of those considerations which might be supposed to operate, whether favorably or otherwise, in connection with their schemes. After some delays the two opposing armies came in sight of each other on the banks of the lovely waters of the Xeres.

"Henceforward this shall be the river of death!" exclaimed the fierce captain of the Arabs, as he looked down at the water flowing before his feet; and the name of "Guadalete," which, in the Arabic, has this signification, consecrated to the purpose by the terrible strife which followed upon the banks of this stream, has clung to it even to the present hour, and will probably cling to it forever. The dark soul of Taric el Tuerto, conscious of its own purpose, was prescient of the awful event about to follow, and he was destined soon to put in exercise all his fearful energies in order to realize his own predictions and desires. Glorious, indeed, was the spectacle then visible upon the borders of this lovely river, so darkly consecrated. On the side of the invaders might be seen a small but formidable army—grim warriors, well armed, compact, accustomed to work together in warfare, expert in the use of their weapons, and yielding to the summons of battle with the exulting spirit of the war horse, impatient of the trumpet. This well-appointed army though but a speck in comparison with the numbers brought into the field by Roderick, wore yet the aspect of a power which might be regarded with respect and apprehension. The order of the well-drilled masses—their compact army—the symmetry and proper relationship of body to body, horse and foot, seeming to co-operate as by some secret sympathy, and without a word—these were signs not to be misunderstood or undervalued by him whose eye hath ever enjoyed the spectacle of combat. The swarthy legions of Taric looked like warriors embrowned by strife on every field in Mauritania. The fiery steeds of the desert, admirably trained by the hand of the Bedouin, gave life and animation to the array, as they coursed over the adjacent plain; and the wild clash of the cymbal, mingled with the jeering cry of the Arabian horsemen, seemed to awaken the very echoes in mockery of the vast but comparatively feeble battallions of the Gothic monarch. But the spectacle that gave most pain and apprehension to the eyes of Roderick was that of the small but formidable body of Christian warriors leagued with the invader against his country. His heart grew cold and sunk within his bosom, when he was shown, a little apart from the array of the Moslem, the command of Count Julian, with his well-known banner waving in the midst. Here were ten thousand of the bravest warriors of the Goth—hardy veterans, daring soldiers, bold, firm and excellently skilled at every weapon. But it was of their leader and not of these he thought; and, turning from the sight with feelings which humbled, and which he did not dare to name to himself nor show to others, he secretly resolved that it was not in this quarter he should seek to find his enemies in battle. The conscience that makes cowards of us all, palsied the valor of the tyrant when he remembered the wrongs that he had done to the daughter of Count Julian, and his heart did not suffer him to join in the frequent maledictions of his nobles, as they shook their vindictive hands towards the tents of the apostate.

A short league lay between the opposing armies. That of Roderick presented a spectacle of unexampled magnificence. The immense number of his host, rated by historians almost as extravagantly as those of the Persians in the invasion of Greece, was itself a sight of marvellous impressiveness. But the splendor of its array put to shame any exhibition of a like character either in ancient or modern times. The habitual luxuries into which the Gothic nobles had fallen, could not be separated from their connection, even though they were about to engage in new toils and perils in which such luxuries were incumbrances only. Details cannot well be given of a display of which all the writers deal in superlatives only. Enough to say that the ostentatious exhibitions of the tournament, in the most glorious periods of chivalry, were translated to that field of death, and crowned it with a magnificence and beauty that contrasted terribly and sadly with the fearful issues of the strife.

Myriads of pennons streamed above the scattered hosts of the Gothic monarch—the tents of their nobles were almost hidden in their ornaments of silk, while their persons, blazing with jewels, were only so many inestimable motives to valorous exertion, on the part of an enemy roused to avarice by the exhibition of a wealth which it required nothing but valor to obtain.

There was yet another army on the field. Scarcely an army, if we regard the mighty legions of Roderick, and the inferior, but still imposing force led by Taric and Julian. This was the little band of Pelayo, the true heir of the Gothic crown. These were his mountaineers, from the Asturian passes, and they occupied a strong position on the side of a hill, in sight of both the opposing armies. They lay quiet but watchful in their camp, as if without a motive or a life; but their prince and leader, Pelayo, was even now a victim in his tent to the bitterest pangs of disappointment and distrust. He who had come to the field under the assurances of the Archbishop Oppas, to find himself seconded by Julian with his forces, now found that Julian himself was but the auxiliar of the infidel invader. It was at the hour of vespers that the army of Roderick pitched its tents on the banks of the Guadalete, and that night Pelayo and the archbishop, his uncle, met midway between his own small array and the multitudes of the tyrant.

"To what feast is this you have brought me?" demanded Pelayo sternly of the archbishop. "A feast where we furnish the food and are ourselves the prey. For whom do we fight here, Lord Oppas? for Roderick or the Moors? for Spain or Africa? Count Julian or yourself? Well, I trow that mine is to be a small share in this business. Why am I here?"

The archbishop's explanations availed nothing.

"Hark ye, Lord Oppas," was the conclusion of Pelayo—"I stand here in most bitter opposition to ye all. You have humbled me to the earth, as you have brought me to a pass where I may but look on the deeds of others, doing nothing of my own. For what should I strive here? If I put in with Count Julian and against Roderick, I but toil for the sons of Islam—the infidel Moor—the swarthy and savage invader. If I strike against him, as it is my mood to do, I strike against my brother's right and against my own—against my father's memory, against Spain, and in behalf of a foul usurper. This is a strife, most like an agony, now working in my soul. My will is feeble and knows not where to turn. My hands are tied—I wist not where to strike. Verily, I must but look on, in waiting for the mood; doing little in this conflict which approaches, unless it be in saving from the scymitar the poor wretches of the land who follow only as they are driven to the fight. Look to it then, lest, in what thou doest to-morrow, thou bring the terrible curse of a foreign sway upon the land which a thousand generations may never shake from its prostrate neck."

They separated, the archbishop failing, with all his art, to disturb the first conclusions to which the honorable mind of Pelayo had attained. Pelayo returned to his heights, and the Lord Oppas proceeded with a guide to another interview in the tents of the Arabian. Here, for the first time, he met with Taric. Here was Count Julian also. Their schemes for the battle were to be adjusted, and the archbishop was to make his conditions. He was to stipulate with Julian and Taric for a certain share of that power which was to accrue from the defeat of Roderick. The ambitious priest had his designs apart from the priesthood. An appetite for power was raging in his heart, with other appetites of which nothing need be said. The Arabian warrior readily conceded to the traitor all that he required. Taric had been impressed with the numerous array of Roderick. Its splendor had dazzled his eyes, and insensibly influenced his apprehensions. He knew his veterans, and he could reasonably judge of the inferior training of the force opposed to him; but he as well knew that such an inequality of numbers as existed between the two armies, was not easily to be reconciled by any inequality of practice or even valor; and he had no reason to suppose, that, if not veteran soldiers, those of Roderick were at all deficient in bravery. He felt the policy, therefore, of acceding to any terms, within certain limits, which might be proposed by Oppas as the price of his treachery on the ensuing day. The archbishop left the tents of "the faithful" for his own, perfectly satisfied with the result of his nocturnal expedition in this quarter.

CHAPTER X.

THE night, according to the Arabian and Spanish historians, was one of auguries and omens to both armies. Those which occurred in the tents of the Arabian were all friendly and auspicious. Taric was cheered by a vision of the prophet, who promised him success, and a prolonged triumph; while, in the tent of Roderick, as he sate quaffing the red wine with some of his favorite nobles, a bearded pilgrim suddenly appeared at the entrance of the tent, and spoke to him, in words, terrible like those which appeared to Belshazzar, written at his fatal feast on the walls ot the chamber: "Thy sway hath departed from thee, Roderick! thy hours are numbered! The Arabian sits within thy palace, and looks out upon thy people for his own! He who would save himself must abandon thee! Wo! wo! to thee and Spain!" Before the king could recover from his consternation at this sudden vision and these awful words, the venerable stranger had disappeared. There are those who assert that the speaker was no other than a Caulian monk, whom the archbishop had suborned for this purpose, and thus tutored, that he might alarm with new fears, and move to treachery like his own, certain of the nobles who sate with Roderick that night. One with such an aspect was known to follow in the army of the archbishop. This event was followed by another of even more inauspicious omen. Going forth with the dawn of day, Roderick summoned to him a noble called Ramiro, to whom he delivered the royal standard, charging him in the usual language, to maintain it faithfully and at the peril of his life. Ramiro received the standard, and as he waved it aloft with a triumphant grace, and a bold delighted spirit, his horse grew unmanageable, and darting away beneath it, flung him under his feet and trampled the royal standard in the dust. When the good knight was lifted from the ground he was found to be dead. His neck was broken. He never stirred once from the moment that he fell. This fatal event, which took place in sight of both armies, was well calculated to encourage the one and to depress the other. But the soul of Roderick seemed to grow stronger because of these sinister aspects in his fortunes. The really brave man is always true to himself; and a prouder feeling, the growth of a noble self-reliance, was kindled in his heart, as, lifting the standard from the ground, he himself rode with it along the plain of Xeres, waving it proudly aloft in the eyes of his assembled legions. The sacrament was administered to Roderick, kneeling in his tent, by the hand of the Bishop Urbino, the Lord Oppas being busy at the time making his own preparations for the battle. "I have sinned before heaven and the sight of man, venerable father!" said the usurper. "I have done cruel wrong to Julian, and my heart shrinks from the meeting with him, alone, of all in the ranks of mine enemy!"

"Be of good cheer, my son," replied the Urbino. "Remember thou goest forth to battle in defence of thy faith and thy country. Thou goest forth representing thy people and thy church, and art not simply the man whom men call Roderick. Forget thyself in thy people and thy God, and holy mother will strengthen thee against thy fear!"

"I repent me from that heavy sin, my father," said the royal criminal, while a deep tremor overspread his frame and grew apparent in the sound of his voice.

"And of all others, my son?"

"I would repent me. I would forswear them, but I am feeble and erring, vicious by blood, and quickly led astray from better resolutions."

"Be thou firm in thy desire for good; be thou faithful to thy fears and sorrows for the evil done, and I grant thee the dispensation which flows abundantly with grace. I assoil thee, Roderick, as thou art thus repentant, from past and present sin. Go forth, for thy God and people, and the strength of thy God and thy people, bring thee safely through the terrors of the foughten field."

Urbino left the camp for a place of safety, while Roderick proceeded to take his last farewell of Egilona. She, with the ladies of the court, had tents assigned her contiguous to that of her husband. It was now the purpose of Roderick to send her with Urbino to some distance from the field. But she refused with a stubbornness of will which had not often been exhibited to her lord, to retire at his bidding. For this resistance she had the secret counsel of the Archbishop Oppas. To afford her husband the succor which he might need, it was essential that she should be near him, and to this desire she religiously adhered. And Roderick's resolution yielded to hers. In truth he had no apprehensions of the issue. He could not doubt the capacity of his numerous masses to overwhelm the inferior armies of his foe. He had no reason to doubt the courage of his people. He did not suspect the treachery in his ranks. The auguries of the night had affected him much less than his nobles, and those of the morning already recited—the death of Ramiro, and the trampling of the consecrated standard in the dust—had not yet taken place. He yielded to the loving and earnest entreaties of his wife, and left her, tearful and full of fears, but glad that she had been permitted to remain in compliance with the calls of duty near the person of her lord. His place in the tent was supplied by the person of Lord Oppas. The last kiss of her husband was yet warm upon her cheeks, when it was removed by the "holy" pressure of other lips. The patriarchal blessing of the archbishop was to be enforced by the imposition of hands, and the mailed glove removed from his fingers—for he was in full armor—they once more wandered in forbidden places. And the pious and unsuspecting woman looked up to the reverend father, and fancied she beheld before her one of those mighty kings among the Jews, who, serving now before the altars of the Lord, and now leading his armies forth to battle, were commissioned with a sort of universal power, in correspondence with the great variety and compass of their moral endowments. And, truly, the Lord Oppas was a person to impose this conviction upon any spectator. We have already spoken of the nobleness and majesty of his frame. He was not wanting in that solicitude which takes care that its habits and ornaments shall properly correspond with what nature has done in his behalf. He was clad from head to foot in armor of jet black, with a noble polish; on his left breast was a cross in gold, and another glittering in blood-red rubies, was above his helmet. He carried himself with the port of a prince. A person more noble moved not that day in all the gorgeous ranks of the Gothic monarch; and it was with a sentiment of delight and exultation that the secret glance of the archbishop detected the eyes of Egilona as they followed the movements of his majestic form, with an expression of admiration, the perfect innocence of which, founded as it was upon her belief in his christian and spotless character, it did not enter his impure spirit to conceive. He left her, with all his loathsome appetites and foul desires and purposes more than ever active, with the secret hope that the events of the day, already begun, were to gratify them with the fullest triumph. Of this we shall see hereafter.

Roderick, destined to be the last king of the Goths, went forth to battle in the luxurious state which had been so much affected by his predecessors. His robes were of gold brocade, his sandals were embroidered with precious stones; he carried the sceptre in his hand, and the royal crown, full of jewels of inestimable value, upon his brows. The chariot in which he rode was of ivory, the axles of silver, the wheels ot burnished gold; the pole was plated with the same precious metal. This sumptuous chariot was canopied with cloth of gold, embossed with armorial devices, studded with jewels, and drawn by four milk white horses, caparisoned in a style of like folly and magnificence. A body guard of a thousand youthful cavaliers surrounded this precious car, which might well suggest the necessity of a far greater force for its defence against a foe so eager and avaricious as the children of Islam. These cavaliers were knighted for the occasion by the king's own hand, and were sworn, as their especial charge, to defend his person to the last. This spectacle of magnificence, according to Arabic historians, seemed to match the sun in heaven. The hosts of Roderick shouted their wonder and delight as he passed along their ranks and enjoined upon them to do their duty as became men fighting for their country and their God. The sight of so much splendor had its effect upon the Africans also. Old Taric, who knew them well, made it the occasion of a speech appealing to their cupidity. "This Roderick," said he, "would save us the pains of looking after his treasure. Would he pay our soldiers or his own with these precious jewels? Dreams he that we know not their value? Hear me, children of the desert, and know, that, from this day, the brave man wears the jewel that he wins!"

The rising of the sun was the signal for the conflict. The two armies drew nigh to each other as his first smiles crimsoned the plain which they were soon to dye in deeper colors. The forces of the Arabian descended in regular order, troop after troop, from the gentle eminence which they occupied. Their advance was wild and picturesque. Their long robes and turbans made their appearance equally majestic and imposing in the sight of their enemies; while their several squadrons, each habited after a fashion of its own, religiously preserving the custom of their homes in the desert, rendered their exhibition quite as various and fanciful, though in a less extravagant and expensive manner, as that of the gorgeous battallions of the Goth. These, with sound of drum and trumpet—with equal show of valor, but far less skill and order—bounded forward to the encounter. Their music was answered by the clash of cymbals, and the wild, piercing cries of the distant horsemen. The sun disappeared from sight as they rushed to the embrace of death; clouds of dust enveloped them, through which could be seen the gleam ot the whizzing javelins and arrows, and could be heard the rattle of a thousand stones. These were the missils of war in that period, and such a stony tempest as raged that day, has left its trace upon the plain of Xeres even to the present. The troops of Roderick, undefended in most part, by shield or buckler—for the criminal prudence of Julian had despoiled the kingdom of the materials of war before his invasion was begun—fought to manifest disadvantage. But their courage was equally manifest, and their swarming multitudes more than compensated for the deficiency. The old valor of the race shone out wondrously in the very moment of its extinction—even as we are confounded at the sudden blazing up into brilliance of the light which has long been dying in the socket. Their efforts promised to prevail.

The Moslems yielded before the reckless masses, as they flung themselves, troop by troop, upon the ranks of the invader, and Taric el Tuerto, borne back by his own legions, tore his beard in the agony of a conviction that the day had gone irretrievably against him. It was at this moment—in the very crisis of his fortunes—that Julian of Consuegra, who had hitherto employed his skirmishers rather than his force, gave orders for the trumpet to sound thrice, a peculiar peal, which had been agreed upon between himself and the archbishop. Scarcely had the sound subsided upon the ear, when piercing and similar notes from the ranks of Roderick, gave significant response from his accomplice.

"Now!" cried Count Julian, rising in his stirrups, and drawing the weapon of vengeance from the sheathe—"Now, Roderick, thy hour has come!"

At the same moment, while the charge of Julian arrested the assailing and pursuing Christians, now closely pressing on the heels of the flying Moslems, the Archbishop Oppas, detaching his squadrons from the rest of the army, led them suddenly against the centre of Roderick's array with a shock that was irresistible. The rout followed—vain was the prowess of the monarch—vain the valor of his nobles. They perished, man by man, fighting bravely to the last. Roderick himself performed prodigies of valor. He had fought from his chariot, sending dart and javelin, with fearful accuracy of direction, against every conspicuous foe; but when, in the defection of Oppas and the terrible onslaught of Julian, the reverses of the field began, he descended from the gorgeous car, and mounted his famous steed Orelia, which had been kept in readiness for such emergencies. Thus mounted, his sword made fearful havoc among the assailants. His valor maintained the fight, and infused new courage into the hearts of his nobles. They emulated the reckless and desperate strength and spirit which he displayed, and yielded themselves to the slaughter, conscious rather that they were smiting as they fell, than of the fearful pang and other trembling emotions of approaching death. Shouting a cheering encouragement to such as survived, Roderick plunged forward to fresh encounters. But a voice, wild and powerful, answered exultingly to his own, from a cloud of combatants in front. It was the voice of Julian. It struck a deep terror to the heart of Roderick. The reins fell upon the neck of his steed—then, as a second time the fearful accents met his ear, he caught them up in his trembling hands, wheeled the animal about, and plunging deeper than ever the rowel into his bleeding sides, he fled from the battle, with a ghastly terror in the shape of the dishonored Cava looking over his shoulders, and a prowling hate, in the aspect of her gigantic father, close pursuing at his heels. He fled—fled wildly from his people—and knew not in what direction his terror led.

CHAPTER XI.

The disappearance of Roderick from the field was the signal for a general rout. The thousand brave young cavaliers who had formed his body-guard, thinned terribly in the previous conflict, now perished to a man in covering his flight. The victory was soon complete, and the Arab and Bedouin horsemen hurried in the dread pursuit, gleaning the fugitives with the edge of the scymitar as they vainly sought refuge among the contiguous hills, or strove with uncertain and fainting footsteps to shelter themselves within the neighboring town of Xeres. The pursuit was unsparing and vindictive, and the slaughter terrible. The panic of the Asturian army was such that they lacked the nerve to rally, and the few bodies of men tha endeavored to hold together, under cool and resolute leaders, were annihilated in the onward sweep of the Moorish squadrons.

It was while the Arabians were thus hotly engaged in the pursuit of the fugitives, or more gratefully occupied still in despoiling the gorgeous camp of Roderick, that the Archbishop Oppas, at the head of a chosen body of men, followed the footsteps of Egilona and the court. This wily priest had so admirably made his arrangements, that his creatures directed the course of the flying cavalcade while his spies followed close and reported to him its direction. It was with feelings of indescribable exultation that he beheld his calculations all verified, and felt himself on the eve of realizing all his audacious hopes. Already the objects of pursuit rose on his vision; and the gorgeous and flowing robes of the women might be seen momently gleaming to his eye, as they wound above the hills lying in the distance on the right of the town of Xeres. The archbishop rose proudly in his stirrups. The prey was already in his grasp, and, urging the pursuit with renewed energy, he overtook the party in a dense thicket of chestnuts. His eye was fastened upon one victim only, and singling her out from the rest, while his troops followed in pursuit and dispersion of the queen's escort, he grasped the bridle rein of her steed, and led his victim aside from the highway. The wife of Roderick and her traitorous confessor, were alone together. He assisted her to dismount from her steed. He smiled upon her—he spoke to her in the ancient fashion of saintly and patriarchal affection. But he now spoke to her in vain. She was aware of his deception; she now felt how fraudulent had been his mission. The lamb's skin had been torn from his shoulders, and she now knew the wolf in his natural aspect. Farther deception was in vain. Her kindling eyes, her haughty and reserved aspect, soon taught him this; and, after a vain attempt to persuade himself that his old arts might yet be renewed with profit, his impatient spirit, vexed at repulse, abandoned all farther attempts at hypocrisy.

"At length," said he "lovely Egilona, I may speak freely. I may declare the passion with which thou hast inspired me so long, and which it has been so maddening to conceal. If I erred, as thine eyes seem to reproach me, it is thy beauties—those very eyes, which are to blame. Thou hast been the cause of my error. For thee I have renounced the church, and put on the armor, with the spirit, of the warrior. Be mine! As the wife of Lord Oppas, thy rule shall be in Spain quite as sufficient and large as when thou wert the wife of Roderick. Roderick lies upon the field of battle, never more to rise. Let the rites of the church bind thee to one, whose love for thee, more true than that of Roderick, is yet more fervent and considerate of the nature which dwells within thy heart."

The answer of Egilona was that of scorn. She was no longer the devotee. She was the woman and the queen.

"False traitor!" she exclaimed. "I loathe thee as the pestilence. Egilona thy wife! Sooner let her perish!"

The face of the priest glowed as with fire beneath his visor. He removed his helmet, and cast it upon the ground.

"Egilona!" said he, "art thou blind? Seest thou not we are alone together?"

"Approach me not, traitor. Forget not that I am the wife of thy sovereign."

"He lives no longer."

"I believe thee not."

"I saw him fall before the sword of Julian."

"Jesu spare and help me! Holy mother be my succor. Strengthen me that I may not give ear to the falsehood of this traitor priest."

Oppas had indeed spoken falsely. He knew nothing of the fate of the monarch. Why should we prolong the parley? Why pursue the conference in which the entreaties and arguments of the disloyal archbishop were answered only by the unvarying scorn and loathing of the royal lady. His passion at length grew stronger than his respect. He laid his hands upon her—not the patriarchal hands, gently and tenderly laid, with which, quite as polluting then as now, he had before done wrong to her sacred person. His touch now was that of open violence. His muscular arms were folded about her delicate and exhausted form, while his lips, priestly no longer, but wholly reckless and passionate, were fastened upon her own with a desperate eagerness which seemed to drink a rapture akin to madness in each draught. Her voice was stifled—her cries were silenced—she sank fainting to the sward, and prayed for death from heaven.

Her prayer was answered in that very moment—not with death, but with safety. The tread of a horse echoed through the grove. A wild strange voice was heard to summon, and the archbishop, furious at the intrusion, turned savagely on the stranger, and hurriedly lifted his sword from the ground where but a moment before he had thrown it. The intruder was a Moor, and by his costume and bearing, a person of distinction. He was armed after the Arab manner, with scymitar and javelin and lance. His person was tall and slight, but eminently graceful and well made. His air was very noble and his features particularly handsome. He was young, scarcely more than twenty; but it could already be seen that he was one destined for great achievement. He had been already heard in counsel, and his deeds were already glorious among the Arabians. He was the son of Musa Ben Nosier, and destined to arrive at distinctions to which even his ambitious sire had never looked even in his fondest dreams of eminence. The noble and chivalrous spirit of Abdalazis—for that was the name of the youthful Ishmaelite—revolted at the spectacle before him; and, heedless of the dignity of Oppas, whom he at once recognised, he called upon him, for shame, to quit his prey.

"By Allah!" said he, "Christian, these be not deeds which shall do thee honor."

"Hence, Moor—away with thee from this presence ere I slay thee. Know me for the Lord Oppas, confederate of Count Julian of Consuegra. Away with thee in pursuit. I will answer for my own deeds."

"I know thee," said the young man, "and will not leave this lady, whom I regard as noble, in thy hands."

Egilona had recovered from her swoon. Her exquisite beauties, her noble air, had fixed the attentions of the Moor.

"Leave me not, I implore thee, to this man! He is mine enemy. Save me, I entreat thee! I am the wife of Don Roderick, the lord and sovereign of the Goth in Spain."

At these words the young man lifted his hand to his turban, and knelt respectfully before the royal lady.

"I will bear thee to a place of safety," he exclaimed.

"Thou!" cried Oppas, who, in his rage, neither recognised the youth, nor knew, perhaps, the rank which he held in the army of Taric. Possibly, even did he know, at that moment he had not heeded the rank of the stranger. "Thou!" he cried, rushing upon him with his weapon. Abdalazis recoiled before the terrible sweep of the sword, drew quickly a javelin from the quiver at his side, and launched the steel with unerring aim and force at the face of the assailant. The action was as quick as light. The shaft sped recklessly to its mark. The bolt penetrated the eye of the archbishop, and the sharp steel was buried in his brain. The gigantic frame of Lord Oppas fell forward heavily upon the earth, which seemed to shake beneath the fall. He writhed but in one convulsion at the feet of Egilona, and his dark passions and fraudful life were at once at an end together.

It may be quite as well to suspend the progress of our story—though for a sin gle instant only—in order to indicate the fortunes of the two persons thus singularly and happily brought together. The events of that meeting between Egilona and Abdalazis constituted but the beginning of an interesting drama, terminating in his final ascent to the throne of Spain, and his marriage with the widow of Roderick the Goth. Let this suffice of their history. The chronicles go a step farther, and it is more than suspected that the pure and lovely Egilona finally won the heart of her Arab lover to the foot of the cross; a triumph of the wife and the devotee which brought them both to the scaffold, victims to the brutal rage of a populace as warmly devoted to Islam as Egilona was to Christ.

CHAPTER XII.

While these exciting events were in progress in one quarter of the field, what was the fate of Roderick, and whither did his footsteps tend? With the vindictive shouts of Julian ringing in his ears, conscience-stricken, he urged his noble steed—the good steed Orelia, of which tradition has deemed it not beneath its care to preserve some pleasing memorials for posterity—to the utmost powers of limb and muscle, in the fond hope of escaping from the avenger. But, as eagerly as he fled did the father of the unhappy Cava pursue. His instincts were all aroused and unerring in the chase, and while the feet of Orelia were laving themselves in the edges of the Guadalete, some seven miles from the field of battle, the steed of Count Julian came thundering down the banks. The oozy surface of the marsh on the sides of the river deceived the unhappy Roderick. Orelia, striving with generous effort, in obedience to the voice and spur of the rider, became entangled in the sedge and mire at the perilous moment, and, compelled to abandon her, Roderick leapt from the saddle to the shore, only to meet with the avenger. Julian was not the first to encounter with the fugitive monarch. This was a fortune reserved to a valiant Moor, the captain of a select body of Bedouin horse, named Maguel el Rami. Their weapons were already opposed, when, hot with haste, weary from hard riding and fighting, and feeble from several wounds, Julian of Consuegra dashed between them, and struck their swords asunder.

"God! how I thank thee that he lives," was the first exclamation of the panting sire! "Moor!" said he, turning to Maguel el Rami, "hadst thou slain him by thy unwitting sword, all Barbary had not saved thee from my wrath. Away! choose thee out other victims—leave this to me!"

He was obeyed! The Moor was in a moment out of sight.

"Roderick!" said Julian, "how I rejoice me thou dost survive this hour—that thou livest to satisfy, however poorly, the hungry passion of revenge which is consuming within my heart."

"Slave!" cried Roderick, with a show of scorn and confidence which he did not feel—"I am still thy king."

"King! to be sure thou art! a king still—but none of mine! it is a part of my rejoicing that I slay in thee a sovereign. The memory of Cava, her bloody wrongs, call for no less a sacrifice. I would not rob thee of a single dignity. Nay, were the passion of my heart once satisfied—could this thing be possible—I would restore thee to thy power—restore myself again to Spain—and all for one small boon which thou hast to bestow."

"And that!" demanded Roderick, somewhat eagerly, deceived by the suddenly subdued tones of the apostate, and the calm and, as he fancied, the gentle expression of his eye. Roderick began to flatter himself with new hopes. He began to think that Julian might possibly relent—might be bought off with new dignities and treasures, and employ his power in repairing the injuries he had done to his country. He built something upon the remorse of the apostate—

"What is that, Julian?" he repeated, as the other remained silent a moment too long for his eager hopes—"What is that?"

"Thy blood! thy blood!—no petty drops—no small tribute, tyrant! idly drawn to show me that thou hast blood in warm and ruddy veins. No! I must rend thy heart from its black caverns! watch its pulsations—note where it beats most quickly and with most life, and there execute my vengeance with keen steel—vexed that so poor a vengeance, after all, must atone to me for my crushed honor, and the tortured innocence of my child! Art thou prepared for this? Art thou ready for thy death?"

"I am no coward, Julian!"

"Would I prate with thee, knew I not this? Hadst thou been, the Moor should have despatched thee in my sight."

"Julian!" said Roderick, "I have wronged thee deeply—sorely have I repented of this wrong—sorely has my kingdom suffered from it, and I stand here ready to await the issue of thy sword in the encounter. But what had thy country done to thee, that thou must gore her with thy cruel weapon? What had these children of the soil—these poor herdlings—the women and the children of the land—that thou shouldst bring the wolf into the fold, and ravage the cities of thy people with the havoc of the African?"

"That is the pang and the shame which thou must answer," said Julian, with the agony of hell speaking in his visage. "Thou hast spoken soothly. Thinkest thou I feel nothing of my shame?—that I loathe not my own crime in this? But it is thy crime, Roderick—it must be revenged on both of us. Come on! I look not to survive this struggle. I am faint with many wounds, but thee I must slay! That I feel and know. Thy doom is on the record! Prepare thee! This hour I give thee to the sword!"

"I am ready! I will fight thee, Julian, to the last—yet not deny heaven's justice if I fight with thee in vain."

Fierce and terrible was the conflict. As if conscious of all his danger, Roderick put on all his coolness and courage. He strove with moderate arm, simply at defence, and his prudence baffled that of the avenger. The sword of Julian was smitten asunder in the struggle. He stood weaponless before his foe. His battle-axe was left upon his saddle bow. He looked aghast upon his enemy. In that one moment Roderick forgot his caution.

"I am safe, Julian! Thou art unarmed, and at my mercy!"

"Traitor and tyrant, in thy teeth thou liest! No! Thou art at mine!"

At the risk of a fearful wound, which took effect upon his shoulder in a deep gash, and upon his neck in a slight one, Julian closed in with his victim, grappled him about the waist with a single arm, and with the hand of the other plucked the dagger from the belt of Roderick, and struck with it, once, twice, thrice, to the very heart of the monarch. This done, he flung him from his grasp—writhing and gasping in a mortal agony upon the sands.

"This to thee, Cava! my child! This to thee, Frandina, the mother of my child! And thou!——"

He turned to look upon Roderick. The eyes of the king were already glazed in death. He himself sunk upon the ground, even as he gazed upon his victim.

"It is over! My limbs fail me! My strength. But it has sufficed. I have lived long enough. My task is ended. Yet! that pang! that agony! It is here!

a dreadful fire in my brain!—Spain! Spain!—it is for thee I burn! Thou wilt curse me! curse me with thy homes made desolate—thy fields ravaged—thy people in captivity. A fearful vision grows up before my sight—the vision of a terrible future from thy enemies and mine. Spare my eyes this spectacle of blood. Ha! it is she! Does she reproach!—my child—my Cava! It was for thee—for thee only that I wrought. Alas! and thou deniest me! thou! thou!——"

He raved. His form writhed beside that of Roderick. He grappled it with his hands. His eyes swam. He no longer saw the objects around him, or he saw them indistinctly. His hand still grasped the dagger with which he had given the fatal blow to his enemy, and as the conviction was renewed in his mind that it was still his enemy that he grappled, he smote again, once, twice, thrice, even as before when he had slain him; then sinking back, he shrieked as with a shuddering and terrible agony. His dying senses caught the sounds of approaching persons—the heavy tread of cavalry. Voices reached his ears.

"Who comes?" he demanded, feebly striving to rise and look around him.

"What is here?" said one. "This surely is Roderick, the Goth. And here is the royal robes and the crown."

"That voice!" exclaimed the dying man: "Is it not Pelayo, son of Witiza, whom I hear?"

"It is!" replied the speaker. "Who art thou?"

"Look on me!"

"Julian!"

"Ay! and nothing. Thy brother—he who loved my daughter—he sleeps by Cueta. I saved him from this day. Thou, Pelayo, art the rightful king in Spain. Save her from the Africans. My prince, place thy sword before me, that I may behold the cross ere I perish. Give it me—in my hands. Give!—give!"

"There! seize it quickly—press it to thy lips. It is thy last refuge!"

"Jesu! mercy!"

In these words the spirit passed. The young prince knelt over the corse in prayer, while his followers, lifting the crown of Roderick from the earth where it lay, placed it upon the brows of Pelayo. The sky then rang with their unanimous shouts as they proclaimed, in a burst of popular enthusiasm, "Pelayo! King of Spain!" He proved himself deserving of the title, and became the real founder of that marvellous race, whose deeds in after centuries, in Europe and America, were among the greatest marvels of human performance. His power did not suffice to expel the Arabs from his country, but he prepared the way for their final expulsion, and preserved the sacred fires of liberty, secure from extinction, in the wild passes of the Asturian mountains.

Pelayo gazed upon the body of Roderick with melancholy contemplation.

"He was the deadly enemy of my home and country. To him we owe the dreadful desolation of this field. But let not the brows which have worn the crown of the Goth, be subject to the indignity of barbarian hoofs. Lift him upon your shoulders, my friends, and let the Xeres bear him to the sea!"

It was done, and vainly did Taric el Tuerto look for the royal victim. The gory head of a noble Gothic cavalier, whose features resembled those of Roderick, was sent, as a sufficient trophy, to the Caliph at Damascus, while the deep waters which could not hide the history and the shame, effectually kept from indignity the person of the "Last King of the Goths!"

THE END.

www.ingramcontent.com/pod-product-compliance
Lightning Source LLC
LaVergne TN
LVHW040758070826
844660LV00025B/1186

* 9 7 8 1 6 1 1 1 7 5 7 5 2 *